George MacDonald (10 December 1824 – 18 September 1905) was a Scottish author, poet and Christian minister. He was a pioneering figure in the field of fantasy literature and the mentor of fellow writer Lewis Carroll. In addition to his fairy tales, MacDonald wrote several works on Christian apologetics. His writings have been cited as a major literary influence by many notable authors including W. H. Auden, J. M. Barrie, Lord Dunsany, Hope Mirrlees, Robert E. Howard, L. Frank Baum, T.H. White, Lloyd Alexander, C. S. Lewis, J. R. R. Tolkien, Walter de la Mare, E. Nesbit, Peter S. Beagle, Neil Gaiman and Madeleine L'Engle. C. S. Lewis wrote that he regarded MacDonald as his "master": "Picking up a copy of Phantastes one day at a train-station bookstall, I began to read. A few hours later", said Lewis, "I knew that I had crossed a great frontier." G. K. Chesterton cited The Princess and the Goblin as a book that had "made a difference to my whole existence". (Source: Wikipedia)

Literary works:
Phantastes: A Fairie Romance for
Men and Women (1858)
"Cross Purposes" (1862)
"The Second Sight" (1864)
Dealings with the Fairies (1867)
At the Back of the North Wind (1871)
Works of Fancy and Imagination (1871)
The Princess and the Goblin (1872)
The Wise Woman: A Parable (1875)
The Gifts of the Child Christ and Other Tales
The Day Boy and the Night Girl (1882)
The Princess and Curdie (1883)

THRONE CLASSICS

A Double Story,
Cross Purposes And The Shadows
&
The History of
Gutta-Percha Willie
George MacDonald

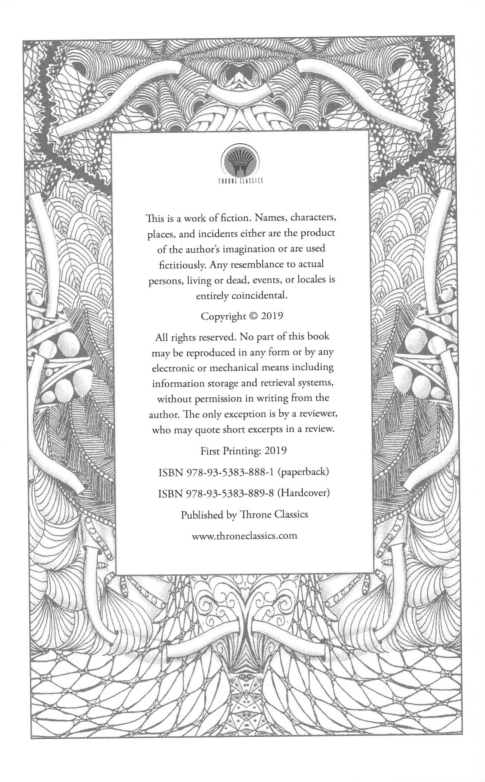

THRONE CLASSICS

First Printing: 2019

ISBN 978-93-5383-888-1 (paperback)

ISBN 978-93-5383-889-8 (Hardcover)

Published by Throne Classics

www.throneclassics.com

Contents

A Double Story,

Cross Purposes And The Shadows

&

The History of

Gutta-Percha Willie

A DOUBLE STORY

I.

There was a certain country where things used to go rather oddly. For instance, you could never tell whether it was going to rain or hail, or whether or not the milk was going to turn sour. It was impossible to say whether the next baby would be a boy, or a girl, or even, after he was a week old, whether he would wake sweet-tempered or cross.

In strict accordance with the peculiar nature of this country of uncertainties, it came to pass one day, that in the midst of a shower of rain that might well be called golden, seeing the sun, shining as it fell, turned all its drops into molten topazes, and every drop was good for a grain of golden corn, or a yellow cowslip, or a buttercup, or a dandelion at least;—while this splendid rain was falling, I say, with a musical patter upon the great leaves of the horse-chestnuts, which hung like Vandyke collars about the necks of the creamy, red-spotted blossoms, and on the leaves of the sycamores, looking as if they had blood in their veins, and on a multitude of flowers, of which some stood up and boldly held out their cups to catch their share, while others cowered down, laughing, under the soft patting blows of the heavy warm drops;—while this lovely rain was washing all the air clean from the motes, and the bad odors, and the poison-seeds that had escaped from their prisons during the long drought;—while it fell, splashing and sparkling, with a hum, and a rush, and a soft clashing—but stop! I am stealing, I find, and not that only, but with clumsy hands spoiling what I steal:—

"O Rain! with your dull twofold sound,

The clash hard by, and the murmur all round:"

—there! take it, Mr. Coleridge;—while, as I was saying, the lovely little rivers whose fountains are the clouds, and which cut their own channels through the air, and make sweet noises rubbing against their banks as they hurry down and down, until at length they are pulled up on a sudden, with a musical plash, in the very heart of an odorous flower, that first gasps and then sighs up a blissful scent, or on the bald head of a stone that never says, Thank you;—while the very sheep felt it blessing them, though it could never reach their skins through the depth of their long wool, and the veriest hedgehog—I mean the one with the longest spikes—came and spiked himself out to impale as many of the drops as he could;—while the rain was thus falling, and the leaves, and the flowers, and the sheep, and the cattle, and the hedgehog, were all busily receiving the golden rain, something happened. It was not a great battle, nor an earthquake, nor a coronation, but something more important than all those put together. A BABY-GIRL WAS BORN; and her father was a king; and her mother was a queen; and her uncles and aunts were princes and princesses; and her first-cousins were dukes and duchesses; and not one of her second-cousins was less than a marquis or marchioness, or of their third-cousins less than an earl or countess: and below a countess they did not care to count. So the little girl was Somebody; and yet for all that, strange to say, the first thing she did was to cry. I told you it was a strange country.

As she grew up, everybody about her did his best to convince her that she was Somebody; and the girl herself was so easily persuaded of it that she quite forgot that anybody had ever told her so, and took it for a fundamental, innate, primary, first-born, self-evident, necessary, and incontrovertible idea and principle that SHE WAS SOMEBODY. And far be it from me to deny it. I will even go so far as to assert that in this odd country there was a huge number of Somebodies. Indeed, it was one of its oddities that every boy and girl in it, was rather too ready to think he or she was Somebody; and the worst of it was that the princess never thought of there being more than one Somebody—and that was herself.

Far away to the north in the same country, on the side of a bleak hill, where a horse-chestnut or a sycamore was never seen, where were no meadows rich with buttercups, only steep, rough, breezy slopes, covered with dry prickly furze and its flowers of red gold, or moister, softer broom with its flowers of yellow gold, and great sweeps of purple heather, mixed with bilberries, and crowberries, and cranberries—no, I am all wrong: there was nothing out yet but a few furze-blossoms; the rest were all waiting behind their doors till they were called; and no full, slow-gliding river with meadow-sweet along its oozy banks, only a little brook here and there, that dashed past without a moment to say, "How do you do?"—there (would you believe it?) while the same cloud that was dropping down golden rain all about the queen's new baby was dashing huge fierce handfuls of hail upon the hills, with such force that they flew spinning off the rocks and stones, went burrowing in the sheep's wool, stung the cheeks and chin of the shepherd with their sharp spiteful little blows, and made his dog wink and whine as they bounded off his hard wise head, and long sagacious nose; only, when they dropped plump down the chimney, and fell hissing in the little fire, they caught it then, for the clever little fire soon sent them up the chimney again, a good deal swollen, and harmless enough for a while, there (what do you think?) among the hailstones, and the heather, and the cold mountain air, another little girl was born, whom the shepherd her father, and the shepherdess her mother, and a good many of her kindred too, thought Somebody. She had not an uncle or an aunt that was less than a shepherd or dairymaid, not a cousin, that was less than a farm-laborer, not a second-cousin that was less than a grocer, and they did not count farther. And yet (would you believe it?) she too cried the very first thing. It WAS an odd country! And, what is still more surprising, the shepherd and shepherdess and the dairymaids and the laborers were not a bit wiser than the king and the queen and the dukes and the marquises and the earls; for they too, one and all, so constantly taught the little woman that she was Somebody, that she also forgot that there were a great many more Somebodies besides herself in the world.

It was, indeed, a peculiar country, very different from ours—so different, that my reader must not be too much surprised when I add the amazing fact, that most of its inhabitants, instead of enjoying the things they had, were always wanting the things they had not, often even the things it was least likely they ever could have. The grown men and women being like this, there is no reason to be further astonished that the Princess Rosamond—the name her parents gave her because it means Rose of the World—should grow up like them, wanting every thing she could and every thing she couldn't have. The things she could have were a great many too many, for her foolish parents always gave her what they could; but still there remained a few things they couldn't give her, for they were only a common king and queen. They could and did give her a lighted candle when she cried for it, and managed by much care that she should not burn her fingers or set her frock on fire; but when she cried for the moon, that they could not give her. They did the worst thing possible, instead, however; for they pretended to do what they could not. They got her a thin disc of brilliantly polished silver, as near the size of the moon as they could agree upon; and, for a time she was delighted.

But, unfortunately, one evening she made the discovery that her moon was a little peculiar, inasmuch as she could not shine in the dark. Her nurse happened to snuff out the candles as she was playing with it; and instantly came a shriek of rage, for her moon had vanished. Presently, through the opening of the curtains, she caught sight of the real moon, far away in the sky, and shining quite calmly, as if she had been there all the time; and her rage increased to such a degree that if it had not passed off in a fit, I do not know what might have come of it.

As she grew up it was still the same, with this difference, that not only must she have every thing, but she got tired of every thing almost as soon as she had it. There was an accumulation of things in her nursery and schoolroom and bedroom that was perfectly appalling. Her mother's wardrobes were almost useless to her, so packed were they with things of which she never took any notice. When she was five years old, they gave her a splendid gold repeater, so close set with diamonds and rubies, that the back was just one crust of gems. In one of her little tempers, as they called her hideously ugly rages, she dashed it against the back of the chimney, after which it never gave a single tick; and some of the diamonds went to the ash-pit. As she grew older still, she became fond of animals, not in a way that brought them much pleasure, or herself much satisfaction. When angry, she would beat them, and try to pull them to pieces, and as soon as she became a little used to them, would neglect them altogether. Then, if they could, they would run away, and she was furious. Some white mice, which she had ceased feeding altogether, did so; and soon the palace was swarming with white mice. Their red eyes might be seen glowing, and their white skins gleaming, in every dark corner; but when it came to the king's finding a nest of them in his second-best crown, he was angry and ordered them to be drowned. The princess heard of it, however, and raised such a clamor, that there they were left until they should run away of themselves; and the poor king had to wear his best crown every day till then. Nothing that was the princess's property, whether she cared for it or not, was to be meddled with.

Of course, as she grew, she grew worse; for she never tried to grow better. She became more and more peevish and fretful every day—dissatisfied not only with what she had, but with all that was around her, and constantly wishing things in general to be different. She found fault with every thing and everybody, and all that happened, and grew more and more disagreeable to every one who had to do with her. At last, when she had nearly killed her nurse, and had all but succeeded in hanging herself, and was miserable from morning to night, her parents thought it time to do something.

A long way from the palace, in the heart of a deep wood of pine-trees, lived a wise woman. In some countries she would have been called a witch; but that would have been a mistake, for she never did any thing wicked, and had more power than any witch could have. As her fame was spread through all the country, the king heard of her; and, thinking she might perhaps be able to suggest something, sent for her. In the dead of the night, lest the princess should know it, the king's messenger brought into the palace a tall woman, muffled from head to foot in a cloak of black cloth. In the presence of both their Majesties, the king, to do her honor, requested her to sit; but she declined, and stood waiting to hear what they had to say. Nor had she to wait long, for almost instantly they began to tell her the dreadful trouble they were in with their only child; first the king talking, then the queen interposing with some yet more dreadful fact, and at times both letting out a torrent of words together, so anxious were they to show the wise woman that their perplexity was real, and their daughter a very terrible one. For a long while there appeared no sign of approaching pause. But the wise woman stood patiently folded in her black cloak, and listened without word or motion. At length silence fell; for they had talked themselves tired, and could not think of any thing more to add to the list of their child's enormities.

After a minute, the wise woman unfolded her arms; and her cloak dropping open in front, disclosed a garment made of a strange stuff, which an old poet who knew her well has thus described:—

"All lilly white, withoutten spot or pride,

That seemd like silke and silver woven neare;

But neither silke nor silver therein did appeare."

"How very badly you have treated her!" said the wise woman. "Poor child!"

"Treated her badly?" gasped the king.

"She is a very wicked child," said the queen; and both glared with indignation.

"Yes, indeed!" returned the wise woman. "She is very naughty indeed, and that she must be made to feel; but it is half your fault too."

"What!" stammered the king. "Haven't we given her every mortal thing she wanted?"

"Surely," said the wise woman: "what else could have all but killed her? You should have given her a few things of the other sort. But you are far too dull to understand me."

"You are very polite," remarked the king, with royal sarcasm on his thin, straight lips.

The wise woman made no answer beyond a deep sigh; and the king and queen sat silent also in their anger, glaring at the wise woman. The silence lasted again for a minute, and then the wise woman folded her cloak around her, and her shining garment vanished like the moon when a great cloud comes over her. Yet another minute passed and the silence endured, for the smouldering wrath of the king and queen choked the channels of their speech. Then the wise woman turned her back on them, and so stood. At this, the rage of the king broke forth; and he cried to the queen, stammering in his fierceness,—

"How should such an old hag as that teach Rosamond good manners? She knows nothing of them herself! Look how she stands!—actually with her back to us."

At the word the wise woman walked from the room. The great folding doors fell to behind her; and the same moment the king and queen were quarrelling like apes as to which of them was to blame for her departure. Before their altercation was over, for it lasted till the early morning, in rushed Rosamond, clutching in her hand a poor little white rabbit, of which she was very fond, and from which, only because it would not come to her when she called it, she was pulling handfuls of fur in the attempt to tear the squealing, pink-eared, red-eyed thing to pieces.

"Rosa, RosaMOND!" cried the queen; whereupon Rosamond threw the rabbit in her mother's face. The king started up in a fury, and ran to seize her. She darted shrieking from the room. The king rushed after her; but, to his amazement, she was nowhere to be seen: the huge hall was empty.—No: just outside the door, close to the threshold, with her back to it, sat the figure of the wise woman, muffled in her dark cloak, with her head bowed over her knees. As the king stood looking at her, she rose slowly, crossed the hall, and walked away down the marble staircase. The king called to her; but she never turned her head, or gave the least sign that she heard him. So quietly did she pass down the wide marble stair, that the king was all but persuaded he had seen only a shadow gliding across the white steps.

For the princess, she was nowhere to be found. The queen went into hysterics; and the rabbit ran away. The king sent out messengers in every direction, but in vain.

In a short time the palace was quiet—as quiet as it used to be before the princess was born. The king and queen cried a little now and then, for the hearts of parents were in that country strangely fashioned; and yet I am afraid the first movement of those very hearts would have been a jump of terror if the ears above them had heard the voice of Rosamond in one of the corridors. As for the rest of the household, they could not have made up a single tear amongst them. They thought, whatever it might be for the princess, it was, for every one else, the best thing that could have happened; and as to what had become of her, if their heads were puzzled, their hearts took no interest in the question. The lord-chancellor alone had an idea about it, but he was far too wise to utter it.

II.

The fact, as is plain, was, that the princess had disappeared in the folds of the wise woman's cloak. When she rushed from the room, the wise woman caught her to her bosom and flung the black garment around her. The princess struggled wildly, for she was in fierce terror, and screamed as loud as choking fright would permit her; but her father, standing in the door, and looking down upon the wise woman, saw never a movement of the cloak, so tight was she held by her captor. He was indeed aware of a most angry crying, which reminded him of his daughter; but it sounded to him so far away, that he took it for the passion of some child in the street, outside the palace-gates. Hence, unchallenged, the wise woman carried the princess down the marble stairs, out at the palace-door, down a great flight of steps outside, across a paved court, through the brazen gates, along half-roused streets where people were opening their shops, through the huge gates of the city, and out into the wide road, vanishing northwards; the princess struggling and screaming all the time, and the wise woman holding her tight. When at length she was too tired to struggle or scream any more, the wise woman unfolded her cloak, and set her down; and the princess saw the light and opened her swollen eyelids. There was nothing in sight that she had ever seen before. City and palace had disappeared. They were upon a wide road going straight on, with a ditch on each side of it, that behind them widened into the great moat surrounding the city. She cast up a terrified look into the wise woman's face, that gazed down upon her gravely and kindly. Now the princess did not in the least understand kindness. She always took it for a sign either of partiality or fear. So when the wise woman looked kindly upon her, she rushed at her, butting with her head like a ram: but the folds of the cloak had closed around the wise woman; and, when the princess ran against it, she found it hard as the cloak of a bronze statue, and fell back upon the road with a great bruise on her head. The wise woman lifted her again, and put her once more under the cloak, where she fell asleep, and where she awoke again only to find that she was still being carried on and on.

When at length the wise woman again stopped and set her down, she saw around her a bright moonlit night, on a wide heath, solitary and houseless. Here she felt more frightened than before; nor was her terror assuaged when, looking up, she saw a stern, immovable countenance, with cold eyes fixedly regarding her. All she knew of the world being derived from nursery-tales, she concluded that the wise woman was an ogress, carrying her home to eat her.

I have already said that the princess was, at this time of her life, such a low-minded creature, that severity had greater influence over her than kindness. She understood terror better far than tenderness. When the wise woman looked at her thus, she fell on her knees, and held up her hands to her, crying,—

"Oh, don't eat me! don't eat me!"

Now this being the best SHE could do, it was a sign she was a low creature. Think of it—to kick at kindness, and kneel from terror. But the sternness on the face of the wise woman came from the same heart and the same feeling as the kindness that had shone from it before. The only thing that could save the princess from her hatefulness, was that she should be made to mind somebody else than her own miserable Somebody.

Without saying a word, the wise woman reached down her hand, took one of Rosamond's, and, lifting her to her feet, led her along through the moonlight. Every now and then a gush of obstinacy would well up in the heart of the princess, and she would give a great ill-tempered tug, and pull her hand away; but then the wise woman would gaze down upon her with such a look, that she instantly sought again the hand she had rejected, in pure terror lest she should be eaten upon the spot. And so they would walk on again; and when the wind blew the folds of the cloak against the princess, she found them soft as her mother's camel-hair shawl.

After a little while the wise woman began to sing to her, and the princess could not help listening; for the soft wind amongst the low dry bushes of the heath, the rustle of their own steps, and the trailing of the wise woman's cloak, were the only sounds beside.

And this is the song she sang:—

Out in the cold,

With a thin-worn fold

Of withered gold

Around her rolled,

Hangs in the air the weary moon.

She is old, old, old;

And her bones all cold,

And her tales all told,

And her things all sold,

And she has no breath to croon.

Like a castaway clout,

She is quite shut out!

She might call and shout,

But no one about

Would ever call back, "Who's there?"

There is never a hut,

Not a door to shut,

Not a footpath or rut,

Long road or short cut,

Leading to anywhere!

She is all alone

Like a dog-picked bone,

The poor old crone!

She fain would groan,

But she cannot find the breath.

She once had a fire;

But she built it no higher,

And only sat nigher

Till she saw it expire;

And now she is cold as death.

She never will smile

All the lonesome while.

Oh the mile after mile,

And never a stile!

And never a tree or a stone!

She has not a tear:

Afar and anear

It is all so drear,

But she does not care,

Her heart is as dry as a bone.

None to come near her!

No one to cheer her!

No one to jeer her!

No one to hear her!

Not a thing to lift and hold!

She is always awake,

But her heart will not break:

She can only quake,

Shiver, and shake:

The old woman is very cold.

As strange as the song, was the crooning wailing tune that the wise woman sung. At the first note almost, you would have thought she wanted to frighten the princess; and so indeed she did. For when people WILL be naughty, they have to be frightened, and they are not expected to like it. The princess grew angry, pulled her hand away, and cried,—

"YOU are the ugly old woman. I hate you!"

Therewith she stood still, expecting the wise woman to stop also, perhaps coax her to go on: if she did, she was determined not to move a step. But the wise woman never even looked about: she kept walking on steadily, the same pace as before. Little Obstinate thought for certain she would turn; for she regarded herself as much too precious to be left behind. But on and on the wise woman went, until she had vanished away in the dim moonlight. Then all at once the princess perceived that she was left alone with the moon, looking down on her from the height of her loneliness. She was horribly frightened, and began to run after the wise woman, calling aloud. But the song she had just heard came back to the sound of her own running feet,—

All all alone,

Like a dog-picked bone!

and again,—

She might call and shout,

And no one about

Would ever call back, "Who's there?"

and she screamed as she ran. How she wished she knew the old woman's name, that she might call it after her through the moonlight!

But the wise woman had, in truth, heard the first sound of her running feet, and stopped and turned, waiting. What with running and crying, however, and a fall or two as she ran, the princess never saw her until she fell right into her arms—and the same moment into a fresh rage; for as soon as any trouble was over the princess was always ready to begin another. The wise woman therefore pushed her away, and walked on; while the princess ran scolding and storming after her. She had to run till, from very fatigue, her rudeness ceased. Her heart gave way; she burst into tears, and ran on silently weeping.

A minute more and the wise woman stooped, and lifting her in her arms, folded her cloak around her. Instantly she fell asleep, and slept as soft and as soundly as if she had been in her own bed. She slept till the moon went down; she slept till the sun rose up; she slept till he climbed the topmost sky; she slept till he went down again, and the poor old moon came peaking and peering out once more: and all that time the wise woman went walking on and on very fast. And now they had reached a spot where a few fir-trees came to meet them through the moonlight.

At the same time the princess awaked, and popping her head out between the folds of the wise woman's cloak—a very ugly little owlet she looked—saw that they were entering the wood. Now there is something awful about every wood, especially in the moonlight; and perhaps a fir-wood is more awful than other woods. For one thing, it lets a little more light through, rendering the darkness a little more visible, as it were; and then the trees go stretching away up towards the moon, and look as if they cared nothing about the creatures below them—not like the broad trees with soft wide leaves that, in the darkness even, look sheltering. So the princess is not to be blamed that she was very much frightened. She is hardly to be blamed either that, assured the wise woman was an ogress carrying her to her castle to eat her up, she began again to kick and scream violently, as those of my readers who are of the same sort as herself will consider the right and natural thing to do. The wrong in her was this—that she had led such a bad life, that she did not know a good woman when she saw her; took her for one like herself, even after she had slept in her arms.

Immediately the wise woman set her down, and, walking on, within a few paces vanished among the trees. Then the cries of the princess rent the air, but the fir-trees never heeded her; not one of their hard little needles gave a single shiver for all the noise she made. But there were creatures in the forest who were soon quite as much interested in her cries as the fir-trees were indifferent to them. They began to hearken and howl and snuff about, and run hither and thither, and grin with their white teeth, and light up the green lamps in their eyes. In a minute or two a whole army of wolves and hyenas were rushing from all quarters through the pillar like stems of the fir-trees, to the place where she stood calling them, without knowing it. The noise she made herself, however, prevented her from hearing either their howls or the soft pattering of their many trampling feet as they bounded over the fallen fir needles and cones.

One huge old wolf had outsped the rest—not that he could run faster, but that from experience he could more exactly judge whence the cries came, and as he shot through the wood, she caught sight at last of his lamping eyes coming swiftly nearer and nearer. Terror silenced her. She stood with her mouth open, as if she were going to eat the wolf, but she had no breath to scream with, and her tongue curled up in her mouth like a withered and frozen leaf. She could do nothing but stare at the coming monster. And now he was taking a few shorter bounds, measuring the distance for the one final leap that should bring him upon her, when out stepped the wise woman from behind the very tree by which she had set the princess down, caught the wolf by the throat half-way in his last spring, shook him once, and threw him from her dead. Then she turned towards the princess, who flung herself into her arms, and was instantly lapped in the folds of her cloak.

But now the huge army of wolves and hyenas had rushed like a sea around them, whose waves leaped with hoarse roar and hollow yell up against the wise woman. But she, like a strong stately vessel, moved unhurt through the midst of them. Ever as they leaped against her cloak, they dropped and slunk away back through the crowd. Others ever succeeded, and ever in their turn fell, and drew back confounded. For some time she walked on attended and assailed on all sides by the howling pack. Suddenly they turned and swept away, vanishing in the depths of the forest. She neither slackened nor hastened her step, but went walking on as before.

In a little while she unfolded her cloak, and let the princess look out. The firs had ceased; and they were on a lofty height of moorland, stony and bare and dry, with tufts of heather and a few small plants here and there. About the heath, on every side, lay the forest, looking in the moonlight like a cloud; and above the forest, like the shaven crown of a monk, rose the bare moor over which they were walking. Presently, a little way in front of them, the princess espied a whitewashed cottage, gleaming in the moon. As they came nearer, she saw that the roof was covered with thatch, over which the moss had grown green. It was a very simple, humble place, not in the least terrible to look at, and yet, as soon as she saw it, her fear again awoke, and always, as soon as her fear awoke, the trust of the princess fell into a dead sleep. Foolish and useless as she might by this time have known it, she once more began kicking and screaming, whereupon, yet once more, the wise woman set her down on the heath, a few yards from the back of the cottage, and saying only, "No one ever gets into my house who does not knock at the door, and ask to come in," disappeared round the corner of the cottage, leaving the princess alone with the moon—two white faces in the cone of the night.

III.

The moon stared at the princess, and the princess stared at the moon; but the moon had the best of it, and the princess began to cry. And now the question was between the moon and the cottage. The princess thought she knew the worst of the moon, and she knew nothing at all about the cottage, therefore she would stay with the moon. Strange, was it not, that she should have been so long with the wise woman, and yet know NOTHING about that cottage? As for the moon, she did not by any means know the worst of her, or even, that, if she were to fall asleep where she could find her, the old witch would certainly do her best to twist her face.

But she had scarcely sat a moment longer before she was assailed by all sorts of fresh fears. First of all, the soft wind blowing gently through the dry stalks of the heather and its thousands of little bells raised a sweet rustling, which the princess took for the hissing of serpents, for you know she had been naughty for so long that she could not in a great many things tell the good from the bad. Then nobody could deny that there, all round about the heath, like a ring of darkness, lay the gloomy fir-wood, and the princess knew what it was full of, and every now and then she thought she heard the howling of its wolves and hyenas. And who could tell but some of them might break from their covert and sweep like a shadow across the heath? Indeed, it was not once nor twice that for a moment she was fully persuaded she saw a great beast coming leaping and bounding through the moonlight to have her all to himself. She did not know that not a single evil creature dared set foot on that heath, or that, if one should do so, it would that instant wither up and cease. If an army of them had rushed to invade it, it would have melted away on the edge of it, and ceased like a dying wave.—She even imagined that the moon was slowly coming nearer and nearer down the sky to take her and freeze her to death in her arms. The wise woman, too, she felt sure, although her cottage looked asleep, was watching her at some little window. In this, however, she would have been quite right, if she had only imagined enough—namely, that the wise woman was watching OVER her from the little window. But after all, somehow, the thought of the wise woman was less frightful than that of any of her other terrors, and at length she began to wonder whether it might not turn out that she was no ogress, but only a rude, ill-bred, tyrannical, yet on the whole not altogether ill-meaning person. Hardly had the possibility arisen in her mind, before she was on her feet: if the woman was any thing short of an ogress, her cottage must be better than that horrible loneliness, with nothing in all the world but a stare; and even an ogress had at least the shape and look of a human being.

She darted round the end of the cottage to find the front. But, to her surprise, she came only to another back, for no door was to be seen. She tried the farther end, but still no door. She must have passed it as she ran—but no—neither in gable nor in side was any to be found.

A cottage without a door!—she rushed at it in a rage and kicked at the wall with her feet. But the wall was hard as iron, and hurt her sadly through her gay silken slippers. She threw herself on the heath, which came up to the walls of the cottage on every side, and roared and screamed with rage. Suddenly, however, she remembered how her screaming had brought the horde of wolves and hyenas about her in the forest, and, ceasing at once, lay still, gazing yet again at the moon. And then came the thought of her parents in the palace at home. In her mind's eye she saw her mother sitting at her embroidery with the tears dropping upon it, and her father staring into the fire as if he were looking for her in its glowing caverns. It is true that if they had both been in tears by her side because of her naughtiness, she would not have cared a straw; but now her own forlorn condition somehow helped her to understand their grief at having lost her, and not only a great longing to be back in her comfortable home, but a feeble flutter of genuine love for her parents awoke in her heart as well, and she burst into real tears—soft, mournful tears—very different from those of rage and disappointment to which she was so much used. And another very remarkable thing was that the moment she began to love her father and mother, she began to wish to see the wise woman again. The idea of her being an ogress vanished utterly, and she thought of her only as one to take her in from the moon, and the loneliness, and the terrors of the forest-haunted heath, and hide her in a cottage with not

27

even a door for the horrid wolves to howl against.

But the old woman—as the princess called her, not knowing that her real name was the Wise Woman—had told her that she must knock at the door: how was she to do that when there was no door? But again she bethought herself—that, if she could not do all she was told, she could, at least, do a part of it: if she could not knock at the door, she could at least knock—say on the wall, for there was nothing else to knock upon—and perhaps the old woman would hear her, and lift her in by some window. Thereupon, she rose at once to her feet, and picking up a stone, began to knock on the wall with it. A loud noise was the result, and she found she was knocking on the very door itself. For a moment she feared the old woman would be offended, but the next, there came a voice, saying,

"Who is there?"

The princess answered,

"Please, old woman, I did not mean to knock so loud."

To this there came no reply.

Then the princess knocked again, this time with her knuckles, and the voice came again, saying,

"Who is there?"

And the princess answered,

"Rosamond."

Then a second time there was silence. But the princess soon ventured to knock a third time.

"What do you want?" said the voice.

"Oh, please, let me in!" said the princess.

"The moon will keep staring at me; and I hear the wolves in the wood."

Then the door opened, and the princess entered. She looked all around, but saw nothing of the wise woman.

It was a single bare little room, with a white deal table, and a few old wooden chairs, a fire of fir-wood on the hearth, the smoke of which smelt sweet, and a patch of thick-growing heath in one corner. Poor as it was, compared to the grand place Rosamond had left, she felt no little satisfaction as she shut the door, and looked around her. And what with the sufferings and terrors she had left outside, the new kind of tears she had shed, the love she had begun to feel for her parents, and the trust she had begun to place in the wise woman, it seemed to her as if her soul had grown larger of a sudden, and she had left the days of her childishness and naughtiness far behind her. People are so ready to think themselves changed when it is only their mood that is changed! Those who are good-tempered because it is a fine day, will be ill-tempered when it rains: their selves are just the same both days; only in the one case, the fine weather has got into them, in the other the rainy. Rosamond, as she sat warming herself by the glow of the peat-fire, turning over in her mind all that had passed, and feeling how pleasant the change in her feelings was, began by degrees to think how very good she had grown, and how very good she was to have grown good, and how extremely good she must always have been that she was able to grow so very good as she now felt she had grown; and she became so absorbed in her self-admiration as never to notice either that the fire was dying, or that a heap of fir-cones lay in a corner near it. Suddenly, a great wind came roaring down the chimney, and scattered the ashes about the floor; a tremendous rain followed, and fell hissing on the embers; the moon was swallowed up, and there was darkness all about her. Then a flash of lightning, followed by a peal of thunder, so terrified the princess, that she cried aloud for the old woman, but there came no answer to her cry.

Then in her terror the princess grew angry, and saying to herself, "She must be somewhere in the place, else who was there to open the door to me?" began to shout and yell, and call the wise woman all the bad names she had been in the habit of throwing at her nurses. But there came not a single sound in reply.

Strange to say, the princess never thought of telling herself now how naughty she was, though that would surely have been reasonable. On the contrary, she thought she had a perfect right to be angry, for was she not most desperately ill used—and a princess too? But the wind howled on, and the rain kept pouring down the chimney, and every now and then the lightning burst out, and the thunder rushed after it, as if the great lumbering sound could ever think to catch up with the swift light!

At length the princess had again grown so angry, frightened, and miserable, all together, that she jumped up and hurried about the cottage with outstretched arms, trying to find the wise woman. But being in a bad temper always makes people stupid, and presently she struck her forehead such a blow against something—she thought herself it felt like the old woman's cloak—that she fell back—not on the floor, though, but on the patch of heather, which felt as soft and pleasant as any bed in the palace. There, worn out with weeping and rage, she soon fell fast asleep.

She dreamed that she was the old cold woman up in the sky, with no home and no friends, and no nothing at all, not even a pocket; wandering, wandering forever, over a desert of blue sand, never to get to anywhere, and never to lie down or die. It was no use stopping to look about her, for what had she to do but forever look about her as she went on and on and on—never seeing any thing, and never expecting to see any thing! The only shadow of a hope she had was, that she might by slow degrees grow thinner and thinner, until at last she wore away to nothing at all; only alas! she could not detect the least sign that she had yet begun to grow thinner. The hopelessness grew at length so unendurable that she woke with a start. Seeing the face of the wise woman bending over her, she threw her arms around her neck and held up her mouth to be kissed. And the kiss of the wise woman was like the rose-gardens of Damascus.

IV.

The wise woman lifted her tenderly, and washed and dressed her far more carefully than even her nurse. Then she set her down by the fire, and prepared her breakfast. The princess was very hungry, and the bread and milk as good as it could be, so that she thought she had never in her life eaten any thing nicer. Nevertheless, as soon as she began to have enough, she said to herself,—

"Ha! I see how it is! The old woman wants to fatten me! That is why she gives me such nice creamy milk. She doesn't kill me now because she's going to kill me then! She IS an ogress, after all!"

Thereupon she laid down her spoon, and would not eat another mouthful—only followed the basin with longing looks, as the wise woman carried it away.

When she stopped eating, her hostess knew exactly what she was thinking; but it was one thing to understand the princess, and quite another to make the princess understand her: that would require time. For the present she took no notice, but went about the affairs of the house, sweeping the floor, brushing down the cobwebs, cleaning the hearth, dusting the table and chairs, and watering the bed to keep it fresh and alive—for she never had more than one guest at a time, and never would allow that guest to go to sleep upon any thing that had no life in it. All the time she was thus busied, she spoke not a word to the princess, which, with the princess, went to confirm her notion of her purposes. But whatever she might have said would have been only perverted by the princess into yet stronger proof of her evil designs, for a fancy in her own head would outweigh any multitude of facts in another's. She kept staring at the fire, and never looked round to see what the wise woman might be doing.

By and by she came close up to the back of her chair, and said,

"Rosamond!"

But the princess had fallen into one of her sulky moods, and shut herself up with her own ugly Somebody; so she never looked round or even answered the wise woman.

"Rosamond," she repeated, "I am going out. If you are a good girl, that is, if you do as I tell you, I will carry you back to your father and mother the moment I return."

The princess did not take the least notice.

"Look at me, Rosamond," said the wise woman.

But Rosamond never moved—never even shrugged her shoulders—perhaps because they were already up to her ears, and could go no farther.

"I want to help you to do what I tell you," said the wise woman. "Look at me."

Still Rosamond was motionless and silent, saying only to herself,

"I know what she's after! She wants to show me her horrid teeth. But I won't look. I'm not going to be frightened out of my senses to please her."

"You had better look, Rosamond. Have you forgotten how you kissed me this morning?"

But Rosamond now regarded that little throb of affection as a momentary weakness into which the deceitful ogress had betrayed her, and almost despised herself for it. She was one of those who the more they are coaxed are the more disagreeable. For such, the wise woman had an awful punishment, but she remembered that the princess had been very ill brought up, and therefore wished to try her with all gentleness first.

She stood silent for a moment, to see what effect her words might have. But Rosamond only said to herself,—

"She wants to fatten and eat me."

And it was such a little while since she had looked into the wise woman's loving eyes, thrown her arms round her neck, and kissed her!

"Well," said the wise woman gently, after pausing as long as it seemed possible she might bethink herself, "I must tell you then without; only whoever listens with her back turned, listens but half, and gets but half the help."

"She wants to fatten me," said the princess.

"You must keep the cottage tidy while I am out. When I come back, I must see the fire bright, the hearth swept, and the kettle boiling; no dust on the table or chairs, the windows clear, the floor clean, and the heather in blossom—which last comes of sprinkling it with water three times a day. When you are hungry, put your hand into that hole in the wall, and you will find a meal."

"She wants to fatten me," said the princess.

"But on no account leave the house till I come back," continued the wise woman, "or you will grievously repent it. Remember what you have already gone through to reach it. Dangers lie all around this cottage of mine; but inside, it is the safest place—in fact the only quite safe place in all the country."

"She means to eat me," said the princess, "and therefore wants to frighten me from running away."

She heard the voice no more. Then, suddenly startled at the thought of being alone, she looked hastily over her shoulder. The cottage was indeed empty of all visible life. It was soundless, too: there was not even a ticking clock or a flapping flame. The fire burned still and smouldering-wise; but it was all the company she had, and she turned again to stare into it.

Soon she began to grow weary of having nothing to do. Then she remembered that the old woman, as she called her, had told her to keep the house tidy.

"The miserable little pig-sty!" she said. "Where's the use of keeping such a hovel clean!"

But in truth she would have been glad of the employment, only just because she had been told to do it, she was unwilling; for there ARE people—however unlikely it may seem—who object to doing a thing for no other reason than that it is required of them.

"I am a princess," she said, "and it is very improper to ask me to do such a thing."

She might have judged it quite as suitable for a princess to sweep away the dust as to sit the centre of a world of dirt. But just because she ought, she wouldn't. Perhaps she feared that if she gave in to doing her duty once, she might have to do it always—which was true enough—for that was the very thing for which she had been specially born.

Unable, however, to feel quite comfortable in the resolve to neglect it, she said to herself, "I'm sure there's time enough for such a nasty job as that!" and sat on, watching the fire as it burned away, the glowing red casting off white flakes, and sinking lower and lower on the hearth.

By and by, merely for want of something to do, she would see what the old woman had left for her in the hole of the wall. But when she put in her hand she found nothing there, except the dust which she ought by this time to have wiped away. Never reflecting that the wise woman had told her she would find food there WHEN SHE WAS HUNGRY, she flew into one of her furies, calling her a cheat, and a thief, and a liar, and an ugly old witch, and an ogress, and I do not know how many wicked names besides. She raged until she was quite exhausted, and then fell fast asleep on her chair. When she awoke the fire was out.

By this time she was hungry; but without looking in the hole, she began again to storm at the wise woman, in which labor she would no doubt have once more exhausted herself, had not something white caught her eye: it was the corner of a napkin hanging from the hole in the wall. She bounded to it, and there was a dinner for her of something strangely good—one of her favorite dishes, only better than she had ever tasted it before. This might surely have at least changed her mood towards the wise woman; but she only grumbled to herself that it was as it ought to be, ate up the food, and lay down on the bed, never thinking of fire, or dust, or water for the heather.

34

The wind began to moan about the cottage, and grew louder and louder, till a great gust came down the chimney, and again scattered the white ashes all over the place. But the princess was by this time fast asleep, and never woke till the wind had sunk to silence. One of the consequences, however, of sleeping when one ought to be awake is waking when one ought to be asleep; and the princess awoke in the black midnight, and found enough to keep her awake. For although the wind had fallen, there was a far more terrible howling than that of the wildest wind all about the cottage. Nor was the howling all; the air was full of strange cries; and everywhere she heard the noise of claws scratching against the house, which seemed all doors and windows, so crowded were the sounds, and from so many directions. All the night long she lay half swooning, yet listening to the hideous noises. But with the first glimmer of morning they ceased.

Then she said to herself, "How fortunate it was that I woke! They would have eaten me up if I had been asleep." The miserable little wretch actually talked as if she had kept them out! If she had done her work in the day, she would have slept through the terrors of the darkness, and awaked fearless; whereas now, she had in the storehouse of her heart a whole harvest of agonies, reaped from the dun fields of the night!

They were neither wolves nor hyenas which had caused her such dismay, but creatures of the air, more frightful still, which, as soon as the smoke of the burning fir-wood ceased to spread itself abroad, and the sun was a sufficient distance down the sky, and the lone cold woman was out, came flying and howling about the cottage, trying to get in at every door and window. Down the chimney they would have got, but that at the heart of the fire there always lay a certain fir-cone, which looked like solid gold red-hot, and which, although it might easily get covered up with ashes, so as to be quite invisible, was continually in a glow fit to kindle all the fir-cones in the world; this it was which had kept the horrible birds—some say they have a claw at the tip of every wing-feather—from tearing the poor naughty princess to pieces, and gobbling her up.

When she rose and looked about her, she was dismayed to see what a state the cottage was in. The fire was out, and the windows were all dim with the wings and claws of the dirty birds, while the bed from which she had just risen was brown and withered, and half its purple bells had fallen. But she consoled herself that she could set all to rights in a few minutes—only she must breakfast first. And, sure enough, there was a basin of the delicious bread and milk ready for her in the hole of the wall!

After she had eaten it, she felt comfortable, and sat for a long time building castles in the air—till she was actually hungry again, without having done an atom of work. She ate again, and was idle again, and ate again. Then it grew dark, and she went trembling to bed, for now she remembered the horrors of the last night. This time she never slept at all, but spent the long hours in grievous terror, for the noises were worse than before. She vowed she would not pass another night in such a hateful haunted old shed for all the ugly women, witches, and ogresses in the wide world. In the morning, however, she fell asleep, and slept late.

Breakfast was of course her first thought, after which she could not avoid that of work. It made her very miserable, but she feared the consequences of being found with it undone. A few minutes before noon, she actually got up, took her pinafore for a duster, and proceeded to dust the table. But the wood-ashes flew about so, that it seemed useless to attempt getting rid of them, and she sat down again to think what was to be done. But there is very little indeed to be done when we will not do that which we have to do.

Her first thought now was to run away at once while the sun was high, and get through the forest before night came on. She fancied she could easily go back the way she had come, and get home to her father's palace. But not the most experienced traveller in the world can ever go back the way the wise woman has brought him.

She got up and went to the door. It was locked! What could the old woman have meant by telling her not to leave the cottage? She was indignant.

The wise woman had meant to make it difficult, but not impossible. Before the princess, however, could find the way out, she heard a hand at the door, and darted in terror behind it. The wise woman opened it, and, leaving it open, walked straight to the hearth. Rosamond immediately slid out, ran a little way, and then laid herself down in the long heather.

V.

The wise woman walked straight up to the hearth, looked at the fire, looked at the bed, glanced round the room, and went up to the table. When she saw the one streak in the thick dust which the princess had left there, a smile, half sad, half pleased, like the sun peeping through a cloud on a rainy day in spring, gleamed over her face. She went at once to the door, and called in a loud voice,

"Rosamond, come to me."

All the wolves and hyenas, fast asleep in the wood, heard her voice, and shivered in their dreams. No wonder then that the princess trembled, and found herself compelled, she could not understand how, to obey the summons. She rose, like the guilty thing she felt, forsook of herself the hiding-place she had chosen, and walked slowly back to the cottage she had left full of the signs of her shame. When she entered, she saw the wise woman on her knees, building up the fire with fir-cones. Already the flame was climbing through the heap in all directions, crackling gently, and sending a sweet aromatic odor through the dusty cottage.

"That is my part of the work," she said, rising. "Now you do yours. But first let me remind you that if you had not put it off, you would have found it not only far easier, but by and by quite pleasant work, much more pleasant than you can imagine now; nor would you have found the time go wearily: you would neither have slept in the day and let the fire out, nor waked at night and heard the howling of the beast-birds. More than all, you would have been glad to see me when I came back; and would have leaped into my arms instead of standing there, looking so ugly and foolish."

As she spoke, suddenly she held up before the princess a tiny mirror, so clear that nobody looking into it could tell what it was made of, or even see it at all—only the thing reflected in it. Rosamond saw a child with dirty fat cheeks, greedy mouth, cowardly eyes—which, not daring to look forward, seemed trying to hide behind an impertinent nose—stooping shoulders, tangled hair, tattered clothes, and smears and stains everywhere. That was what she had made herself. And to tell the truth, she was shocked at the sight, and immediately began, in her dirty heart, to lay the blame on the wise woman, because she had taken her away from her nurses and her fine clothes; while all the time she knew well enough that, close by the heather-bed, was the loveliest little well, just big enough to wash in, the water of which was always springing fresh from the ground, and running away through the wall. Beside it lay the whitest of linen towels, with a comb made of mother-of-pearl, and a brush of fir-needles, any one of which she had been far too lazy to use. She dashed the glass out of the wise woman's hand, and there it lay, broken into a thousand pieces!

Without a word, the wise woman stooped, and gathered the fragments—did not leave searching until she had gathered the last atom, and she laid them all carefully, one by one, in the fire, now blazing high on the hearth. Then she stood up and looked at the princess, who had been watching her sulkily.

"Rosamond," she said, with a countenance awful in its sternness, "until you have cleansed this room—"

"She calls it a room!" sneered the princess to herself.

"You shall have no morsel to eat. You may drink of the well, but nothing else you shall have. When the work I set you is done, you will find food in the same place as before. I am going from home again; and again I warn you not to leave the house."

"She calls it a house!—It's a good thing she's going out of it anyhow!" said the princess, turning her back for mere rudeness, for she was one who, even if she liked a thing before, would dislike it the moment any person in authority over her desired her to do it.

When she looked again, the wise woman had vanished.

Thereupon the princess ran at once to the door, and tried to open it; but open it would not. She searched on all sides, but could discover no way of getting out. The windows would not open—at least she could not open them;

and the only outlet seemed the chimney, which she was afraid to try because of the fire, which looked angry, she thought, and shot out green flames when she went near it. So she sat down to consider. One may well wonder what room for consideration there was—with all her work lying undone behind her. She sat thus, however, considering, as she called it, until hunger began to sting her, when she jumped up and put her hand as usual in the hole of the wall: there was nothing there. She fell straight into one of her stupid rages; but neither her hunger nor the hole in the wall heeded her rage. Then, in a burst of self-pity, she fell a-weeping, but neither the hunger nor the hole cared for her tears. The darkness began to come on, and her hunger grew and grew, and the terror of the wild noises of the last night invaded her. Then she began to feel cold, and saw that the fire was dying. She darted to the heap of cones, and fed it. It blazed up cheerily, and she was comforted a little. Then she thought with herself it would surely be better to give in so far, and do a little work, than die of hunger. So catching up a duster, she began upon the table. The dust flew about and nearly choked her. She ran to the well to drink, and was refreshed and encouraged. Perceiving now that it was a tedious plan to wipe the dust from the table on to the floor, whence it would have all to be swept up again, she got a wooden platter, wiped the dust into that, carried it to the fire, and threw it in. But all the time she was getting more and more hungry and, although she tried the hole again and again, it was only to become more and more certain that work she must if she would eat.

At length all the furniture was dusted, and she began to sweep the floor, which happily, she thought of sprinkling with water, as from the window she had seen them do to the marble court of the palace. That swept, she rushed again to the hole—but still no food! She was on the verge of another rage, when the thought came that she might have forgotten something. To her dismay she found that table and chairs and every thing was again covered with dust—not so badly as before, however. Again she set to work, driven by hunger, and drawn by the hope of eating, and yet again, after a second careful wiping, sought the hole. But no! nothing was there for her! What could it mean?

Her asking this question was a sign of progress: it showed that she expected the wise woman to keep her word. Then she bethought her that she had forgotten the household utensils, and the dishes and plates, some of which wanted to be washed as well as dusted.

Faint with hunger, she set to work yet again. One thing made her think of another, until at length she had cleaned every thing she could think of. Now surely she must find some food in the hole!

When this time also there was nothing, she began once more to abuse the wise woman as false and treacherous;—but ah! there was the bed unwatered! That was soon amended.—Still no supper! Ah! there was the hearth unswept, and the fire wanted making up!—Still no supper! What else could there be? She was at her wits' end, and in very weariness, not laziness this time, sat down and gazed into the fire. There, as she gazed, she spied something brilliant,—shining even, in the midst of the fire: it was the little mirror all whole again; but little she knew that the dust which she had thrown into the fire had helped to heal it. She drew it out carefully, and, looking into it, saw, not indeed the ugly creature she had seen there before, but still a very dirty little animal; whereupon she hurried to the well, took off her clothes, plunged into it, and washed herself clean. Then she brushed and combed her hair, made her clothes as tidy as might be, and ran to the hole in the wall: there was a huge basin of bread and milk!

Never had she eaten any thing with half the relish! Alas! however, when she had finished, she did not wash the basin, but left it as it was, revealing how entirely all the rest had been done only from hunger. Then she threw herself on the heather, and was fast asleep in a moment. Never an evil bird came near her all that night, nor had she so much as one troubled dream.

In the morning as she lay awake before getting up, she spied what seemed a door behind the tall eight-day clock that stood silent in the corner.

"Ah!" she thought, "that must be the way out!" and got up instantly. The first thing she did, however, was to go to the hole in the wall. Nothing was there.

"Well, I am hardly used!" she cried aloud. "All that cleaning for the cross old woman yesterday, and this for my trouble,—nothing for breakfast! Not even a crust of bread! Does Mistress Ogress fancy a princess will bear that?"

The poor foolish creature seemed to think that the work of one day ought to serve for the next day too! But that is nowhere the way in the whole universe. How could there be a universe in that case? And even she never dreamed of applying the same rule to her breakfast.

"How good I was all yesterday!" she said, "and how hungry and ill used I am to-day!"

But she would NOT be a slave, and do over again to-day what she had done only last night! SHE didn't care about her breakfast! She might have it no doubt if she dusted all the wretched place again, but she was not going to do that—at least, without seeing first what lay behind the clock!

Off she darted, and putting her hand behind the clock found the latch of a door. It lifted, and the door opened a little way. By squeezing hard, she managed to get behind the clock, and so through the door. But how she stared, when instead of the open heath, she found herself on the marble floor of a large and stately room, lighted only from above. Its walls were strengthened by pilasters, and in every space between was a large picture, from cornice to floor. She did not know what to make of it. Surely she had run all round the cottage, and certainly had seen nothing of this size near it! She forgot that she had also run round what she took for a hay-mow, a peat-stack, and several other things which looked of no consequence in the moonlight.

"So, then," she cried, "the old woman IS a cheat! I believe she's an ogress, after all, and lives in a palace—though she pretends it's only a cottage, to keep people from suspecting that she eats good little children like me!"

Had the princess been tolerably tractable, she would, by this time, have known a good deal about the wise woman's beautiful house, whereas she had never till now got farther than the porch. Neither was she at all in its innermost places now.

But, king's daughter as she was, she was not a little daunted when, stepping forward from the recess of the door, she saw what a great lordly hall it was. She dared hardly look to the other end, it seemed so far off: so she began to gaze at the things near her, and the pictures first of all, for she had a great liking for pictures. One in particular attracted her attention. She came back to it several times, and at length stood absorbed in it.

A blue summer sky, with white fleecy clouds floating beneath it, hung over a hill green to the very top, and alive with streams darting down its sides toward the valley below. On the face of the hill strayed a flock of sheep feeding, attended by a shepherd and two dogs. A little way apart, a girl stood with bare feet in a brook, building across it a bridge of rough stones. The wind was blowing her hair back from her rosy face. A lamb was feeding close beside her; and a sheepdog was trying to reach her hand to lick it.

"Oh, how I wish I were that little girl!" said the princess aloud. "I wonder how it is that some people are made to be so much happier than others! If I were that little girl, no one would ever call me naughty."

She gazed and gazed at the picture. At length she said to herself,

"I do not believe it is a picture. It is the real country, with a real hill, and a real little girl upon it. I shall soon see whether this isn't another of the old witch's cheats!"

She went close up to the picture, lifted her foot, and stepped over the frame.

"I am free, I am free!" she exclaimed; and she felt the wind upon her cheek.

The sound of a closing door struck on her ear. She turned—and there was a blank wall, without door or window, behind her. The hill with the sheep was before her, and she set out at once to reach it.

Now, if I am asked how this could be, I can only answer, that it was a result of the interaction of things outside and things inside, of the wise woman's skill, and the silly child's folly. If this does not satisfy my questioner, I can only add, that the wise woman was able to do far more wonderful things than this.

VI.

Meantime the wise woman was busy as she always was; and her business now was with the child of the shepherd and shepherdess, away in the north. Her name was Agnes.

Her father and mother were poor, and could not give her many things. Rosamond would have utterly despised the rude, simple playthings she had. Yet in one respect they were of more value far than hers: the king bought Rosamond's with his money; Agnes's father made hers with his hands.

And while Agnes had but few things—not seeing many things about her, and not even knowing that there were many things anywhere, she did not wish for many things, and was therefore neither covetous nor avaricious.

She played with the toys her father made her, and thought them the most wonderful things in the world—windmills, and little crooks, and water-wheels, and sometimes lambs made all of wool, and dolls made out of the leg-bones of sheep, which her mother dressed for her; and of such playthings she was never tired. Sometimes, however, she preferred playing with stones, which were plentiful, and flowers, which were few, or the brooks that ran down the hill, of which, although they were many, she could only play with one at a time, and that, indeed, troubled her a little—or live lambs that were not all wool, or the sheep-dogs, which were very friendly with her, and the best of playfellows, as she thought, for she had no human ones to compare them with. Neither was she greedy after nice things, but content, as well she might be, with the homely food provided for her. Nor was she by nature particularly self-willed or disobedient; she generally did what her father and mother wished, and believed what they told her. But by degrees they had spoiled her; and this was the way: they were so proud of her that they always repeated every thing she said, and told every thing she did, even when she was present; and so full of admiration of their child were they, that they wondered and laughed at and praised things in her which in another child would never have struck them as the least remarkable, and some things even which would in another have disgusted them altogether. Impertinent and rude things done by THEIR child they thought SO clever! laughing at them as something quite marvellous; her commonplace speeches were said over again as if they had been the finest poetry; and the pretty ways which every moderately good child has were extolled as if the result of her excellent taste, and the choice of her judgment and will. They would even say sometimes that she ought not to hear her own praises for fear it should make her vain, and then whisper them behind their hands, but so loud that she could not fail to hear every word. The consequence was that she soon came to believe—so soon, that she could not recall the time when she did not believe, as the most absolute fact in the universe, that she was SOMEBODY; that is, she became most immoderately conceited.

Now as the least atom of conceit is a thing to be ashamed of, you may fancy what she was like with such a quantity of it inside her!

At first it did not show itself outside in any very active form; but the wise woman had been to the cottage, and had seen her sitting alone, with such a smile of self-satisfaction upon her face as would have been quite startling to her, if she had ever been startled at any thing; for through that smile she could see lying at the root of it the worm that made it. For some smiles are like the ruddiness of certain apples, which is owing to a centipede, or other creeping thing, coiled up at the heart of them. Only her worm had a face and shape the very image of her own; and she looked so simpering, and mawkish, and self-conscious, and silly, that she made the wise woman feel rather sick.

Not that the child was a fool. Had she been, the wise woman would have only pitied and loved her, instead of feeling sick when she looked at her. She had very fair abilities, and were she once but made humble, would be capable not only of doing a good deal in time, but of beginning at once to grow to no end. But, if she were not made humble, her growing would be to a mass of distorted shapes all huddled together; so that, although the body she now showed might grow up straight and well-shaped and comely to behold, the new body that was growing inside of it, and would come out of it when she died, would be ugly, and crooked this way and that, like an aged hawthorn that has lived hundreds of years exposed upon all sides to salt sea-winds.

44

As time went on, this disease of self-conceit went on too, gradually devouring the good that was in her. For there is no fault that does not bring its brothers and sisters and cousins to live with it. By degrees, from thinking herself so clever, she came to fancy that whatever seemed to her, must of course be the correct judgment, and whatever she wished, the right thing; and grew so obstinate, that at length her parents feared to thwart her in any thing, knowing well that she would never give in. But there are victories far worse than defeats; and to overcome an angel too gentle to put out all his strength, and ride away in triumph on the back of a devil, is one of the poorest.

So long as she was left to take her own way and do as she would, she gave her parents little trouble. She would play about by herself in the little garden with its few hardy flowers, or amongst the heather where the bees were busy; or she would wander away amongst the hills, and be nobody knew where, sometimes from morning to night; nor did her parents venture to find fault with her.

She never went into rages like the princess, and would have thought Rosamond—oh, so ugly and vile! if she had seen her in one of her passions. But she was no better, for all that, and was quite as ugly in the eyes of the wise woman, who could not only see but read her face. What is there to choose between a face distorted to hideousness by anger, and one distorted to silliness by self-complacency? True, there is more hope of helping the angry child out of her form of selfishness than the conceited child out of hers; but on the other hand, the conceited child was not so terrible or dangerous as the wrathful one. The conceited one, however, was sometimes very angry, and then her anger was more spiteful than the other's; and, again, the wrathful one was often very conceited too. So that, on the whole, of two very unpleasant creatures, I would say that the king's daughter would have been the worse, had not the shepherd's been quite as bad. But, as I have said, the wise woman had her eye upon her: she saw that something special must be done, else she would be one of those who kneel to their own shadows till feet grow on their knees; then go down on their hands till their hands grow into feet; then lay their faces on the ground till they grow into snouts; when at last they are a hideous sort of lizards, each of which believes himself the best, wisest, and loveliest being in the world, yea, the very centre of the universe. And so they run about forever looking for their own shadows, that they may worship them, and miserable because they cannot find them, being themselves too near the ground to have any shadows; and what becomes of them at last there is but one who knows.

The wise woman, therefore, one day walked up to the door of the shepherd's cottage, dressed like a poor woman, and asked for a drink of water. The shepherd's wife looked at her, liked her, and brought her a cup of milk. The wise woman took it, for she made it a rule to accept every kindness that was offered her.

Agnes was not by nature a greedy girl, as I have said; but self-conceit will go far to generate every other vice under the sun. Vanity, which is a form of self-conceit, has repeatedly shown itself as the deepest feeling in the heart of a horrible murderess.

That morning, at breakfast, her mother had stinted her in milk—just a little—that she might have enough to make some milk-porridge for their dinner. Agnes did not mind it at the time, but when she saw the milk now given to a beggar, as she called the wise woman—though, surely, one might ask a draught of water, and accept a draught of milk, without being a beggar in any such sense as Agnes's contemptuous use of the word implied—a cloud came upon her forehead, and a double vertical wrinkle settled over her nose. The wise woman saw it, for all her business was with Agnes though she little knew it, and, rising, went and offered the cup to the child, where she sat with her knitting in a corner. Agnes looked at it, did not want it, was inclined to refuse it from a beggar, but thinking it would show her consequence to assert her rights, took it and drank it up. For whoever is possessed by a devil, judges with the mind of that devil; and hence Agnes was guilty of such a meanness as many who are themselves capable of something just as bad will consider incredible.

The wise woman waited till she had finished it—then, looking into the empty cup, said:

"You might have given me back as much as you had no claim upon!"

Agnes turned away and made no answer—far less from shame than indignation.

The wise woman looked at the mother.

"You should not have offered it to her if you did not mean her to have it," said the mother, siding with the devil in her child against the wise woman and her child too. Some foolish people think they take another's part when they take the part he takes.

The wise woman said nothing, but fixed her eyes upon her, and soon the mother hid her face in her apron weeping. Then she turned again to Agnes, who had never looked round but sat with her back to both, and suddenly lapped her in the folds of her cloak. When the mother again lifted her eyes, she had vanished.

Never supposing she had carried away her child, but uncomfortable because of what she had said to the poor woman, the mother went to the door, and called after her as she toiled slowly up the hill. But she never turned her head; and the mother went back into her cottage.

The wise woman walked close past the shepherd and his dogs, and through the midst of his flock of sheep. The shepherd wondered where she could be going—right up the hill. There was something strange about her too, he thought; and he followed her with his eyes as she went up and up.

It was near sunset, and as the sun went down, a gray cloud settled on the top of the mountain, which his last rays turned into a rosy gold. Straight into this cloud the shepherd saw the woman hold her pace, and in it she vanished. He little imagined that his child was under her cloak.

He went home as usual in the evening, but Agnes had not come in. They were accustomed to such an absence now and then, and were not at first frightened; but when it grew dark and she did not appear, the husband set out with his dogs in one direction, and the wife in another, to seek their child. Morning came and they had not found her. Then the whole country-side arose to search for the missing Agnes; but day after day and night after night passed, and nothing was discovered of or concerning her, until at length all gave up the search in despair except the mother, although she was nearly convinced now that the poor woman had carried her off.

One day she had wandered some distance from her cottage, thinking she might come upon the remains of her daughter at the foot of some cliff, when she came suddenly, instead, upon a disconsolate-looking creature sitting on a stone by the side of a stream.

Her hair hung in tangles from her head; her clothes were tattered, and through the rents her skin showed in many places; her cheeks were white, and worn thin with hunger; the hollows were dark under her eyes, and they stood out scared and wild. When she caught sight of the shepherdess, she jumped to her feet, and would have run away, but fell down in a faint.

At first sight the mother had taken her for her own child, but now she saw, with a pang of disappointment, that she had mistaken. Full of compassion, nevertheless, she said to herself:

"If she is not my Agnes, she is as much in need of help as if she were. If I cannot be good to my own, I will be as good as I can to some other woman's; and though I should scorn to be consoled for the loss of one by the presence of another, I yet may find some gladness in rescuing one child from the death which has taken the other."

Perhaps her words were not just like these, but her thoughts were. She took up the child, and carried her home. And this is how Rosamond came to occupy the place of the little girl whom she had envied in the picture.

VII.

Notwithstanding the differences between the two girls, which were, indeed, so many that most people would have said they were not in the least alike, they were the same in this, that each cared more for her own fancies and desires than for any thing else in the world. But I will tell you another difference: the princess was like several children in one—such was the variety of her moods; and in one mood she had no recollection or care about any thing whatever belonging to a previous mood—not even if it had left her but a moment before, and had been so violent as to make her ready to put her hand in the fire to get what she wanted. Plainly she was the mere puppet of her moods, and more than that, any cunning nurse who knew her well enough could call or send away those moods almost as she pleased, like a showman pulling strings behind a show. Agnes, on the contrary, seldom changed her mood, but kept that of calm assured self-satisfaction. Father nor mother had ever by wise punishment helped her to gain a victory over herself, and do what she did not like or choose; and their folly in reasoning with one unreasonable had fixed her in her conceit. She would actually nod her head to herself in complacent pride that she had stood out against them. This, however, was not so difficult as to justify even the pride of having conquered, seeing she loved them so little, and paid so little attention to the arguments and persuasions they used. Neither, when she found herself wrapped in the dark folds of the wise woman's cloak, did she behave in the least like the princess, for she was not afraid. "She'll soon set me down," she said, too self-important to suppose that any one would dare do her an injury.

Whether it be a good thing or a bad not to be afraid depends on what the fearlessness is founded upon. Some have no fear, because they have no knowledge of the danger: there is nothing fine in that. Some are too stupid to be afraid: there is nothing fine in that. Some who are not easily frightened would yet turn their backs and run, the moment they were frightened: such never had more courage than fear. But the man who will do his work in spite of his fear is a man of true courage. The fearlessness of Agnes was only ignorance: she did not know what it was to be hurt; she had never read a single story of giant, or ogress or wolf; and her mother had never carried out one of her threats of punishment. If the wise woman had but pinched her, she would have shown herself an abject little coward, trembling with fear at every change of motion so long as she carried her.

Nothing such, however, was in the wise woman's plan for the curing of her. On and on she carried her without a word. She knew that if she set her down she would never run after her like the princess, at least not before the evil thing was already upon her. On and on she went, never halting, never letting the light look in, or Agnes look out. She walked very fast, and got home to her cottage very soon after the princess had gone from it.

But she did not set Agnes down either in the cottage or in the great hall. She had other places, none of them alike. The place she had chosen for Agnes was a strange one—such a one as is to be found nowhere else in the wide world.

It was a great hollow sphere, made of a substance similar to that of the mirror which Rosamond had broken, but differently compounded. That substance no one could see by itself. It had neither door, nor window, nor any opening to break its perfect roundness.

The wise woman carried Agnes into a dark room, there undressed her, took from her hand her knitting-needles, and put her, naked as she was born, into the hollow sphere.

What sort of a place it was she could not tell. She could see nothing but a faint cold bluish light all about her. She could not feel that any thing supported her, and yet she did not sink. She stood for a while, perfectly calm, then sat down. Nothing bad could happen to HER—she was so important! And, indeed, it was but this: she had cared only for Somebody, and now she was going to have only Somebody. Her own choice was going to be carried a good deal farther for her than she would have knowingly carried it for herself.

After sitting a while, she wished she had something to do, but nothing came. A little longer, and it grew wearisome. She would see whether she could not walk out of the strange luminous dusk that surrounded her.

Walk she found she could, well enough, but walk out she could not. On and on she went, keeping as much in a straight line as she might, but after walking until she was thoroughly tired, she found herself no nearer out of her prison than before. She had not, indeed, advanced a single step; for, in whatever direction she tried to go, the sphere turned round and round, answering her feet accordingly. Like a squirrel in his cage she but kept placing another spot of the cunningly suspended sphere under her feet, and she would have been still only at its lowest point after walking for ages.

At length she cried aloud; but there was no answer. It grew dreary and drearier—in her, that is: outside there was no change. Nothing was overhead, nothing under foot, nothing on either hand, but the same pale, faint, bluish glimmer. She wept at last, then grew very angry, and then sullen; but nobody heeded whether she cried or laughed. It was all the same to the cold unmoving twilight that rounded her. On and on went the dreary hours—or did they go at all?—"no change, no pause, no hope;"—on and on till she FELT she was forgotten, and then she grew strangely still and fell asleep.

The moment she was asleep, the wise woman came, lifted her out, and laid her in her bosom; fed her with a wonderful milk, which she received without knowing it; nursed her all the night long, and, just ere she woke, laid her back in the blue sphere again.

When first she came to herself, she thought the horrors of the preceding day had been all a dream of the night. But they soon asserted themselves as facts, for here they were!—nothing to see but a cold blue light, and nothing to do but see it. Oh, how slowly the hours went by! She lost all notion of time. If she had been told that she had been there twenty years, she would have believed it—or twenty minutes—it would have been all the same: except for weariness, time was for her no more.

Another night came, and another still, during both of which the wise woman nursed and fed her. But she knew nothing of that, and the same one dreary day seemed ever brooding over her.

All at once, on the third day, she was aware that a naked child was seated beside her. But there was something about the child that made her shudder. She never looked at Agnes, but sat with her chin sunk on her chest, and her eyes staring at her own toes. She was the color of pale earth, with a pinched nose, and a mere slit in her face for a mouth.

"How ugly she is!" thought Agnes. "What business has she beside me!"

But it was so lonely that she would have been glad to play with a serpent, and put out her hand to touch her. She touched nothing. The child, also, put out her hand—but in the direction away from Agnes. And that was well, for if she had touched Agnes it would have killed her. Then Agnes said, "Who are you?" And the little girl said, "Who are you?" "I am Agnes," said Agnes; and the little girl said, "I am Agnes." Then Agnes thought she was mocking her, and said, "You are ugly;" and the little girl said, "You are ugly."

Then Agnes lost her temper, and put out her hands to seize the little girl; but lo! the little girl was gone, and she found herself tugging at her own hair. She let go; and there was the little girl again! Agnes was furious now, and flew at her to bite her. But she found her teeth in her own arm, and the little girl was gone—only to return again; and each time she came back she was tenfold uglier than before. And now Agnes hated her with her whole heart.

The moment she hated her, it flashed upon her with a sickening disgust that the child was not another, but her Self, her Somebody, and that she was now shut up with her for ever and ever—no more for one moment ever to be alone. In her agony of despair, sleep descended, and she slept.

When she woke, there was the little girl, heedless, ugly, miserable, staring at her own toes. All at once, the creature began to smile, but with such an odious, self-satisfied expression, that Agnes felt ashamed of seeing her. Then she began to pat her own cheeks, to stroke her own body, and examine her finger-ends, nodding her head with satisfaction. Agnes felt that there could not be such another hateful, ape-like creature, and at the same time was perfectly aware she was only doing outside of her what she herself had been doing, as long as she could remember, inside of her.

She turned sick at herself, and would gladly have been put out of existence, but for three days the odious companionship went on. By the third day, Agnes was not merely sick but ashamed of the life she had hitherto led, was despicable in her own eyes, and astonished that she had never seen the truth concerning herself before.

The next morning she woke in the arms of the wise woman; the horror had vanished from her sight, and two heavenly eyes were gazing upon her. She wept and clung to her, and the more she clung, the more tenderly did the great strong arms close around her.

When she had lain thus for a while, the wise woman carried her into her cottage, and washed her in the little well; then dressed her in clean garments, and gave her bread and milk. When she had eaten it, she called her to her, and said very solemnly,—

"Agnes, you must not imagine you are cured. That you are ashamed of yourself now is no sign that the cause for such shame has ceased. In new circumstances, especially after you have done well for a while, you will be in danger of thinking just as much of yourself as before. So beware of yourself. I am going from home, and leave you in charge of the house. Do just as I tell you till my return."

She then gave her the same directions she had formerly given Rosamond—with this difference, that she told her to go into the picture-hall when she pleased, showing her the entrance, against which the clock no longer stood—and went away, closing the door behind her.

VIII.

As soon as she was left alone, Agnes set to work tidying and dusting the cottage, made up the fire, watered the bed, and cleaned the inside of the windows: the wise woman herself always kept the outside of them clean. When she had done, she found her dinner—of the same sort she was used to at home, but better—in the hole of the wall. When she had eaten it, she went to look at the pictures.

By this time her old disposition had begun to rouse again. She had been doing her duty, and had in consequence begun again to think herself Somebody. However strange it may well seem, to do one's duty will make any one conceited who only does it sometimes. Those who do it always would as soon think of being conceited of eating their dinner as of doing their duty. What honest boy would pride himself on not picking pockets? A thief who was trying to reform would. To be conceited of doing one's duty is then a sign of how little one does it, and how little one sees what a contemptible thing it is not to do it. Could any but a low creature be conceited of not being contemptible? Until our duty becomes to us common as breathing, we are poor creatures.

So Agnes began to stroke herself once more, forgetting her late self-stroking companion, and never reflecting that she was now doing what she had then abhorred. And in this mood she went into the picture-gallery.

The first picture she saw represented a square in a great city, one side of which was occupied by a splendid marble palace, with great flights of broad steps leading up to the door. Between it and the square was a marble-paved court, with gates of brass, at which stood sentries in gorgeous uniforms, and to which was affixed the following proclamation in letters of gold, large enough for Agnes to read:—

"By the will of the King, from this time until further notice, every stray child found in the realm shall be brought without a moment's delay to the palace. Whoever shall be found having done otherwise shall straightway lose his head by the hand of the public executioner."

Agnes's heart beat loud, and her face flushed.

"Can there be such a city in the world?" she said to herself. "If I only knew where it was, I should set out for it at once. THERE would be the place for a clever girl like me!"

Her eyes fell on the picture which had so enticed Rosamond. It was the very country where her father fed his flocks. Just round the shoulder of the hill was the cottage where her parents lived, where she was born and whence she had been carried by the beggar-woman.

"Ah!" she said, "they didn't know me there. They little thought what I could be, if I had the chance. If I were but in this good, kind, loving, generous king's palace, I should soon be such a great lady as they never saw! Then they would understand what a good little girl I had always been! And I shouldn't forget my poor parents like some I have read of. I would be generous. I should never be selfish and proud like girls in story-books!"

As she said this, she turned her back with disdain upon the picture of her home, and setting herself before the picture of the palace, stared at it with wide ambitious eyes, and a heart whose every beat was a throb of arrogant self-esteem.

The shepherd-child was now worse than ever the poor princess had been. For the wise woman had given her a terrible lesson one of which the princess was not capable, and she had known what it meant; yet here she was as bad as ever, therefore worse than before. The ugly creature whose presence had made her so miserable had indeed crept out of sight and mind too—but where was she? Nestling in her very heart, where most of all she had her company, and least of all could see her. The wise woman had called her out, that Agnes might see what sort of creature she was herself; but now she was snug in her soul's bed again, and she did not even suspect she was there.

After gazing a while at the palace picture, during which her ambitious pride rose and rose, she turned yet again in condescending mood, and honored the home picture with one stare more.

"What a poor, miserable spot it is compared with this lordly palace!" she said.

But presently she spied something in it she had not seen before, and drew nearer. It was the form of a little girl, building a bridge of stones over one of the hill-brooks.

"Ah, there I am myself!" she said. "That is just how I used to do.—No," she resumed, "it is not me. That snub-nosed little fright could never be meant for me! It was the frock that made me think so. But it IS a picture of the place. I declare, I can see the smoke of the cottage rising from behind the hill! What a dull, dirty, insignificant spot it is! And what a life to lead there!"

She turned once more to the city picture. And now a strange thing took place. In proportion as the other, to the eyes of her mind, receded into the background, this, to her present bodily eyes, appeared to come forward and assume reality. At last, after it had been in this way growing upon her for some time, she gave a cry of conviction, and said aloud,—

"I do believe it is real! That frame is only a trick of the woman to make me fancy it a picture lest I should go and make my fortune. She is a witch, the ugly old creature! It would serve her right to tell the king and have her punished for not taking me to the palace—one of his poor lost children he is so fond of! I should like to see her ugly old head cut off. Anyhow I will try my luck without asking her leave. How she has ill used me!"

But at that moment, she heard the voice of the wise woman calling, "Agnes!" and, smoothing her face, she tried to look as good as she could, and walked back into the cottage. There stood the wise woman, looking all round the place, and examining her work. She fixed her eyes upon Agnes in a way that confused her, and made her cast hers down, for she felt as if she were reading her thoughts. The wise woman, however, asked no questions, but began to talk about her work, approving of some of it, which filled her with arrogance, and showing how some of it might have been done better, which filled her with resentment. But the wise woman seemed to take no care of what she might be thinking, and went straight on with her lesson. By the time it was over, the power of reading thoughts would not have been necessary to a knowledge of what was in the mind of Agnes, for it had all come to the surface—that is up into her face, which is the surface of the mind. Ere it had time to sink down again, the wise woman caught up the little mirror, and held it before her: Agnes saw her Somebody—the very embodiment of miserable conceit and ugly ill-temper. She gave such a scream of horror that the wise woman pitied her, and laying aside the mirror, took her upon her knees, and talked to her most kindly and solemnly; in particular about the necessity of destroying the ugly things that come out of the heart—so ugly that they make the very face over them ugly also.

And what was Agnes doing all the time the wise woman was talking to her? Would you believe it?—instead of thinking how to kill the ugly things in her heart, she was with all her might resolving to be more careful of her face, that is, to keep down the things in her heart so that they should not show in her face, she was resolving to be a hypocrite as well as a self-worshipper. Her heart was wormy, and the worms were eating very fast at it now.

Then the wise woman laid her gently down upon the heather-bed, and she fell fast asleep, and had an awful dream about her Somebody.

When she woke in the morning, instead of getting up to do the work of the house, she lay thinking—to evil purpose. In place of taking her dream as a warning, and thinking over what the wise woman had said the night before, she communed with herself in this fashion:—

"If I stay here longer, I shall be miserable, It is nothing better than slavery. The old witch shows me horrible things in the day to set me dreaming horrible things in the night. If I don't run away, that frightful blue prison and the disgusting girl will come back, and I shall go out of my mind. How I do wish I could find the way to the good king's palace! I shall go and look at the picture again—if it be a picture—as soon as I've got my clothes on. The work can wait. It's not my work. It's the old witch's; and she ought to do it herself."

She jumped out of bed, and hurried on her clothes. There was no wise woman to be seen; and she hastened into the hall. There was the picture, with the marble palace, and the proclamation shining in letters of gold upon its gates of brass. She stood before it, and gazed and gazed; and all the time it kept growing upon her in some strange way, until at last she was fully persuaded that it was no picture, but a real city, square, and marble palace, seen through a framed opening in the wall. She ran up to the frame, stepped over it, felt the wind blow upon her cheek, heard the sound of a closing door behind her, and was free. FREE was she, with that creature inside her?

The same moment a terrible storm of thunder and lightning, wind and rain, came on. The uproar was appalling. Agnes threw herself upon the ground, hid her face in her hands, and there lay until it was over. As soon as she felt the sun shining on her, she rose. There was the city far away on the horizon. Without once turning to take a farewell look of the place she was leaving, she set off, as fast as her feet would carry her, in the direction of the city. So eager was she, that again and again she fell, but only to get up, and run on faster than before.

IX.

The shepherdess carried Rosamond home, gave her a warm bath in the tub in which she washed her linen, made her some bread-and-milk, and after she had eaten it, put her to bed in Agnes's crib, where she slept all the rest of that day and all the following night.

When at last she opened her eyes, it was to see around her a far poorer cottage than the one she had left—very bare and uncomfortable indeed, she might well have thought; but she had come through such troubles of late, in the way of hunger and weariness and cold and fear, that she was not altogether in her ordinary mood of fault-finding, and so was able to lie enjoying the thought that at length she was safe, and going to be fed and kept warm. The idea of doing any thing in return for shelter and food and clothes, did not, however, even cross her mind.

But the shepherdess was one of that plentiful number who can be wiser concerning other women's children than concerning their own. Such will often give you very tolerable hints as to how you ought to manage your children, and will find fault neatly enough with the system you are trying to carry out; but all their wisdom goes off in talking, and there is none left for doing what they have themselves said. There is one road talk never finds, and that is the way into the talker's own hands and feet. And such never seem to know themselves—not even when they are reading about themselves in print. Still, not being specially blinded in any direction but their own, they can sometimes even act with a little sense towards children who are not theirs. They are affected with a sort of blindness like that which renders some people incapable of seeing, except sideways.

She came up to the bed, looked at the princess, and saw that she was better. But she did not like her much. There was no mark of a princess about her, and never had been since she began to run alone. True, hunger had brought down her fat cheeks, but it had not turned down her impudent nose, or driven the sullenness and greed from her mouth. Nothing but the wise woman could do that—and not even she, without the aid of the princess herself. So the shepherdess thought what a poor substitute she had got for her own lovely Agnes—who was in fact equally repulsive, only in a way to which she had got used; for the selfishness in her love had blinded her to the thin pinched nose and the mean self-satisfied mouth. It was well for the princess, though, sad as it is to say, that the shepherdess did not take to her, for then she would most likely have only done her harm instead of good.

"Now, my girl," she said, "you must get up, and do something. We can't keep idle folk here."

"I'm not a folk," said Rosamond; "I'm a princess."

"A pretty princess—with a nose like that! And all in rags too! If you tell such stories, I shall soon let you know what I think of you."

Rosamond then understood that the mere calling herself a princess, without having any thing to show for it, was of no use. She obeyed and rose, for she was hungry; but she had to sweep the floor ere she had any thing to eat.

The shepherd came in to breakfast, and was kinder than his wife. He took her up in his arms and would have kissed her; but she took it as an insult from a man whose hands smelt of tar, and kicked and screamed with rage. The poor man, finding he had made a mistake, set her down at once. But to look at the two, one might well have judged it condescension rather than rudeness in such a man to kiss such a child. He was tall, and almost stately, with a thoughtful forehead, bright eyes, eagle nose, and gentle mouth; while the princess was such as I have described her.

Not content with being set down and let alone, she continued to storm and scold at the shepherd, crying she was a princess, and would like to know what right he had to touch her! But he only looked down upon her from the height of his tall person with a benignant smile, regarding her as a spoiled little ape whose mother had flattered her by calling her a princess.

"Turn her out of doors, the ungrateful hussy!" cried his wife. "With your bread and your milk inside her ugly body, this is what she gives you for it! Troth, I'm paid for carrying home such an ill-bred tramp in my arms! My own poor angel Agnes! As if that ill-tempered toad were one hair like her!"

These words drove the princess beside herself; for those who are most given to abuse can least endure it. With fists and feet and teeth, as was her wont, she rushed at the shepherdess, whose hand was already raised to deal her a sound box on the ear, when a better appointed minister of vengeance suddenly showed himself. Bounding in at the cottage-door came one of the sheep-dogs, who was called Prince, and whom I shall not refer to with a WHICH, because he was a very superior animal indeed, even for a sheep-dog, which is the most intelligent of dogs: he flew at the princess, knocked her down, and commenced shaking her so violently as to tear her miserable clothes to pieces. Used, however, to mouthing little lambs, he took care not to hurt her much, though for her good he left her a blue nip or two by way of letting her imagine what biting might be. His master, knowing he would not injure her, thought it better not to call him off, and in half a minute he left her of his own accord, and, casting a glance of indignant rebuke behind him as he went, walked slowly to the hearth, where he laid himself down with his tail toward her. She rose, terrified almost to death, and would have crept again into Agnes's crib for refuge; but the shepherdess cried—

"Come, come, princess! I'll have no skulking to bed in the good daylight. Go and clean your master's Sunday boots there."

"I will not!" screamed the princess, and ran from the house.

"Prince!" cried the shepherdess, and up jumped the dog, and looked in her face, wagging his bushy tail.

"Fetch her back," she said, pointing to the door.

With two or three bounds Prince caught the princess, again threw her down, and taking her by her clothes dragged her back into the cottage, and dropped her at his mistress' feet, where she lay like a bundle of rags.

"Get up," said the shepherdess.

Rosamond got up as pale as death.

"Go and clean the boots."

"I don't know how."

"Go and try. There are the brushes, and yonder is the blacking-pot."

Instructing her how to black boots, it came into the thought of the shepherdess what a fine thing it would be if she could teach this miserable little wretch, so forsaken and ill-bred, to be a good, well-behaved, respectable child. She was hardly the woman to do it, but every thing well meant is a help, and she had the wisdom to beg her husband to place Prince under her orders for a while, and not take him to the hill as usual, that he might help her in getting the princess into order.

When the husband was gone, and his boots, with the aid of her own finishing touches, at last quite respectably brushed, the shepherdess told the princess that she might go and play for a while, only she must not go out of sight of the cottage-door.

The princess went right gladly, with the firm intention, however, of getting out of sight by slow degrees, and then at once taking to her heels. But no sooner was she over the threshold than the shepherdess said to the dog, "Watch her;" and out shot Prince.

The moment she saw him, Rosamond threw herself on her face, trembling from head to foot. But the dog had no quarrel with her, and of the violence against which he always felt bound to protest in dog fashion, there was no sign in the prostrate shape before him; so he poked his nose under her, turned her over, and began licking her face and hands. When she saw that he meant to be friendly, her love for animals, which had had no indulgence for a long time now, came wide awake, and in a little while they were romping and rushing about, the best friends in the world.

Having thus seen one enemy, as she thought, changed to a friend, she began to resume her former plan, and crept cunningly farther and farther. At length she came to a little hollow, and instantly rolled down into it. Finding then that she was out of sight of the cottage, she ran off at full speed.

But she had not gone more than a dozen paces, when she heard a growling rush behind her, and the next instant was on the ground, with the dog standing over her, showing his teeth, and flaming at her with his eyes. She threw her arms round his neck, and immediately he licked her face, and let her get up. But the moment she would have moved a step farther from the cottage, there he was it front of her, growling, and showing his teeth. She saw it was of no use, and went back with him.

Thus was the princess provided with a dog for a private tutor—just the right sort for her.

Presently the shepherdess appeared at the door and called her. She would have disregarded the summons, but Prince did his best to let her know that, until she could obey herself, she must obey him. So she went into the cottage, and there the shepherdess ordered her to peel the potatoes for dinner. She sulked and refused. Here Prince could do nothing to help his mistress, but she had not to go far to find another ally.

"Very well, Miss Princess!" she said; "we shall soon see how you like to go without when dinner-time comes."

Now the princess had very little foresight, and the idea of future hunger would have moved her little; but happily, from her game of romps with Prince, she had begun to be hungry already, and so the threat had force. She took the knife and began to peel the potatoes.

By slow degrees the princess improved a little. A few more outbreaks of passion, and a few more savage attacks from Prince, and she had learned to try to restrain herself when she felt the passion coming on; while a few dinnerless afternoons entirely opened her eyes to the necessity of working in order to eat. Prince was her first, and Hunger her second dog-counsellor.

But a still better thing was that she soon grew very fond of Prince. Towards the gaining of her affections, he had three advantages: first, his nature was inferior to hers; next, he was a beast; and last, she was afraid of him; for so spoiled was she that she could more easily love what was below than what was above her, and a beast, than one of her own kind, and indeed could hardly have ever come to love any thing much that she had not first learned to fear,

63

and the white teeth and flaming eyes of the angry Prince were more terrible to her than any thing had yet been, except those of the wolf, which she had now forgotten. Then again, he was such a delightful playfellow, that so long as she neither lost her temper, nor went against orders, she might do almost any thing she pleased with him. In fact, such was his influence upon her, that she who had scoffed at the wisest woman in the whole world, and derided the wishes of her own father and mother, came at length to regard this dog as a superior being, and to look up to him as well as love him. And this was best of all.

The improvement upon her, in the course of a month, was plain. She had quite ceased to go into passions, and had actually begun to take a little interest in her work and try to do it well.

Still, the change was mostly an outside one. I do not mean that she was pretending. Indeed she had never been given to pretence of any sort. But the change was not in HER, only in her mood. A second change of circumstances would have soon brought a second change of behavior; and, so long as that was possible, she continued the same sort of person she had always been. But if she had not gained much, a trifle had been gained for her: a little quietness and order of mind, and hence a somewhat greater possibility of the first idea of right arising in it, whereupon she would begin to see what a wretched creature she was, and must continue until she herself was right.

Meantime the wise woman had been watching her when she least fancied it, and taking note of the change that was passing upon her. Out of the large eyes of a gentle sheep she had been watching her—a sheep that puzzled the shepherd; for every now and then she would appear in his flock, and he would catch sight of her two or three times in a day, sometimes for days together, yet he never saw her when he looked for her, and never when he counted the flock into the fold at night. He knew she was not one of his; but where could she come from, and where could she go to? For there was no other flock within many miles, and he never could get near enough to her to see whether or not she was marked. Nor was Prince of the least use to him for the unravelling of the mystery; for although, as often as he told him to fetch the strange sheep, he went bounding to her at once, it was only to lie down at her feet.

At length, however, the wise woman had made up her mind, and after that the strange sheep no longer troubled the shepherd.

As Rosamond improved, the shepherdess grew kinder. She gave her all Agnes's clothes, and began to treat her much more like a daughter. Hence she had a great deal of liberty after the little work required of her was over, and would often spend hours at a time with the shepherd, watching the sheep and the dogs, and learning a little from seeing how Prince, and the others as well, managed their charge—how they never touched the sheep that did as they were told and turned when they were bid, but jumped on a disobedient flock, and ran along their backs, biting, and barking, and half choking themselves with mouthfuls of their wool.

Then also she would play with the brooks, and learn their songs, and build bridges over them. And sometimes she would be seized with such delight of heart that she would spread out her arms to the wind, and go rushing up the hill till her breath left her, when she would tumble down in the heather, and lie there till it came back again.

A noticeable change had by this time passed also on her countenance. Her coarse shapeless mouth had begun to show a glimmer of lines and curves about it, and the fat had not returned with the roses to her cheeks, so that her eyes looked larger than before; while, more noteworthy still, the bridge of her nose had grown higher, so that it was less of the impudent, insignificant thing inherited from a certain great-great-great-grandmother, who had little else to leave her. For a long time, it had fitted her very well, for it was just like her; but now there was ground for alteration, and already the granny who gave it her would not have recognized it. It was growing a little liker Prince's; and Prince's was a long, perceptive, sagacious nose,—one that was seldom mistaken.

One day about noon, while the sheep were mostly lying down, and the shepherd, having left them to the care of the dogs, was himself stretched under the shade of a rock a little way apart, and the princess sat knitting, with Prince at her feet, lying in wait for a snap at a great fly, for even he had his follies—Rosamond saw a poor woman come toiling up the hill, but took little notice of her until she was passing, a few yards off, when she heard her utter the dog's name in a low voice.

Immediately on the summons, Prince started up and followed her—with hanging head, but gently-wagging tail. At first the princess thought he was merely taking observations, and consulting with his nose whether she was respectable or not, but she soon saw that he was following her in meek submission. Then she sprung to her feet and cried, "Prince, Prince!" But Prince only turned his head and gave her an odd look, as if he were trying to smile, and could not. Then the princess grew angry, and ran after him, shouting, "Prince, come here directly." Again Prince turned his head, but this time to growl and show his teeth.

The princess flew into one of her forgotten rages, and picking up a stone, flung it at the woman. Prince turned and darted at her, with fury in his eyes, and his white teeth gleaming. At the awful sight the princess turned also, and would have fled, but he was upon her in a moment, and threw her to the ground, and there she lay.

It was evening when she came to herself. A cool twilight wind, that somehow seemed to come all the way from the stars, was blowing upon her. The poor woman and Prince, the shepherd and his sheep, were all gone, and she was left alone with the wind upon the heather.

She felt sad, weak, and, perhaps, for the first time in her life, a little ashamed. The violence of which she had been guilty had vanished from her spirit, and now lay in her memory with the calm morning behind it, while in front the quiet dusky night was now closing in the loud shame betwixt a double peace. Between the two her passion looked ugly. It pained her to remember. She felt it was hateful, and HERS.

But, alas, Prince was gone! That horrid woman had taken him away! The fury rose again in her heart, and raged—until it came to her mind how her dear Prince would have flown at her throat if he had seen her in such a passion. The memory calmed her, and she rose and went home. There, perhaps, she would find Prince, for surely he could never have been such a silly dog as go away altogether with a strange woman!

She opened the door and went in. Dogs were asleep all about the cottage, it seemed to her, but nowhere was Prince. She crept away to her little bed, and cried herself asleep.

In the morning the shepherd and shepherdess were indeed glad to find she had come home, for they thought she had run away.

"Where is Prince?" she cried, the moment she waked.

"His mistress has taken him," answered the shepherd.

"Was that woman his mistress?"

"I fancy so. He followed her as if he had known her all his life. I am very sorry to lose him, though."

The poor woman had gone close past the rock where the shepherd lay. He saw her coming, and thought of the strange sheep which had been feeding beside him when he lay down. "Who can she be?" he said to himself; but when he noted how Prince followed her, without even looking up at him as he passed, he remembered how Prince had come to him. And this was how: as he lay in bed one fierce winter morning, just about to rise, he heard the voice of a woman call to him through the storm, "Shepherd, I have brought you a dog. Be good to him. I will come again and fetch him away." He dressed as quickly as he could, and went to the door. It was half snowed up, but on the top of the white mound before it stood Prince. And now he had gone as mysteriously as he had come, and he felt sad.

Rosamond was very sorry too, and hence when she saw the looks of the shepherd and shepherdess, she was able to understand them. And she tried for a while to behave better to them because of their sorrow. So the loss of the dog brought them all nearer to each other.

X.

After the thunder-storm, Agnes did not meet with a single obstruction or misadventure. Everybody was strangely polite, gave her whatever she desired, and answered her questions, but asked none in return, and looked all the time as if her departure would be a relief. They were afraid, in fact, from her appearance, lest she should tell them that she was lost, when they would be bound, on pain of public execution, to take her to the palace.

But no sooner had she entered the city than she saw it would hardly do to present herself as a lost child at the palace-gates; for how were they to know that she was not an impostor, especially since she really was one, having run away from the wise woman? So she wandered about looking at every thing until she was tired, and bewildered by the noise and confusion all around her. The wearier she got, the more was she pushed in every direction. Having been used to a whole hill to wander upon, she was very awkward in the crowded streets, and often on the point of being run over by the horses, which seemed to her to be going every way like a frightened flock. She spoke to several persons, but no one stopped to answer her; and at length, her courage giving way, she felt lost indeed, and began to cry. A soldier saw her, and asked what was the matter.

"I've nowhere to go to," she sobbed.

"Where's your mother?" asked the soldier.

"I don't know," answered Agnes. "I was carried off by an old woman, who then went away and left me. I don't know where she is, or where I am myself."

"Come," said the soldier, "this is a case for his Majesty."

So saying, he took her by the hand, led her to the palace, and begged an audience of the king and queen. The porter glanced at Agnes, immediately admitted them, and showed them into a great splendid room, where the king and queen sat every day to review lost children, in the hope of one day thus finding their Rosamond. But they were by this time beginning to get tired of it. The moment they cast their eyes upon Agnes, the queen threw back her head, threw up her hands, and cried, "What a miserable, conceited, white-faced little ape!" and the king turned upon the soldier in wrath, and cried, forgetting his own decree, "What do you mean by bringing such a dirty, vulgar-looking, pert creature into my palace? The dullest soldier in my army could never for a moment imagine a child like THAT, one hair's-breadth like the lovely angel we lost!"

"I humbly beg your Majesty's pardon," said the soldier, "but what was I to do? There stands your Majesty's proclamation in gold letters on the brazen gates of the palace."

"I shall have it taken down," said the king. "Remove the child."

"Please your Majesty, what am I to do with her?"

"Take her home with you."

"I have six already, sire, and do not want her."

"Then drop her where you picked her up."

"If I do, sire, some one else will find her and bring her back to your Majesties."

"That will never do," said the king. "I cannot bear to look at her."

"For all her ugliness," said the queen, "she is plainly lost, and so is our Rosamond."

"It may be only a pretence, to get into the palace," said the king.

"Take her to the head scullion, soldier," said the queen, "and tell her to make her useful. If she should find out she has been pretending to be lost, she must let me know."

The soldier was so anxious to get rid of her, that he caught her up in his arms, hurried her from the room, found his way to the scullery, and gave her, trembling with fear, in charge to the head maid, with the queen's message.

As it was evident that the queen had no favor for her, the servants did as they pleased with her, and often treated her harshly. Not one amongst them liked her, nor was it any wonder, seeing that, with every step she took from the wise woman's house, she had grown more contemptible, for she had grown more conceited. Every civil answer given her, she attributed to the impression she made, not to the desire to get rid of her; and every kindness, to approbation of her looks and speech, instead of friendliness to a lonely child. Hence by this time she was twice as odious as before; for whoever has had such severe treatment as the wise woman gave her, and is not the better for it, always grows worse than before. They drove her about, boxed her ears on the smallest provocation, laid every thing to her charge, called her all manner of contemptuous names, jeered and scoffed at her awkwardnesses, and made her life so miserable that she was in a fair way to forget every thing she had learned, and know nothing but how to clean saucepans and kettles.

They would not have been so hard upon her, however, but for her irritating behavior. She dared not refuse to do as she was told, but she obeyed now with a pursed-up mouth, and now with a contemptuous smile. The only thing that sustained her was her constant contriving how to get out of the painful position in which she found herself. There is but one true way, however, of getting out of any position we may be in, and that is, to do the work of it so well that we grow fit for a better: I need not say this was not the plan upon which Agnes was cunning enough to fix.

She had soon learned from the talk around her the reason of the proclamation which had brought her hither.

"Was the lost princess so very beautiful?" she said one day to the youngest of her fellow-servants.

"Beautiful!" screamed the maid; "she was just the ugliest little toad you ever set eyes upon."

"What was she like?" asked Agnes.

"She was about your size, and quite as ugly, only not in the same way; for she had red cheeks, and a cocked little nose, and the biggest, ugliest mouth you ever saw."

Agnes fell a-thinking.

"Is there a picture of her anywhere in the palace?" she asked.

"How should I know? You can ask a housemaid."

Agnes soon learned that there was one, and contrived to get a peep of it. Then she was certain of what she had suspected from the description given of her, namely, that she was the same she had seen in the picture at the wise woman's house. The conclusion followed, that the lost princess must be staying with her father and mother, for assuredly in the picture she wore one of her frocks.

She went to the head scullion, and with humble manner, but proud heart, begged her to procure for her the favor of a word with the queen.

"A likely thing indeed!" was the answer, accompanied by a resounding box on the ear.

She tried the head cook next, but with no better success, and so was driven to her meditations again, the result of which was that she began to drop hints that she knew something about the princess. This came at length to the queen's ears, and she sent for her.

Absorbed in her own selfish ambitions, Agnes never thought of the risk to which she was about to expose her parents, but told the queen that in her wanderings she had caught sight of just such a lovely creature as she described the princess, only dressed like a peasant—saying, that, if the king would permit her to go and look for her, she had little doubt of bringing her back safe and sound within a few weeks.

But although she spoke the truth, she had such a look of cunning on her pinched face, that the queen could not possibly trust her, but believed that she made the proposal merely to get away, and have money given her for her journey. Still there was a chance, and she would not say any thing until she had consulted the king.

Then they had Agnes up before the lord chancellor, who, after much questioning of her, arrived at last, he thought, at some notion of the part of the country described by her—that was, if she spoke the truth, which, from her looks and behavior, he also considered entirely doubtful. Thereupon she was ordered back to the kitchen, and a band of soldiers, under a clever lawyer, sent out to search every foot of the supposed region. They were commanded not to return until they brought with them, bound hand and foot, such a shepherd pair as that of which they received a full description.

And now Agnes was worse off than before. For to her other miseries was added the fear of what would befall her when it was discovered that the persons of whom they were in quest, and whom she was certain they must find, were her own father and mother.

By this time the king and queen were so tired of seeing lost children, genuine or pretended—for they cared for no child any longer than there seemed a chance of its turning out their child—that with this new hope, which, however poor and vague at first, soon began to grow upon such imaginations as they had, they commanded the proclamation to be taken down from the palace gates, and directed the various sentries to admit no child whatever, lost or found, be the reason or pretence what it might, until further orders.

"I'm sick of children!" said the king to his secretary, as he finished dictating the direction.

XI.

After Prince was gone, the princess, by degrees, fell back into some of her bad old ways, from which only the presence of the dog, not her own betterment, had kept her. She never grew nearly so selfish again, but she began to let her angry old self lift up its head once more, until by and by she grew so bad that the shepherdess declared she should not stop in the house a day longer, for she was quite unendurable.

"It is all very well for you, husband," she said, "for you haven't her all day about you, and only see the best of her. But if you had her in work instead of play hours, you would like her no better than I do. And then it's not her ugly passions only, but when she's in one of her tantrums, it's impossible to get any work out of her. At such times she's just as obstinate as—as—as"—

She was going to say "as Agnes," but the feelings of a mother overcame her, and she could not utter the words.

"In fact," she said instead, "she makes my life miserable."

The shepherd felt he had no right to tell his wife she must submit to have her life made miserable, and therefore, although he was really much attached to Rosamond, he would not interfere; and the shepherdess told her she must look out for another place.

The princess was, however, this much better than before, even in respect of her passions, that they were not quite so bad, and after one was over, she was really ashamed of it. But not once, ever since the departure of Prince had she tried to check the rush of the evil temper when it came upon her. She hated it when she was out of it, and that was something; but while she was in it, she went full swing with it wherever the prince of the power of it pleased to carry her. Nor was this all: although she might by this time have known well enough that as soon as she was out of it she was certain to be ashamed of it, she would yet justify it to herself with twenty different arguments that looked very good at the time, but would have looked very poor indeed afterwards, if then she had ever remembered them.

She was not sorry to leave the shepherd's cottage, for she felt certain of soon finding her way back to her father and mother; and she would, indeed, have set out long before, but that her foot had somehow got hurt when Prince gave her his last admonition, and she had never since been able for long walks, which she sometimes blamed as the cause of her temper growing worse. But if people are good-tempered only when they are comfortable, what thanks have they?—Her foot was now much better; and as soon as the shepherdess had thus spoken, she resolved to set out at once, and work or beg her way home. At the moment she was quite unmindful of what she owed the good people, and, indeed, was as yet incapable of understanding a tenth part of her obligation to them. So she bade them good by without a tear, and limped her way down the hill, leaving the shepherdess weeping, and the shepherd looking very grave.

When she reached the valley she followed the course of the stream, knowing only that it would lead her away from the hill where the sheep fed, into richer lands where were farms and cattle. Rounding one of the roots of the hill she saw before her a poor woman walking slowly along the road with a burden of heather upon her back, and presently passed her, but had gone only a few paces farther when she heard her calling after her in a kind old voice—

"Your shoe-tie is loose, my child."

But Rosamond was growing tired, for her foot had become painful, and so she was cross, and neither returned answer, nor paid heed to the warning. For when we are cross, all our other faults grow busy, and poke up their ugly heads like maggots, and the princess's old dislike to doing any thing that came to her with the least air of advice about it returned in full force.

"My child," said the woman again, "if you don't fasten your shoe-tie, it will make you fall."

"Mind your own business," said Rosamond, without even turning her head, and had not gone more than three steps when she fell flat on her face on the path. She tried to get up, but the effort forced from her a scream, for she had sprained the ankle of the foot that was already lame.

The old woman was by her side instantly.

"Where are you hurt, child?" she asked, throwing down her burden and kneeling beside her.

"Go away," screamed Rosamond. "YOU made me fall, you bad woman!"

The woman made no reply, but began to feel her joints, and soon discovered the sprain. Then, in spite of Rosamond's abuse, and the violent pushes and even kicks she gave her, she took the hurt ankle in her hands, and stroked and pressed it, gently kneading it, as it were, with her thumbs, as if coaxing every particle of the muscles into its right place. Nor had she done so long before Rosamond lay still. At length she ceased, and said:—

"Now, my child, you may get up."

"I can't get up, and I'm not your child," cried Rosamond. "Go away."

Without another word the woman left her, took up her burden, and continued her journey.

In a little while Rosamond tried to get up, and not only succeeded, but found she could walk, and, indeed, presently discovered that her ankle and foot also were now perfectly well.

"I wasn't much hurt after all," she said to herself, nor sent a single grateful thought after the poor woman, whom she speedily passed once more upon the road without even a greeting.

Late in the afternoon she came to a spot where the path divided into two, and was taking the one she liked the look of better, when she started at the sound of the poor woman's voice, whom she thought she had left far behind, again calling her. She looked round, and there she was, toiling under her load of heather as before.

"You are taking the wrong turn, child." she cried.

"How can you tell that?" said Rosamond. "You know nothing about where I want to go."

"I know that road will take you where you won't want to go," said the woman.

"I shall know when I get there, then," returned Rosamond, "and no thanks to you."

She set off running. The woman took the other path, and was soon out of sight.

By and by, Rosamond found herself in the midst of a peat-moss—a flat, lonely, dismal, black country. She thought, however, that the road would soon lead her across to the other side of it among the farms, and went on without anxiety. But the stream, which had hitherto been her guide, had now vanished; and when it began to grow dark, Rosamond found that she could no longer distinguish the track. She turned, therefore, but only to find that the same darkness covered it behind as well as before. Still she made the attempt to go back by keeping as direct a line as she could, for the path was straight as an arrow. But she could not see enough even to start her in a line, and she had not gone far before she found herself hemmed in, apparently on every side, by ditches and pools of black, dismal, slimy water. And now it was so dark that she could see nothing more than the gleam of a bit of clear sky now and then in the water. Again and again she stepped knee-deep in black mud, and once tumbled down in the shallow edge of a terrible pool; after which she gave up the attempt to escape the meshes of the watery net, stood still, and began to cry bitterly, despairingly. She saw now that her unreasonable anger had made her foolish as well as rude, and felt that she was justly punished for her wickedness to the poor woman who had been so friendly to her. What would Prince think of her, if he knew? She cast herself on the ground, hungry, and cold, and weary.

Presently, she thought she saw long creatures come heaving out of the black pools. A toad jumped upon her, and she shrieked, and sprang to her feet, and would have run away headlong, when she spied in the distance a faint glimmer. She thought it was a Will-o'-the-wisp. What could he be after? Was he looking for her? She dared not run, lest he should see and pounce upon her. The light came nearer, and grew brighter and larger. Plainly, the little fiend was looking for her—he would torment her. After many twistings and turnings among the pools, it came straight towards her, and she would have shrieked, but that terror made her dumb.

It came nearer and nearer, and lo! it was borne by a dark figure, with a burden on its back: it was the poor woman, and no demon, that was looking for her! She gave a scream of joy, fell down weeping at her feet, and clasped her knees. Then the poor woman threw away her burden, laid down her lantern, took the princess up in her arms, folded her cloak around her, and having taken up her lantern again, carried her slowly and carefully through the midst of the black pools, winding hither and thither. All night long she carried her thus, slowly and wearily, until at length the darkness grew a little thinner, an uncertain hint of light came from the east, and the poor woman, stopping on the brow of a little hill, opened her cloak, and set the princess down.

"I can carry you no farther," she said. "Sit there on the grass till the light comes. I will stand here by you."

Rosamond had been asleep. Now she rubbed her eyes and looked, but it was too dark to see any thing more than that there was a sky over her head. Slowly the light grew, until she could see the form of the poor woman standing in front of her; and as it went on growing, she began to think she had seen her somewhere before, till all at once she thought of the wise woman, and saw it must be she. Then she was so ashamed that she bent down her head, and could look at her no longer. But the poor woman spoke, and the voice was that of the wise woman, and every word went deep into the heart of the princess.

"Rosamond," she said, "all this time, ever since I carried you from your father's palace, I have been doing what I could to make you a lovely creature: ask yourself how far I have succeeded."

All her past story, since she found herself first under the wise woman's cloak, arose, and glided past the inner eyes of the princess, and she saw, and in a measure understood, it all. But she sat with her eyes on the ground, and made no sign.

Then said the wise woman:—

"Below there is the forest which surrounds my house. I am going home. If you pledge to come there to me, I will help you, in a way I could not do now, to be good and lovely. I will wait you there all day, but if you start at once, you may be there long before noon. I shall have your breakfast waiting for you. One thing more: the beasts have not yet all gone home to their holes; but I give you my word, not one will touch you so long as you keep coming nearer to my house."

She ceased. Rosamond sat waiting to hear something more; but nothing came. She looked up; she was alone.

Alone once more! Always being left alone, because she would not yield to what was right! Oh, how safe she had felt under the wise woman's cloak! She had indeed been good to her, and she had in return behaved like one of the hyenas of the awful wood! What a wonderful house it was she lived in! And again all her own story came up into her brain from her repentant heart.

"Why didn't she take me with her?" she said. "I would have gone gladly." And she wept. But her own conscience told her that, in the very middle of her shame and desire to be good, she had returned no answer to the words of the wise woman; she had sat like a tree-stump, and done nothing. She tried to say there was nothing to be done; but she knew at once that she could have told the wise woman she had been very wicked, and asked her to take her with her. Now there was nothing to be done.

"Nothing to be done!" said her conscience. "Cannot you rise, and walk down the hill, and through the wood?"

"But the wild beasts!"

"There it is! You don't believe the wise woman yet! Did she not tell you the beasts would not touch you?"

"But they are so horrid!"

"Yes, they are; but it would be far better to be eaten up alive by them than live on—such a worthless creature as you are. Why, you're not fit to be thought about by any but bad ugly creatures."

This was how herself talked to her.

XII.

All at once she jumped to her feet, and ran at full speed down the hill and into the wood. She heard howlings and yellings on all sides of her, but she ran straight on, as near as she could judge. Her spirits rose as she ran. Suddenly she saw before her, in the dusk of the thick wood, a group of some dozen wolves and hyenas, standing all together right in her way, with their green eyes fixed upon her staring. She faltered one step, then bethought her of what the wise woman had promised, and keeping straight on, dashed right into the middle of them. They fled howling, as if she had struck them with fire. She was no more afraid after that, and ere the sun was up she was out of the wood and upon the heath, which no bad thing could step upon and live. With the first peep of the sun above the horizon, she saw the little cottage before her, and ran as fast as she could run towards it, When she came near it, she saw that the door was open, and ran straight into the outstretched arms of the wise woman.

The wise woman kissed her and stroked her hair, set her down by the fire, and gave her a bowl of bread and milk.

When she had eaten it she drew her before her where she sat, and spoke to her thus:—

"Rosamond, if you would be a blessed creature instead of a mere wretch, you must submit to be tried."

"Is that something terrible?" asked the princess, turning white.

"No, my child; but it is something very difficult to come well out of. Nobody who has not been tried knows how difficult it is; but whoever has come well out of it, and those who do not overcome never do come out of it, always looks back with horror, not on what she has come through, but on the very idea of the possibility of having failed, and being still the same miserable creature as before."

"You will tell me what it is before it begins?" said the princess.

"I will not tell you exactly. But I will tell you some things to help you. One great danger is that perhaps you will think you are in it before it has really begun, and say to yourself, 'Oh! this is really nothing to me. It may be a trial to some, but for me I am sure it is not worth mentioning.' And then, before you know, it will be upon you, and you will fail utterly and shamefully."

"I will be very, very careful," said the princess. "Only don't let me be frightened."

"You shall not be frightened, except it be your own doing. You are already a brave girl, and there is no occasion to try you more that way. I saw how you rushed into the middle of the ugly creatures; and as they ran from you, so will all kinds of evil things, as long as you keep them outside of you, and do not open the cottage of your heart to let them in. I will tell you something more about what you will have to go through.

"Nobody can be a real princess—do not imagine you have yet been any thing more than a mock one—until she is a princess over herself, that is, until, when she finds herself unwilling to do the thing that is right, she makes herself do it. So long as any mood she is in makes her do the thing she will be sorry for when that mood is over, she is a slave, and no princess. A princess is able to do what is right even should she unhappily be in a mood that would make another unable to do it. For instance, if you should be cross and angry, you are not a whit the less bound to be just, yes, kind even—a thing most difficult in such a mood—though ease itself in a good mood, loving and sweet. Whoever does what she is bound to do, be she the dirtiest little girl in the street, is a princess, worshipful, honorable. Nay, more; her might goes farther than she could send it, for if she act so, the evil mood will wither and die, and leave her loving and clean.—Do you understand me, dear Rosamond?"

As she spoke, the wise woman laid her hand on her head and looked—oh, so lovingly!—into her eyes.

"I am not sure," said the princess, humbly.

"Perhaps you will understand me better if I say it just comes to this, that you must NOT DO what is wrong, however much you are inclined to do it, and you must DO what is right, however much you are disinclined to do it."

"I understand that," said the princess.

"I am going, then, to put you in one of the mood-chambers of which I have many in the house. Its mood will come upon you, and you will have to deal with it."

She rose and took her by the hand. The princess trembled a little, but never thought of resisting.

The wise woman led her into the great hall with the pictures, and through a door at the farther end, opening upon another large hall, which was circular, and had doors close to each other all round it. Of these she opened one, pushed the princess gently in, and closed it behind her.

The princess found herself in her old nursery. Her little white rabbit came to meet her in a lumping canter as if his back were going to tumble over his head. Her nurse, in her rocking-chair by the chimney corner, sat just as she had used. The fire burned brightly, and on the table were many of her wonderful toys, on which, however, she now looked with some contempt. Her nurse did not seem at all surprised to see her, any more than if the princess had but just gone from the room and returned again.

"Oh! how different I am from what I used to be!" thought the princess to herself, looking from her toys to her nurse. "The wise woman has done me so much good already! I will go and see mamma at once, and tell her I am very glad to be at home again, and very sorry I was so naughty."

She went towards the door.

"Your queen-mamma, princess, cannot see you now," said her nurse.

"I have yet to learn that it is my part to take orders from a servant," said the princess with temper and dignity.

"I beg your pardon, princess," returned her nurse, politely; "but it is my duty to tell you that your queen-mamma is at this moment engaged. She is alone with her most intimate friend, the Princess of the Frozen Regions."

"I shall see for myself," returned the princess, bridling, and walked to the door.

Now little bunny, leap-frogging near the door, happened that moment to get about her feet, just as she was going to open it, so that she tripped and fell against it, striking her forehead a good blow. She caught up the rabbit in a rage, and, crying, "It is all your fault, you ugly old wretch!" threw it with violence in her nurse's face.

Her nurse caught the rabbit, and held it to her face, as if seeking to sooth its fright. But the rabbit looked very limp and odd, and, to her amazement, Rosamond presently saw that the thing was no rabbit, but a pocket-handkerchief. The next moment she removed it from her face, and Rosamond beheld—not her nurse, but the wise woman—standing on her own hearth, while she herself stood by the door leading from the cottage into the hall.

"First trial a failure," said the wise woman quietly.

Overcome with shame, Rosamond ran to her, fell down on her knees, and hid her face in her dress.

"Need I say any thing?" said the wise woman, stroking her hair.

"No, no," cried the princess. "I am horrid."

"You know now the kind of thing you have to meet: are you ready to try again?"

"MAY I try again?" cried the princess, jumping up. "I'm ready. I do not think I shall fail this time."

"The trial will be harder."

Rosamond drew in her breath, and set her teeth. The wise woman looked at her pitifully, but took her by the hand, led her to the round hall, opened the same door, and closed it after her.

The princess expected to find herself again in the nursery, but in the wise woman's house no one ever has the same trial twice. She was in a beautiful garden, full of blossoming trees and the loveliest roses and lilies. A lake was in the middle of it, with a tiny boat. So delightful was it that Rosamond forgot all about how or why she had come there, and lost herself in the joy of the flowers and the trees and the water. Presently came the shout of a child, merry and glad, and from a clump of tulip trees rushed a lovely little boy, with his arms stretched out to her. She was charmed at the sight, ran to meet him, caught him up in her arms, kissed him, and could hardly let him go again. But the moment she set him down he ran from her towards the lake, looking back as he ran, and crying "Come, come."

She followed. He made straight for the boat, clambered into it, and held out his hand to help her in. Then he caught up the little boat-hook, and pushed away from the shore: there was a great white flower floating a few yards off, and that was the little fellow's goal. But, alas! no sooner had Rosamond caught sight of it, huge and glowing as a harvest moon, than she felt a great desire to have it herself. The boy, however, was in the bows of the boat, and caught it first. It had a long stem, reaching down to the bottom of the water, and for a moment he tugged at it in vain, but at last it gave way so suddenly, that he tumbled back with the flower into the bottom of the boat. Then Rosamond, almost wild at the danger it was in as he struggled to rise, hurried to save it, but somehow between them it came in pieces, and all its petals of fretted silver were scattered about the boat. When the boy got up, and saw the ruin his companion had occasioned, he burst into tears, and having the long stalk of the flower still in his hand, struck her with it across the face. It did not hurt her much, for he was a very little fellow, but it was wet and slimy. She tumbled rather than rushed at him, seized him in her arms, tore him from his frightened grasp, and flung him into the water. His head struck on the boat as he fell, and he sank at once to the bottom, where he lay looking up at her with white face and open eyes.

The moment she saw the consequences of her deed she was filled with horrible dismay. She tried hard to reach down to him through the water, but it was far deeper than it looked, and she could not. Neither could she get her eyes to leave the white face: its eyes fascinated and fixed hers; and there she lay leaning over the boat and staring at the death she had made. But a voice crying, "Ally! Ally!" shot to her heart, and springing to her feet she saw a lovely lady come running down the grass to the brink of the water with her hair flying about her head.

"Where is my Ally?" she shrieked.

But Rosamond could not answer, and only stared at the lady, as she had before stared at her drowned boy.

Then the lady caught sight of the dead thing at the bottom of the water, and rushed in, and, plunging down, struggled and groped until she reached it. Then she rose and stood up with the dead body of her little son in her arms, his head hanging back, and the water streaming from him.

"See what you have made of him, Rosamond!" she said, holding the body out to her; "and this is your second trial, and also a failure."

The dead child melted away from her arms, and there she stood, the wise woman, on her own hearth, while Rosamond found herself beside the little well on the floor of the cottage, with one arm wet up to the shoulder. She threw herself on the heather-bed and wept from relief and vexation both.

The wise woman walked out of the cottage, shut the door, and left her alone. Rosamond was sobbing, so that she did not hear her go. When at length she looked up, and saw that the wise woman was gone, her misery returned afresh and tenfold, and she wept and wailed. The hours passed, the shadows of evening began to fall, and the wise woman entered.

XIII.

She went straight to the bed, and taking Rosamond in her arms, sat down with her by the fire.

"My poor child!" she said. "Two terrible failures! And the more the harder! They get stronger and stronger. What is to be done?"

"Couldn't you help me?" said Rosamond piteously.

"Perhaps I could, now you ask me," answered the wise woman. "When you are ready to try again, we shall see."

"I am very tired of myself," said the princess. "But I can't rest till I try again."

"That is the only way to get rid of your weary, shadowy self, and find your strong, true self. Come, my child; I will help you all I can, for now I CAN help you."

Yet again she led her to the same door, and seemed to the princess to send her yet again alone into the room. She was in a forest, a place half wild, half tended. The trees were grand, and full of the loveliest birds, of all glowing gleaming and radiant colors, which, unlike the brilliant birds we know in our world, sang deliciously, every one according to his color. The trees were not at all crowded, but their leaves were so thick, and their boughs spread so far, that it was only here and there a sunbeam could get straight through. All the gentle creatures of a forest were there, but no creatures that killed, not even a weasel to kill the rabbits, or a beetle to eat the snails out of their striped shells. As to the butterflies, words would but wrong them if they tried to tell how gorgeous they were. The princess's delight was so great that she neither laughed nor ran, but walked about with a solemn countenance and stately step.

"But where are the flowers?" she said to herself at length.

They were nowhere. Neither on the high trees, nor on the few shrubs that grew here and there amongst them, were there any blossoms; and in the grass that grew everywhere there was not a single flower to be seen.

"Ah, well!" said Rosamond again to herself, "where all the birds and butterflies are living flowers, we can do without the other sort."

Still she could not help feeling that flowers were wanted to make the beauty of the forest complete.

Suddenly she came out on a little open glade; and there, on the root of a great oak, sat the loveliest little girl, with her lap full of flowers of all colors, but of such kinds as Rosamond had never before seen. She was playing with them—burying her hands in them, tumbling them about, and every now and then picking one from the rest, and throwing it away. All the time she never smiled, except with her eyes, which were as full as they could hold of the laughter of the spirit—a laughter which in this world is never heard, only sets the eyes alight with a liquid shining. Rosamond drew nearer, for the wonderful creature would have drawn a tiger to her side, and tamed him on the way. A few yards from her, she came upon one of her cast-away flowers and stooped to pick it up, as well she might where none grew save in her own longing. But to her amazement she found, instead of a flower thrown away to wither, one fast rooted and quite at home. She left it, and went to another; but it also was fast in the soil, and growing comfortably in the warm grass. What could it mean? One after another she tried, until at length she was satisfied that it was the same with every flower the little girl threw from her lap.

She watched then until she saw her throw one, and instantly bounded to the spot. But the flower had been quicker than she: there it grew, fast fixed in the earth, and, she thought, looked at her roguishly. Something evil moved in her, and she plucked it.

"Don't! don't!" cried the child. "My flowers cannot live in your hands."

Rosamond looked at the flower. It was withered already. She threw it from her, offended. The child rose, with difficulty keeping her lapful together, picked it up, carried it back, sat down again, spoke to it, kissed it, sang to it—oh! such a sweet, childish little song!—the princess never could recall a word of it—and threw it away. Up rose its little head, and there it was, busy growing again!

Rosamond's bad temper soon gave way: the beauty and sweetness of the child had overcome it; and, anxious to make friends with her, she drew near, and said:

"Won't you give me a little flower, please, you beautiful child?"

"There they are; they are all for you," answered the child, pointing with her outstretched arm and forefinger all round.

"But you told me, a minute ago, not to touch them."

"Yes, indeed, I did."

"They can't be mine, if I'm not to touch them."

"If, to call them yours, you must kill them, then they are not yours, and never, never can be yours. They are nobody's when they are dead."

"But you don't kill them."

"I don't pull them; I throw them away. I live them."

"How is it that you make them grow?"

"I say, 'You darling!' and throw it away and there it is."

"Where do you get them?"

"In my lap."

"I wish you would let me throw one away."

"Have you got any in your lap? Let me see."

"No; I have none."

"Then you can't throw one away, if you haven't got one."

"You are mocking me!" cried the princess.

"I am not mocking you," said the child, looking her full in the face, with reproach in her large blue eyes.

"Oh, that's where the flowers come from!" said the princess to herself, the moment she saw them, hardly knowing what she meant.

Then the child rose as if hurt, and quickly threw away all the flowers she had in her lap, but one by one, and without any sign of anger. When they were all gone, she stood a moment, and then, in a kind of chanting cry, called, two or three times, "Peggy! Peggy! Peggy!"

A low, glad cry, like the whinny of a horse, answered, and, presently, out of the wood on the opposite side of the glade, came gently trotting the loveliest little snow-white pony, with great shining blue wings, half-lifted from his shoulders. Straight towards the little girl, neither hurrying nor lingering, he trotted with light elastic tread.

Rosamond's love for animals broke into a perfect passion of delight at the vision. She rushed to meet the pony with such haste, that, although clearly the best trained animal under the sun, he started back, plunged, reared, and struck out with his fore-feet ere he had time to observe what sort of a creature it was that had so startled him. When he perceived it was a little girl, he dropped instantly upon all fours, and content with avoiding her, resumed his quiet trot in the direction of his mistress. Rosamond stood gazing after him in miserable disappointment.

When he reached the child, he laid his head on her shoulder, and she put her arm up round his neck; and after she had talked to him a little, he turned and came trotting back to the princess.

Almost beside herself with joy, she began caressing him in the rough way which, not-withstanding her love for them, she was in the habit of using with animals; and she was not gentle enough, in herself even, to see that he did not like it, and was only putting up with it for the sake of his mistress. But when, that she might jump upon his back, she laid hold of one of his wings, and ruffled some of the blue feathers, he wheeled suddenly about, gave his long tail a sharp whisk which threw her flat on the grass, and, trotting back to his mistress, bent down his head before her as if asking excuse for ridding himself of the unbearable.

The princess was furious. She had forgotten all her past life up to the time when she first saw the child: her beauty had made her forget, and yet she was now on the very borders of hating her. What she might have done, or rather tried to do, had not Peggy's tail struck her down with such force that for a moment she could not rise, I cannot tell.

But while she lay half-stunned, her eyes fell on a little flower just under them. It stared up in her face like the living thing it was, and she could not take her eyes off its face. It was like a primrose trying to express doubt instead of confidence. It seemed to put her half in mind of something, and she felt as if shame were coming. She put out her hand to pluck it; but the moment her fingers touched it, the flower withered up, and hung as dead on its stalks as if a flame of fire had passed over it.

Then a shudder thrilled through the heart of the princess, and she thought with herself, saying—"What sort of a creature am I that the flowers wither when I touch them, and the ponies despise me with their tails? What a wretched, coarse, ill-bred creature I must be! There is that lovely child giving life instead of death to the flowers, and a moment ago I was hating her! I am made horrid, and I shall be horrid, and I hate myself, and yet I can't help being myself!"

She heard the sound of galloping feet, and there was the pony, with the child seated betwixt his wings, coming straight on at full speed for where she lay.

"I don't care," she said. "They may trample me under their feet if they like. I am tired and sick of myself—a creature at whose touch the flowers wither!"

On came the winged pony. But while yet some distance off, he gave a great bound, spread out his living sails of blue, rose yards and yards above her in the air, and alighted as gently as a bird, just a few feet on the other side of her. The child slipped down and came and kneeled over her.

"Did my pony hurt you?" she said. "I am so sorry!"

"Yes, he hurt me," answered the princess, "but not more than I deserved, for I took liberties with him, and he did not like it."

"Oh, you dear!" said the little girl. "I love you for talking so of my Peggy. He is a good pony, though a little playful sometimes. Would you like a ride upon him?"

"You darling beauty!" cried Rosamond, sobbing. "I do love you so, you are so good. How did you become so sweet?"

"Would you like to ride my pony?" repeated the child, with a heavenly smile in her eyes.

"No, no; he is fit only for you. My clumsy body would hurt him," said Rosamond.

"You don't mind me having such a pony?" said the child.

"What! mind it?" cried Rosamond, almost indignantly. Then remembering certain thoughts that had but a few moments before passed through her mind, she looked on the ground and was silent.

"You don't mind it, then?" repeated the child.

"I am very glad there is such a you and such a pony, and that such a you has got such a pony," said Rosamond, still looking on the ground. "But I do wish the flowers would not die when I touch them. I was cross to see you make them grow, but now I should be content if only I did not make them wither."

As she spoke, she stroked the little girl's bare feet, which were by her, half buried in the soft moss, and as she ended she laid her cheek on them and kissed them.

"Dear princess!" said the little girl, "the flowers will not always wither at your touch. Try now—only do not pluck it. Flowers ought never to be plucked except to give away. Touch it gently."

A silvery flower, something like a snow-drop, grew just within her reach.

Timidly she stretched out her hand and touched it. The flower trembled, but neither shrank nor withered.

"Touch it again," said the child.

It changed color a little, and Rosamond fancied it grew larger.

"Touch it again," said the child.

It opened and grew until it was as large as a narcissus, and changed and deepened in color till it was a red glowing gold.

Rosamond gazed motionless. When the transfiguration of the flower was perfected, she sprang to her feet with clasped hands, but for very ecstasy of joy stood speechless, gazing at the child.

"Did you never see me before, Rosamond?" she asked.

"No, never," answered the princess. "I never saw any thing half so lovely."

"Look at me," said the child.

And as Rosamond looked, the child began, like the flower, to grow larger. Quickly through every gradation of growth she passed, until she stood before her a woman perfectly beautiful, neither old nor young; for hers was the old age of everlasting youth.

Rosamond was utterly enchanted, and stood gazing without word or movement until she could endure no more delight. Then her mind collapsed to the thought—had the pony grown too? She glanced round. There was no pony, no grass, no flowers, no bright-birded forest—but the cottage of the wise woman—and before her, on the hearth of it, the goddess-child, the only thing unchanged.

She gasped with astonishment.

"You must set out for your father's palace immediately," said the lady.

"But where is the wise woman?" asked Rosamond, looking all about.

"Here," said the lady.

And Rosamond, looking again, saw the wise woman, folded as usual in her long dark cloak.

"And it was you all the time?" she cried in delight, and kneeled before her, burying her face in her garments.

"It always is me, all the time," said the wise woman, smiling.

"But which is the real you?" asked Rosamond; "this or that?"

"Or a thousand others?" returned the wise woman. "But the one you have just seen is the likest to the real me that you are able to see just yet—but—. And that me you could not have seen a little while ago.—But, my darling child," she went on, lifting her up and clasping her to her bosom, "you must not think, because you have seen me once, that therefore you are capable of seeing me at all times. No; there are many things in you yet that must be changed before that can be. Now, however, you will seek me. Every time you feel you want me, that is a sign I am wanting you. There are yet many rooms in my house you may have to go through; but when you need no more of them, then you will be able to throw flowers like the little girl you saw in the forest."

The princess gave a sigh.

"Do not think," the wise woman went on, "that the things you have seen in my house are mere empty shows. You do not know, you cannot yet think, how living and true they are.—Now you must go."

She led her once more into the great hall, and there showed her the picture of her father's capital, and his palace with the brazen gates.

"There is your home," she said. "Go to it."

The princess understood, and a flush of shame rose to her forehead. She turned to the wise woman and said:

"Will you forgive ALL my naughtiness, and ALL the trouble I have given you?"

"If I had not forgiven you, I would never have taken the trouble to punish you. If I had not loved you, do you think I would have carried you away in my cloak?"

"How could you love such an ugly, ill-tempered, rude, hateful little wretch?"

"I saw, through it all, what you were going to be," said the wise woman, kissing her. "But remember you have yet only BEGUN to be what I saw."

"I will try to remember," said the princess, holding her cloak, and looking up in her face.

"Go, then," said the wise woman.

Rosamond turned away on the instant, ran to the picture, stepped over the frame of it, heard a door close gently, gave one glance back, saw behind her the loveliest palace-front of alabaster, gleaming in the pale-yellow light of an early summer-morning, looked again to the eastward, saw the faint outline of her father's city against the sky, and ran off to reach it.

It looked much further off now than when it seemed a picture, but the sun was not yet up, and she had the whole of a summer day before her.

XIV.

The soldiers sent out by the king, had no great difficulty in finding Agnes's father and mother, of whom they demanded if they knew any thing of such a young princess as they described. The honest pair told them the truth in every point—that, having lost their own child and found another, they had taken her home, and treated her as their own; that she had indeed called herself a princess, but they had not believed her, because she did not look like one; that, even if they had, they did not know how they could have done differently, seeing they were poor people, who could not afford to keep any idle person about the place; that they had done their best to teach her good ways, and had not parted with her until her bad temper rendered it impossible to put up with her any longer; that, as to the king's proclamation, they heard little of the world's news on their lonely hill, and it had never reached them; that if it had, they did not know how either of them could have gone such a distance from home, and left their sheep or their cottage, one or the other, uncared for.

"You must learn, then, how both of you can go, and your sheep must take care of your cottage," said the lawyer, and commanded the soldiers to bind them hand and foot.

Heedless of their entreaties to be spared such an indignity, the soldiers obeyed, bore them to a cart, and set out for the king's palace, leaving the cottage door open, the fire burning, the pot of potatoes boiling upon it, the sheep scattered over the hill, and the dogs not knowing what to do.

Hardly were they gone, however, before the wise woman walked up, with Prince behind her, peeped into the cottage, locked the door, put the key in her pocket, and then walked away up the hill. In a few minutes there arose a great battle between Prince and the dog which filled his former place—a well-meaning but dull fellow, who could fight better than feed. Prince was not long in showing him that he was meant for his master, and then, by his efforts, and directions to the other dogs, the sheep were soon gathered again, and out of danger from foxes and bad dogs. As soon as this was done, the wise woman left them in charge of Prince, while she went to the next farm to arrange for the folding of the sheep and the feeding of the dogs.

When the soldiers reached the palace, they were ordered to carry their prisoners at once into the presence of the king and queen, in the throne room. Their two thrones stood upon a high dais at one end, and on the floor at the foot of the dais, the soldiers laid their helpless prisoners. The queen commanded that they should be unbound, and ordered them to stand up. They obeyed with the dignity of insulted innocence, and their bearing offended their foolish majesties.

Meantime the princess, after a long day's journey, arrived at the palace, and walked up to the sentry at the gate.

"Stand back," said the sentry.

"I wish to go in, if you please," said the princess gently.

"Ha! ha! ha!" laughed the sentry, for he was one of those dull people who form their judgment from a person's clothes, without even looking in his eyes; and as the princess happened to be in rags, her request was amusing, and the booby thought himself quite clever for laughing at her so thoroughly.

"I am the princess," Rosamond said quietly.

"WHAT princess?" bellowed the man.

"The princess Rosamond. Is there another?" she answered and asked.

But the man was so tickled at the wondrous idea of a princess in rags, that he scarcely heard what she said for laughing. As soon as he recovered a little, he proceeded to chuck the princess under the chin, saying—

"You're a pretty girl, my dear, though you ain't no princess."

Rosamond drew back with dignity.

"You have spoken three untruths at once," she said. "I am NOT pretty, and I AM a princess, and if I were dear to you, as I ought to be, you would not laugh at me because I am badly dressed, but stand aside, and let me go to my father and mother."

The tone of her speech, and the rebuke she gave him, made the man look at her; and looking at her, he began to tremble inside his foolish body, and wonder whether he might not have made a mistake. He raised his hand in salute, and said—

"I beg your pardon, miss, but I have express orders to admit no child whatever within the palace gates. They tell me his majesty the king says he is sick of children."

"He may well be sick of me!" thought the princess; "but it can't mean that he does not want me home again.—I don't think you can very well call me a child," she said, looking the sentry full in the face.

"You ain't very big, miss," answered the soldier, "but so be you say you ain't a child, I'll take the risk. The king can only kill me, and a man must die once."

He opened the gate, stepped aside, and allowed her to pass. Had she lost her temper, as every one but the wise woman would have expected of her, he certainly would not have done so.

She ran into the palace, the door of which had been left open by the porter when he followed the soldiers and prisoners to the throne-room, and bounded up the stairs to look for her father and mother. As she passed the door of the throne-room she heard an unusual noise in it, and running to the king's private entrance, over which hung a heavy curtain, she peeped past the edge of it, and saw, to her amazement, the shepherd and shepherdess standing like culprits before the king and queen, and the same moment heard the king say—

"Peasants, where is the princess Rosamond?"

"Truly, sire, we do not know," answered the shepherd.

"You ought to know," said the king.

"Sire, we could keep her no longer."

97

"You confess, then," said the king, suppressing the outbreak of the wrath that boiled up in him, "that you turned her out of your house."

For the king had been informed by a swift messenger of all that had passed long before the arrival of the prisoners.

"We did, sire; but not only could we keep her no longer, but we knew not that she was the princess."

"You ought to have known, the moment you cast your eyes upon her," said the king. "Any one who does not know a princess the moment he sees her, ought to have his eyes put out."

"Indeed he ought," said the queen.

To this they returned no answer, for they had none ready.

"Why did you not bring her at once to the palace," pursued the king, "whether you knew her to be a princess or not? My proclamation left nothing to your judgment. It said EVERY CHILD."

"We heard nothing of the proclamation, sire."

"You ought to have heard," said the king. "It is enough that I make proclamations; it is for you to read them. Are they not written in letters of gold upon the brazen gates of this palace?"

"A poor shepherd, your majesty—how often must he leave his flock, and go hundreds of miles to look whether there may not be something in letters of gold upon the brazen gates? We did not know that your majesty had made a proclamation, or even that the princess was lost."

"You ought to have known," said the king.

The shepherd held his peace.

"But," said the queen, taking up the word, "all that is as nothing, when I think how you misused the darling."

The only ground the queen had for saying thus, was what Agnes had told her as to how the princess was dressed; and her condition seemed to the

98

queen so miserable, that she had imagined all sorts of oppression and cruelty.

But this was more than the shepherdess, who had not yet spoken, could bear.

"She would have been dead, and NOT buried, long ago, madam, if I had not carried her home in my two arms."

"Why does she say her TWO arms?" said the king to himself. "Has she more than two? Is there treason in that?"

"You dressed her in cast-off clothes," said the queen.

"I dressed her in my own sweet child's Sunday clothes. And this is what I get for it!" cried the shepherdess, bursting into tears.

"And what did you do with the clothes you took off her? Sell them?"

"Put them in the fire, madam. They were not fit for the poorest child in the mountains. They were so ragged that you could see her skin through them in twenty different places."

"You cruel woman, to torture a mother's feelings so!" cried the queen, and in her turn burst into tears.

"And I'm sure," sobbed the shepherdess, "I took every pains to teach her what it was right for her to know. I taught her to tidy the house and"—

"Tidy the house!" moaned the queen. "My poor wretched offspring!"

"And peel the potatoes, and"—

"Peel the potatoes!" cried the queen. "Oh, horror!"

"And black her master's boots," said the shepherdess.

"Black her master's boots!" shrieked the queen. "Oh, my white-handed princess! Oh, my ruined baby!"

"What I want to know," said the king, paying no heed to this maternal duel, but patting the top of his sceptre as if it had been the hilt of a sword which he was about to draw, "is, where the princess is now."

The shepherd made no answer, for he had nothing to say more than he had said already.

"You have murdered her!" shouted the king. "You shall be tortured till you confess the truth; and then you shall be tortured to death, for you are the most abominable wretches in the whole wide world."

"Who accuses me of crime?" cried the shepherd, indignant.

"I accuse you," said the king; "but you shall see, face to face, the chief witness to your villany. Officer, bring the girl."

Silence filled the hall while they waited. The king's face was swollen with anger. The queen hid hers behind her handkerchief. The shepherd and shepherdess bent their eyes on the ground, wondering. It was with difficulty Rosamond could keep her place, but so wise had she already become that she saw it would be far better to let every thing come out before she interfered.

At length the door opened, and in came the officer, followed by Agnes, looking white as death and mean as sin.

The shepherdess gave a shriek, and darted towards her with arms spread wide; the shepherd followed, but not so eagerly.

"My child! my lost darling! my Agnes!" cried the shepherdess.

"Hold them asunder," shouted the king. "Here is more villany! What! have I a scullery-maid in my house born of such parents? The parents of such a child must be capable of any thing. Take all three of them to the rack. Stretch them till their joints are torn asunder, and give them no water. Away with them!"

The soldiers approached to lay hands on them. But, behold! a girl all in rags, with such a radiant countenance that it was right lovely to see, darted between, and careless of the royal presence, flung herself upon the shepherdess, crying,—

"Do not touch her. She is my good, kind mistress."

But the shepherdess could hear or see no one but her Agnes, and pushed her away. Then the princess turned, with the tears in her eyes, to the shepherd, and threw her arms about his neck and pulled down his head and kissed him. And the tall shepherd lifted her to his bosom and kept her there, but his eyes were fixed on his Agnes.

"What is the meaning of this?" cried the king, starting up from his throne. "How did that ragged girl get in here? Take her away with the rest. She is one of them, too."

But the princess made the shepherd set her down, and before any one could interfere she had run up the steps of the dais and then the steps of the king's throne like a squirrel, flung herself upon the king, and begun to smother him with kisses.

All stood astonished, except the three peasants, who did not even see what took place. The shepherdess kept calling to her Agnes, but she was so ashamed that she did not dare even lift her eyes to meet her mother's, and the shepherd kept gazing on her in silence. As for the king, he was so breathless and aghast with astonishment, that he was too feeble to fling the ragged child from him, as he tried to do. But she left him, and running down the steps of the one throne and up those of the other, began kissing the queen next. But the queen cried out,—

"Get away, you great rude child!—Will nobody take her to the rack?"

Then the princess, hardly knowing what she did for joy that she had come in time, ran down the steps of the throne and the dais, and placing herself between the shepherd and shepherdess, took a hand of each, and stood looking at the king and queen.

Their faces began to change. At last they began to know her. But she was so altered—so lovelily altered, that it was no wonder they should not have known her at the first glance; but it was the fault of the pride and anger and injustice with which their hearts were filled, that they did not know her at the second.

The king gazed and the queen gazed, both half risen from their thrones, and looking as if about to tumble down upon her, if only they could be right sure that the ragged girl was their own child. A mistake would be such a dreadful thing!

"My darling!" at last shrieked the mother, a little doubtfully.

"My pet of pets?" cried the father, with an interrogative twist of tone.

Another moment, and they were half way down the steps of the dais.

"Stop!" said a voice of command from somewhere in the hall, and, king and queen as they were, they stopped at once half way, then drew themselves up, stared, and began to grow angry again, but durst not go farther.

The wise woman was coming slowly up through the crowd that filled the hall. Every one made way for her. She came straight on until she stood in front of the king and queen.

"Miserable man and woman!" she said, in words they alone could hear, "I took your daughter away when she was worthy of such parents; I bring her back, and they are unworthy of her. That you did not know her when she came to you is a small wonder, for you have been blind in soul all your lives: now be blind in body until your better eyes are unsealed."

She threw her cloak open. It fell to the ground, and the radiance that flashed from her robe of snowy whiteness, from her face of awful beauty, and from her eyes that shone like pools of sunlight, smote them blind.

Rosamond saw them give a great start, shudder, waver to and fro, then sit down on the steps of the dais; and she knew they were punished, but knew not how. She rushed up to them, and catching a hand of each said—

"Father, dear father! mother dear! I will ask the wise woman to forgive you."

"Oh, I am blind! I am blind!" they cried together. "Dark as night! Stone blind!"

Rosamond left them, sprang down the steps, and kneeling at her feet, cried, "Oh, my lovely wise woman! do let them see. Do open their eyes, dear, good, wise woman."

The wise woman bent down to her, and said, so that none else could hear, "I will one day. Meanwhile you must be their servant, as I have been yours. Bring them to me, and I will make them welcome."

Rosamond rose, went up the steps again to her father and mother, where they sat like statues with closed eyes, half-way from the top of the dais where stood their empty thrones, seated herself between them, took a hand of each, and was still.

All this time very few in the room saw the wise woman. The moment she threw off her cloak she vanished from the sight of almost all who were present. The woman who swept and dusted the hall and brushed the thrones, saw her, and the shepherd had a glimmering vision of her; but no one else that I know of caught a glimpse of her. The shepherdess did not see her. Nor did Agnes, but she felt her presence upon her like the beat of a furnace seven times heated.

As soon as Rosamond had taken her place between her father and mother, the wise woman lifted her cloak from the floor, and threw it again around her. Then everybody saw her, and Agnes felt as if a soft dewy cloud had come between her and the torrid rays of a vertical sun. The wise woman turned to the shepherd and shepherdess.

"For you," she said, "you are sufficiently punished by the work of your own hands. Instead of making your daughter obey you, you left her to be a slave to herself; you coaxed when you ought to have compelled; you praised when you ought to have been silent; you fondled when you ought to have punished; you threatened when you ought to have inflicted—and there she stands, the full-grown result of your foolishness! She is your crime and your punishment. Take her home with you, and live hour after hour with the pale-hearted disgrace you call your daughter. What she is, the worm at her heart has begun to teach her. When life is no longer endurable, come to me."

"Madam," said the shepherd, "may I not go with you now?"

"You shall," said the wise woman.

"Husband! husband!" cried the shepherdess, "how are we two to get home without you?"

"I will see to that," said the wise woman. "But little of home you will find it until you have come to me. The king carried you hither, and he shall carry you back. But your husband shall not go with you. He cannot now if he would."

The shepherdess looked and saw that the shepherd stood in a deep sleep. She went to him and sought to rouse him, but neither tongue nor hands were of the slightest avail.

The wise woman turned to Rosamond.

"My child," she said, "I shall never be far from you. Come to me when you will. Bring them to me."

Rosamond smiled and kissed her hand, but kept her place by her parents. They also were now in a deep sleep like the shepherd.

The wise woman took the shepherd by the hand, and led him away.

And that is all my double story. How double it is, if you care to know, you must find out. If you think it is not finished—I never knew a story that was. I could tell you a great deal more concerning them all, but I have already told more than is good for those who read but with their foreheads, and enough for those whom it has made look a little solemn, and sigh as they close the book.

CROSS PURPOSES AND THE SHADOWS

CROSS PURPOSES

CHAPTER I.

Once upon a time, the Queen of Fairyland, finding her own subjects far too well-behaved to be amusing, took a sudden longing to have a mortal or two at her Court. So, after looking about her for some time, she fixed upon two to bring to Fairyland.

But how were they to be brought?

"Please your majesty," said at last the daughter of the prime-minister,

"I will bring the girl."

The speaker, whose name was Peaseblossom, after her great-great-grandmother, looked so graceful, and hung her head so apologetically, that the Queen said at once,—

"How will you manage it, Peaseblossom?"

"I will open the road before her, and close it behind her."

"I have heard that you have pretty ways of doing things; so you may try."

The court happened to be held in an open forest-glade of smooth turf, upon which there was just one mole-heap. As soon as the Queen had given her permission to Peaseblossom, up through the mole-heap came the head of a goblin, which cried out,—

"Please your majesty, I will bring the boy."

"You!" exclaimed the Queen. "How will you do it?"

The goblin began to wriggle himself out of the earth, as if he had been a snake, and the whole world his skin, till the court was convulsed with laughter. As soon as he got free, he began to roll over and over, in every possible manner, rotatory and cylindrical, all at once, until he reached the wood. The courtiers followed, holding their sides, so that the Queen was left sitting upon her throne in solitary state.

When they reached the wood, the goblin, whose name was Toadstool, was nowhere to be seen. While they were looking for him, out popped his head from the mole-heap again, with the words,—

"So, your majesty."

"You have taken your own time to answer," said the Queen, laughing.

"And my own way too, eh! your majesty?" rejoined Toadstool, grinning.

"No doubt. Well, you may try."

And the goblin, making as much of a bow as he could with only half his neck above ground, disappeared under it.

CHAPTER II.

No mortal, or fairy either, can tell where Fairyland begins and where it ends. But somewhere on the borders of Fairyland there was a nice country village, in which lived some nice country people.

Alice was the daughter of the squire, a pretty, good-natured girl, whom her friends called fairy-like, and others called silly.

One rosy summer evening, when the wall opposite her window was flaked all over with rosiness, she threw herself down on her bed, and lay gazing at the wall. The rose-colour sank through her eyes and dyed her brain, and she began to feel as if she were reading a story-book. She thought she was looking at a western sea, with the waves all red with sunset. But when the colour died out, Alice gave a sigh to see how commonplace the wall grew. "I wish it was always sunset!" she said, half aloud. "I don't like gray things."

"I will take you where the sun is always setting, if you like, Alice," said a sweet, tiny voice near her. She looked down on the coverlet of the bed, and there, looking up at her, stood a lovely little creature. It seemed quite natural that the little lady should be there; for many things we never could believe, have only to happen, and then there is nothing strange about them. She was dressed in white, with a cloak of sunset-red—the colours of the sweetest of sweet-peas. On her head was a crown of twisted tendrils, with a little gold beetle in front.

"Are you a fairy?" said Alice.

"Yes. Will you go with me to the sunset?"

"Yes, I will."

When Alice proceeded to rise, she found that she was no bigger than the fairy; and when she stood up on the counterpane, the bed looked like a great hall with a painted ceiling. As she walked towards Peaseblossom, she stumbled several times over the tufts that made the pattern. But the fairy took her by the hand and led her towards the foot of the bed. Long before they reached it, however, Alice saw that the fairy was a tall, slender lady, and that she herself was quite her own size. What she had taken for tufts on the counterpane were really bushes of furze, and broom, and heather, on the side of a slope.

"Where are we?" asked Alice.

"Going on," answered the fairy.

Alice, not liking the reply, said,—

"I want to go home."

"Good-bye, then!" answered the fairy.

Alice looked round. A wide, hilly country lay all about them. She could not even tell from what quarter they had come.

"I must go with you, I see," she said.

Before they reached the bottom, they were walking over the loveliest meadow-grass. A little stream went cantering down beside them, without channel or bank, sometimes running between the blades, sometimes sweeping the grass all one way under it. And it made a great babbling for such a little stream and such a smooth course.

Gradually the slope grew gentler, and the stream flowed more softly and spread out wider. At length they came to a wood of long, straight poplars, growing out of the water, for the stream ran into the wood, and there stretched out into a lake. Alice thought they could go no farther; but Peaseblossom led her straight on, and they walked through.

It was now dark; but everything under the water gave out a pale, quiet light. There were deep pools here and there, but there was no mud, or frogs, or water-lizards, or eels. All the bottom was pure, lovely grass, brilliantly green. Down the banks of the pools she saw, all under water, primroses and violets and pimpernels. Any flower she wished to see she had only to look for, and she was sure to find it. When a pool came in their way, the fairy swam, and Alice swam by her; and when they got out they were quite dry, though the water was as delightfully wet as water should be. Besides the trees, tall, splendid lilies grew out of it, and hollyhocks and irises and sword-plants, and many other long-stemmed flowers. From every leaf and petal of these, from every branch-tip and tendril, dropped bright water. It gathered slowly at each point, but the points were so many that there was a constant musical plashing of diamond rain upon the still surface of the lake. As they went on, the moon rose and threw a pale mist of light over the whole, and the diamond drops turned to half-liquid pearls, and round every tree-top was a halo of moonlight, and the water went to sleep, and the flowers began to dream.

"Look," said the fairy; "those lilies are just dreaming themselves into a child's sleep. I can see them smiling. This is the place out of which go the things that appear to children every night."

"Is this dreamland, then?" asked Alice.

"If you like," answered the fairy.

"How far am I from home?"

"The farther you go, the nearer home you are."

Then the fairy lady gathered a bundle of poppies and gave it to Alice. The next deep pool that they came to, she told her to throw it in. Alice did so, and following it, laid her head upon it. That moment she began to sink. Down and down she went, till at last she felt herself lying on the long, thick grass at the bottom of the pool, with the poppies under her head and the clear water high over it. Up through it she saw the moon, whose bright face looked sleepy too, disturbed only by the little ripples of the rain from the tall flowers on the edges of the pool.

She fell fast asleep, and all night dreamed about home.

CHAPTER III.

Richard—which is name enough for a fairy story—was the son of a widow in Alice's village. He was so poor that he did not find himself generally welcome; so he hardly went anywhere, but read books at home, and waited upon his mother. His manners, therefore, were shy, and sufficiently awkward to give an unfavourable impression to those who looked at outsides. Alice would have despised him; but he never came near enough for that.

Now Richard had been saving up his few pence in order to buy an umbrella for his mother; for the winter would come, and the one she had was almost torn to ribands. One bright summer evening, when he thought umbrellas must be cheap, he was walking across the market-place to buy one: there, in the middle of it, stood an odd-looking little man, actually selling umbrellas. Here was a chance for him! When he drew nearer, he found that the little man, while vaunting his umbrellas to the skies, was asking such absurdly small prices for them, that no one would venture to buy one. He had opened and laid them all out at full stretch on the market-place—about five-and-twenty of them, stick downwards, like little tents—and he stood beside, haranguing the people. But he would not allow one of the crowd to touch his umbrellas. As soon as his eye fell upon Richard, he changed his tone, and said, "Well, as nobody seems inclined to buy, I think, my dear umbrellas, we had better be going home." Whereupon the umbrellas got up, with some difficulty, and began hobbling away. The people stared at each other with open mouths, for they saw that what they had taken for a lot of umbrellas, was in reality a flock of black geese. A great turkey-cock went gobbling behind them, driving them all down a lane towards the forest. Richard thought with himself, "There is more in this than I can account for. But an umbrella that could lay eggs would be a very jolly umbrella." So by the time the people were beginning to laugh at each other, Richard was half-way down the lane at the heels of the geese. There he stooped and caught one of them, but instead of a goose he had a huge hedgehog in his hands, which he dropped in dismay; whereupon it waddled away a goose as before, and the whole of them began cackling and hissing in a way that he could not mistake. For the turkey-cock, he gobbled and gabbled and choked himself and got right again in the most ridiculous manner. In fact, he seemed sometimes to forget that he was a turkey, and laughed like a fool. All at once, with a simultaneous long-necked hiss, they flew into the wood, and the turkey after them. But Richard soon got up with them again, and found them all hanging by their feet from the trees, in two rows, one on each side of the path, while the turkey was walking on. Him Richard followed; but the moment he reached the middle of the suspended geese, from every side arose the most frightful hisses, and their necks grew longer and longer, till there were nearly thirty broad bills close to his head, blowing in his face, in his ears, and at the back of his neck. But the turkey, looking round and seeing what was going on, turned and walked back. When he reached the place, he looked up at the first and gobbled at him in the wildest manner. That goose grew silent and dropped from the tree. Then he went to the next, and the next, and so on, till he had gobbled them all off the trees, one after another. But when Richard expected to see them go after the turkey, there was nothing there but a flock of huge mushrooms and puff-balls.

"I have had enough of this," thought Richard. "I will go home again."

"Go home, Richard," said a voice close to him.

Looking down, he saw, instead of the turkey, the most comical-looking little man he had ever seen.

"Go home, Master Richard," repeated he, grinning.

"Not for your bidding," answered Richard.

"Come on, then, Master Richard."

"Nor that either, without a good reason."

"I will give you such an umbrella for your mother."

"I don't take presents from strangers."

"Bless you, I'm no stranger here! Oh, no! not at all." And he set off in the manner usual with him, rolling every way at once.

Richard could not help laughing and following. At length Toadstool plumped into a great hole full of water. "Served him right!" thought Richard. "Served him right!" bawled the goblin, crawling out again, and shaking the water from him like a spaniel. "This is the very place I wanted, only I rolled too fast." However, he went on rolling again faster than before, though it was now uphill, till he came to the top of a considerable height, on which grew a number of palm-trees.

"Have you a knife, Richard?" said the goblin, stopping all at once, as if he had been walking quietly along, just like other people.

Richard pulled out a pocket-knife and gave it to the creature, who instantly cut a deep gash in one of the trees. Then he bounded to another and did the same, and so on till he had gashed them all. Richard, following him, saw that a little stream, clearer than the clearest water, began to flow from each, increasing in size the longer it flowed. Before he had reached the last there was quite a tinkling and rustling of the little rills that ran down the stems of the palms. This grew and grew, till Richard saw that a full rivulet was flowing down the side of the hill.

"Here is your knife, Richard," said the goblin; but by the time he had put it in his pocket, the rivulet had grown to a small torrent.

"Now, Richard, come along," said Toadstool, and threw himself into the torrent.

"I would rather have a boat," returned Richard.

"Oh, you stupid!" cried Toadstool crawling up the side of the hill, down which the stream had already carried him some distance.

With every contortion that labour and difficulty could suggest, yet with incredible rapidity, he crawled to the very top of one of the trees, and tore down a huge leaf, which he threw on the ground, and himself after it, rebounding like a ball. He then laid the leaf on the water, held it by the stem, and told Richard to get upon it. He did so. It went down deep in the middle with his weight. Toadstool let it go, and it shot down the stream like an arrow. This began the strangest and most delightful voyage. The stream rushed careering and curveting down the hill-side, bright as a diamond, and soon reached a meadow plain. The goblin rolled alongside of the boat like a bundle of weeds; but Richard rode in triumph through the low grassy country upon the back of his watery steed. It went straight as an arrow, and, strange to tell, was heaped up on the ground, like a ridge of water or a wave, only rushing on endways. It needed no channel, and turned aside for no opposition. It flowed over everything that crossed its path, like a great serpent of water, with folds fitting into all the ups and downs of the way. If a wall came in its course it flowed against it, heaping itself up on itself till it reached the top, whence it plunged to the foot on the other side, and flowed on. Soon he found that it was running gently up a grassy hill. The waves kept curling back as if the wind blew them, or as if they could hardly keep from running down again. But still the stream mounted and flowed, and the waves with it. It found it difficult, but it could do it. When they reached the top, it bore them across a heathy country, rolling over purple heather, and blue harebells, and delicate ferns, and tall foxgloves crowded with bells purple and white. All the time the palm-leaf curled its edges away from the water, and made a delightful boat for Richard, while Toadstool tumbled along in the stream like a porpoise. At length the water began to run very fast, and went faster and faster, till suddenly it plunged them into a deep lake, with a great splash, and stopped there. Toadstool went out of sight, and came up gasping and grinning, while Richard's boat tossed and heaved like a vessel in a storm at sea; but not a drop of water came in. Then the goblin began to swim, and pushed and tugged the boat along. But the lake was so still, and the motion so pleasant, that Richard fell fast asleep.

CHAPTER IV.

When he woke he found himself still afloat upon the broad palm-leaf. He was alone in the middle of a lake, with flowers and trees growing in and out of it everywhere. The sun was just over the tree-tops. A drip of water from the flowers greeted him with music; the mists were dissolving away, and where the sunlight fell on the lake the water was clear as glass. Casting his eyes downward, he saw, just beneath him, far down at the bottom, Alice drowned, as he thought. He was in the act of plunging in, when he saw her open her eyes, and at the same moment begin to float up. He held out his hand, but she repelled it with disdain, and swimming to a tree, sat down on a low branch, wondering how ever the poor widow's son could have found his way into Fairyland. She did not like it. It was an invasion of privilege.

"How did you come here, young Richard?" she asked, from six yards off.

"A goblin brought me."

"Ah! I thought so. A fairy brought me."

"Where is your fairy?"

"Here I am," said Peaseblossom, rising slowly to the surface just by the tree on which Alice was seated.

"Where is your goblin?" retorted Alice.

"Here I am," bawled Toadstool, rushing out of the water like a salmon, and casting a summersault in the air before he fell in again with a tremendous splash. His head rose again close beside Peaseblossom, who being used to such creatures only laughed.

"Isn't he handsome?" he grinned.

"Yes, very. He wants polishing, though."

"You could do that for yourself, you know. Shall we change?"

"I don't mind. You'll find her rather silly."

"That's nothing. The boy's too sensible for me."

He dived, and rose at Alice's feet. She shrieked with terror. The fairy floated away like a water-lily towards Richard. "What a lovely creature!" thought he; but hearing Alice shriek again, he said,

"Don't leave Alice; she's frightened at that queer creature.—I don't think there's any harm in him, though, Alice."

"Oh, no! He won't hurt her," said Peaseblossom. "I'm tired of her. He's going to take her to the court, and I will take you."

"I don't want to go."

"But you must. You can't go home again. You don't know the way."

"Richard! Richard!" cried Alice, in an agony.

Richard sprang from his boat, and was by her side in a moment.

"He pinched me," cried Alice.

Richard hit the goblin a terrible blow on the head; but it took no more effect upon him than if his head had been a round ball of india-rubber. He gave Richard a furious look, however, and bawling out, "You'll repent that, Dick!" vanished under the water.

"Come along, Richard; make haste; he will murder you," cried the fairy.

"It is all your fault," said Richard. "I won't leave Alice."

Then the fairy saw it was all over with her and Toadstool; for they can do nothing with mortals against their will. So she floated away across the water in Richard's boat, holding her robe for a sail, and vanished, leaving the two alone in the lake.

"You have driven away my fairy!" cried Alice. "I shall never get home now. It is all your fault, you naughty young man."

"I drove away the goblin," remonstrated Richard.

"Will you please to sit on the other side of the tree? I wonder what my papa would say if he saw me talking to you!"

"Will you come to the next tree, Alice?" said Richard, after a pause.

Alice, who had been crying all the time that Richard was thinking, said "I won't." Richard, therefore, plunged into the water without her, and swam for the tree. Before he had got half-way, however, he heard Alice crying "Richard! Richard!" This was just what he wanted. So he turned back, and Alice threw herself into the water. With Richard's help she swam pretty well, and they reached the tree. "Now for the next!" said Richard; and they swam to the next, and then to the third. Every tree they reached was larger than the last, and every tree before them was larger still. So they swam from tree to tree, till they came to one that was so large that they could not see round it. What was to be done? Clearly to climb this tree. It was a dreadful prospect for Alice, but Richard proceeded to climb; and by putting her feet where he put his, and now and then getting hold of his ankle, she managed to make her way up. There were a great many stumps where branches had withered off, and the bark was nearly as rough as a hill-side, so there was plenty of foothold for them. When they had climbed a long time, and were getting very tired indeed, Alice cried out, "Richard, I shall drop—I shall. Why did you come this way?" And she began once more to cry. But at that moment Richard caught hold of a branch above his head, and reaching down his other hand got hold of Alice, and held her till she had recovered a little. In a few moments more they reached the fork of the tree, and there they sat and rested. "This is capital!" said Richard, cheerily.

"What is?" asked Alice, sulkily.

"Why, we have room to rest, and there's no hurry for a minute or two. I'm tired."

"You selfish creature!" said Alice. "If you are tired, what must I be!"

"Tired too," answered Richard. "But we've got on bravely. And look! what's that?"

By this time the day was gone, and the night so near, that in the shadows of the tree all was dusky and dim. But there was still light enough to discover that in a niche of the tree sat a huge horned owl, with green spectacles on his beak, and a book in one foot. He took no heed of the intruders, but kept muttering to himself. And what do you think the owl was saying? I will tell you. He was talking about the book that he held upside down in his foot.

"Stupid book this-s-s-s! Nothing in it at all! Everything upside down!

Stupid ass-s-s-s! Says owls can't read! I can read backwards!"

"I think that is the goblin again," said Richard, in a whisper. "However, if you ask a plain question, he must give you a plain answer, for they are not allowed to tell downright lies in Fairyland."

"Don't ask him, Richard; you know you gave him a dreadful blow."

"I gave him what he deserved, and he owes me the same.—Hallo! which is the way out?"

He wouldn't say if you please, because then it would not have been a plain question.

"Down-stairs," hissed the owl, without ever lifting his eyes from the book, which all the time he read upside down, so learned was he.

"On your honour, as a respectable old owl?" asked Richard.

"No," hissed the owl; and Richard was almost sure that he was not really an owl. So he stood staring at him for a few moments, when all at once, without lifting his eyes from the book, the owl said, "I will sing a song," and began:—

"Nobody knows the world but me.

When they're all in bed, I sit up to see

I'm a better student than students all,

For I never read till the darkness fall;

And I never read without my glasses,

And that is how my wisdom passes.

Howlowlwhoolhoolwoolool.

"I can see the wind. Now who can do that?

I see the dreams that he has in his hat;

I see him snorting them out as he goes—

Out at his stupid old trumpet-nose.

Ten thousand things that you couldn't think

I write them down with pen and ink.

Howlowlwhooloolwhitit that's wit.

"You may call it learning—'tis mother-wit.

No one else sees the lady-moon sit

On the sea, her nest, all night, but the owl,

Hatching the boats and the long-legged fowl.

When the oysters gape to sing by rote,

She crams a pearl down each stupid throat.

Howlowlwhitit that's wit, there's a fowl!"

And so singing, he threw the book in Richard's face, spread out his great, silent, soft wings, and sped away into the depths of the tree. When the book struck Richard, he found that it was only a lump of wet moss.

While talking to the owl he had spied a hollow behind one of the branches. Judging this to be the way the owl meant, he went to see, and found a rude, ill-defined staircase going down into the very heart of the trunk. But so large was the tree that this could not have hurt it in the least. Down this stair, then, Richard scrambled as best he could, followed by Alice—not of her own will, she gave him clearly to understand, but because she could do no better. Down, down they went, slipping and falling sometimes, but never very far, because the stair went round and round. It caught Richard when he slipped, and he caught Alice when she did. They had begun to fear that there was no end to the stair, it went round and round so steadily, when, creeping through a crack, they found themselves in a great hall, supported by thousands of pillars of gray stone. Where the little light came from they could not tell. This hall they began to cross in a straight line, hoping to reach one side, and intending to walk along it till they came to some opening. They kept straight by going from pillar to pillar, as they had done before by the trees. Any honest plan will do in Fairyland, if you only stick to it. And no plan will do if you do not stick to it.

It was very silent, and Alice disliked the silence more than the dimness,— so much, indeed, that she longed to hear Richard's voice. But she had always been so cross to him when he had spoken, that he thought it better to let her speak first; and she was too proud to do that. She would not even let him walk alongside of her, but always went slower when he wanted to wait for her; so that at last he strode on alone. And Alice followed. But by degrees the horror of silence grew upon her, and she felt at last as if there was no one in the universe but herself. The hall went on widening around her; their footsteps made no noise; the silence grew so intense that it seemed on the point of taking shape. At last she could bear it no longer. She ran after Richard, got up with him, and laid hold of his arm.

He had been thinking for some time what an obstinate, disagreeable girl Alice was, and wishing he had her safe home to be rid of her, when, feeling a hand, and looking round, he saw that it was the disagreeable girl. She soon began to be companionable after a fashion, for she began to think, putting everything together, that Richard must have been several times in Fairyland before now. "It is very strange," she said to herself; "for he is quite a poor boy, I am sure of that. His arms stick out beyond his jacket like the ribs of his mother's umbrella. And to think of me wandering about Fairyland with him!"

The moment she touched his arm, they saw an arch of blackness before them. They had walked straight to a door—not a very inviting one, for it opened upon an utterly dark passage. Where there was only one door, however, there was no difficulty about choosing. Richard walked straight through it; and from the greater fear of being left behind, Alice faced the lesser fear of going on. In a moment they were in total darkness. Alice clung to Richard's arm, and murmured, almost against her will, "Dear Richard!" It was strange that fear should speak like love; but it was in Fairyland. It was strange, too, that as soon as she spoke thus, Richard should fall in love with her all at once. But what was more curious still was, that, at the same moment, Richard saw her face. In spite of her fear, which had made her pale, she looked very lovely.

"Dear Alice!" said Richard, "how pale you look!"

"How can you tell that, Richard, when all is as black as pitch?"

"I can see your face. It gives out light. Now I see your hands. Now I can see your feet. Yes, I can see every spot where you are going to—No, don't put your foot there. There is an ugly toad just there."

The fact was, that the moment he began to love Alice, his eyes began to send forth light. What he thought came from Alice's face, really came from his eyes. All about her and her path he could see, and every minute saw better; but to his own path he was blind. He could not see his hand when he held it straight before his face, so dark was it. But he could see Alice, and that was better than seeing the way—ever so much.

At length Alice too began to see a face dawning through the darkness. It was Richard's face; but it was far handsomer than when she saw it last. Her eyes had begun to give light too. And she said to herself—"Can it be that I love the poor widow's son?—I suppose that must be it," she answered herself, with a smile; for she was not disgusted with herself at all. Richard saw the smile, and was glad. Her paleness had gone, and a sweet rosiness had taken its place. And now she saw Richard's path as he saw hers, and between the two sights they got on well.

They were now walking on a path betwixt two deep waters, which never moved, shining as black as ebony where the eyelight fell. But they saw ere long that this path kept growing narrower and narrower. At last, to Alice's dismay, the black waters met in front of them.

"What is to be done now, Richard?" she said.

When they fixed their eyes on the water before them, they saw that it was swarming with lizards, and frogs, and black snakes, and all kinds of strange and ugly creatures, especially some that had neither heads, nor tails, nor legs, nor fins, nor feelers, being, in fact, only living lumps. These kept jumping out and in, and sprawling upon the path. Richard thought for a few moments before replying to Alice's question, as, indeed, well he might. But he came to the conclusion that the path could not have gone on for the sake of stopping there; and that it must be a kind of finger that pointed on where it was not allowed to go itself. So he caught up Alice in his strong arms, and jumped into the middle of the horrid swarm. And just as minnows vanish if you throw anything amongst them, just so these wretched creatures vanished, right and left and every way.

He found the water broader than he had expected; and before he got over, he found Alice heavier than he could have believed; but upon a firm, rocky bottom, Richard waded through in safety. When he reached the other side, he found that the bank was a lofty, smooth, perpendicular rock, with some rough steps cut in it. By and by the steps led them right into the rock, and they were in a narrow passage once more, but, this time, leading up. It wound round and round, like the thread of a great screw. At last, Richard knocked his head against something, and could go no farther. The place was close and hot. He put up his hands, and pushed what felt like a warm stone: it moved a little.

"Go down, you brutes!" growled a voice above, quivering with anger. "You'll upset my pot and my cat, and my temper too, if you push that way. Go down!"

Richard knocked very gently, and said: "Please let us out."

"Oh, yes, I dare say! Very fine and soft-spoken! Go down, you goblin brutes! I've had enough of you. I'll scald the hair off your ugly heads if you do that again. Go down, I say!"

Seeing fair speech was of no avail, Richard told Alice to go down a little, out of the way; and, setting his shoulders to one end of the stone, heaved it up; whereupon down came the other end, with a pot, and a fire, and a cat which had been asleep beside it. She frightened Alice dreadfully as she rushed past her, showing nothing but her green lamping eyes.

Richard, peeping up, found that he had turned a hearth-stone upside down. On the edge of the hole stood a little crooked old man, brandishing a mop-stick in a tremendous rage, and hesitating only where to strike him. But Richard put him out of his difficulty by springing up and taking the stick from him. Then, having lifted Alice out, he returned it with a bow, and, heedless of the maledictions of the old man, proceeded to get the stone and the pot up again. For puss, she got out of herself.

Then the old man became a little more friendly, and said: "I beg your pardon, I thought you were goblins. They never will let me alone. But you must allow, it was rather an unusual way of paying a morning call." And the creature bowed conciliatingly.

"It was, indeed," answered Richard. "I wish you had turned the door to us instead of the hearth-stone." For he did not trust the old man. "But," he added, "I hope you will forgive us."

"Oh, certainly, certainly, my dear young people! Use your freedom. But such young people have no business to be out alone. It is against the rules."

"But what is one to do—I mean two to do—when they can't help it?"

"Yes, yes, of course; but now, you know, I must take charge of you. So you sit there, young gentleman; and you sit there, young lady."

He put a chair for one at one side of the hearth, and for the other at the other side, and then drew his chair between them. The cat got upon his hump, and then set up her own. So here was a wall that would let through no moonshine. But although both Richard and Alice were very much amused, they did not like to be parted in this peremptory manner. Still they thought it better not to anger the old man any more—in his own house, too.

But he had been once angered, and that was once too often, for he had made it a rule never to forgive without taking it out in humiliation.

It was so disagreeable to have him sitting there between them, that they felt as if they were far asunder. In order to get the better of the fancy, they wanted to hold each other's hand behind the dwarf's back. But the moment their hands began to approach, the back of the cat began to grow long, and its hump to grow high; and, in a moment more, Richard found himself crawling wearily up a steep hill, whose ridge rose against the stars, while a cold wind blew drearily over it. Not a habitation was in sight; and Alice had vanished from his eyes. He felt, however, that she must be somewhere on the other side, and so climbed and climbed to get over the brow of the hill, and down to where he thought she must be. But the longer he climbed, the farther off the top of the hill seemed; till at last he sank quite exhausted, and—must I confess it?—very nearly began to cry. To think of being separated from Alice all at once, and in such a disagreeable way! But he fell a-thinking instead, and soon said to himself: "This must be some trick of that wretched old man. Either this mountain is a cat or it is not. If it is a mountain, this won't hurt it; if it is a cat, I hope it will." With that, he pulled out his pocket-knife, and feeling for a soft place, drove it at one blow up to the handle in the side of the mountain.

A terrific shriek was the first result; and the second, that Alice and he sat looking at each other across the old man's hump, from which the cat-a-mountain had vanished. Their host sat staring at the blank fireplace, without ever turning round, pretending to know nothing of what had taken place.

"Come along, Alice," said Richard, rising. "This won't do. We won't stop here."

Alice rose at once, and put her hand in his. They walked towards the door. The old man took no notice of them. The moon was shining brightly through the window; but instead of stepping out into the moonlight when they opened the door, they stepped into a great beautiful hall, through the high gothic windows of which the same moon was shining. Out of this hall they could find no way, except by a staircase of stone which led upwards. They ascended it together. At the top Alice let go Richard's hand to peep into a little room, which looked all the colours of the rainbow, just like the inside of a diamond. Richard went a step or two along a corridor, but finding she had left him, turned and looked into the chamber. He could see her nowhere. The room was full of doors; and she must have mistaken the door. He heard her voice calling him, and hurried in the direction of the sound. But he could see nothing of her. "More tricks," he said to himself. "It is of no use to stab this one. I must wait till I see what can be done." Still he heard Alice calling him, and still he followed, as well as he could. At length he came to a doorway, open to the air, through which the moonlight fell. But when he reached it, he found that it was high up in the side of a tower, the wall of which went straight down from his feet, without stair or descent of any kind. Again he heard Alice call him, and lifting his eyes, saw her, across a wide castle-court, standing at another door just like the one he was at, with the moon shining full upon her.

"All right, Alice!" he cried. "Can you hear me?"

"Yes," answered she.

"Then listen. This is all a trick. It is all a lie of that old wretch in the kitchen. Just reach out your hand, Alice dear."

Alice did as Richard asked her; and, although they saw each other many yards off across the court, their hands met.

"There! I thought so!" exclaimed Richard triumphantly. "Now, Alice, I don't believe it is more than a foot or two down to the court below, though it looks like a hundred feet. Keep fast hold of my hand, and jump when I count three." But Alice drew her hand from him in sudden dismay; whereupon Richard said, "Well, I will try first," and jumped. The same moment his cheery laugh came to Alice's ears, and she saw him standing safe on the ground, far below.

"Jump, dear Alice, and I will catch you," said he.

130

"I can't; I am afraid," answered she.

"The old man is somewhere near you. You had better jump," said Richard.

Alice sprang from the wall in terror, and only fell a foot or two into Richard's arms. The moment she touched the ground, they found themselves outside the door of a little cottage which they knew very well, for it was only just within the wood that bordered on their village. Hand in hand they ran home as fast as they could. When they reached a little gate that led into her father's grounds, Richard bade Alice good-bye. The tears came in her eyes. Richard and she seemed to have grown quite man and woman in Fairyland, and they did not want to part now. But they felt that they must. So Alice ran in the back way, and reached her own room before anyone had missed her. Indeed, the last of the red had not quite faded from the west.

As Richard crossed the market-place on his way home, he saw an umbrella-man just selling the last of his umbrellas. He thought the man gave him a queer look as he passed, and felt very much inclined to punch his head. But remembering how useless it had been to punch the goblin's head, he thought it better not.

In reward of their courage, the Fairy Queen sent them permission to visit Fairyland as often as they pleased; and no goblin or fairy was allowed to interfere with them.

For Peaseblossom and Toadstool, they were both banished from court, and compelled to live together, for seven years, in an old tree that had just one green leaf upon it.

Toadstool did not mind it much, but Peaseblossom did.

THE SHADOWS

Old Ralph Rinkelmann made his living by comic sketches, and all but lost it again by tragic poems. So he was just the man to be chosen king of the fairies, for in Fairyland the sovereignty is elective.

It is no doubt very strange that fairies should desire to have a mortal king; but the fact is, that with all their knowledge and power, they cannot get rid of the feeling that some men are greater than they are, though they can neither fly nor play tricks. So at such times as there happens to be twice the usual number of sensible electors, such a man as Ralph Rinkelmann gets to be chosen.

They did not mean to insist on his residence; for they needed his presence only on special occasions. But they must get hold of him somehow, first of all, in order to make him king. Once he was crowned, they could get him as often as they pleased; but before this ceremony there was a difficulty. For it is only between life and death that the fairies have power over grown-up mortals, and can carry them off to their country. So they had to watch for an opportunity.

Nor had they to wait long. For old Ralph was taken dreadfully ill; and while hovering between life and death, they carried him off, and crowned him king of Fairyland. But after he was crowned, it was no wonder, considering the state of his health, that he should not be able to sit quite upright on the throne of Fairyland; or that, in consequence, all the gnomes and goblins, and ugly, cruel things that live in the holes and corners of the kingdom, should take advantage of his condition, and run quite wild, playing him, king as he was, all sorts of tricks; crowding about his throne, climbing up the steps, and actually scrambling and quarrelling like mice about his ears and eyes, so that he could see and think of nothing else. But I am not going to tell anything more about this part of his adventures just at present. By strong and sustained efforts, he succeeded, after much trouble and suffering, in reducing his rebellious subjects to order. They all vanished to their respective holes and corners; and King Ralph, coming to himself, found himself in his bed, half propped up with pillows.

But the room was full of dark creatures, which gambolled about in the firelight in such a strange, huge, though noiseless fashion, that he thought at first that some of his rebellious goblins had not been subdued with the rest, but had followed him beyond the bounds of Fairyland into his own private house in London. How else could these mad, grotesque hippopotamus-calves make their ugly appearance in Ralph Rinkelmann's bed-room? But he soon found out that although they were like the underground goblins, they were very different as well, and would require quite different treatment. He felt convinced that they were his subjects too, but that he must have overlooked them somehow at his late coronation—if indeed they had been present; for he could not recollect that he had seen anything just like them before. He resolved, therefore, to pay particular attention to their habits, ways, and characters; else he saw plainly that they would soon be too much for him; as indeed this intrusion into his chamber, where Mrs. Rinkelmann, who must be queen if he was king, sat taking some tea by the fireside, evidently foreshadowed. But she, perceiving that he was looking about him with a more composed expression than his face had worn for many days, started up, and came quickly and quietly to his side, and her face was bright with gladness. Whereupon the fire burned up more cheerily; and the figures became more composed and respectful in their behaviour, retreating towards the wall like

134

well-trained attendants. Then the king of Fairyland had some tea and dry toast, and leaning back on his pillows, nearly fell asleep; but not quite, for he still watched the intruders.

Presently the queen left the room to give some of the young princes and princesses their tea; and the fire burned lower, and behold, the figures grew as black and as mad in their gambols as ever! Their favourite games seemed to be Hide and Seek; Touch and Go; Grin and Vanish; and many other such; and all in the king's bed-chamber, too; so that it was quite alarming. It was almost as bad as if the house had been haunted by certain creatures which shall be nameless in a fairy story, because with them Fairyland will not willingly have much to do.

"But it is a mercy that they have their slippers on!" said the king to himself; for his head ached.

As he lay back, with his eyes half shut and half open, too tired to pay longer attention to their games, but, on the whole, considerably more amused than offended with the liberties they took, for they seemed good-natured creatures, and more frolicsome than positively ill-mannered, he became suddenly aware that two of them had stepped forward from the walls, upon which, after the manner of great spiders, most of them preferred sprawling, and now stood in the middle of the floor at the foot of his majesty's bed, becking and bowing and ducking in the most grotesquely obsequious manner; while every now and then they turned solemnly round upon one heel, evidently considering that motion the highest token of homage they could show.

"What do you want?" said the king.

"That it may please your majesty to be better acquainted with us," answered they. "We are your majesty's subjects."

135

"I know you are. I shall be most happy," answered the king.

"We are not what your majesty takes us for, though. We are not so foolish as your majesty thinks us."

"It is impossible to take you for anything that I know of," rejoined the king, who wished to make them talk, and said whatever came uppermost;— "for soldiers, sailors, or anything: you will not stand still long enough. I suppose you really belong to the fire brigade; at least, you keep putting its light out."

"Don't jest, please your majesty." And as they said the words—for they both spoke at once throughout the interview—they performed a grave somerset towards the king.

"Not jest!" retorted he; "and with you? Why, you do nothing but jest.

What are you?"

"The Shadows, sire. And when we do jest, sire, we always jest in earnest. But perhaps your majesty does not see us distinctly."

"I see you perfectly well," returned the king.

"Permit me, however," rejoined one of the Shadows; and as he spoke he approached the king; and lifting a dark forefinger, he drew it lightly but carefully across the ridge of his forehead, from temple to temple. The king felt the soft gliding touch go, like water, into every hollow, and over the top of every height of that mountain-chain of thought. He had involuntarily closed his eyes during the operation, and when he unclosed them again, as soon as the finger was withdrawn, he found that they were opened in more senses than one. The room appeared to have extended itself on all sides, till he could not exactly see where the walls were; and all about it stood the

Shadows motionless. They were tall and solemn; rather awful, indeed, in their appearance, notwithstanding many remarkable traits of grotesqueness, for they looked just like the pictures of Puritans drawn by Cavaliers, with long arms, and very long, thin legs, from which hung large loose feet, while in their countenances length of chin and nose predominated. The solemnity of their mien, however, overcame all the oddity of their form, so that they were very eerie indeed to look at, dressed as they all were in funereal black. But a single glance was all that the king was allowed to have; for the former operator waved his dusky palm across his vision, and once more the king saw only the fire-lighted walls, and dark shapes flickering about upon them. The two who had spoken for the rest seemed likewise to have vanished. But at last the king discovered them, standing one on each side of the fireplace. They kept close to the chimney-wall, and talked to each other across the length of the chimney-piece; thus avoiding the direct rays of the fire, which, though light is necessary to their appearing to human eyes, do not agree with them at all—much less give birth to them, as the king was soon to learn. After a few minutes they again approached the bed, and spoke thus:—

"It is now getting dark, please your majesty. We mean, out of doors in the snow. Your majesty may see, from where he is lying, the cold light of its great winding-sheet—a famous carpet for the Shadows to dance upon, your majesty. All our brothers and sisters will be at church now, before going to their night's work."

"Do they always go to church before they go to work?"

"They always go to church first."

"Where is the church?"

"In Iceland. Would your majesty like to see it?"

"How can I go and see it, when, as you know very well, I am ill in bed? Besides, I should be sure to take cold in a frosty night like this, even if I put on the blankets, and took the feather-bed for a muff."

A sort of quivering passed over their faces, which seemed to be their mode of laughing. The whole shape of the face shook and fluctuated as if it had been some dark fluid; till by slow degrees of gathering calm, it settled into its former rest. Then one of them drew aside the curtains of the bed, and the window-curtains not having been yet drawn, the king beheld the white glimmering night outside, struggling with the heaps of darkness that tried to quench it; and the heavens full of stars, flashing and sparkling like live jewels. The other Shadow went towards the fire and vanished in it.

Scores of Shadows immediately began an insane dance all about the room; disappearing, one after the other, through the uncovered window, and gliding darkly away over the face of the white snow; for the window looked at once on a field of snow. In a few moments, the room was quite cleared of them; but instead of being relieved by their absence, the king felt immediately as if he were in a dead-house, and could hardly breathe for the sense of emptiness and desolation that fell upon him. But as he lay looking out on the snow, which stretched blank and wide before him, he spied in the distance a long dark line which drew nearer and nearer, and showed itself at last to be all the Shadows, walking in a double row, and carrying in the midst of them something like a bier. They vanished under the window, but soon reappeared, having somehow climbed up the wall of the house; for they entered in perfect order by the window, as if melting through the transparency of the glass.

They still carried the bier or litter. It was covered with richest furs, and skins of gorgeous wild beasts, whose eyes were replaced by sapphires and emeralds, that glittered and gleamed in the fire and snow light. The outermost

138

skin sparkled with frost, but the inside ones were soft and warm and dry as the down under a swan's wing. The Shadows approached the bed, and set the litter upon it. Then a number of them brought a huge fur robe, and wrapping it round the king, laid him on the litter in the midst of the furs. Nothing could be more gentle and respectful than the way in which they moved him; and he never thought of refusing to go. Then they put something on his head, and, lifting the litter, carried him once round the room, to fall into order. As he passed the mirror he saw that he was covered with royal ermine, and that his head wore a wonderful crown of gold, set with none but red stones: rubies and carbuncles and garnets, and others whose names he could not tell, glowed gloriously around his head, like the salamandrine essence of all the Christmas fires over the world. A sceptre lay beside him—a rod of ebony, surmounted by a cone-shaped diamond, which, cut in a hundred facets, flashed all the hues of the rainbow, and threw coloured gleams on every side, that looked like Shadows too, but more ethereal than those that bore him. Then the Shadows rose gently to the window, passed through it, and sinking slowing upon the field of outstretched snow, commenced an orderly gliding rather than march along the frozen surface. They took it by turns to bear the king, as they sped with the swiftness of thought, in a straight line towards the north. The pole-star rose above their heads with visible rapidity; for indeed they moved quite as fast as sad thoughts, though not with all the speed of happy desires. England and Scotland slid past the litter of the king of the Shadows. Over rivers and lakes they skimmed and glided. They climbed the high mountains, and crossed the valleys with a fearless bound; till they came to John-o'-Groat's house and the Northern Sea. The sea was not frozen; for all the stars shone as clear out of the deeps below as they shone out of the deeps above; and as the bearers slid along the blue-gray surface, with never a furrow in their track, so pure was the water beneath that the king saw neither surface, bottom, nor substance to it, and seemed to be gliding only through the blue sphere of heaven, with the stars above him, and the stars below him, and between the stars and him nothing but an emptiness, where, for the first time in his life, his soul felt that it had room enough.

At length they reached the rocky shores of Iceland. There they landed, still pursuing their journey. All this time the king felt no cold; for the red stones in his crown kept him warm, and the emerald and sapphire eyes of the wild beasts kept the frosts from settling upon his litter.

Oftentimes upon their way they had to pass through forests, caverns, and rock-shadowed paths, where it was so dark that at first the king feared he should lose his Shadows altogether. But as soon as they entered such places, the diamond in his sceptre began to shine and glow, and flash, sending out streams of light of all the colours that painter's soul could dream of; in which light the Shadows grew livelier and stronger than ever, speeding through the dark ways with an all but blinding swiftness. In the light of the diamond, too, some of their forms became more simple and human, while others seemed only to break out into a yet more untamable absurdity. Once, as they passed through a cave, the king actually saw some of their eyes—strange shadow-eyes; he had never seen any of their eyes before. But at the same moment when he saw their eyes, he knew their faces too, for they turned them full upon him for an instant; and the other Shadows, catching sight of these, shrank and shivered, and nearly vanished. Lovely faces they were; but the king was very thoughtful after he saw them, and continued rather troubled all the rest of the journey. He could not account for those faces being there, and the faces of Shadows, too, with living eyes.

But he soon found that amongst the Shadows a man must learn never to be surprised at anything; for if he does not, he will soon grow quite stupid, in consequence of the endless recurrence of surprises.

At last they climbed up the bed of a little stream, and then, passing through a narrow rocky defile, came out suddenly upon the side of a mountain, overlooking a blue frozen lake in the very heart of mighty hills. Overhead, the aurora borealis was shivering and flashing like a battle of ten thousand spears. Underneath, its beams passed faintly over the blue ice and the sides of the snow-clad mountains, whose tops shot up like huge icicles all about, with here and there a star sparkling on the very tip of one. But as the northern lights in the sky above, so wavered and quivered, and shot hither and thither, the Shadows on the surface of the lake below; now gathering in groups, and now shivering asunder; now covering the whole surface of the lake, and anon condensed into one dark knot in the centre. Every here and there on the white mountains might be seen two or three shooting away towards the tops, to vanish beyond them, so that their number was gradually, though not visibly, diminishing.

"Please your majesty," said the Shadows, "this is our church—the

Church of the Shadows."

And so saying, the king's body-guard set down the litter upon a rock, and plunged into the multitudes below. They soon returned, however, and bore the king down into the middle of the lake. All the Shadows came crowding round him, respectfully but fearlessly; and sure never such a grotesque assembly revealed itself before to mortal eyes. The king had seen all kind of gnomes, goblins, and kobolds at his coronation; but they were quite rectilinear figures compared with the insane lawlessness of form in which the Shadows rejoiced; and the wildest gambols of the former were orderly dances of ceremony beside the apparently aimless and wilful contortions of figure, and metamorphoses of shape, in which the latter indulged. They retained, however, all the time, to the surprise of the king, an identity, each of his own type, inexplicably perceptible through every change. Indeed this preservation of the primary idea of each form was more wonderful than the bewildering and ridiculous alterations to which the form itself was every moment subjected.

"What are you?" said the king, leaning on his elbow, and looking around him.

"The Shadows, your majesty," answered several voices at once.

"What Shadows?"

"The human Shadows. The Shadows of men, and women, and their children."

"Are you not the shadows of chairs and tables, and pokers and tongs, just as well?"

At this question a strange jarring commotion went through the assembly with a shock. Several of the figures shot up as high as the aurora, but instantly settled down again to human size, as if overmastering their feelings, out of respect to him who had roused them. One who had bounded to the highest visible icy peak, and as suddenly returned, now elbowed his way through the rest, and made himself spokesman for them during the remaining part of the dialogue.

"Excuse our agitation, your majesty," said he. "I see your majesty has not yet thought proper to make himself acquainted with our nature and habits."

"I wish to do so now," replied the king.

"We are the Shadows," repeated the Shadow solemnly.

"Well?" said the king.

"We do not often appear to men."

"Ha!" said the king.

"We do not belong to the sunshine at all. We go through it unseen, and only by a passing chill do men recognize an unknown presence."

"Ha!" said the king again.

"It is only in the twilight of the fire, or when one man or woman is alone with a single candle, or when any number of people are all feeling the same thing at once, making them one, that we show ourselves, and the truth of things."

"Can that be true that loves the night?" said the king.

"The darkness is the nurse of light," answered the Shadow.

"Can that be true which mocks at forms?" said the king.

"Truth rides abroad in shapeless storms," answered the Shadow.

"Ha! ha!" thought Ralph Rinkelmann, "it rhymes. The Shadow caps my questions with his answers. Very strange!" And he grew thoughtful again.

The Shadow was the first to resume.

"Please your majesty, may we present our petition?"

"By all means," replied the king. "I am not well enough to receive it in proper state."

"Never mind, your majesty. We do not care for much ceremony; and indeed none of us are quite well at present. The subject of our petition weighs upon us."

"Go on," said the king.

"Sire," began the Shadow, "our very existence is in danger. The various sorts of artificial light, both in houses and in men, women, and children, threaten to end our being. The use and the disposition of gaslights, especially high in the centres, blind the eyes by which alone we can be perceived. We are all but banished from towns. We are driven into villages and lonely houses, chiefly old farm-houses, out of which, even, our friends the fairies are fast disappearing. We therefore petition our king, by the power of his art, to restore us to our rights in the house itself, and in the hearts of its inhabitants."

"But," said the king, "you frighten the children."

"Very seldom, your majesty; and then only for their good. We seldom seek to frighten anybody. We mostly want to make people silent and thoughtful; to awe them a little, your majesty."

"You are much more likely to make them laugh," said the king.

"Are we?" said the Shadow.

And approaching the king one step, he stood quite still for a moment. The diamond of the king's sceptre shot out a vivid flame of violet light, and the king stared at the Shadow in silence, and his lip quivered. He never told what he saw then; but he would say:

"Just fancy what it might be if some flitting thoughts were to persist in staying to be looked at."

"It is only," resumed the Shadow, "when our thoughts are not fixed upon any particular object, that our bodies are subject to all the vagaries of elemental influences. Generally, amongst worldly men and frivolous women, we only attach ourselves to some article of furniture or of dress; and they never doubt that we are mere foolish and vague results of the dashing of the waves of the light against the solid forms of which their houses are full. We do not care to tell them the truth, for they would never see it. But let the worldly man—or the frivolous woman—and then—"

At each of the pauses indicated, the mass of Shadows throbbed and heaved with emotion; but they soon settled again into comparative stillness. Once more the Shadow addressed himself to speak. But suddenly they all looked up, and the king, following their gaze, saw that the aurora had begun to pale.

"The moon is rising," said the Shadow. "As soon as she looks over the mountains into the valley, we must be gone, for we have plenty to do by the moon; we are powerful in her light. But if your majesty will come here to-morrow night, your majesty may learn a great deal more about us, and judge for himself whether it be fit to accord our petition; for then will be our grand annual assembly, in which we report to our chiefs the things we have attempted, and the good or bad success we have had."

"If you send for me," returned the king, "I will come."

Ere the Shadow could reply, the tip of the moon's crescent horn peeped up from behind an icy pinnacle, and one slender ray fell on the lake. It shone upon no Shadows. Ere the eye of the king could again seek the earth after beholding the first brightness of the moon's resurrection, they had vanished; and the surface of the lake glittered gold and blue in the pale moonlight.

There the king lay, alone in the midst of the frozen lake, with the moon staring at him. But at length he heard from somewhere a voice that he knew.

145

"Will you take another cup of tea, dear?" said Mrs. Rinkelmann.

And Ralph, coming slowly to himself, found that he was lying in his own bed.

"Yes, I will," he answered; "and rather a large piece of toast, if you please; for I have been a long journey since I saw you last."

"He has not come to himself quite," said Mrs. Rinkelmann, between her and herself.

"You would be rather surprised," continued Ralph, "if I told you where I had been."

"I dare say I should," responded his wife.

"Then I will tell you," rejoined Ralph.

But at that moment, a great Shadow bounced out of the fire with a single huge leap, and covered the whole room. Then it settled in one corner, and Ralph saw it shaking its fist at him from the end of a preposterous arm. So he took the hint, and held his peace. And it was as well for him. For I happen to know something about the Shadows too; and I know that if he had told his wife all about it just then, they would not have sent for him the following evening.

But as the king, after finishing his tea and toast, lay and looked about him, the Shadows dancing in his room seemed to him odder and more inexplicable than ever. The whole chamber was full of mystery. So it generally was, but now it was more mysterious than ever. After all that he had seen in the Shadow-church, his own room and its Shadows were yet more wonderful and unintelligible than those.

This made it the more likely that he had seen a true vision; for instead of making common things look commonplace, as a false vision would have done, it had made common things disclose the wonderful that was in them.

"The same applies to all arts as well," thought Ralph Rinkelmann.

The next afternoon, as the twilight was growing dusky, the king lay wondering whether or not the Shadows would fetch him again. He wanted very much to go, for he had enjoyed the journey exceedingly, and he longed, besides, to hear some of the Shadows tell their stories. But the darkness grew deeper and deeper, and the shadows did not come. The cause was, that Mrs. Rinkelmann sat by the fire in the gloaming; and they could not carry off the king while she was there. Some of them tried to frighten her away by playing the oddest pranks on the walls, and floor, and ceiling; but altogether without effect; the queen only smiled, for she had a good conscience. Suddenly, however, a dreadful scream was heard from the nursery, and Mrs. Rinkelmann rushed upstairs to see what was the matter. No sooner had she gone than the two warders of the chimney-corners stepped out into the middle of the room, and said, in a low voice,—

"Is your majesty ready?"

"Have you no hearts?" said the king; "or are they as black as your faces? Did you not hear the child scream? I must know what is the matter with her before I go."

"Your majesty may keep his mind easy on that point," replied the warders. "We had tried everything we could think of to get rid of her majesty the queen, but without effect. So a young madcap Shadow, half against the will of the older ones of us, slipped upstairs into the nursery; and has, no doubt, succeeded in appalling the baby, for he is very lithe and long-legged.—

Now, your majesty."

"I will have no such tricks played in my nursery," said the king, rather angrily. "You might put the child beside itself."

"Then there would be twins, your majesty. And we rather like twins."

"None of your miserable jesting! You might put the child out of her wits."

"Impossible, sire; for she has not got into them yet."

"Go away," said the king.

"Forgive us, your majesty. Really, it will do the child good; for that

Shadow will, all her life, be to her a symbol of what is ugly and bad.

When she feels in danger of hating or envying anyone, that Shadow will

come back to her mind and make her shudder."

"Very well," said the king. "I like that. Let us go."

The Shadows went through the same ceremonies and preparations as before; during which, the young Shadow before-mentioned contrived to make such grimaces as kept the baby in terror, and the queen in the nursery, till all was ready. Then with a bound that doubled him up against the ceiling, and a kick of his legs six feet out behind him, he vanished through the nursery door, and reached the king's bed-chamber just in time to take his place with the last who were melting through the window in the rear of the litter, and settling down upon the snow beneath. Away they went as before, a gliding blackness over the white carpet. And it was Christmas-eve.

When they came in sight of the mountain-lake, the king saw that it was crowded over its whole surface with a changeful intermingling of Shadows. They were all talking and listening alternately, in pairs, trios, and groups of every size. Here and there large companies were absorbed in attention to one elevated above the rest, not in a pulpit, or on a platform, but on the stilts of his own legs, elongated for the nonce. The aurora, right overhead, lighted up the lake and the sides of the mountains, by sending down from the zenith, nearly to the surface of the lake, great folded vapours, luminous with all the colours of a faint rainbow.

Many, however, as the words were that passed on all sides, not a shadow of a sound reached the ears of the king: the shadow-speech could not enter his corporeal organs. One of his guides, however, seeing that the king wanted to hear and could not, went through a strange manipulation of his head and ears; after which he could hear perfectly, though still only the voice to which, for the time, he directed his attention. This, however, was a great advantage, and one which the king longed to carry back with him to the world of men.

The king now discovered that this was not merely the church of the Shadows, but their news exchange at the same time. For, as the shadows have no writing or printing, the only way in which they can make each other acquainted with their doings and thinkings, is to meet and talk at this word-mart and parliament of shades. And as, in the world, people read their favourite authors, and listen to their favourite speakers, so here the Shadows seek their favourite Shadows, listen to their adventures, and hear generally what they have to say.

Feeling quite strong, the king rose and walked about amongst them, wrapped in his ermine robe, with his red crown on his head, and his diamond sceptre in his hand. Every group of Shadows to which he drew near, ceased talking as soon as they saw him approach; but at a nod they went on again directly, conversing and relating and commenting, as if no one was there of other kind or of higher rank than themselves. So the king heard a good many stories. At some of them he laughed, and at some of them he cried. But if the stories that the Shadows told were printed, they would make a book that no publisher could produce fast enough to satisfy the buyers. I will record some of the things that the king heard, for he told them to me soon after. In fact, I was for some time his private secretary.

"I made him confess before a week was over," said a gloomy old Shadow.

"But what was the good of that?" rejoined a pert young one. "That could not undo what was done."

"Yes, it could."

"What! bring the dead to life?"

"No; but comfort the murderer. I could not bear to see the pitiable misery he was in. He was far happier with the rope round his neck, than he was with the purse in his pocket. I saved him from killing himself too."

"How did you make him confess?"

"Only by wallowing on the wall a little."

"How could that make him tell?"

"He knows."

The Shadow was silent; and the king turned to another, who was preparing to speak.

"I made a fashionable mother repent."

"How?" broke from several voices, in whose sound was mingled a touch of incredulity.

"Only by making a little coffin on the wall," was the reply.

"Did the fashionable mother confess too?"

"She had nothing more to confess than everybody knew."

"What did everybody know then?"

"That she might have been kissing a living child, when she followed a dead one to the grave.—The next will fare better."

"I put a stop to a wedding," said another.

"Horrid shade!" remarked a poetic imp.

"How?" said others. "Tell us how."

"Only by throwing a darkness, as if from the branch of a sconce, over the forehead of a fair girl.—They are not married yet, and I do not think they will be. But I loved the youth who loved her. How he started! It was a revelation to him."

"But did it not deceive him?"

"Quite the contrary."

"But it was only a shadow from the outside, not a shadow coming through from the soul of the girl."

"Yes. You may say so. But it was all that was wanted to make the meaning of her forehead manifest—yes, of her whole face, which had now and then, in the pauses of his passion, perplexed the youth. All of it, curled nostrils, pouting lips, projecting chin, instantly fell into harmony with that darkness between her eyebrows. The youth understood it in a moment, and went home miserable. And they're not married yet."

"I caught a toper alone, over his magnum of port," said a very dark Shadow; "and didn't I give it him! I made delirium tremens first; and then I settled into a funeral, passing slowly along the length of the opposite wall. I gave him plenty of plumes and mourning coaches. And then I gave him a funeral service, but I could not manage to make the surplice white, which was all the better for such a sinner. The wretch stared till his face passed from purple to grey, and actually left his fifth glass only, unfinished, and took refuge with his wife and children in the drawing-room, much to their surprise. I believe he actually drank a cup of tea; and although I have often looked in since, I have never caught him again, drinking alone at least."

"But does he drink less? Have you done him any good?"

"I hope so; but I am sorry to say I can't feel sure about it."

"Humph! Humph! Humph!" grunted various shadow throats.

"I had such fun once!" cried another. "I made such game of a young clergyman!"

"You have no right to make game of anyone."

"Oh yes, I have—when it is for his good. He used to study his sermons—where do you think?"

"In his study, of course. Where else should it be?"

"Yes and no. Guess again."

"Out amongst the faces in the streets."

"Guess again."

"In still green places in the country?"

"Guess again."

"In old books?"

"Guess again."

"No, no. Tell us."

"In the looking glass. Ha! ha! ha!"

"He was fair game; fair shadow game."

"I thought so. And I made such fun of him one night on the wall! He had sense enough to see that it was himself, and very like an ape. So he got ashamed, turned the mirror with its face to the wall, and thought a little more about his people, and a little less about himself. I was very glad; for, please your majesty,"—and here the speaker turned towards the king—"we don't like the creatures that live in the mirrors. You call them ghosts, don't you?"

Before the king could reply, another had commenced. But the story about the clergyman had made the king wish to hear one of the shadow-sermons. So he turned him towards a long Shadow, who was preaching to a very quiet and listening crowd. He was just concluding his sermon.

"Therefore, dear Shadows, it is the more needful that we love one another as much as we can, because that is not much. We have no such excuse for not loving as mortals have, for we do not die like them. I suppose it is the thought of that death that makes them hate so much. Then again, we go to sleep all day, most of us, and not in the night, as men do. And you know that we forget everything that happened the night before; therefore, we ought to love well, for the love is short. Ah! dear Shadow, whom I love now with all my shadowy

153

soul, I shall not love thee to-morrow eve, I shall not know thee; I shall pass thee in the crowd and never dream that the Shadow whom I now love is near me then. Happy Shades! for we only remember our tales until we have told them here, and then they vanish in the shadow-churchyard, where we bury only our dead selves. Ah! brethren, who would be a man and remember? Who would be a man and weep? We ought indeed to love one another, for we alone inherit oblivion; we alone are renewed with eternal birth; we alone have no gathered weight of years. I will tell you the awful fate of one Shadow who rebelled against his nature, and sought to remember the past. He said, 'I will remember this eve.' He fought with the genial influences of kindly sleep when the sun rose on the awful dead day of light; and although he could not keep quite awake, he dreamed of the foregone eve, and he never forgot his dream. Then he tried again the next night, and the next, and the next; and he tempted another Shadow to try it with him. But at last their awful fate overtook them; for, instead of continuing to be Shadows, they began to cast shadows, as foolish men say; and so they thickened and thickened till they vanished out of our world. They are now condemned to walk the earth, a man and a woman, with death behind them, and memories within them. Ah, brother Shades! let us love one another, for we shall soon forget. We are not men, but Shadows."

The king turned away, and pitied the poor Shadows far more than they pitied men.

"Oh! how we played with a musician one night!" exclaimed a Shadow in another group, to which the king had first directed a passing thought, and then had stopped to listen.—"Up and down we went, like the hammers and dampers on his piano. But he took his revenge on us. For after he had watched us for half an hour in the twilight, he rose and went to his instrument, and played a shadow-dance that fixed us all in sound for ever. Each could tell the very notes meant for him; and as long as he played, we could not stop, but went on dancing and dancing after the music, just as the magician—I mean the musician—pleased. And he punished us well; for he nearly danced us all off our legs and out of shape into tired heaps of collapsed and palpitating darkness. We won't go near him for some time again, if we can only remember it. He had been very miserable all day, he was so poor; and we could not think of any way of comforting him except making him laugh. We did not succeed, with our wildest efforts; but it turned out better than we had expected, after all; for his shadow-dance got him into notice, and he is quite popular now, and making money fast.—If he does not take care, we shall have other work to do with him by and by, poor fellow!"

"I and some others did the same for a poor play-writer once. He had a Christmas piece to write, and [not] being an original genius, it was not so easy for him to find a subject as it is for most of his class. I saw the trouble he was in, and collecting a few stray Shadows, we acted, in dumb-show of course, the funniest bit of nonsense we could think of; and it was quite successful. The poor fellow watched every motion, roaring with laughter at us, and delight at the ideas we put into his head. He turned it all into words, and scenes, and actions; and the piece came off with a splendid success."

"But how long we have to look for a chance of doing anything worth doing," said a long, thin, especially lugubrious Shadow. "I have only done one thing worth telling ever since we met last. But I am proud of that."

"What was it? What was it?" rose from twenty voices.

"I crept into a dining-room, one twilight, soon after Christmas-day. I had been drawn thither by the glow of a bright fire shining through red

155

window-curtains. At first I thought there was no one there, and was on the point of leaving the room, and going out again into the snowy street, when I suddenly caught the sparkle of eyes. I found that they belonged to a little boy who lay very still on a sofa. I crept into a dark corner by the sideboard, and watched him. He seemed very sad, and did nothing but stare into the fire. At last he sighed out,—'I wish mamma would come home.' 'Poor boy!' thought I, 'there is no help for that but mamma.' Yet I would try to while away the time for him. So out of my corner I stretched a long shadow arm, reaching all across the ceiling, and pretended to make a grab at him. He was rather frightened at first; but he was a brave boy, and soon saw that it was all a joke. So when I did it again, he made a clutch at me; and then we had such fun! For though he often sighed and wished mamma would come home, he always began again with me; and on we went with the wildest games. At last his mother's knock came to the door, and starting up in delight, he rushed into the hall to meet her, and forgot all about poor black me. But I did not mind that in the least; for when I glided out after him into the hall, I was well repaid for my trouble by hearing his mother say to him,—'Why, Charlie, my dear, you look ever so much better since I left you!' At that moment I slipped through the closing door, and as I ran across the snow, I heard the mother say,—'What shadow can that be, passing so quickly?' And Charlie answered with a merry laugh,—'Oh! mamma, I suppose it must be the funny shadow that has been playing such games with me all the time you were out.' As soon as the door was shut, I crept along the wall and looked in at the dining-room window. And I heard his mamma say, as she led him into the room, 'What an imagination the boy has!' Ha! ha! ha! Then she looked at him, and the tears came in her eyes; and she stooped down over him, and I heard the sounds of a mingling kiss and sob."

156

"I always look for nurseries full of children," said another; "and this winter I have been very fortunate. I am sure children belong especially to us. One evening, looking about in a great city, I saw through the window into a large nursery, where the odious gas had not yet been lighted. Round the fire sat a company of the most delightful children I had ever seen. They were waiting patiently for their tea. It was too good an opportunity to be lost. I hurried away, and gathering together twenty of the best Shadows I could find, returned in a few moments; and entering the nursery, we danced on the walls one of our best dances. To be sure it was mostly extemporized; but I managed to keep it in harmony by singing this song, which I made as we went on. Of course the children could not hear it; they only saw the motions that answered to it; but with them they seemed to be very much delighted indeed, as I shall presently prove to you. This was the song:—

'Swing, swang, swingle, swuff,

Flicker, flacker, fling, fluff!

Thus we go,

To and fro;

Here and there,

Everywhere,

Born and bred;

Never dead,

Only gone.

'On! Come on.

Looming, glooming,

Spreading, fuming,

Shattering, scattering,

Parting, darting,

Settling, starting,

All our life

Is a strife,

And a wearying for rest

On the darkness' friendly breast.

'Joining, splitting,

Rising, sitting,

Laughing, shaking,

Sides all aching,

Grumbling, grim, and gruff.

Swingle, swangle, swuff!

'Now a knot of darkness;

Now dissolved gloom;

Now a pall of blackness

Hiding all the room.

Flicker, flacker, fluff!

Black, and black enough!

'Dancing now like demons;

Lying like the dead;

Gladly would we stop it,

And go down to bed!

But our work we still must do,

Shadow men, as well as you.

'Rooting, rising, shooting,

Heaving, sinking, creeping;

Hid in corners crooning;

Splitting, poking, leaping,

Gathering, towering, swooning.

When we're lurking,

Yet we're working,

For our labour we must do,

Shadow men, as well as you.

Flicker, flacker, fling, fluff!

Swing, swang, swingle, swuff!'

"'How thick the Shadows are!' said one of the children—a thoughtful little girl.

"'I wonder where they come from,' said a dreamy little boy.

"'I think they grow out of the wall,' answered the little girl; 'for I have been watching them come; first one and then another, and then a whole lot of them. I am sure they grow out of the walls.'

"'Perhaps they have papas and mammas,' said an older boy, with a smile.

"'Yes, yes; and the doctor brings them in his pocket,' said another, a consequential little maiden.

"'No; I'll tell you,' said the older boy: 'they're ghosts.'

"'But ghosts are white.'

"'Oh! but these have got black coming down the chimney.'

"'No,' said a curious-looking, white-faced boy of fourteen, who had been reading by the firelight, and had stopped to hear the little ones talk; 'they're body ghosts; they're not soul ghosts.'

"'A silence followed, broken by the first, the dreamy-eyed boy, who said,—

"'I hope they didn't make me;' at which they all burst out laughing. Just then the nurse brought in their tea, and when she proceeded to light the gas, we vanished."

"I stopped a murder," cried another.

"How? How? How?"

"I will tell you. I had been lurking about a sick-room for some time, where a miser lay, apparently dying. I did not like the place at all, but I felt as if I should be wanted there. There were plenty of lurking-places about, for the room was full of all sorts of old furniture, especially cabinets, chests, and presses. I believe he had in that room every bit of the property he had spent a long life in gathering. I found that he had gold and gold in those places; for one night, when his nurse was away, he crept out of bed, mumbling and shaking, and managed to open one of his chests, though he nearly fell down with the effort. I was peeping over his shoulder, and such a gleam of gold fell upon me, that it nearly killed me. But hearing his nurse coming, he slammed the lid down, and I recovered.

"I tried very hard, but I could not do him any good. For although I made all sorts of shapes on the walls and ceiling, representing evil deeds that he had done, of which there were plenty to choose from, I could make no shapes on his brain or conscience. He had no eyes for anything but gold. And it so happened that his nurse had neither eyes nor heart for anything else either.

"'One day, as she was seated beside his bed, but where he could not see her, stirring some gruel in a basin, to cool it from him, I saw her take a little phial from her bosom, and I knew by the expression of her face both what it was and what she was going to do with it. Fortunately the cork was a little hard to get out, and this gave me one moment to think.

"The room was so crowded with all sorts of things, that although there were no curtains on the four-post bed to hide from the miser the sight of his precious treasures, there was yet but one small part of the ceiling suitable for casting myself upon in the shape I wished to assume. And this spot was hard to reach. But having discovered that upon this very place lay a dull gleam of firelight thrown from a strange old dusty mirror that stood away in some corner, I got in front of the fire, spied where the mirror was, threw myself upon it, and bounded from its face upon the oval pool of dim light on the ceiling, assuming, as I passed, the shape of an old stooping hag, who poured something from a phial into a basin. I made the handle of the spoon with my own nose, ha! ha!" And the shadow-hand caressed the shadow-tip of the shadow-nose, before the shadow-tongue resumed.

"The old miser saw me: he would not taste the gruel that night, although his nurse coaxed and scolded till they were both weary. She pretended to taste it herself, and to think it very good; but at last retired into a corner, and after making as if she were eating it, took good care to pour it all out into the ashes."

"But she must either succeed, or starve him, at last," interposed a Shadow.

"I will tell you."

"And," interposed a third, "he was not worth saving."

"He might repent," suggested another who was more benevolent.

"No chance of that," returned the former. "Misers never do. The love of money has less in it to cure itself than any other wickedness into which wretched men can fall. What a mercy it is to be born a Shadow! Wickedness does not stick to us. What do we care for gold!—Rubbish!"

"Amen! Amen! Amen!" came from a hundred shadow-voices.

"You should have let her murder him, and so you would have been quit of him."

"And besides, how was he to escape at last? He could never get rid of her, you know."

"I was going to tell you," resumed the narrator, "only you had so many shadow-remarks to make, that you would not let me."

"Go on; go on."

"There was a little grandchild who used to come and see him sometimes— the only creature the miser cared for. Her mother was his daughter; but the old man would never see her, because she had married against his will. Her husband was now dead, but he had not forgiven her yet. After the shadow he had seen, however, he said to himself, as he lay awake that night—I saw the words on his face—'How shall I get rid of that old devil? If I don't eat I shall die; and if I do eat I shall be poisoned. I wish little Mary would come. Ah! her mother would never have served me so.' He lay awake, thinking such things over and over again, all night long, and I stood watching him from a dark corner, till the dayspring came and shook me out. When I came back next night, the room was tidy and clean. His own daughter, a sad-faced but beautiful woman, sat by his bedside; and little Mary was curled up on the floor by the fire, imitating us, by making queer shadows on the ceiling with her twisted hands. But she could not think how ever they got there. And no wonder, for I helped her to some very unaccountable ones."

"I have a story about a granddaughter, too," said another, the moment that speaker ceased.

"Tell it. Tell it."

"Last Christmas-day," he began, "I and a troop of us set out in the twilight to find some house where we could all have something to do; for we had made up our minds to act together. We tried several, but found objections to them all. At last we espied a large lonely country-house, and hastening to it, we found great preparations making for the Christmas dinner. We rushed into it, scampered all over it, and made up our minds in a moment that it would do. We amused ourselves in the nursery first, where there were several children being dressed for dinner. We generally do go to the nursery first, your majesty. This time we were especially charmed with a little girl about five years old, who clapped her hands and danced about with delight at the antics we performed; and we said we would do something for her if we had a chance. The company began to arrive; and at every arrival we rushed to the hall, and cut wonderful capers of welcome. Between times we scudded away to see how the dressing went on. One girl about eighteen was delightful. She dressed herself as if she did not care much about it, but could not help doing it prettily. When she took her last look at the phantom in the glass, she half smiled to it.—But we do not like those creatures that come into the mirrors at all, your majesty. We don't understand them. They are dreadful to us.— She looked rather sad and pale, but very sweet and hopeful. So we wanted to know all about her, and soon found out that she was a distant relation and a great favourite of the gentleman of the house, an old man, in whose face benevolence was mingled with obstinacy and a deep shade of the tyrannical. We could not admire him much; but we would not make up our minds all at once: Shadows never do.

"The dinner-bell rang, and down we hurried. The children all looked happy, and we were merry. But there was one cross fellow among the servants, and didn't we plague him! and didn't we get fun out of him! When he was bringing up dishes, we lay in wait for him at every corner, and sprang upon him from the floor, and from over the banisters, and down from the cornices. He started and stumbled and blundered so in consequence, that his fellow-servants thought he was tipsy. Once he dropped a plate, and had to pick up the pieces, and hurry away with them; and didn't we pursue him as he went! It was lucky for him his master did not see how he went on; but we took care not to let him get into any real scrape, though he was quite dazed with the dodging of the unaccountable shadows. Sometimes he thought the walls were coming down upon him; sometimes that the floor was gaping to swallow him; sometimes that he would be knocked to pieces by the hurrying to and fro, or be smothered in the black crowd.

"When the blazing plum-pudding was carried in we made a perfect shadow-carnival about it, dancing and mumming in the blue flames, like mad demons. And how the children screamed with delight!

"The old gentleman, who was very fond of children, was laughing his heartiest laugh, when a loud knock came to the hall-door. The fair maiden started, turned paler, and then red as the Christmas fire. I saw it, and flung my hands across her face. She was very glad, and I know she said in her heart, 'You kind Shadow!' which paid me well. Then I followed the rest into the hall, and found there a jolly, handsome, brown-faced sailor, evidently a son of the house. The old man received him with tears in his eyes, and the children with shouts of joy. The maiden escaped in the confusion, just in time to save herself from fainting. We crowded about the lamp to hide her retreat, and nearly put it out; and the butler could not get it to burn up before she had glided into her place again, relieved to find the room so dark. The sailor only had seen her go, and now he sat down beside her, and, without a word, got hold of her hand in the gloom. When we all scattered to the walls and the corners, and the lamp blazed up again, he let her hand go.

"During the rest of the dinner the old man watched the two, and saw that there was something between them, and was very angry. For he was an

165

important man in his own estimation, and they had never consulted him. The fact was, they had never known their own minds till the sailor had gone upon his last voyage, and had learned each other's only this moment.—We found out all this by watching them, and then talking together about it afterwards.—The old gentleman saw, too, that his favourite, who was under such obligation to him for loving her so much, loved his son better than him; and he grew by degrees so jealous that he overshadowed the whole table with his morose looks and short answers. That kind of shadowing is very different from ours; and the Christmas dessert grew so gloomy that we Shadows could not bear it, and were delighted when the ladies rose to go to the drawing-room. The gentlemen would not stay behind the ladies, even for the sake of the well-known wine. So the moody host, notwithstanding his hospitality, was left alone at the table in the great silent room. We followed the company upstairs to the drawing-room, and thence to the nursery for snap-dragon; but while they were busy with this most shadowy of games, nearly all the Shadows crept downstairs again to the dining-room, where the old man still sat, gnawing the bone of his own selfishness. They crowded into the room, and by using every kind of expansion—blowing themselves out like soap-bubbles—they succeeded in heaping up the whole room with shade upon shade. They clustered thickest about the fire and the lamp, till at last they almost drowned them in hills of darkness.

"Before they had accomplished so much, the children, tired with fun and frolic, had been put to bed. But the little girl of five years old, with whom we had been so pleased when first we arrived, could not go to sleep. She had a little room of her own; and I had watched her to bed, and now kept her awake by gambolling in the rays of the night-light. When her eyes were once fixed upon me, I took the shape of her grandfather, representing him on the wall as he sat in his chair, with his head bent down and his arms hanging listlessly by his sides. And the child remembered that that was just as she had seen him last; for she had happened to peep in at the dining-room door after all the rest had gone upstairs. 'What if he should be sitting there still,' thought she, 'all alone in the dark!' She scrambled out of bed and crept down.

"Meantime the others had made the room below so dark, that only the face and white hair of the old man could be dimly discerned in the shadowy crowd. For he had filled his own mind with shadows, which we Shadows wanted to draw out of him. Those shadows are very different from us, your majesty knows. He was thinking of all the disappointments he had had in life, and of all the ingratitude he had met with. And he thought far more of the good he had done, than the good others had got. 'After all I have done for them,' said he, with a sigh of bitterness, 'not one of them cares a straw for me. My own children will be glad when I am gone!'—At that instant he lifted up his eyes and saw, standing close by the door, a tiny figure in a long night-gown. The door behind her was shut. It was my little friend, who had crept in noiselessly. A pang of icy fear shot to the old man's heart, but it melted away as fast, for we made a lane through us for a single ray from the fire to fall on the face of the little sprite; and he thought it was a child of his own that had died when just the age of her child-niece, who now stood looking for her grandfather among the Shadows. He thought she had come out of her grave in the cold darkness to ask why her father was sitting alone on Christmas-day. And he felt he had no answer to give his little ghost, but one he would be ashamed for her to hear. But his grandchild saw him now, and walked up to him with a childish stateliness, stumbling once or twice on what seemed her long shroud. Pushing through the crowded shadows, she reached him, climbed upon his knee, laid her little long-haired head on his shoulders, and said,—'Ganpa! you goomy? Isn't it your Kissy-Day too, ganpa?'

"A new fount of love seemed to burst from the clay of the old man's heart. He clasped the child to his bosom, and wept. Then, without a word, he rose with her in his arms, carried her up to her room, and laying her down in her bed, covered her up, kissed her sweet little mouth unconscious of reproof, and then went to the drawing-room.

"As soon as he entered, he saw the culprits in a quiet corner alone. He went up to them, took a hand of each, and joining them in both his, said, 'God bless you!' Then he turned to the rest of the company, and 'Now,' said he, 'let's have a Christmas carol.'—And well he might; for though I have paid many visits to the house, I have never seen him cross since; and I am sure that must cost him a good deal of trouble."

"We have just come from a great palace," said another, "where we knew there were many children, and where we thought to hear glad voices, and see royally merry looks. But as soon as we entered, we became aware that one mighty Shadow shrouded the whole; and that Shadow deepened and deepened, till it gathered in darkness about the reposing form of a wise prince. When we saw him, we could move no more, but clung heavily to the walls, and by our stillness added to the sorrow of the hour. And when we saw the mother of her people weeping with bowed head for the loss of him in whom she had trusted, we were seized with such a longing to be Shadows no more, but winged angels, which are the white shadows cast in heaven from the Light of Light, so as to gather around her, and hover over her with comforting, that we vanished from the walls, and found ourselves floating high above the towers of the palace, where we met the angels on their way, and knew that our service was not needed."

168

By this time there was a glimmer of approaching moonlight, and the king began to see several of those stranger Shadows, with human faces and eyes, moving about amongst the crowd. He knew at once that they did not belong to his dominion. They looked at him, and came near him, and passed slowly, but they never made any obeisance, or gave sign of homage. And what their eyes said to him, the king only could tell. And he did not tell.

"What are those other Shadows that move through the crowd?" said he to one of his subjects near him.

The Shadow started, looked round, shivered slightly, and laid his finger on his lips. Then leading the king a little aside, and looking carefully about him once more,—

"I do not know," said he in a low tone, "what they are. I have heard of them often, but only once did I ever see any of them before. That was when some of us one night paid a visit to a man who sat much alone, and was said to think a great deal. We saw two of those sitting in the room with him, and he was as pale as they were. We could not cross the threshold, but shivered and shook, and felt ready to melt away. Is not your majesty afraid of them too?"

But the king made no answer; and before he could speak again, the moon had climbed above the mighty pillars of the church of the Shadows, and looked in at the great window of the sky.

The shapes had all vanished; and the king, again lifting up his eyes, saw but the wall of his own chamber, on which flickered the Shadow of a Little Child. He looked down, and there, sitting on a stool by the fire, he saw one of his own little ones, waiting to say good-night to his father, and go to bed early, that he might rise early too, and be very good and happy all Christmas-day.

And Ralph Rinkelmann rejoiced that he was a man, and not a Shadow.

But as the Shadows vanished they left the sense of song in the king's brain. And the words of their song must have been something like these:—

"Shadows, Shadows, Shadows all!

Shadow birth and funeral!

Shadow moons gleam overhead;

Over shadow-graves we tread.

Shadow-hope lives, grows, and dies.

Shadow-love from shadow-eyes

Shadow-ward entices on

To shadow-words on shadow-stone,

Closing up the shadow-tale

With a shadow-shadow-wail.

"Shadow-man, thou art a gloom

Cast upon a shadow-tomb

Through the endless shadow air,

From the shadow sitting there,

On a moveless shadow-throne,

Glooming through the ages gone;

North and south, and in and out,

East and west, and all about,

Flinging Shadows everywhere

On the shadow-painted air

Shadow-man, thou hast no story;

Nothing but a shadow-glory."

But Ralph Rinkelmann said to himself,—

"They are but Shadows that sing thus; for a Shadow can see but Shadows.

A man sees a man where a Shadow sees only a Shadow."

And he was comforted in himself.

THE HISTORY OF GUTTA-PERCHA WILLIE

CHAPTER I. WHO HE WAS AND WHERE HE WAS.

When he had been at school for about three weeks, the boys called him Six-fingered Jack; but his real name was Willie, for his father and mother gave it him—not William, but Willie, after a brother of his father, who died young, and had always been called Willie. His name in full was Willie Macmichael. It was generally pronounced Macmickle, which was, by a learned anthropologist, for certain reasons about to appear in this history, supposed to have been the original form of the name, dignified in the course of time into Macmichael. It was his own father, however, who gave him the name of Gutta-Percha Willie, the reason of which will also show itself by and by.

Mr Macmichael was a country doctor, living in a small village in a thinly-peopled country; the first result of which was that he had very hard work, for he had often to ride many miles to see a patient, and that not unfrequently in the middle of the night; and the second that, for this hard work, he had very little pay, for a thinly-peopled country is generally a poor country, and those who live in it are poor also, and cannot spend much even upon their health. But the doctor not only preferred a country life, although he would have been glad to have richer patients, and within less distances of each other, but he would say to any one who expressed surprise that, with his reputation, he should remain where he was—"What's to become of my little flock if I go away, for there are very few doctors of my experience who would feel inclined to come and undertake my work. I know every man, woman, and child in the whole country-side, and that makes all the difference." You see, therefore, that he was a good kind-hearted man, and loved his work, for the sake of those whom he helped by it, better than the money he received for it.

Their home was necessarily a very humble one—a neat little cottage in the village of Priory Leas—almost the one pretty spot thereabout. It lay in a valley in the midst of hills, which did not look high, because they rose with a gentle slope, and had no bold elevations or grand-shaped peaks. But they rose to a good height notwithstanding, and the weather on the top of them in the wintertime was often bitter and fierce—bitter with keen frost, and fierce with as wild winds as ever blew. Of both frost and wind the village at their feet had its share too, but of course they were not so bad down below, for the hills were a shelter from the wind, and it is always colder the farther you go up and away from the heart of this warm ball of rock and earth upon which we live. When Willie's father was riding across the great moorland of those desolate hills, and the people in the village would be saying to each other how bitterly cold it was, he would be thinking how snug and warm it was down there, and how nice it would be to turn a certain corner on the road back, and slip at once out of the freezing wind that had it all its own way up among the withered gorse and heather of the wide expanse where he pursued his dreary journey.

For his part, Willie cared very little what the weather was, but took it as it came. In the hot summer, he would lie in the long grass and get cool; in the cold winter, he would scamper about and get warm. When his hands were as cold as icicles, his cheeks would be red as apples. When his mother took his hands in hers, and chafed them, full of pity for their suffering, as she thought it, Willie first knew that they were cold by the sweet warmth of the kind hands that chafed them: he had not thought of it before. Climbing amongst the ruins of the Priory, or playing with Farmer Thomson's boys and girls about the ricks in his yard, in the thin clear saffron twilight which came so early after noon, when, to some people, every breath seemed full of needle-points, so sharp was the cold, he was as comfortable and happy as if he had been a creature of the winter only, and found himself quite at home in it.

For there were ruins, and pretty large ruins too, which they called the Priory. It was not often that monks chose such a poor country to settle in, but I suppose they had their reasons. And I dare say they were not monks at all, but begging friars, who founded it when they wanted to reprove the luxury and greed of the monks; and perhaps by the time they had grown as bad themselves, the place was nearly finished, and they could not well move it. They had, however, as I have indicated, chosen the one pretty spot, around which, for a short distance on every side, the land was tolerably good, and grew excellent oats if poor wheat, while the gardens were equal to apples and a few pears, besides abundance of gooseberries, currants, and strawberries.

The ruins of the Priory lay behind Mr Macmichael's cottage—indeed, in the very garden—of which, along with the house, he had purchased the fen—that is, the place was his own, so long as he paid a small sum—not more than fifteen shillings a year, I think—to his superior. How long it was since the Priory had come to be looked upon as the mere encumbrance of a cottage garden, nobody thereabouts knew; and although by this time I presume archaeologists have ferreted out everything concerning it, nobody except its owner had then taken the trouble to make the least inquiry into its history. To Willie it was just the Priory, as naturally in his father's garden as if every garden had similar ruins to adorn or encumber it, according as the owner might choose to regard its presence.

The ruins were of considerable extent, with remains of Gothic arches, and carvings about the doors—all open to the sky except a few places on the ground-level which were vaulted. These being still perfectly solid, were used by the family as outhouses to store wood and peats, to keep the garden tools in, and for such like purposes. In summer, golden flowers grew on the broken walls; in winter, grey frosts edged them against the sky.

I fancy the whole garden was but the space once occupied by the huge building, for its surface was the most irregular I ever saw in a garden. It was up and down, up and down, in whatever direction you went, mounded with heaps of ruins, over which the mould had gathered. For many years bushes and flowers had grown upon them, and you might dig a good way without coming to the stones, though come to them you must at last. The walks wound about between the heaps, and through the thick walls of the ruin, overgrown with lichens and mosses, now and then passing through an arched door or window of the ancient building. It was a generous garden in old-fashioned flowers and vegetables. There were a few apple and pear trees also on a wall that faced the south, which were regarded by Willie with mingled respect and desire, for he was not allowed to touch them, while of the gooseberries he was allowed to eat as many as he pleased when they were ripe, and of the currants too, after his mother had had as many as she wanted for preserves.

Some spots were much too shady to allow either fruit or flowers to grow in them, so high and close were the walls. But I need not say more about the garden now, for I shall have occasion to refer to it again and again, and I must not tell all I know at once, else how should I make a story of it?

CHAPTER II. WILLIE'S EDUCATION.

Willie was a good deal more than nine years of age before he could read a single word. It was not that he was stupid, as we shall soon see, but that he had not learned the good of reading, and therefore had not begun to wish to read; and his father had unusual ideas about how he ought to be educated. He said he would no more think of making Willie learn to read before he wished to be taught than he would make him eat if he wasn't hungry. The gift of reading, he said, was too good a thing to give him before he wished to have it, or knew the value of it. "Would you give him a watch," he would say, "before he cares to know whether the sun rises in the east or the west, or at what hour dinner will be ready?"

Now I am not very sure how this would work with some boys and girls. I am afraid they might never learn to read until they had boys and girls of their own whom they wanted to be better off than, because of their ignorance, they had been themselves. But it worked well in Willie's case, who was neither lazy nor idle. And it must not be supposed that he was left without any education at all. For one thing, his father and mother used to talk very freely before him—much more so than most parents do in the presence of their children; and nothing serves better for teaching than the conversation of good and thoughtful people. While they talked, Willie would sit listening intently, trying to understand what he heard; and although it not unfrequently took very strange shapes in his little mind, because at times he understood neither the words nor the things the words represented, yet there was much that he did understand and make a good use of. For instance, he soon came to know that his father and mother had very little money to spare, and that his father had to work hard to get what money they had. He learned also that everything that came into the house, or was done for them, cost money; therefore, for one thing, he must not ill-use his clothes. He learned, too, that there was a great deal of suffering in the world, and that his father's business was to try to make it less, and help people who were ill to grow well again, and be able to do their work; and this made him see what a useful man his father was, and wish to be also of some good in the world. Then he looked about him and saw that there were a great many ways of getting money, that is, a great many things for doing which people would give money; and he saw that some of those ways were better than others, and he thought his father's way the very best of all. I give these as specimens of the lessons he learned by listening to his father and mother as they talked together. But he had another teacher.

Down the street of the village, which was very straggling, with nearly as many little gardens as houses in it, there was a house occupied by several poor people, in one end of which, consisting just of a room and a closet, an old woman lived who got her money by spinning flax into yarn for making linen. She was a kind-hearted old creature—widow, without any relation near to help her or look after her. She had had one child, who died before he was as old as Willie. That was forty years before, but she had never forgotten her little Willie, for that was his name too, and she fancied our Willie was like him. Nothing, therefore, pleased her better than to get him into her little room, and talk to him. She would take a little bit of sugar-candy or liquorice out of her cupboard for him, and tell him some strange old fairy tale or legend, while she sat spinning, until at last she had made him so fond of her that he would often go and stay for hours with her. Nor did it make much difference when his mother begged Mrs Wilson to give him something sweet only now and then, for she was afraid of his going to see the old woman merely for what she gave him, which would have been greedy. But the fact was, he liked her stories better than her sugar-candy and liquorice; while above all things he delighted in watching the wonderful wheel go round and round so fast that he could not find out whether her foot was making it spin, or it was making her foot dance up and down in that curious way. After she had explained it to him as well as she could, and he thought he understood it, it seemed to him only the more wonderful and mysterious; and ever as it went whirring round, it sung a song of its own, which was also the song of the story, whatever it was, that the old woman was telling him, as he sat listening in her high soft chair, covered with long-faded chintz, and cushioned like a nest. For Mrs Wilson had had a better house to live in once, and this chair, as well as the chest of drawers of dark mahogany, with brass handles, that stood opposite the window, was part of the furniture she saved when she had to sell the rest; and well it was, she used to say, for her old rheumatic bones that she had saved the chair at least. In that chair, then, the little boy would sit coiled up as nearly into a ball as might be, like a young bird or a rabbit in its nest, staring at the wheel, and listening with two ears and one heart to its song and the old woman's tale both at once.

One sultry summer afternoon, his mother not being very well and having gone to lie down, his father being out, as he so often was, upon Scramble the old horse, and Tibby, their only servant, being busy with the ironing, Willie ran off to Widow Wilson's, and was soon curled up in the chair, like a little Hindoo idol that had grown weary of sitting upright, and had tumbled itself into a corner.

Now, before he came, the old woman had been thinking about him, and wishing very much that he would come; turning over also in her mind, as she spun, all her stock of stories, in the hope of finding in some nook or other one she had not yet told him; for although he had not yet begun to grow tired even of those he knew best, it was a special treat to have a new one; for by this time Mrs Wilson's store was all but exhausted, and a new one turned up very rarely. This time, however, she was successful, and did call to mind one that she had not thought of before. It had not only grown very dusty, but was full of little holes, which she at once set about darning up with the needle and thread of her imagination, so that, by the time Willie arrived, she had a treat, as she thought, quite ready for him.

I am not going to tell you the story, which was about a poor boy who received from a fairy to whom he had shown some kindness the gift of a marvelous wand, in the shape of a common blackthorn walking-stick, which nobody could suspect of possessing such wonderful virtue. By means of it, he was able to do anything he wished, without the least trouble; and so, upon a trial of skill, appointed by a certain king, in order to find out which of the craftsmen of his realm was fittest to aid him in ruling it, he found it easy to surpass every one of them, each in his own trade. He produced a richer damask than any of the silk-weavers; a finer linen than any of the linen-weavers; a more complicated as well as ornate cabinet, with more drawers and

179

quaint hiding-places, than any of the cabinet-makers; a sword-blade more cunningly damasked, and a hilt more gorgeously jewelled, than any of the sword-makers; a ring set with stones more precious, more brilliant in colour, and more beautifully combined, than any of the jewellers: in short, as I say, without knowing a single device of one of the arts in question, he surpassed every one of the competitors in his own craft, won the favour of the king and the office he wished to confer, and, if I remember rightly, gained at length the king's daughter to boot.

For a long time Willie had not uttered a single exclamation, and when the old woman looked up, fancying he must be asleep, she saw, to her disappointment, a cloud upon his face—amounting to a frown.

"What's the matter with you, Willie, my chick?" she asked. "Have you got a headache?"

"No, thank you, Mrs Wilson," answered Willie; "but I don't like that story at all."

"I'm sorry for that. I thought I should be sure to please you this time; it is one I never told you before, for I had quite forgotten it myself till this very afternoon. Why don't you like it?"

"Because he was a cheat. He couldn't do the things; it was only the fairy's wand that did them."

"But he was such a good lad, and had been so kind to the fairy."

"That makes no difference. He wasn't good. And the fairy wasn't good either, or she wouldn't have set him to do such wicked things."

"They weren't wicked things. They were all first-rate—everything that he made—better than any one else could make them."

"But he didn't make them. There wasn't one of those poor fellows he cheated that wasn't a better man than he. The worst of them could do something with his own hands, and I don't believe he could do anything, for if he had ever tried he would have hated to be such a sneak. He cheated the king, too, and the princess, and everybody. Oh! shouldn't I like to have been there, and to have beaten him wand and all! For somebody might have been able to make the things better still, if he had only known how."

Mrs Wilson was disappointed—perhaps a little ashamed that she had not thought of this before; anyhow she grew cross; and because she was cross, she grew unfair, and said to Willie—

"You think a great deal of yourself, Master Willie! Pray what could those idle little hands of yours do, if you were to try?"

"I don't know, for I haven't tried," answered Willie.

"It's a pity you shouldn't," she rejoined, "if you think they would turn out so very clever."

She didn't mean anything but crossness when she said this—for which probably a severe rheumatic twinge which just then passed through her shoulder was also partly to blame. But Willie took her up quite seriously, and asked in a tone that showed he wanted it accounted for—

"Why haven't I ever done anything, Mrs Wilson?"

"You ought to know that best yourself," she answered, still cross. "I suppose because you don't like work. Your good father and mother work very hard, I'm sure. It's a shame of you to be so idle."

This was rather hard on a boy of seven, for Willie was no more then. It made him look very grave indeed, if not unhappy, for a little while, as he sat turning over the thing in his mind.

"Is it wrong to play about, Mrs Wilson?" he asked, after a pause of considerable duration.

"No, indeed, my dear," she answered; for during the pause she had begun to be sorry for having spoken so roughly to her little darling.

"Does everybody work?"

"Everybody that's worth anything, and is old enough," she added.

"Does God work?" he asked, after another pause, in a low voice.

"No, child. What should He work for?"

"If everybody works that is good and old enough, then I think God must work," answered Willie. "But I will ask my papa. Am I old enough?"

"Well, you're not old enough to do much, but you might do something."

"What could I do? Could I spin, Mrs Wilson?"

"No, child; that's not an easy thing to do; but you could knit."

"Could I? What good would it do?"

"Why, you could knit your mother a pair of stockings."

"Could I though? Will you teach me, Mrs Wilson?"

Mrs Wilson very readily promised, foreseeing that so she might have a good deal more of the little man's company, if indeed he was in earnest; for she was very lonely, and was never so happy as when he was with her. She said she would get him some knitting-needles—wires she called them—that very evening; she had some wool, and if he came to-morrow, she would soon see whether he was old enough and clever enough to learn to knit. She advised him, however, to say nothing about it to his mother till she had made up her mind whether or not he could learn; for if he could, then he might surprise her by taking her something of his own knitting—at least a pair of muffetees to keep her wrists warm in the winter. Willie went home solemn with his secret.

The next day he began to learn, and although his fingers annoyed him a good deal at first by refusing to do exactly as he wanted them, they soon became more obedient; and before the new year arrived, he had actually knitted a pair of warm white lamb's-wool stockings for his mother. I am bound to confess that when first they were finished they were a good deal soiled by having been on the way so long, and perhaps partly by the little hands not always being so clean as they might have been when he turned from play to work; but Mrs Wilson washed them herself, and they looked, if not as white as snow, at least as white as the whitest lamb you ever saw. I will not attempt to describe the delight of his mother, the triumph of Willie, or the gratification of his father, who saw in this good promise of his boy's capacity; for all that I have written hitherto is only introductory to my story, and I long to begin and tell it you in a regular straightforward fashion.

Before I begin, however, I must not forget to tell you that Willie did ask his father the question with Mrs Wilson's answer to which he had not been satisfied—I mean the question whether God worked; and his father's answer, after he had sat pondering for a while in his chair, was something to this effect:—

"Yes, Willie; it seems to me that God works more than anybody—for He works all night and all day, and, if I remember rightly, Jesus tells us somewhere that He works all Sunday too. If He were to stop working, everything would stop being. The sun would stop shining, and the moon and the stars; the corn would stop growing; there would be no more apples or gooseberries; your eyes would stop seeing; your ears would stop hearing; your fingers couldn't move an inch; and, worst of all, your little heart would stop loving."

"No, papa," cried Willie; "I shouldn't stop loving, I'm sure."

"Indeed you would, Willie."

"Not you and mamma."

"Yes; you wouldn't love us any more than if you were dead asleep without dreaming."

"That would be dreadful."

"Yes it would. So you see how good God is to us—to go on working, that we may be able to love each other."

"Then if God works like that all day long, it must be a fine thing to work," said Willie.

"You are right. It is a fine thing to work—the finest thing in the world, if it comes of love, as God's work does."

This conversation made Willie quite determined to learn to knit; for if God worked, he would work too. And although the work he undertook was a very small work, it was like all God's great works, for every loop he made had a little love looped up in it, like an invisible, softest, downiest lining to the stockings. And after those, he went on knitting a pair for his father; and indeed, although he learned to work with a needle as well, and to darn the stockings he had made, and even tried his hand at the spinning—of which, however, he could not make much for a long time—he had not left off knitting when we come to begin the story in the next chapter.

CHAPTER III. HE IS TURNED INTO SOMETHING HE NEVER WAS BEFORE.

Hitherto I have been mixing up summer and winter and everything all together, but now I am going to try to keep everything in its own place.

Willie was now nine years old. His mother had been poorly for some time—confined to her room, as she not unfrequently was in the long cold winters. It was winter now; and one morning, when all the air was dark with falling snow, he was standing by the parlour window, looking out on it, and wondering whether the angels made it up in the sky; for he thought it might be their sawdust, which, when they had too much, they shook down to get melted and put out of the way; when Tibby came into the room very softly, and looking, he thought, very strange.

"Willie, your mamma wants you," she said; and Willie hastened upstairs to his mother's room. Dark as was the air outside, he was surprised to find how dark the room was. And what surprised him more was a curious noise which he heard the moment he entered it, like the noise of a hedgehog, or some other little creature of the fields or woods. But he crept gently up to his mother's bed, saying—

"Are you better this morning, mamma?"

And she answered in a feeble sweet voice—

"Yes, Willie, very much better. And, Willie, God has sent you a little sister."

"O-o-o-oh!" cried Willie. "A little sister! Did He make her Himself?"

"Yes; He made her Himself, and sent her to you last night."

"How busy He must have been lately!" said Willie. "Where is she? I should like to see her. Is she my very own sister?"

"Yes, your very own sister, Willie—to love and take care of always."

"Where is she?"

"Go and ask nurse to let you see her."

Then Willie saw that there was a strange woman in the room, with something lying on her lap. He went up to her, and she folded back the corner of a blanket, and revealed a face no bigger than that of the big doll at the clergyman's house, but alive, quite alive—such a pretty little face! He stood staring at it for a while.

"May I kiss her, nurse?"

"Yes—gently—quite gently."

He kissed her, half afraid, he did not know of what. Her cheek was softer and smoother than anything he had ever touched before. He sped back to his mother, too full of delight to speak. But she was not yet well enough to talk to him, and his father coming in, led him down-stairs again, where he began once more to watch the snow, wondering now if it had anything to do with baby's arrival.

In the afternoon, it was found that the lock of his mother's room not only would not catch easily, but made a noise that disturbed her. So his father got a screwdriver and removed it, making as little noise as he could. Next he contrived a way, with a piece of string, for keeping the door shut, and as that would not hold it close enough, hung a shawl over it to keep the draught out—all which proceeding Willie watched. As soon as he had finished, and the nurse had closed the door behind them, Mr Macmichael set out to take the lock to the smithy, and allowed Willie to go with him. By the time they reached it, the snow was an inch deep on their shoulders, on Willie's cap, and on his father's hat. How red the glow of the smith's fire looked! It was a great black cavern with a red heart to it in the midst of whiteness.

The smith was a great powerful man, with bare arms, and blackened face. When they entered, he and two other men were making the axle of a wheel. They had a great lump of red-hot iron on the anvil, and were knocking a big hole through it—not boring it, but knocking it through with a big punch. One of the men, with a pair of tongs-like pincers, held the punch steady in the hole, while the other two struck the head of it with alternate blows of mighty hammers called sledges, each of which it took the strength of two brawny arms to heave high above the head with a great round swing over the shoulder, that it might come down with right good force, and drive the punch through the glowing iron, which was, I should judge, four inches thick. All this Willie thought he could understand, for he knew that fire made the hardest metal soft; but what he couldn't at all understand was this: every now and then they stopped heaving their mighty sledges, the third man took the punch out of the hole, and the smith himself, whose name was Willet (and will it he did with a vengeance, when he had anything on the anvil before him), caught up his tongs in his hand, then picked up a little bit of black coal with the tongs, and dropped it into the hole where the punch had been, where it took fire immediately and blazed up. Then in went the punch again, and again the huge hammering commenced, with such bangs and blows, that the smith was wise to have no floor to his smithy, for they would surely have knocked a hole in that, though they were not able to knock the anvil down halfway into the earth, as the giant smith in the story did.

While this was going on, Mr Macmichael, perceiving that the operation ought not to be interrupted any more than a surgical one, stood quite still waiting, and Willie stood also—absorbed in staring, and gradually creeping nearer and nearer to the anvil, for there were no sparks flying about to make it dangerous to the eyes, as there would have been if they had been striking the iron itself instead of the punch.

As soon as the punch was driven through, and the smith had dropped his sledge-hammer, and begun to wipe his forehead, Willie spoke.

"Mr Willet," he said, for he knew every man of any standing in the village by name and profession, "why did you put bits of coal into the hole you were making? I should have thought it would be in the way rather than help you."

"So it would, my little man," answered Willet, with no grim though grimy smile, "if it didn't take fire and keep getting out of the way all the time it kept up the heat. You see we depend on the heat for getting through, and it's much less trouble to drop a bit of coal or two into the hole, than to take

187

up the big axle and lay it in the fire again, not to mention the time and the quantity of coal it would take to heat it up afresh."

"But such little bits of coal couldn't do much?" said Willie.

"They could do enough, and all that's less after that is saving," said the smith, who was one of those men who can not only do a thing right but give a reason for it. "You see I was able to put the little bits just in the right place."

"I see! I see!" cried Willie. "I understand! But, papa, do you think Mr

Willet is the proper person to ask to set your lock right?"

"I haven't a doubt of it," said Mr Macmichael, taking it out of his greatcoat pocket, and unfolding the piece of paper in which he had wrapped it. "Why do you make a question of it?"

"Because look what great big huge things he does! How could those tremendous hammers set such a little thing as that right? They would knock it all to pieces. Don't you think you had better take it to the watchmaker?"

"If I did, Willie, do you know what you would say the moment you saw him at work?"

"No, papa. What should I say?"

"You would say, 'Don't you think, papa, you had better take it back to the smith?'

"But why should I say that?"

"Because, when you saw his tools beside this lock, you would think the tools so small and the lock so huge, that nothing could be done between them. Yet I daresay the watchmaker could set the lock all right if he chose to try. Don't you think so, Mr Willet?"

"Not a doubt of it," answered the smith.

"Had we better go to him then?"

"Well," answered the smith, smiling, "I think perhaps he would ask you why you hadn't come to me. No doubt he could do it, but I've got better tools for the purpose. Let me look at the lock. I'm sure I shall be able to set it right."

"Not with that great big hammer, then," said Willie.

"No; I have smaller hammers than that. When do you want it, sir?"

"Could you manage to do it at once, and let me take it home, for there's a little baby there, just arrived?"

"You don't mean it!" said the smith, looking surprised. "I wish you joy, sir."

"And this is the lock of the room she's in," continued the doctor.

"And you're afraid of her getting out and flying off again!" said the smith. "I will do it at once. There isn't much wrong with it, I daresay. I hope Mrs Macmichael is doing well, sir."

He took the lock, drew several screws from it, and then forced it open.

"It's nothing but the spring gone," he said, as he took out something and threw it away.

Then he took out several more pieces, and cleaned them all. Then he searched in a box till he found another spring, which he put in instead of the broken one, after snipping off a little bit with a pair of pincers. Then he put all the pieces in, put on the cover of it, gave something a few taps with a tiny hammer, replaced the screws, and said—

"Shall I come and put it on for you, sir?"

"No, no; I am up to that much," said Mr Macmichael. "I can easily manage that. Come, Willie. I'm much obliged to you for doing it at once. Good-night."

Then out they went into the snowstorm again, Willie holding fast by his father's hand.

"This is good," said his father. "Your mother will have a better day all to-morrow, and perhaps a longer sleep to-night for it. You see how easy it is to be both useful and kind sometimes. The smith did more for your mother in those few minutes than ten doctors could have done. Think of his great black fingers making a little more sleep and rest and warmth for her—and all in those few minutes!"

"Suppose he couldn't have done it," said Willie. "Do you think the watchmaker could?"

"That I can't tell, but I don't think it likely. We should most probably have had to get a new one."

"Suppose you couldn't get a new one?"

"Then we should have had to set our wits to work, and contrive some other way of fastening the door, so that mamma shouldn't take cold by its being open, nor yet be disturbed by the noise of it."

"It would be so nice to be able to do everything!" said Willie.

"So it would; but nobody can; and it's just as well, for then we should not need so much help from each other, and would be too independent."

"Then shouldn't a body try to do as many things as he can?"

"Yes, for there's no fear of ever being able to do without other people, and you would be so often able to help them. Both the smith and the watch maker could mend a lock, but neither of them could do without the other for all that."

When Willie went to bed, he lay awake a long time, thinking how, if the lock could not have been mended, and there had been no other to be had, he could have contrived to keep the door shut properly. In the morning, however, he told his father that he had not thought of any way that would do, for though he could contrive to shut and open the door well enough, he could not think how a person outside might be able to do it; and he thought the best way, if such a difficulty should occur, would be to take the lock off his door, and put it on mamma's till a better one could be got. Of this suggestion his father, much to Willie's satisfaction, entirely approved.

CHAPTER IV. HE SERVES AN APPRENTICESHIP.

Willie's mother grew better, and Willie's sister grew bigger; and the strange nurse went away, and Willie and his mother and Tibby, with a little occasional assistance from the doctor, managed the baby amongst them. Considering that she had been yet only a short time at school, she behaved wonderfully well. She never cried except she was in some trouble, and even then you could seldom have seen a tear on her face. She did all that was required of her, grew longer and broader and heavier, and was very fond of a lighted candle. The only fault she had was that she wouldn't give Willie quite so many smiles as he wanted. As to the view she took of affairs, she seemed for a long time to be on the whole very well satisfied with life and its gifts. But when at last its troubles began to overtake her, she did not approve of them at all. The first thing she objected to was being weaned, which she evidently considered a very cruel and unnecessary experience. But her father said it must be, and her mother, believing him to know best, carried out his decree. Little Agnes endured it tolerably well in the daytime, but in the night protested lustily—was indeed so outrageously indignant, that one evening the following conversation took place at the tea-table, where Willie sat and heard it.

"Really, my dear," said Mrs Macmichael, "I cannot have your rest disturbed in this way another night. You must go to Willie's room, and let me manage the little squalling thing myself."

"Why shouldn't I take my share of the trouble?" objected her husband.

"Because you may be called up any moment, and have no more sleep till next night; and it is not fair that what sleep your work does let you have should be so unnecessarily broken. It's not as if I couldn't manage without you."

"But Willie's bed is not big enough for both of us," he objected.

"Then Willie can come and sleep with me."

"But Willie wants his sleep as much as I do mine."

"There's no fear of him: he would sleep though all the babies in Priory Leas were crying in the room."

"Would I really?" thought Willie, feeling rather ashamed of himself.

"But who will get up and warm the milk-and-water for you?" pursued his father.

"Oh! I can manage that quite well."

"Couldn't I do that, mamma?" said Willie, very humbly, for he thought of what his mother had said about his sleeping powers.

"No, my pet," she answered; and he said no more.

"It seems to me," said his father, "a very clumsy necessity. I have been thinking over it. To keep a fire in all night only to warm such a tiny drop of water as she wants, I must say, seems like using a steam-engine to sweep up the crumbs. If you would just get a stone bottle, fill it with boiling water, wrap a piece of flannel about it, and lay it anywhere in the bed, it would be quite hot enough even in the morning to make the milk as warm as she ought to have it."

"If you will go to Willie's room, and let Willie come and sleep with me, I will try it," she said.

Mr Macmichael consented; and straightway Willie was filled with silent delight at the thought of sleeping with his mother and the baby. Nor because of that only; for he resolved within himself that he would try to get a share in the business of the night: why should his mother have too little sleep rather than himself? They might at least divide the too little between them! So he went to bed early, full of the thought of waking up as soon as Agnes should begin to cry, and finding out what he could do. Already he had begun to be useful in the daytime, and had twice put her to sleep when both his mother and Tibby had failed. And although he quite understood that in all probability he would not have succeeded if they hadn't tried first, yet it had been some relief to them, and they had confessed it.

But when he woke, there lay his mother and his sister both sound asleep; the sun was shining through the blind; he heard Tibby about the house; and, in short, it was time to get up.

At breakfast, his father said to him—

"Well, Willie, how did Agnes behave herself last night?"

"So well!" answered Willie; "she never cried once."

"O Willie!" said his mother, laughing, "she screamed for a whole hour, and was so hungry after it that she emptied her bottle without stopping once. You were sound asleep all the time, and never stirred."

Willie was so much ashamed of himself, although he wasn't in the least to blame, that he could hardly keep from crying. He did not say another word, except when he was spoken to, all through breakfast, and his father and mother were puzzled to think what could be the matter with him: He went about the greater part of the morning moodily thinking; then for advice betook himself to Mrs Wilson, who gave him her full attention, and suggested several things, none of which, however, seemed to him likely to succeed.

"If I could but go to bed after mamma was asleep," he said, "I could tie a string to my hair, and then slip a loop at the other end over mamma's wrist, so that when she sat up to attend to Agnes, she would pull my hair and wake me. Wouldn't she wonder what it was when she felt it pulling her?"

He had to go home without any help from Mrs Wilson. All the way he kept thinking with himself something after this fashion—

"Mamma won't wake me, and Agnes can't; and the worst of it is that everybody else will be just as fast asleep as I shall be. Let me see—who is there that's awake all night? There's the cat: I think she is, but then she wouldn't know when to wake me, and even if I could teach her to wake me the moment Agnes cried, I don't think she would be a nice one to do it; for if I didn't come awake with a pat of her velvety pin-cushions, she might turn out the points of the pins in them, and scratch me awake. There's the clock; it's always awake;

but it can't tell you the time till you go and ask it. I think it might be made to wind up a string that should pull me when the right time came; but I don't think I could teach it. And when it came to the pull, the pull might stop the clock, and what would papa say then? They tell me the owls are up all night, but they're no good, I'm certain. I don't see what I am to do. I wonder if God would wake me if I were to ask Him?"

I don't know whether Willie did or did not ask God to wake him. I did not inquire, for what goes on of that kind, it is better not to talk much about. What I do know is, that he fell asleep with his head and heart full of desire to wake and help his mother; and that, in the middle of the night, he did wake up suddenly, and there was little Agnes screaming with all her might. He sat up in bed instantly.

"What's the matter, Willie?" said his mother. "Lie down and go to sleep."

"Baby's crying," said Willie.

"Never you mind. I'll manage her."

"Do you know, mamma, I think I was waked up just in time to help you.

I'll take her from you, and perhaps she will take her drink from me."

"Nonsense, Willie. Lie down, my pet."

"But I've been thinking about it, mamma. Do you remember, yesterday, Agnes would not take her bottle from you, and screamed and screamed; but when Tibby took her, she gave in and drank it all? Perhaps she would do the same with me."

As he spoke he slipped out of bed, and held out his arms to take the baby. The light was already coming in, just a little, through the blind, for it was summer. He heard a cow lowing in the fields at the back of the house, and he wondered whether her baby had woke her. The next moment he had little Agnes in his arms, for his mother thought he might as well try, seeing he was awake.

"Do take care and don't let her fall, Willie."

"That I will, mamma. I've got her tight. Now give me the bottle, please."

"I haven't got it ready yet; for you woke the minute she began to cry."

So Willie walked about the room with Agnes till his mother had got her bottle filled with nice warm milk-and-water and just a little sugar. When she gave it to him, he sat down with the baby on his knees, and, to his great delight, and the satisfaction of his mother as well, she stopped crying, and began to drink the milk-and-water.

"Why, you're a born nurse, Willie!" said his mother. But the moment the baby heard her mother's voice, she forsook the bottle, and began to scream, wanting to go to her.

"O mamma! you mustn't speak, please; for of course she likes you better than the bottle; and when you speak that reminds her of you. It was just the same with Tibby yesterday. Or if you must speak, speak with some other sound, and not in your own soft, sweet way."

A few moments after, Willie was so startled by a gruff voice in the room that he nearly dropped the bottle; but it was only his mother following his directions. The plan was quite successful, for the baby had not a suspicion that the voice was her mother's, paid no heed to it, and attended only to her bottle.

Mr Macmichael, who had been in the country, was creeping up the stair to his room, fearful of disturbing his wife, when what should he hear but a man's voice as he supposed! and what should he think but that robbers had broken in! Of course he went to his wife's room first. There he heard the voice plainly enough through the door, but when he opened it he could see no one except Willie feeding the baby on an ottoman at the foot of the bed. When his wife had explained what and why it was, they both laughed heartily over Willie's suggestion for leaving the imagination of little Agnes in repose; and henceforth he was installed as night-nurse, so long as the process of weaning should last; and very proud of his promotion he was. He slept as sound as ever, for he had no anxiety about waking; his mother always woke him the instant Agnes began to cry.

"Willie!" she would say, "Willie! here's your baby wanting you."

And up Willie would start, sometimes before he was able to open his eyes, for little boys' eyelids are occasionally obstinate. And once he jumped out of bed crying, "Where is she, mamma? I've lost her!" for he had been dreaming about her.

You may be sure his mamma let him have a long sleep in the morning always, to make up for being disturbed in the night.

Agnes throve well, notwithstanding the weaning. She soon got reconciled to the bottle, and then Willie slept in peace.

CHAPTER V. HE GOES TO LEARN A TRADE.

Time passed, and Willie grew. Have my readers ever thought what is meant by growing? It is far from meaning only that you get bigger and stronger. It means that you become able both to understand and to wonder at more of the things about you. There are people who the more they understand, wonder the less; but such are not growing straight; they are growing crooked. There are two ways of growing. You may be growing up, or you may be growing down; and if you are doing both at once, then you are growing crooked. There are people who are growing up in understanding, but down in goodness. It is a beautiful fact, however, that you can't grow up in goodness and down in understanding; while the great probability is, that, if you are not growing better, you will by and by begin to grow stupid. Those who are growing the right way, the more they understand, the more they wonder; and the more they learn to do, the more they want to do. Willie was a boy of this kind. I don't care to write about boys and girls, or men and women, who are not growing the right way. They are not interesting enough to write about.

But he was not the only one to grow: Agnes grew as well; and the more Willie grew capable of helping her, the more he found Agnes required of him. It was a long time, however, before he knew how much he was obliged to Agnes for requiring so much of him.

She grew and grew until she was capable of a doll; when of course a doll was given her—not a new one just bought, but a most respectable old doll, a big one that had been her mother's when she was a little girl, and which she had been wise enough to put in her trunk before she left her mother's house to go home with Mr Macmichael. She made some new clothes for it now, and Tibby made a cloak and bonnet for her to wear when she went out of doors. But it struck Willie that her shoes, which were only of cloth, were very unfit for walking, and he thought that in a doctor's family it was something quite amazing that, while head and shoulders were properly looked after, the feet should remain utterly neglected. It was clear that must be his part in the affair; it could not be anybody else's, for in that case some one else would have attended to it. He must see about it.

I think I have said before that Willie knew almost everybody in the village, and I might have added that everybody without exception knew him. He was a favourite—first of all, because his father was much loved and trusted; next, because his mother spoke as kindly to her husband's poor patients as to the richer ones; and last, because he himself spoke to everybody with proper respect. Some of the people, however, he knew of course better than others. Of these Mrs Wilson we know was one. But I believe I also mentioned that in the house in which she lived there were other poor people. In the room opposite to hers, on the ground-floor, lived and worked a shoemaker—a man who had neither wife nor child, nor, so far as people knew, any near relative at all. He was far from being in good health, and although he worked from morning to night, had a constant pain in his back, which was rather crooked, having indeed a little hump on it. If his temper was not always of the best, I wonder what cleverest of watches or steam-engines would go as well as he did with such a twist in its back? To see him seated on his low stool—in which, by the way, as if it had not been low enough, he sat in a leather-covered hole, perhaps for the sake of the softness and spring of the leather—with his head and body bent forward over his lapstone or his last, and his right hand with the quick broad-headed hammer hammering up and down on a piece of sole-leather; or with both his hands now meeting as if for a little friendly chat about something small, and then suddenly starting asunder as if in astonished anger, with a portentous hiss, you might have taken him for an automaton moved by springs, and imitating human actions in a very wonderful manner—so regular and machine-like were his motions, and so little did he seem to think about what he was at. A little passing attention, a hint now and then from his head, was sufficient to keep his hands right, for they were so used to their work, and had been so well taught by his head, that they could pretty nearly have made a pair of shoes of themselves; so that the shoemaking trade is one that admits of a great deal of thought going on in the head that hangs over the work, like a sun over the earth ripening its harvest. Shoemakers have distinguished themselves both in poetry and in prose; and if Hector Macallaster had done so in neither, he could yet think, and that is what some people who write both poetry and prose cannot do. But it is of infinitely more importance to be able to think well than merely to write ever so well; and, besides, to think well is what everybody ought to be or to become able to do.

Hector had odd ways of looking at things, but I need not say more about that, for it will soon be plain enough. Ever since the illness from which he had risen with a weak spine, and ever-working brain, and a quiet heart, he had shown himself not merely a good sort of man, for such he had always been, but a religious man; not by saying much, for he was modest even to shyness with grown people, but by the solemnity of his look when a great word was spoken, by his unblamable behaviour, and by the readiness with which he would lend or give of his small earnings to his poor neighbours. The only thing of which anybody could complain was his temper; but it showed itself only occasionally, and almost everybody made excuse for it on the ground of his bodily ailments. He gave it no quarter himself, however. He said once to the clergyman, to whom he had been lamenting the trouble he had with it, and who had sought to comfort him by saying that it was caused by the weakness of his health—

"No, sir—excuse me; nobody knows how much I am indebted to my crooked back. If it weren't for that I might have a bad temper and never know it. But that drives it out of its hole, and when I see the ugly head of it I know it's there, and try once more to starve it to death. But oh dear! it's such a creature to burrow! When I think I've built it in all round, out comes its head again at a place where I never looked to see it, and it's all to do over again!"

You will understand by this already that the shoemaker thought after his own fashion, which is the way everybody who can think does think. What he thought about his trade and some other things we shall see by and by.

When Willie entered his room, he greeted him with a very friendly nod; for not only was he fond of children, but he had a special favour for Willie, chiefly because he considered himself greatly indebted to him for something he had said to Mrs Wilson, and which had given him a good deal to think about. For Mrs Wilson often had a chat with Hector, and then she would not unfrequently talk about Willie, of whose friendship she was proud. She had told him of the strange question he had put to her as to whether God worked, and the shoemaker, thinking over it, had come to the same conclusion as Willie's father, and it had been a great comfort and help to him.

"What can I do for you to-day, Willie?" he said; for in that part of the country they do not say Master and Miss. "You look," he added, "if you wanted something."

"I want you to teach me, please," answered Willie.

"To teach you what?" asked Hector.

"To make shoes, please," answered Willie.

"Ah! but do you think that would be prudent of me? Don't you see, if I were to teach you to make shoes, people would be coming to you to make their shoes for them, and what would become of me then?"

"But I only want to make shoes for Aggy's doll. She oughtn't to go without shoes in this weather, you know."

"Certainly not. Well, if you will bring me the doll I will take her measure and make her a pair."

"But I don't think papa could afford to pay for shoes for a doll as well as for all of us. You see, though it would be better, it's not necessary that a doll should have strong shoes. She has shoes good enough for indoors, and she needn't walk in the wet. Don't you think so yourself, Hector?"

"But," returned Hector, "I shall be happy to make Agnes a present of a pair of shoes for her doll. I shouldn't think of charging your papa for that. He is far too good a man to be made to pay for everything."

"But," objected Willie, "to let you make them for nothing would be as bad as to make papa pay for them when they are not necessary. Please, you must let me make them for Aggy. Besides, she's not old enough yet even to say thank you for them."

"Then she won't be old enough to say thank you to you either," said Hector, who, all this time, had been losing no moment from his work, but was stitching away, with a bore, and a twiddle, and a hiss, at the sole of a huge boot.

"Ah! but you see, she's my own—so it doesn't matter!"

If I were writing a big book, instead of a little one, I should be tempted to say not only that this set Hector a thinking, but what it made him think as well. Instead of replying, however, he laid down his boot, rose, and first taking from a shelf a whole skin of calf-leather, and next a low chair from a corner of the room, he set the latter near his own seat opposite the window.

"Sit down there, then, Willie," he said; adding, as he handed him the calf-skin, "There's your leather, and my tools are at your service. Make your shoes, and welcome. I shall be glad of your company."

Having thus spoken, he sat down again, caught up his boot hurriedly, and began stitching away as if for bare life.

Willie took the calf-skin on his lap, somewhat bewildered. If he had been asked to cut out a pair of seven-leagued boots for the ogre, there would have seemed to his eyes enough of leather for them in that one skin. But how ever was he to find two pieces small enough for doll's shoes in such an ocean of leather? He began to turn it round and round, looking at it all along the edge, while Hector was casting sidelong glances at him in the midst of his busyness, with a curiosity on his face which his desire to conceal it caused to look grim instead of amused.

Willie, although he had never yet considered how shoes are made, had seen at once that nothing could be done until he had got the command of a manageable bit of leather; he found too much only a shade better than too little; and he saw that it wouldn't be wise to cut a piece out anywhere, for that might spoil what would serve for a large pair of shoes or even boots. Therefore he kept turning the skin round until he came to a small projecting piece. This he contemplated for some time, trying to recall the size of Dolly's feet, and to make up his mind whether it would not be large enough for one or even for both shoes. A smile passed over Hector's face—a smile of satisfaction.

"That's it!" he said at last. "I think you'll do. That's the first thing—

to consider your stuff, and see how much you can make of it. Waste is a thing that no good shoemaker ever yet could endure. It's bad in itself, and so unworkmanlike! Yes, I think that corner will do. Shall I cut it off for you?"

"No, thank you—not yet, please. I think I must go and look at her feet, for I can't recollect quite how big they are. I'll just run home and look."

"Do you think you will be able to carry the exact size in your head, and bring it back with you?"

"Yes, I think I shall."

"I don't. I never could trust myself so far as that, nearly. You might be pretty nigh it one way and all wrong another, for you have to consider length and breadth and roundabout. I will tell you the best way for you to do. Set the doll standing on a bit of paper, and draw a pencil all round her foot with the point close to it on the paper. Both feet will be better, for it would be a mistake to suppose they must be of the same size. That will give you the size of the sole. Then take a strip of paper and see how long a piece it takes to go round the thickest part of the foot, and cut it off to that length. That will be sufficient measurement for a doll's shoe, for even if it should not fit exactly, she won't mind either being pinched a little or having to walk a little loose."

Willie got up at once to go and do as Hector had told him; but Hector was not willing to part with him so soon, for it was not often he had anybody to talk to while he went on with his work. Therefore he said—

"But don't you think, Willie, before you set about it, you had better see how I do? It would be a pity to spend your labour in finding out for yourself what shoemakers have known for hundreds of years, and which you could learn so easily by letting me show you."

"Thank you," said Willie, sitting down again.

"I should like that very much. I will sit and look at you. I know what you are doing. You are fastening on the sole of a boot."

"Yes. Do you see how it's done?"

"I'm not sure. I don't see yet quite. Of course I see you are sewing the one to the other. I've often wondered how you could manage with small shoes like mine to get in your hand to pull the needle through; but I see you don't use a needle, and I see that you are sewing it all on the outside of the boot, and don't put your hand inside at all. I can't get to understand it."

"You will in a minute. You see how, all round the edge of the upper, as we call it, I have sewn on a strong narrow strip, so that one edge of the strip sticks out all round, while the other is inside. To the edge that sticks out I sew on the sole, drawing my threads so tight that when I pare the edges off smooth, it will look like one piece, and puzzle anybody who did not know how it was done."

"I think I understand. But how do you get your thread so sharp and stiff as to go through the holes you make? I find it hard enough sometimes to get a thread through the eye of a needle; for though the thread is ever so much smaller than yours, I have to sharpen and sharpen it often before I can get it through. But yours, though it is so thick, keeps so sharp that it goes through the holes at once—two threads at once—one from each side!"

"Ah! but I don't sharpen my thread; I put a point upon it."

"Doesn't that mean the same thing?"

"Well, it may generally; but I don't mean the same thing by it. Look here."

"I see!" cried Willie; "there is a long bit of something else, not thread, upon it. What is it? It looks like a hair, only thicker, and it is so sharp at the point!"

"Can't you guess?"

"No; I can't."

"Then I will tell you. It is a bristle out of a hog's back. I don't know what a shoemaker would do without them. Look, here's a little bunch of them."

"That's a very clever use to put them to," said Willie.

"Do you go and pluck them out of the pigs?"

"No; we buy them at the shop. We want a good many, for they wear out. They get too soft, and though they don't break right off, they double up in places, so that they won't go through."

"How do you fasten them to the thread?"

"Look here," said Hector.

He took several strands of thread together, and drew them through and through a piece of cobbler's wax, then took a bristle and put it in at the end cunningly, in a way Willie couldn't quite follow; and then rolled and rolled threads and all over and over between his hand and his leather apron, till it seemed like a single dark-coloured cord.

"There, you see, is my needle and thread all in one."

"And what is the good of rubbing it so much with the cobbler's wax?"

"There are several good reasons for doing that. In the first place, it makes all the threads into one by sticking them together. Next it would be worn out before I had drawn it many times through but for the wax, which keeps the rubbing from wearing it. The wax also protects it afterwards, and keeps the wet from rotting it. The waxed thread fills the hole better too, and what is of as much consequence as anything, it sticks so that the last stitch doesn't slacken before the next comes, but holds so tight that, although the leather is very springy, it cannot make it slip. The two pieces are thus got so close together that they are like one piece, as you will see when I pare the joined edges."

I should tire my reader if I were to recount all the professional talk that followed; for although Willie found it most interesting, and began to feel as if he should soon be able to make a shoe himself, it is a very different thing merely to read about it—the man's voice not in your ears, and the work not going on before your eyes. But the shoemaker cared for other things besides shoemaking, and after a while he happened to make a remark which led to the following question from Willie:—

"Do you understand astronomy, Hector?"

"No. It's not my business, you see, Willie."

"But you've just been telling me so much about the moon, and the way she keeps turning her face always to us—in the politest manner, as you said!"

"I got it all out of Mr Dick's book. I don't understand it. I don't know why she does so. I know a few things that are not my business, just as you know a little about shoemaking, that not being your business; but I don't understand them for all that."

"Whose business is astronomy then?"

"Well," answered Hector, a little puzzled, "I don't see how it can well be anybody's business but God's, for I'm sure no one else can lay a hand to it."

"And what's your business, Hector?" asked Willie, in a half-absent mood.

Some readers may perhaps think this a stupid question, and perhaps so it was; but Willie was not therefore stupid. People sometimes appear stupid because they have more things to think about than they can well manage; while those who think only about one or two things may, on the contrary, appear clever when just those one or two things happen to be talked about.

"What is my business, Willie? Why, to keep people out of the dirt, of course."

"How?" asked Willie again.

"By making and mending their shoes. Mr Dick, now, when he goes out to look at the stars through his telescope, might get his death of cold if his shoemaker did not know his business. Of the general business, it's a part God keeps to Himself to see that the stars go all right, and that the sun rises and sets at the proper times. For the time's not the same any two mornings running, you see, and he might make a mistake if he wasn't looked after, and that would be serious. But I told you I don't understand about astronomy, because it's not my business. I'm set to keep folk's feet off the cold and wet earth, and stones and broken glass; for however much a man may be an astronomer and look up at the sky, he must touch the earth with some part of him, and generally does so with his feet."

"And God sets you to do it, Hector?"

"Yes. It's the way He looks after people's feet. He's got to look after everything, you know, or everything would go wrong. So He gives me the leather and the tools and the hands—and I must say the head, for it wants no little head to make a good shoe to measure—and it is as if He said to me—'There! you make shoes, while I keep the stars right.' Isn't it a fine thing to have a hand in the general business?"

And Hector looked up with shining eyes in the face of the little boy, while he pulled at his rosin-ends as if he would make the boot strong enough to keep out evil spirits.

"I think it's a fine thing to have to make nice new shoes," said Willie; "but I don't think I should like to mend them when they are soppy and muddy and out of shape."

"If you would take your share in the general business, you mustn't be particular. It won't do to be above your business, as they say: for my part, I would say below your business. There's those boots in the corner now. They belong to your papa. And they come next. Don't you think it's an honour to keep the feet of such a good man dry and warm as he goes about from morning to night comforting people? Don't you think it's an honour to mend boots for him, even if they should be dirty?"

"Oh, yes—for papa!" said Willie, as if his papa must be an exception to any rule.

"Well," resumed Hector, "look at these great lace-boots. I shall have to fill the soles of them full of hobnails presently. They belong to the best ploughman in the parish—John Turnbull. Don't you think it's an honour to mend boots for a man who makes the best bed for the corn to die in?"

"I thought it was to grow in," said Willie.

"All the same," returned Hector. "When it dies it grows—and not till then, as you will read in the New Testament. Isn't it an honour, I say, to mend boots for John Turnbull?"

"Oh, yes—for John Turnbull! I know John," said Willie, as if it made any difference to his merit whether Willie knew him or not!

"And there," Hector went on, "lies a pair of slippers that want patching. They belong to William Webster, the weaver, round the corner. They're very much down at heel too. But isn't it an honour to patch or set up slippers for a man who keeps his neighbours in fine linen all the days of their lives?"

"Yes, yes. I know William. It must be nice to do anything for William Webster."

"Suppose you didn't know him, would that make any difference?"

"No," said Willie, after thinking a little. "Other people would know him if I didn't."

"Yes, and if nobody knew him, God would know him; and anybody God has thought worth making, it's an honour to do anything for. Believe me, Willie, to have to keep people's feet dry and warm is a very important appointment."

"Your own shoes aren't very good, Hector," said Willie, who had been casting glances from time to time at his companion's feet, which were shod in a manner that, to say the least of it, would have prejudiced no one in favour of his handiwork. "Isn't it an honour to make shoes for yourself Hector?"

"There can't be much honour in doing anything for yourself," replied Hector, "so far as I can see. I confess my shoes are hardly decent, but then I can make myself a pair at any time; and indeed I've been thinking I would for the last three months, as soon as a slack time came; but I've been far too busy as yet, and, as I don't go out much till after it's dusk, nobody sees them."

"But if you should get your feet wet, and catch cold?"

"Ah! that might be the death of me!" said Hector. "I really must make myself a pair. Well now—let me see—as soon as I have mended those two pairs—I can do them all to-morrow—I will begin. And I'll tell you what," he added, after a thoughtful pause, "if you'll come to me the day after to-morrow, I will take that skin, and cut out a pair of shoes for myself, and you shall see how I do it, and everything about the making of them;—yes, you shall do some part of them yourself, and that shall be your first lesson in shoemaking."

"But Dolly's shoes!" suggested Willie.

"Dolly can wait a bit. She won't take her death of cold from wet feet. And let me tell you it is harder to make a small pair well than a large pair. You will do Dolly's ever so much better after you know how to make a pair for me."

CHAPTER VI. HOW WILLIE LEARNED TO READ BEFORE HE KNEW HIS LETTERS.

The next day his thoughts, having nothing particular to engage them, kept brooding over two things. These two things came together all at once, and a resolution was the consequence. I shall soon explain what I mean.

The one thing was, that Hector had shown considerable surprise when he found that Willie could not read. Now Willie was not in the least ashamed that he could not read: why should he be? It was nowhere written in the catechism he had learnt that it was his duty to be able to read; and if the catechism had merely forgotten to mention it, his father and mother would have told him. Neither was it a duty he ought to have known of himself—for then he would have known it. So why should he be ashamed?

People are often ashamed of what they need not be ashamed of. Again, they are often not at all ashamed of what they ought to be ashamed of, and will turn up their faces to the sun when they ought to hide them in the dust. If, for instance, Willie had ever put on a sulky face when his mother asked him to hold the baby for her, that would have been a thing for shame of which the skin of his face might well try to burn itself off; but not to be able to read before he had even been made to think about it, was not at all a thing to be ashamed of: it would have been more of a shame to be ashamed. Now that it had been put into his head, however, to think what a good thing reading was, all this would apply no longer. It was a very different thing now.

The other subject which occupied his thoughts was this:

Everybody was so kind to him—so ready to do things for him—and, what was of far more consequence, to teach him to do them himself; while he, so far as he could think, did nothing for anybody! That could not be right; it could not be—for it was not reasonable. Not to mention his father and mother, there was Mrs Wilson, who had taught him to knit, and even given him a few lessons in spinning, though that had not come to much; and here was Hector Macallaster going to teach him to make shoes; and not one thing that he could think of was he capable of doing in return! This must be looked into, for things could not be allowed to go on like that. All at once it struck him that Hector had said, with some regret in his voice, that though he had plenty of time to think, he had very little time to read; also that although he could see well enough by candlelight to work at his trade, he could not see well enough to read. What a fine thing it would be to learn to read to Hector! It would be such fun to surprise him too, by all at once reading him something!

The sun was not at his full height when Willie received this illumination. Before the sun went down he knew and could read at sight at least a dozen words.

For the moment he saw that he ought to learn to read, he ran to his mother, and asked her to teach him. She was delighted, for she had begun to be a little doubtful whether his father's plan of leaving him alone till he wanted to learn was the right one. But at that precise moment she was too busy with something that must be done for his father to lay it down and begin teaching him his letters. Willie was so eager to learn, however, that he could not rest without doing something towards it. He bethought himself a little—then ran and got Dr Watts's hymns for children. He knew "How doth the little busy bee" so well as to be able to repeat it without a mistake, for his mother had taught it him, and he had understood it. You see, he was not like a child of five, taught to repeat by rote lines which could give him no notions but mistaken ones. Besides, he had a good knowledge of words, and could use them well in talk, although he could not read; and it is a great thing if a child can talk well before he begins to learn to read.

He opened the little book at the Busy Bee, and knowing already enough to be able to divide the words the one from the other, he said to himself—

"The first word must be How. There it is, with a gap between it and the next word. I will look and see if I can find another How anywhere."

He looked a long time before he found one; for the capital H was in the way. Of course there were a good many how's, but not many with a big H, and he didn't know that the little h was just as good for the mere word. Then he looked for doth, and he found several doth's. Of the's he found as great a swarm as if they had been the bees themselves with which the little song was concerned. Busy was scarce; I am not sure whether he found it at all; but he looked at it until he was pretty sure he should know it again when he saw it. After he had gone over in this way every word of the first verse, he tried himself, by putting his finger at random here and there upon it, and seeing whether he could tell the word it happened to touch. Sometimes he could, and sometimes he couldn't. However, as I said, before the day was over, he knew at least a dozen words perfectly well at sight.

Nor let any one think this was other than a great step in the direction of reading. It would be easy for Willie afterwards to break up these words into letters.

It took him two days more—for during part of each he was learning to make shoes—to learn to know anywhere every word he had found in that hymn.

Next he took a hymn he had not learned, and applied to his mother when he came to a word he did not know, which was very often. As soon as she told him one, he hunted about until he found another and another specimen of the same, and so went on until he had fixed it quite in his mind.

At length he began to compare words that were like each other, and by discovering wherein they looked the same, and wherein they looked different, he learned something of the sound of the letters. For instance, in comparing the and these, although the one sound of the two letters, t and h, puzzled him, and likewise the silent e, he conjectured that the s must stand for the hissing sound; and when he looked at other words which had that sound, and perceived an s in every one of them, then he was sure of it. His mother had no idea how fast he was learning; and when about a fortnight after he had begun, she was able to take him in hand, she found, to her astonishment, that he could read a great many words, but that, when she wished him to spell one, he had not the least notion what she meant.

"Isn't that a b?" she said, wishing to help him to find out a certain word for himself.

"I don't know," answered Willie. "It's not the busy bee," he added, laughing;—"I should know him. It must be the lazy one, I suppose."

"Don't you know your letters?" asked his mother.

"No, mamma. Which are they? Are the rest yours and papa's?"

"Oh, you silly dear!" she said.

"Of course I am!" he returned;—"very silly! How could any of them be mine before I know the names of them! When I know them all, then they'll all be mine, I suppose—and everybody else's who knows them.—So that's Mr B—is it?"

"Yes. And that's C," said his mother.

"I'm glad to see you, Mr C," said Willie, merrily, nodding to the letter. "We shall know each other when we meet again.—I suppose this is D, mamma. How d'e do, Mr D? And what's this one with its mouth open, and half its tongue cut off?"

His mother told him it was E.

"Then this one, with no foot to stand on, is Fe, I suppose."

His mother laughed; but whoever gave it the name it has, would have done better to call it Fe, as Willie did. It would be much better also, in teaching children, at least, to call H, He, and W, We, and Y, Ye, and Z, Ze, as Willie called them. But it was easy enough for him to learn their names after he knew so much of what they could do.

What gave him a considerable advantage was, that he had begun with verse, and not dry syllables and stupid sentences. The music of the verse repaid him at once for the trouble of making it out—even before he got at the meaning, while the necessity of making each line go right, and the rhymes too, helped him occasionally to the pronunciation of a word.

The farther he got on, the faster he got on; and before six weeks were over, he could read anything he was able to understand pretty well at sight.

By this time, also, he understood all the particulars as to how a shoe is made, and had indeed done a few stitches himself, a good deal of hammering both of leather and of hob-nails, and a little patching, at which last the smallness of his hands was an advantage.

At length, one day, he said to the shoemaker—

"Shall I read a little poem to you, Hector?"

"You told me you couldn't read, Willie."

"I can now though."

"Do then," said Hector.

Looking for but a small result in such a short time, he was considerably astonished to find how well the boy could read; for he not merely gave the words correctly, but the sentences, which is far more difficult; that is, he read so that Hector could understand what the writer meant. It is a great thing to read well. Few can. Whoever reads aloud and does not read well, is a sort of deceiver; for he pretends to introduce one person to another, while he misrepresents him.

In after life, Willie continued to pay a good deal of attention not merely to reading for its own sake, but to reading for the sake of other people, that is, to reading aloud. As often as he came, in the course of his own reading, to any verse that he liked very much, he always read it aloud in order to teach himself how it ought to be read; doing his best—first, to make it sound true, that is, to read it according to the sense; next, to make it sound beautiful, that is, to read it according to the measure of the verse and the melody of the words.

He now read a great deal to Hector. There came to be a certain time every day at which Willie Macmichael was joyfully expected by the shoemaker—to read to him for an hour and a half—beyond which time his father did not wish the reading to extend.

CHAPTER VII. SOME THINGS THAT CAME OF WILLIE'S GOING TO SCHOOL.

When his father found that he had learned to read, then he judged it good for him to go to school. Willie was very much pleased. His mother said she would make him a bag to carry his books in; but Willie said there was no occasion to trouble herself; for, if she would give him the stuff, he would make it. So she got him a nice bit of green baize, and in the afternoon he made his bag—no gobble-stitch work, but good, honest back-stitching, except the string-case, which was only run, that it might draw easier and tighter. He passed the string through with a bodkin, fixed it in the middle, tied the two ends, and carried the bag to his mother, who pronounced it nearly as well made as if she had done it herself.

At school he found it more and more plain what a good thing it is that we haven't to find out every thing for ourselves from the beginning; that people gather into books what they and all who went before them have learned, so that we come into their property, as it were; and, after being taught of them, have only to begin our discoveries from where they leave off. In geography, for instance, what a number of voyages and journeys have had to be made, and books to record them written; then what a number of these books to be read, and the facts gathered out of them, before a single map could be drawn, not to say a geography book printed! Whereas now he could learn a multitude of things about the various countries, their peoples and animals and plants, their mountains and rivers and lakes and cities, without having set his foot beyond the parish in which he was born. And so with everything else after its kind. But it is more of what Willie learned to do than what he learned to know that I have to treat.

When he went to school, his father made him a present of a pocket-knife. He had had one before, but not a very good one; and this, having three blades, all very sharp, he found a wonderful treasure of recourse. His father also bought him a nice new slate.

Now there was another handy boy at school, a couple of years older than Willie, whose father was a carpenter. He had cut on the frame of his slate, not his initials only, but his whole name and address,—Alexander Spelman, Priory Leas. Willie thought how nice it would be with his new knife also to cut his name on his slate; only he would rather make some difference in the way of doing it. What if, instead of sinking the letters in the frame, he made them stand up from the frame by cutting it away to some depth all round them. There was not much originality in this, for it was only reversing what Spelman had done; but it was more difficult, and would, he thought, be prettier. Then what was he thus to carve? One would say, "Why, William Macmichael, of course, and, if he liked, Priory Leas" But Willie was a peculiar little fellow, and began to reason with himself whether he had any right to put his own name on the slate. "My father did not give me the slate," he said, "to be my very own. He gave me the knife like that, but not the slate. When I am grown up, it will belong to Agnes. What shall I put on it? What's mine's papa's, and what's papa's is his own," argued Willie.—"I know!" he said to himself at last.

The boys couldn't imagine what he meant to do when they saw him draw first a D and then an O on the frame. But when they saw a C and a T follow, they thought what a conceited little prig Willie was!

"Do you think you're a doctor because your father is, you little ape?" they said.

"No, no," answered Willie, laughing heartily, but thinking, as he went on with his work, that he might be one some day.

When the drawing of the letters was finished, there stood, all round the slate, "Doctor Macmichael's Willie, The Ruins, Priory Leas."

Then out came his knife. But it was a long job, for Willie was not one of those slovenly boys that scamp their work. Such boys are nothing but soft, pulpy creatures, who, when they grow to be men, will be too soft for any of the hard work of the world. They will be fit only for buffers, to keep the working men from breaking their heads against each other in their eagerness. But the carving was at length finished, and gave much satisfaction—first to

Willie himself, because it was finished; next, to Alexander Spelman, Priory Leas, because, being a generous-minded boy, he admired Willie's new and superior work; third, to Mr and Mrs Macmichael, because they saw in it, not the boy's faculty merely, but his love to his father as well; for the recognition of a right over us is one of the sweetest forms love can take. "I am yours" is the best and greatest thing one can say, if to the right person.

It led to a strong friendship between him and Spelman, and to his going often to the workshop of the elder Spelman, the carpenter.

He was a solemn, long-faced, and long-legged man, with reddish hair and pale complexion, who seldom or ever smiled, and at the bench always looked as if he were standing on a stool, he stooped so immoderately. A greater contrast than that between him and the shoemaker could hardly have been found, except in this, that the carpenter also looked sickly. He was in perfect health, however, only oppressed with the cares of his family, and the sickness of his wife, who was a constant invalid, with more children her husband thought than she could well manage, or he well provide for. But if he had thought less about it he would have got on better. He worked hard, but little fancied how many fewer strokes of his plane he made in an hour just because he was brooding over his difficulties, and imagining what would be the consequences if this or that misfortune were to befall him—of which he himself sought and secured the shadow beforehand, to darken and hinder the labour which might prevent its arrival. But he was a good man nevertheless, for his greatest bugbear was debt. If he could only pay off every penny he owed in the world, and if only his wife were so far better as to enjoy life a little, he would, he thought, be perfectly happy. His wife, however, was tolerably happy, notwithstanding her weak health, and certainly enjoyed life a good deal—far more at least than her husband was able to believe.

Mr Macmichael was very kind and attentive to Mrs Spelman; though, as the carpenter himself said, he hadn't seen the colour of his money for years. But the Doctor knew that Spelman was a hard-working man, and would rather have given him a little money than have pressed him for a penny. He told him one day, when he was lamenting that he couldn't pay him even yet, that he was only too glad to do anything in the least little bit like what the

Saviour did when he was in the world—"a carpenter like you, Spelman—think of that," added the Doctor.

So Spelman was as full of gratitude as he could hold. Except Hector Macallaster, the Doctor was almost his only creditor. Medicine and shoes were his chief trials: he kept on paying for the latter, but the debt for the former went on accumulating.

Hence it came that when Willie began to haunt his shop, though he had hardly a single smile to give the little fellow, he was more than pleased;—gave him odds and ends of wood; lent him whatever tools he wanted except the adze—that he would not let him touch; would drop him a hint now and then as to the use of them; would any moment stop his own work to attend to a difficulty the boy found himself in; and, in short, paid him far more attention than he would have thought required of him if Willie had been his apprentice.

From the moment he entered the workshop, Willie could hardly keep his hands off the tools. The very shape of them, as they lay on the bench or hung on the wall, seemed to say over and over, "Come, use me; come, use me." They looked waiting, and hungry for work. They wanted stuff to shape and fashion into things, and join into other things. They wanted to make bigger tools than themselves—for ploughing the earth, for carrying the harvest, or for some one or other of ten thousand services to be rendered in the house or in the fields. It was impossible for Willie to see the hollow lip of the gouge, the straight lip of the chisel, or the same lip fitted with another lip, and so made into the mouth of the plane, the worm-like auger, or the critical spokeshave, the hammer which will have it so, or the humble bradawl which is its pioneer—he could see none of them without longing to send his life into theirs, and set them doing in the world—for was not this what their dumb looks seemed ever to implore? At that time young Spelman was busy making a salt-box for his mother out of the sound bits of an old oak floor which his father had taken up because it was dry-rotted. It was hard wood to work, but Willie bore a hand in planing the pieces, and was initiated into the mysteries of dovetailing and gluing. Before the lid was put on by the hinges, he carved the initials of the carpenter and his wife in relief upon it, and many years after they used to show his work. But the first thing he set about making for himself was a water-wheel.

If he had been a seaside boy, his first job would have been a boat; if he had lived in a flat country, it would very likely have been a windmill; but the most noticeable thing in that neighbourhood was a mill for grinding corn driven by a water-wheel.

When Willie was a tiny boy, he had gone once with Farmer Thomson's man and a load of corn to see the mill; and the miller had taken him all over it. He saw the corn go in by the hopper into the trough which was the real hopper, for it kept constantly hopping to shake the corn down through a hole in the middle of the upper stone, which went round and round against the lower, so that between them they ground the corn to meal, which, in the story beneath, he saw pouring, a solid stream like an avalanche, from a wooden spout. But the best of it all was the wheel outside, and the busy rush of the water that made it go. So Willie would now make a water-wheel.

The carpenter having given him a short lecture on the different kinds of water-wheels, he decided on an undershot, and with Sandy's help proceeded to construct it—with its nave of mahogany, its spokes of birch, its floats of deal, and its axle of stout iron-wire, which, as the friction would not be great, was to run in gudgeon-blocks of some hard wood, well oiled. These blocks were fixed in a frame so devised that, with the help of a few stones to support it, the wheel might be set going in any small stream.

There were many tiny brooks running into the river, and they fixed upon one of them which issued from the rising ground at the back of the village: just where it began to run merrily down the hill, they constructed in its channel a stonebed for the water-wheel—not by any means for it to go to sleep in!

It went delightfully, and we shall hear more of it by and by. For the present, I have only to confess that, after a few days, Willie got tired of it—and small blame to him, for it was of no earthly use beyond amusement, and that which can only amuse can never amuse long. I think the reason children get tired of their toys so soon is just that it is against human nature to be really interested in what is of no use. If you say that a beautiful thing is always interesting, I answer, that a beautiful thing is of the highest use. Is not a diamond that flashes all its colours into the heart of a poet as useful as the diamond with which the glazier divides the sheets of glass into panes for our windows? Anyhow, the reason Willie got tired of his water-wheel was that it went round and round, and did nothing but go round. It drove no machinery, ground no grain of corn—"did nothing for _no_body," Willie said, seeking to be emphatic. So he carried it home, and put it away in a certain part of the ruins where he kept odds and ends of things that might some day come in useful.

Mr Macmichael was so devoted to his profession that he desired nothing better for Willie than that he too should be a medical man, and he was more than pleased to find how well Willie's hands were able to carry out his contrivances; for he judged it impossible for a country doctor to have too much mechanical faculty. The exercise of such a skill alone might secure the instant relief of a patient, and be the saving of him. But, more than this, he believed that nothing tended so much to develop common sense—the most precious of faculties—as the doing of things with the hands. Hence he not only encouraged Willie in everything he undertook, but, considering the five hours of school quite sufficient for study of that sort, requested the master not to give him any lessons to do at home. So Willie worked hard during school, and after it had plenty of time to spend in carpentering, so that he soon came to use all the common bench-tools with ease, and Spelman was proud of his apprentice, as he called him—so much so, that the burden of his debt grew much lighter upon his shoulders.

But Willie did not forget his older friend, Hector Macallaster. Every half-holiday he read to him for a couple of hours, chiefly, for some time, from Dick's Astronomy. Neither of them understood all he read, but both understood much, and Hector could explain some of the things that puzzled Willie. And when he found that everything went on in such order, above and below and all about him, he began to see that even a thing well done was worth a good deal more when done at the right moment or within the set time; and that the heavens themselves were like a great clock, ordering the time for everything.

Neither did he give up shoemaking, for he often did a little work for Hector, who had made him a leather apron, and cut him out bits of stout leather to protect his hands from the thread when he was sewing. For twelve months, however, his chief employment lay in the workshop of the carpenter.

CHAPTER VIII. WILLIE DIGS AND FINDS WHAT HE DID NOT EXPECT.

He had been reading to Hector Sir Walter Scott's "Antiquary," in which occurs the narration of a digging for treasure in ruins not unlike these, only grander. It was of little consequence to Willie that no treasure had been found there: the propriety of digging remained the same; for in a certain spot he had often fancied that a hollow sound, when he stamped hard, indicated an empty place underneath. I believe myself that it came from above, and not from beneath; for although a portion of the vaulted roof of the little chamber had been broken in, the greater part of it still remained, and might have caused a reverberation. The floor was heaped up with fallen stones and rubbish.

One Wednesday afternoon, instead of going to Hector, whom he had told not to expect him, he got a pickaxe and spade, and proceeded to dig in the trodden heap. At the first blow of the pickaxe he came upon large stones—the job of clearing out which was by no means an easy one—so far from it, indeed, that, after working for half an hour, and only getting out two large and half a dozen smaller ones, he resolved to ask Sandy Spelman to help him. So he left his pickaxe with one point fast between two stones, and ran to the shop. Sandy was at work, but his father was quite willing to let him go. Willie told them he was digging for a treasure, and they all laughed over it; but at the same time Willie thought with himself—"Who knows? People have found treasures buried in old places like that. The Antiquary did not—but he is only in a story, not in a high story" (for that was Willie's derivation of the word history). "The place sounds likely enough. Anyhow, where's the harm in trying?"

They were both so eager—for Sandy liked the idea of digging in the ruins much better than the work he was at—that they set off at full speed the moment they were out of the shop, and never slackened until they stood panting by the anchored pickaxe, upon which Spelman pounced, and being stronger than Willie, and more used to hard work, had soon dislodged both the stones which held it. They were so much larger, however, than any Willie had come upon before, that they had to roll them out of the little chamber, instead of lifting them; after which they got on better, and had soon piled a good heap against the wall outside. After they had had their tea, they set to work again, and worked till the twilight grew dark about them—by which time they had got the heap down to what seemed the original level of the floor. Still there were stones below, but what with fatigue and darkness, they were now compelled to stop, and Sandy went home, after promising to come as early as he could in the morning and call Willie, who was to leave the end of a string hanging out of the staircase window, whose other end should pass through the keyhole of his door and be tied to his wrist. He seemed to have hardly been in bed an hour, when he woke with his arm at full length, and the pulling going on as if it would pull him out of bed. He tugged again in reply, and jumped out.

It was a lovely summer morning—the sun a few yards up the sky; the grass glittering with dew; the birds singing as if they were singing their first and would sing their last; the whole air, even in his little room, filled with a cool odour as of blessed thoughts, and just warm enough to let him know that the noontide would be hot. And there was Sandy waiting in the street to help him dig for the treasure! In a few minutes he had opened the street door and admitted him. They went straight to the scene of their labour.

Having got out a few more stones, they began to fancy they heard a curious sound, which they agreed was more like that of running water than anything else they could think of. Now, except a well in the street, just before the cottage, there was no water they knew of much nearer than the river, and they wondered a good deal.

At length Sandy's pickaxe got hold of a stone which he could not move, do what he would. He tried another, and succeeded, but soon began to suspect that there was some masonry there. Contenting himself therefore with clearing out only the loose stones, he soon found plainly enough that he was working in a narrow space, around which was a circular wall of solid stone and lime. The sound of running water was now clear enough, and the earth in the hole was very damp. Sandy had now got down three or four feet below the level.

"It's an old well," he said. "There can be no doubt of it."

"Does it smell bad?" asked Willie, peeping down disappointed.

"Not a bit," answered Sandy.

"Then it's not stagnant," said Willie.

"You might have told that by your ears without troubling your nose," said Sandy. "Didn't you hear it running?"

"How can it be running when it's buried away down there?" said Willie.

"How can it make a noise if it isn't running?" retorted Sandy—to which question Willie attempted no reply.

It was now serious work to get the stones up, for Sandy's head only was above the level of the ground; it was all he could do to lift some of the larger ones out of the hole, and Willie saw that he must contrive to give him some help. He ran therefore to the house, and brought a rope which he had seen lying about. One end of it Sandy tied round whatever stone was too heavy for him, and Willie, laying hold of the other, lifted along with him. They got on faster now, and in a few minutes Sandy exclaimed—

"Here it is at last!"

"The treasure?" cried Willie. "Oh, jolly!"

Sandy burst out laughing, and shouted—

"The water!"

"Bother the water!" growled Willie. "But go on, Sandy; the iron chest may be at the bottom of the water, you know."

"All very well for you up there!" retorted Sandy. "But though I can get the stones out, I can't get the water out. And I've no notion of diving where there's pretty sure to be nothing to dive for. Besides, a body can't dive in a stone pipe like this. I should want weights to sink me, and I mightn't get them off in time. I want my breakfast dreadful, Willie."

So saying, he scrambled up the side of the well, and the last of him that appeared, his boots, namely, bore testimony enough to his having reached the water. Willie peered down into the well, and caught the dull glimmer of it through the stones; then, a good deal disappointed, followed Sandy as he strode away towards the house.

"You'll come and have your breakfast with me, Sandy, won't you?" he said from behind him.

"No, thank you," answered Sandy. "I don't like any porridge but my mother's."

And without looking behind him, he walked right through the cottage, and away home.

Before Willie had finished his porridge, he had got over his disappointment, and had even begun to see that he had never really expected to find a treasure. Only it would have been fun to hand it over to his father!

All through morning school, however, his thoughts would go back to the little vault, so cool and shadowy, sheltering its ancient well from the light that lorded it over all the country outside. No doubt the streams rejoiced in it, but even for them it would be too much before the evening came to cool and console them; while the slow wells in the marshy ground up on the mountains must feel faint in an hour of its burning eye. This well had always been, and always would be, cool and blessed and sweet, like—like a precious thing you can only think about. And wasn't it a nice thing to have a well of your own? Tibby needn't go any more to the village pump—which certainly was nearer, but stood in the street, not in their own ground. Of course, as yet, she could not draw a bucketful, for the water hardly came above the stones; but he would soon get out as many as would make it deep enough—only, if it was all Sandy could do to get out the big ones, and that with his help too, how was he to manage it alone? There was the rub!

I must go back a little to explain how he came to think of a plan.

After Hector and he had gone as far in Dr Dick's astronomy as they could understand, they found they were getting themselves into what seemed quite a jungle of planets, and suns, and comets, and constellations.

"It seems to me," said the shoemaker, "that to understand anything you must understand everything."

So they laid the book aside for the present; and Hector, searching about for another with which to fill up the remainder of the afternoon, came upon one in which the mechanical powers were treated after a simple fashion.

Of this book Willie had now read a good deal. I cannot say that he had yet come to understand the mechanical power so thoroughly as to see that the lever and the wheel-and-axle are the same in kind, or that the screw, the inclined plane, and the wedge are the same power in different shapes; but he did understand that while a single pulley gives you no advantage except by enabling you to apply your strength in the most effective manner, a second pulley takes half the weight off you. Hence, with the difficulty in which he now found himself, came at once the thought of a block with a pulley in it, which he had seen lying about in the carpenter's shop. He remembered also that there was a great iron staple or eye in the vault just over the well; and if he could only get hold of a second pulley, the thing was as good as done—the well as good as cleared out to whatever depth he could reach below the water.

As soon as school was over, he ran to Mr Spelman, and found to his delight that he could lend him not only that pulley but another as well. Each ran in a block which had an iron hook attached to it. With the aid of a ladder he put the hook of one of the blocks through the staple, and then fastened the end of his rope to the block. Next he got another bit of rope, and having pulled off his shoes and stockings, and got down into the well, tied it round the largest stone within reach, loosely enough to allow the hook of the second pulley to lay hold of it. Then, as a sailor would say, he rove the end of the long rope through this block, and getting up on the ladder again, rove it also through the first block which he had left hanging to the staple. All preparations thus completed, he stood by the well, and hauled away at the rope. It came slipping through the pulleys, and up rose the stone from the well as if by magic. As soon as it came clear of the edge, he drew it towards him, lowered it to the ground, took off its rope collar, and rolled it out of the doorway. Then he got into the well again, tied the collar about another stone, drew down the pulley, thrust its hook through the collar, got out of the well, and hauled up the second stone.

In this way he had soon got out so many that he was standing far above his ankles in the water, which was so cold that he was glad to get out to pull up every stone. By this time it was perfectly explained how the water made a noise, for he saw it escape by an opening in the side of the well.

He came at last to a huge stone, round which it was with difficulty he managed to fasten the rope. He had to pull away smaller stones from beneath it, and pass the rope through under it. Having lifted it a little way with the powerful help of his tackle, to try if all was right before he got out to haul in earnest, he saw that his knot was slipping, and lowered the stone again so as to set it on one end, leaning against the side of the well—when he discovered that his rope collar had got so frayed, that one of the strands was cut through; it would probably break and let the stone fall again into the well, when he would still more probably tumble after it. He was getting tired too, and it was growing very dusky in the ruins. He thought it better to postpone further proceedings, and getting out of the well, caught up his shoes and stockings, and went into the house.

CHAPTER IX. A MARVEL.

Early the next morning Mr Macmichael, as he was dressing, heard a laugh of strange delight in the garden, and, drawing up the blind, looked out. There, some distance off, stood Willie, the one moment staring motionless at something at his feet, the other dancing and skipping and singing, but still looking down at something at his feet. His father could not see what this something was, for Willie was on the other side of one of the mounds, and was turning away to finish his dressing, when from another direction a peculiar glitter caught his eye.

"What can this mean?" he said to himself. "Water in the garden! There's been no rain; and there's neither river nor reservoir to overflow! I can hardly believe my eyes!"

He hurried on the remainder of his clothes, and went out. But he had not gone many steps when what should he meet but a merry little brook coming cantering down between two of the mounds! It had already worn itself a channel in the path. He followed it up, wondering much, bewildered indeed; and had got to a little turfy hollow, down the middle of which it came bubbling and gabbling along, when Willie caught sight of him, and bounded to meet him with a radiant countenance and almost inarticulate cries of delight.

"Am I awake, Willie? or am I dreaming?" he asked.

"Wide awake, papa," answered Willie.

"Then what is the meaning of this? You seem to be in the secret: where does this water come from? I feel as if I were in a fairy tale."

"Isn't it lovely?" cried Willie. "I'll show you where it comes from. This way. You'll spoil your boots there. Look at the rhubarb-bed; it's turned into a swamp."

"The garden will be ruined," said his father.

"No, no, papa; we won't let it come to that. I've been watching it.

There's no soil carried away yet. Do come and see."

In mute astonishment, his father followed.

As I have already described it, the ground was very uneven, with many heights and hollows, whence it came that the water took an amazing number of twists and turns. Willie led his father as straight as he could, but I don't know how often they crossed the little brook before they came to where, from the old stone shaft, like the crater of a volcano, it rolled over the brim, an eruption of cool, clear, lucid water. Plenteous it rose and overflowed, like a dark yet clear molten gem, tumbling itself into the open world. How deliciously wet it looked in the shadow I—-how it caught the sun the moment it left the chamber, grew merry, and trotted and trolled and cantered along!

"Is this your work, Willie?" asked his father, who did not know which of twenty questions to ask first.

"Mostly," said Willie.

"You little wizard! what have you been about? I can't understand it. We must make a drain for it at once."

"Bury a beauty like that in a drain!" cried Willie. "O papa!"

"Well, I don't know what else to do with it. How is it that it never found its way out before—somewhere or other?"

"I'll soon show you that," said Willie. "I'll soon send it about its business."

He had thought, when he first saw the issuing water, that the weight of the fallen stones and the hard covering of earth being removed, the spring had burst out with tenfold volume and vigour; but had satisfied himself by thinking about it, that the cause of the overflow must be the great stone he had set leaning against the side the last thing before dropping work the previous night: it must have blocked up the opening, and prevented the water from getting out as fast as before, that is, as fast as the spring rose. Therefore he now laid hold of the rope, which was still connected with the stone, and, not aware of how the water would help him by partly floating it, was astonished to find how easily he moved it. At once it swung away from the side into the middle of the well; the water ceased to run over the edge, with a loud gurgling began to sink, and sank down and down and down until the opening by which it escaped was visible.

"Ah! now, now I understand!" cried Mr Macmichael. "It's the old well of the Priory you've come upon, you little burrowing mole."

"Sandy helped me out with the stones. I thought there might be a treasure down there, and that set me digging. It was a funny treasure to find—wasn't it? No treasure could have been prettier though."

"If this be the Prior's Well, and all be true they said about it in old times," returned his father, "it may turn out a greater treasure than you even hoped for, Willie. Why, as I found some time ago in an old book about the monasteries of the country, people used to come from great distances to drink the water of the Prior's Well, believing it a cure for every disease under the sun. Run into the house and fetch me a jug."

"Yes, papa," said Willie, and bounded off.

There was no little brook careering through the garden now—only a few pools here and there—and its channel would soon be dry in the hot sun. But Willie thought how delightful it was to be able to have one there whenever he pleased. And it might be a much bigger brook too, for, instead of using the stone which could but partly block the water from the underground way, he would cut a piece of wood large enough to cover the opening, and rounded a little to fit the side of the well; then he would put the big stone just so far from the opening that the piece of wood could get through between it and the side of the well, and so be held tight. Then all the water would be forced to mount up, get out at the top, and run through the garden.

Meantime Mr Macmichael, having gone to see what course the water had taken, and how it had left the garden, found that, after a very circuitous route, it had run through the hedge into a surface drain in the field, and so down the hill towards the river.

When Willie brought him the jug, he filled it from the well, and carried the water into his surgery. There he put a little of it into several different glasses, and dropping something out of one bottle into one glass, and something out of another bottle into another glass, soon satisfied himself that it contained medicinal salts in considerable quantities. There could be no doubt that Willie had found the Prior's Well.

"It's a good thing," said his father at breakfast, "that you didn't flood the house, Willie! One turn more and the stream would have been in at the back-door."

"It wouldn't have done much harm," said Willie. "It would have run along the slabs in the passage and out again, for the front door is lower than the back. It would have been such fun!"

"You mischievous little thing!" said his mother, pretending to scold him,—"you don't think what trouble you would have given Tibby!"

"But wouldn't it have been fun? And wouldn't it have been lovely—running through the house all the hot summer day?"

"There may be a difference of opinion about that, Master Willie," said his mother. "You, for instance, might like to walk through water every time you went from the parlour to the kitchen, but I can't say I should."

Curious to know whether the village pump might not be supplied from his well, Mr Macmichael next analysed the water of that also, and satisfied himself that there was no connection between them. Within the next fortnight Willie discovered that as often as the stream ran through the garden, the little brook in which he had set his water-wheel going was nearly dry.

He had soon made a nice little channel for it, so that it should not get into any of the beds. He laid down turf along its banks in some parts, and sowed grass and daisy-seed in others; and when he found a pretty stone or shell, or bit of coloured glass or bright crockery or broken mirror, he would always throw it in, that the water might have the prettier path to run upon. Indeed, he emptied his store of marbles into it. He was not particularly fond of playing with marbles, but he had a great fancy for those of real white marble with lovely red streaks, and had collected some twenty or thirty of them. He kept them in the brook now, instead of in a calico bag.

The summer was a very hot and dry one. More than any of the rest of the gardens in the village, that of The Ruins suffered from such weather; for not only was there a deep gravel-bed under its mould, but a good part of its produce grew on the mounds, which were mostly heaps of stones, and neither gravel nor stones could retain much moisture. Willie watered it a good deal out of the Prior's Well; but it was hard work, and did not seem to be of much use.

One evening, when he had set the little brook free to run through the garden, and the sun was setting huge and red, with the promise of another glowing day to-morrow, and the air was stifling, and not a breath of wind stirring, so that the flowers hung their heads oppressed, and the leaves and little buttons of fruit on the trees looked ready to shrivel up and drop from the boughs, the thought came to him whether he could not turn the brook into a little Nile, causing it to overflow its banks and enrich the garden. He could not, of course, bring it about in the same way; for the Nile overflows from the quantities of rain up in the far-off mountains, making huge torrents rush into it faster than its channel, through a slow, level country, can carry the water away, so that there is nothing for it but overflow. If, however, he could not make more water run out of the well, he could make it more difficult for what did come from it to get away. First, he stopped up the outlet through the hedge with stones, and clay, and bits of board; then watched as it spread, until he saw where it would try to escape next, and did the same; and so on, taking care especially to keep it from the house. The mounds were a great assistance to him in hemming it in, but he had hard enough work of it notwithstanding; and soon perceived that at one spot it would get the better of him in a few minutes, and make straight for the back-door. He ran at once and opened the sluice in the well, and away the stream gurgled underground.

Before morning the water it left had all disappeared. It had soaked through the mounds, and into the gravel, but comforting the hot roots as it went, and feeding them with dissolved minerals. Doubtless, also, it lay all night in many a little hidden pool, which the heat of the next day's sun drew up, comforting again, through the roots in the earth, and through the leaves in the air, up into the sky. Willie could not help thinking that the garden looked refreshed; the green was brighter, he thought, and the flowers held up their heads a little better; the carrots looked more feathery, and the ferns more palmy; everything looked, he said, just as he felt after a good drink out of the Prior's Well. At all events, he resolved to do the same every night after sunset while the hot weather lasted—that was, if his father had no objection.

Mr Macmichael said he might try it, only he must mind and not go to bed and leave the water running, else they would have a cartload of mud in the house before morning.

So Willie strengthened and heightened his barriers, and having built a huge one at the last point where the water had tried to get away, as soon as the sun was down shut the sluice, and watched the water as it surged up in the throat of the well, and rushed out to be caught in the toils he had made for it. Before it could find a fresh place to get out at, the whole upper part of the garden was one network of lakes and islands.

Willie kept walking round and round it, as if it had been a wild beast trying to get out of its cage, and he had to watch and prevent it at every weak spot; or as if he were a magician, busily sustaining the charm by which he confined the gad-about creature. The moment he saw it beginning to get the better of him, he ran to the sluice and banished it to the regions below. Then he fetched an old newspaper, and sitting down on the borders of his lake, fashioned boat after boat out of the paper, and sent them sailing like merchant ships from isle to blooming isle.

Night after night he flooded the garden, and always before morning the water had sunk away through the gravel. Soon there was no longer any doubt that everything was mightily refreshed by it; the look of exhaustion and hopelessness was gone, and life was busy in flower and tree and plant. This year there was not a garden, even on the banks of the river, to compare with it; and when the autumn came, there was more fruit than Mr Macmichael remembered ever to have seen before.

CHAPTER X. A NEW ALARUM.

Willie was always thinking what uses he could put things to. Only he was never tempted to set a fine thing to do dirty work, as dull-hearted money-grubbers do—mill-owners, for instance, when they make the channel of a lovely mountain-stream serve for a drain to carry off the filth from their works. If Dante had known any such, I know where he would have put them, but I would rather not describe the place. I have told you what Willie made the prisoned stream do for the garden; I will now tell you what he made the running stream do for himself, and you shall judge whether or not that was fit work for him to require of it.

Ever since he had ceased being night-nurse to little Agnes, he had wished that he had some one to wake him every night, about the middle of it, that he might get up and look out of the window. For, after he had fed his baby-sister and given her back to his mother in a state of contentment, before getting into bed again he had always looked out of the window to see what the night was like—not that he was one bit anxious about the weather, except, indeed, he heard his papa getting up to go out, or knew that he had to go; for he could enjoy weather of any sort and all sorts, and never thought what the next day would be like—but just to see what Madame Night was thinking about—how she looked, and what she was doing. For he had soon found her such a changeful creature that, every time he looked at her, she looked at him with another face from that she had worn last time. Before he had made this acquaintance with the night, he would often, ere he fell asleep, lie wondering what he was going to dream about; for, with all his practical tendencies, Willie was very fond of dreaming; but after he had begun in this manner to make acquaintance with her, he would just as often fall asleep wondering what the day would be dreaming about—for, in his own fanciful way of thinking, he had settled that the look of the night was what the day was dreaming. Hence, when Agnes required his services no longer, he fell asleep the first night with the full intention of waking just as before, and getting up to have a peep into the day's dream, whatever it might be, that night, and every night thereafter.

But he was now back in his own room, and there was nothing to wake him, so he slept sound until the day had done dreaming, and the morning was wide awake.

Neither had he awoke any one night since, or seen what marvel there might be beyond his windowpanes.

Does any little boy or girl wonder what there can be going on when we are asleep? Sometimes the stars, sometimes the moon, sometimes the clouds, sometimes the wind, sometimes the snow, sometimes the frost, sometimes all of them together, are busy. Sometimes the owl and the moth and the beetle, and the bat and the cat and the rat, are all at work. Sometimes there are flowers in bloom that love the night better than the day, and are busy all through the darkness pouring out on the still air the scent they withheld during the sunlight. Sometimes the lightning and the thunder, sometimes the moon-rainbow, sometimes the aurora borealis, is busy. And the streams are running all night long, and seem to babble louder than in the day time, for the noises of the working world are still, so that we hear them better. Almost the only daylight thing awake, is the clock ticking with nobody to heed it, and that sounds to me very dismal. But it was the look of the night, the meaning on her face that Willie cared most about, and desired so much to see, that he was at times quite unhappy to think that he never could wake up, not although ever so many strange and lovely dreams might be passing before his window. He often dreamed that he had waked up, and was looking out on some gorgeous and lovely show, but in the morning he knew sorrowfully that he had only dreamed his own dream, not gazed into that of the sleeping day. Again and again he had worked his brains to weariness, trying and trying to invent some machine that should wake him. But although he was older and cleverer now, he fared no better than when he wanted to wake himself to help his mother with Agnes. He must have some motive power before he could do anything, and the clock was still the only power he could think of, and that he was afraid to meddle with, for its works were beyond him, and it was so essential to the well-being of the house that he would not venture putting it in jeopardy.

One day, however, when he was thinking nothing about it, all at once it struck him that he had another motive power at his command, and the thought had hardly entered his mind, before he saw also how it was possible to turn it to account. His motive power was the stream from the Prior's Well, and the means of using it for his purpose stood on a shelf in the ruins, in the shape of the toy water-wheel which he had laid aside as distressingly useless. He set about the thing at once.

First of all, he made a second bit of channel for the stream, like a little loop to the first, so that he could, when he pleased, turn a part of the water into it, and let it again join the principal channel a little lower down. This was, in fact, his mill-race. Just before it joined the older part again, right opposite his window, he made it run for a little way in a direct line towards the house, and in this part of the new channel he made preparations for his water-wheel. Into the channel he laid a piece of iron pipe, which had been lying about useless for years; and just where the water would issue in a concentrated rush from the lower end of it, he constructed a foundation for his wheel, similar to that Sandy and he had built for it before. The water, as it issued from the pipe, should strike straight upon its floats, and send it whirling round. It took him some time to build it, for he wanted this to be a good and permanent job. He had stones at command: he had a well, he said, that yielded both stones and water, which was more than everybody could say; and in order to make it a sound bit of work, he fetched a lump of quick-lime from the kiln, where they burned quantities of it to scatter over the clay-soil, and first wetting it with water till it fell into powder, and then mixing it with sand which he riddled from the gravel he dug from the garden, he made it into good strong mortar. When its bed was at length made for it, he took the wheel and put in a longer axis, to project on one side beyond the gudgeon-block, or hollow in which it turned; and upon this projecting piece he fixed a large reel. Then, having put the wheel in its place, he asked his father for sixpence, part of which he laid out on a large ball of pack-thread. The outside end of the ball he fastened to the reel, then threw the ball through the open window into his room, and there undid it from the inside end, laying the thread in coils on the floor. When it was time to go to bed, he ran out and turned the water first into the garden, and then into the new channel; when suddenly the wheel began to spin about, and wind the pack-thread on to the reel. He ran to his room, and undressed faster than he had ever done before, tied the other end of the thread around his wrist, and, although kept awake much longer than usual by his excitement, at length fell fast asleep, and dreamed that the thread had waked him, and drawn him to the window, where he saw the water-wheel flashing like a fire-wheel, and the water rushing away from under it in a green flame. When he did wake it was broad day; the coils of pack-thread were lying on the floor scarcely diminished; the brook was singing in the garden, and when he went to the window, he saw the wheel spinning merrily round. He dressed in haste, ran out, and found that the thread had got entangled amongst the bushes on its way to the wheel, and had stuck fast; whereupon the wheel had broken it to get loose, and had been spinning round and round all night for nothing, like the useless thing it was before.

That afternoon he set poles up for guides, along the top of which the thread might run, and so keep clear of the bushes. But he fared no better the next night, for he never waked until the morning, when he found that the wheel stood stock still, for the thread, having filled the reel, had slipped off, and so wound itself about the wheel that it was choked in its many windings. Indeed, the thread was in a wonderful tangle about the whole machine, and it took him a long time to unwind—turning the wheel backwards, so as not to break the thread.

In order to remove the cause of this fresh failure, he went to the turner, whose name was William Burt, and asked him to turn for him a large reel or spool, with deep ends, and small cylinder between. William told him he was very busy just then, but he would fix a suitable piece of wood for him on his old lathe, with which, as he knew him to be a handy boy, he might turn what he wanted for himself. This was his first attempt at the use of the turning-lathe; but he had often watched William at work, and was familiar with the way in which he held his tool. Hence the result was tolerably satisfactory. Long before he had reached the depth of which he wished to make the spool, he had learned to manage his chisel with some nicety. Burt finished it off for him with just a few touches; and, delighted with his acquisition of the rudiments of a new trade, he carried the spool home with him, to try once more the possibility of educating his water-wheel into a watchman.

236

That night the pull did indeed come, but, alas before he had even fallen asleep.

Something seemed to be always going wrong! He concluded already that it was a difficult thing to make a machine which should do just what the maker wished. The spool had gone flying round, and had swallowed up the thread incredibly fast. He made haste to get the end off his wrist, and saw it fly through the little hole in the window frame, and away after the rest of it, to be wound on the whirling spool.

Disappointing as this was, however, there was progress in it: he had got the thing to work, and all that remained was to regulate it. But this turned out the most difficult part of the affair by far. He saw at once that if he were only to make the thread longer, which was the first mode that suggested itself, he would increase the constant danger there was of its getting fouled, not to mention the awkwardness of using such a quantity of it. If the kitten were to get into the room, for instance, after he had laid it down, she would ruin his every hope for the time being; and in Willie's eyes sixpence was a huge sum to ask from his father. But if, on the contrary, he could find out any mode of making the machine wind more slowly, he might then be able to shorten instead of lengthening the string.

At length, after much pondering, he came to see that if, instead of the spool, he were to fix on the axis a small cogged wheel—that is, a wheel with teeth—and then make these cogs fit into the cogs of a much larger wheel, the small wheel, which would turn once with every turn of the water-wheel, must turn a great many times before it could turn the big wheel once. Then he must fix the spool on the axis of this great slow wheel, when, turning only as often as the wheel turned, the spool would wind the thread so much the more slowly.

I will not weary my reader with any further detail of Willie's efforts and failures. It is enough to say that he was at last so entirely successful in timing his machine, for the run of the water was always the same, that he could tell exactly how much thread it would wind in a given time. Having then measured off the thread with a mark of ink for the first hour, two for the second, and so on, he was able to set his alarum according to the time at which he wished to be woke by the pull at his wrist.

But if any one had happened to go into the garden after the household was asleep, and had come upon the toy water-wheel, working away in starlight or moonlight, how little, even if he had caught sight of the nearly invisible thread, and had discovered that the wheel was winding it up, would he have thought what the tiny machine was about! How little would he have thought that its business was with the infinite! that it was in connection with the window of an eternal world—namely, Willie's soul—from which at a given moment it would lift the curtains, namely, the eyelids, and let the night of the outer world in upon the thought and feeling of the boy! To use a likeness, the wheel was thus ever working to draw up the slide of a camera obscura, and let in whatever pictures might be abroad in the dreams of the day, that the watcher within might behold them.

Indeed, one night as he came home from visiting a patient, soon after Willie had at length taught his watchman his duty, Mr Macmichael did come upon the mill, and was just going to turn the water off at the well, which he thought Willie had forgotten to do, when he caught sight of the winding thread—for the moon was full, and the Doctor was sharp-sighted.

"What can this be now?" he said to himself. "Some new freak of Willie's, of course. Yes; the thread goes right up to his window! I dare say if I were to stop and watch I should see something happen in consequence. But I am too tired, and must go to bed."

Just as he thought thus with himself, the wheel stopped. The next moment the blind of Willie's window was drawn up, and there stood Willie, his face and his white gown glimmering in the moonlight. He caught sight of his father, and up went the sash.

"O papa!" he cried; "I didn't think it was you I was going to see!"

"Who was it then you thought to see?" asked his father.

"Oh, nobody!—only the night herself, and the moon perhaps."

"What new freak of yours is this, my boy?" said his father, smiling.

"Wait a minute, and I'll tell you all about it," answered Willie.

Out he came in his night-shirt, his bare feet dancing with pleasure at having his father for his midnight companion. On the grass, beside the ruins, in the moonlight, by the gurgling water, he told him all about it.

"Yes, my boy; you are right," said his father. "God never sleeps; and it would be a pity if we never saw Him at his night-work."

CHAPTER XI. SOME OF THE SIGHTS WILLIE SAW.

I fancy some of my readers would like to hear what were some of the scenes Willie saw on such occasions. The little mill went on night after night—almost everynight in the summer, and those nights in the winter when the frost wasn't so hard that it would have frozen up the machinery. But to attempt to describe the variety of the pictures Willie saw would be an endless labour.

Sometimes, when he looked out, it was a simple, quiet, thoughtful night that met his gaze, without any moon, but as full of stars as it could hold, all flashing and trembling through the dew that was slowly sinking down the air to settle upon the earth and its thousand living things below. On such a night Willie never went to bed again without wishing to be pure in heart, that he might one day see the God whose thought had taken the shape of such a lovely night. For although he could not have expressed himself thus at that time, he felt that it must be God's thinking that put it all there.

Other times, the stars would be half blotted out—all over the heavens—not with mist, but with the light of the moon. Oh, how lovely she was!—so calm! so all alone in the midst of the great blue ocean! the sun of the night! She seemed to hold up the tent of the heavens in a great silver knot. And, like the stars above, all the flowers below had lost their colour and looked pale and wan, sweet and sad. It was just like what the schoolmaster had been telling him about the Elysium of the Greek and Latin poets, to which they fancied the good people went when they died—not half so glad and bright and busy as the daylight world which they had left behind them, and to which they always wanted to go back that they might eat and drink and be merry again—but oh, so tender and lovely in its mournfulness!

Several times in winter, looking out, he saw a strange sight—the air so full of great snowflakes that he could not see the moon through them, although her light was visible all about them. They came floating slowly down through the dusky light, just as if they had been a precipitate from that solution of moonbeams. He could hardly persuade himself to go to bed, so fascinating was the sight; but the cold would drive him to his nest again.

Once the wheel-watchman pulled him up in the midst of a terrible thunder-storm—when the East and the West were answering each other with alternate flashes of forked lightning that seemed to split the black clouds with cracks of blinding blue, awful in their blasting silence—followed by great, billowy, shattering rolls of thunder, as loud as if the sky had been a huge kettledrum, on which the clubs of giant drummers were beating a terrible onset; while at sudden intervals, down came the big-dropped rain, pattering to the earth as if beaten out of the clouds by the blows of the thunder. But Willie was not frightened, though the lightning blinded and the thunder deafened him—not frightened any more than the tiniest flower in the garden below, which, if she could have thought about it, would have thought it all being done only that she might feel cooler and stronger, and be able to hold up her head better.

And once he saw a glorious dance of the aurora borealis—in all the colours of a faint rainbow. The frosty snow sparkled underneath, and the cold stars of winter sparkled above, and between the snow and the stars, shimmered and shifted, vanished and came again, a serried host of spears. Willie had been reading the "Paradise Lost," and the part which pleased him, boy-like, the most, was the wars of the angels in the sixth book. Hence it came that the aurora looked to him like the crowding of innumerable spears— in the hands of angels, themselves invisible—clashed together and shaken asunder, however, as in the convolutions of a mazy dance of victory, rather than brandished and hurtled as in the tumult of the battle.

Another vision that would greatly delight him was a far more common one: the moon wading through clouds blown slowly across the sky—especially if by an upper wind, unfelt below. Now she would be sinking helpless in a black faint—growing more and more dim, until at last she disappeared from the night—was blotted from the face of nature, leaving only a dim memorial light behind her; now her soul would come into her again, and she was there once more—doubtful indeed: but with a slow, solemn revival, her light would grow and grow, until the last fringe of the great cloud swung away from off her face, and she dawned out stately and glorious, to float for a space in queenly triumph across a lake of clearest blue. And Willie was philosopher enough to say to himself, that all this fainting and reviving, all this defeat and conquest, were but appearances; that the moon was her own bright self all the time, basking contented in the light of her sun, between whom and her the cloud could not creep, only between her and Willie.

But what delighted him most of all was to catch the moon dreaming. That was when the old moon, tumbled over on her back, would come floating up the east, like a little boat on the rising tide of the night, looking lost on the infinite sea! Dreaming she must be surely!—she looked nothing but dreaming; for she seemed to care about nothing—not even that she was old and worn, and withered and dying,—not even that, instead of sinking down in the west, into some deep bed of dim repose, she was drifting, haggard and battered, untidy and weak and sleepy, up and up into the dazzling halls of the sun. Did she know that his light would clothe her as with a garment, and hide her in the highest recesses of his light-filled ceiling? or was it only that she was dreaming, dreaming—sweet, cool, tender dreams of her own, and neither knew nor cared about anything around her? What a strange look all the night wore while the tired old moon was thus dreaming of the time when she would come again, back through the vanishing and the darkness—a single curved thread of a baby moon, to grow and grow to a great full-grown lady moon, able to cross with fearless gaze the gulf of the vaulted heavens—alone, with neither sleep nor dreams to protect her!

There were many other nights, far more commonplace, which yet Willie liked well to look out upon, but which could not keep him long from his bed. There was, for instance, the moonless and cloudy night, when, if he had been able to pierce the darkness to the core, he would have found nothing but blackness. It had a power of its own, but one cannot say it had much to look at. On such a night he would say to himself that the day was so sound asleep he was dreaming of nothing at all, and make haste to his nest. Then again there was the cold night of black frost, when there was cloud enough to hide the stars and the moon, and yet a little light came soaking through, enough to reveal how hopeless and dreary the earth was. For in such nights of cold, when there is no snow to cover them, the flowers that have crept into their roots to hide from the winter are not even able to dream of the spring;—they grow quite stupid and benumbed, and sleep outright like a polar bear or a dormouse. He never could look long at such a night.

Neither did he care to look long when a loud wind was out—except the moon was bright; for the most he could distinguish was the trees blowing against the sky, and they always seemed not to like it, and to want to stop. And if the big strong trees did not like it, how could the poor little delicate flowers, shivering and shaking and tossed to and fro? If he could have seen the wind itself, it would have been a different thing; but as it was, he could enjoy it more by lying in bed and listening to it. Then as he listened he could fancy himself floating out through miles and miles of night and wind, and moon-and-star-light, or moony snowflakes, or even thick darkness and rain; until, falling asleep in the middle of his fancy, it would thicken around him into a dream of delight.

Once there was to be an eclipse of the moon about two o'clock in the morning.

"It's a pity it's so late, or rather so early," said Mr Macmichael.

"You, Willie, won't be able to see it."

"Oh, yes, I shall, father," answered Willie.

"I can't let you sit up so late. I shall be in the middle of Sedgy Moor most likely when it begins—and who is to wake you? I won't have your mother disturbed, and Tibby's not much to depend upon. She's too hard-worked to wake when she likes, poor old thing."

"Oh, I can be woke without anybody to do it!" said Willie.

"You don't mean you can depend on your water-wheel to wake you at the right time, do you?"

"Yes, I do, father. If you will tell me exactly when the eclipse is going to begin, I will set my wakener so that it shall wake me a quarter-of-an-hour before, that I may be sure of seeing the very first of it."

"Well, it will be worth something to you, if it can do that!" said Mr

Macmichael.

"It's been worth a great deal to me, already," said Willie. "It would have shown me an eclipse before now, only there hasn't been one since I set it going."

And wake him it did. While his father was riding across the moor, in the strange hush of the blotted moon, Willie was out in the garden beside his motionless wheel, watching the fell shadow of the earth passing over the blessed face of the moon, and leaving her pure and clear, and nothing the worse.

CHAPTER XII. A NEW SCHEME.

I have said that Willie's father and mother used to talk without restraint in his presence. They had no fear of Willie's committing an indiscretion by repeating what he heard. One day at dinner the following conversation took place between them.

"I've had a letter from my mother, John," said Mrs Macmichael to her husband. "It's wonderful how well she manages to write, when she sees so badly."

"She might see well enough—at least a great deal better—if she would submit to an operation, said the doctor.

"At her age, John!" returned his wife in an expostulatory tone. "Do you really think it worth while—for the few years that are left her?"

"Worth while to see well for a few years!" exclaimed the doctor.

"Indeed, I do."

"But there's another thing I want to talk to you about now," said Mrs Macmichael. "Since old Ann's death, six months ago, she says she has been miserable, and if she goes on like this, it will shorten the few days that are left her. Effie, the only endurable servant she has had since Ann, is going to leave at the end of her half-year, and she says the thought of another makes her wretched. She may be a little hard to please, but after being used to one for so many years, it is no wonder if she be particular. I don't know what is to be done."

"I don't know, either—except you make her a present of Tibby," said her husband.

"John!" exclaimed Mrs Macmichael; and "John" burst out laughing.

"You don't think they'd pull together?" he said.

"Two old people—each with her own ways, and without any memories in common to bind them together! I'm surprised at your dreaming of such a thing," exclaimed his wife.

"But I didn't even dream of it; I only said it," returned her husband.

"It's time you knew when I was joking, wifie."

"You joke so dreadfully like earnest!" she answered.

"If only we had one more room in the house!" said the doctor, thoughtfully.

"Ah!" returned his wife, eagerly, "that would be a blessing! And though Tibby would be a thorn in every inch of grandmamma's body, if they were alone together, I have no doubt they would get on very well with me between them."

"I don't doubt it," said her husband, still thoughtfully.

"Couldn't we manage it somehow, John?" said Mrs Macmichael, half timidly, after a pause of some duration.

"I can't say I see how—at this moment," answered the doctor, "much as I should like it. But there's time yet, and we'll think it over, and talk about it, and perhaps we may hit upon some plan or other. Most things may be done; and everything necessary can be done _some_how. So we won't bother our minds about it, but only our brains, and see what they can do for us."

With this he rose and went to his laboratory.

Willie rose also and went straight to his own room. Having looked all round it thoughtfully several times, he went out again on the landing, whence a ladder led up into a garret running the whole length of the roof of the cottage.

"My room would do for grannie," he said to himself; "and I could sleep up there. A shake-down in the corner would do well enough for me."

He climbed the ladder, pushed open the trap-door, crept half through, and surveyed the gloomy place.

246

"There's no window but a skylight!" he said; and his eyes smarted as if the tears were about to rush into them. "What shall I do? Wheelie will be useless!—Well, I can't help it; and if I can't help it, I can bear it. To have grannie comfortable will be better than to look out of the window ever so much."

He drew in his head, came down the ladder with a rush, and hurried off to school.

At supper he laid his scheme before his father and mother.

They looked very much pleased with their boy. But his father said at once—

"No, no, Willie. It won't do. I'm glad you've been the first to think of something—only, unfortunately, your plan won't work. You can't sleep there."

"I'll engage to sleep wherever there's room to lie down; and if there isn't I'll engage to sleep sitting or standing," said Willie, whose mother had often said she wished she could sleep like Willie. "And as I don't walk in my sleep," he added, "the trap-door needn't be shut."

"Mice, Willie!" said his mother, in a tone of much significance.

"The cat and I are good friends," returned Willie. "She'll be pleased enough to sleep with me."

"You don't hit the thing at all," said his father. "I wonder a practical man like you, Willie, doesn't see it at once. Even if I were at the expense of ceiling the whole roof with lath and plaster, we should find you, some morning in summer, baked black as a coal; or else, some morning in winter frozen so stiff that, when we tried to lift you, your arm snapped off like a dry twig of elder."

"Ho! ho! ho!" laughed Willie; "then there would be the more room for grannie."

His father laughed with him, but his mother looked a little shocked.

"No, Willie," said his father again; "you must make another attempt. You must say with Hamlet when he was puzzled for a plan—'About my brains!' Perhaps they will suggest something wiser next time."

Willie lay so long awake that night, thinking, that Wheelie pulled him before he had had a wink of sleep. He got up, of course, and looked from the window.

The day was dreaming grandly. The sky was pretty clear in front, and full of sparkles of light, for the stars were kept in the background by the moon, which was down a little towards the west. She had sunk below the top of a huge towering cloud, the edges of whose jags and pinnacles she bordered with a line of silvery light. Now this cloud rose into the sky from just behind the ruins, and looking a good deal like upheaved towers and spires, made Willie think within himself what a grand place the priory must have been, when its roofs and turrets rose up into the sky.

"They say a lot of people lived in it then!" he thought with himself as he stood gazing at the cloud.

Suddenly he gave a great jump, and clapped his hands so loud that he woke his father.

"Is anything the matter, my boy?" he asked, opening Willie's door, and peeping in.

"No, papa, nothing," answered Willie. "Only something that came into my head with a great bounce!"

"Ah!—Where did it come from, Willie?"

"Out of that cloud there. Isn't it a grand one?"

"Grand enough certainly to put many thoughts into a body's head, Willie.

What did it put into yours?"

"Please, I would rather not tell just yet," answered Willie, "—if you don't mind, father."

"Not a bit, my boy. Tell me just when you please, or don't tell me at all.

I should like to hear it, but only at your pleasure, Willie."

"Thank you, father. I do want to tell you, you know, but not just yet."

"Very well, my boy. Now go to bed, and sleep may better the thought before the morning."

Willie soon fell asleep now, for he believed he had found what he wanted.

He was up earlier than usual the next morning, and out in the garden.

"Surely," he said to himself, "those ruins, which once held so many monks, might manage even yet to find room for me!"

He went wandering about amongst them, like an undecided young bird looking for the very best possible spot to build its nest in. The spot Willie sought was that which would require the least labour and least material to make it into a room.

Before he heard the voice of Tibby, calling him to come to his porridge, he had fixed upon one; and in the following chapter I will tell you what led him to choose it. All the time between morning and afternoon school, he spent in the same place; and when he came home in the evening, he was accompanied by Mr Spelman, who went with him straight to the ruins. There they were a good while together; and when Willie at length came in, his mother saw that his face was more than usually radiant, and was certain he had some new scheme or other in his head.

CHAPTER XIII. WILLIE'S NEST IN THE RUINS.

The spot he had fixed upon was in the part of the ruins next the cottage, not many yards from the back door of it. I have said there were still a few vaulted places on the ground-level used by the family. The vault over the wood-house was perfectly sound and weather-tight, and, therefore, as Willie and the carpenter agreed, quite safe to roost upon. In a corner outside, and now open to the elements, had once been a small winding stone stair, which led to the room above, on the few broken fragments of which, projecting from the two sides of the corner, it was just possible to climb, and so reach the top of the vault. Willie had often got up to look out through a small, flat-arched window into the garden of the manse. When Mr Shepherd, the clergyman, who often walked in his garden, caught sight of him, he always came nearer, and had a chat with him; for he did not mind such people as Willie looking into his garden, and seeing what he was about. Sometimes also little Mona, a girl of his own age, would be running about; and she also, if she caught sight of Willie, was sure to come hopping and skipping like a bird to have a talk with him, and beg him to take her up, which, he as often assured her, was all but impossible. To this place Mr Spelman and Willie climbed, and there held consultation whether and how it could be made habitable. The main difficulty was, how to cover it in; for although the walls were quite sound a long way up, it lay open to the sky. But about ten feet over their heads they saw the opposing holes in two of the walls where the joists formerly sustaining the floor of the chamber above had rested; and Mr Spelman thought that, without any very large outlay either of time or material, he could there lay a floor, as it were, and then turn it into a roof by covering it with cement, or pitch, or something of the sort, concerning which he would take counsel with his friend Mortimer, the mason.

"But," said Willie, "that would turn it into the bottom of a cistern; for the walls above would hold the rain in, and what would happen then? Either it must gather till it reached the top, or the weight of it would burst the walls, or perhaps break through my roof and drown me."

"It is easy to avoid that," said Mr Spelman. "We have only to lay on the cement a little thicker at one side, and slope the surface down to the other, where a hole through the wall, with a pipe in it, would let the water off."

"I know!" cried Willie. "That's what they called a gurgoyle!"

"I don't know anything about that," said the carpenter; "I know it will carry off the water."

"To be sure," said Willie. "It's capital."

"But," said Mr Spelman, "it's rather too serious a job this to set about before asking the doctor's leave. It will cost money."

"Much?" asked Willie, whose heart sank within him.

"Well, that depends on what you count much," answered Spelman. "All I can say is, it wouldn't be anything out of your father's pocket."

"I don't see how that can be," said Willie. "—Cost money, and yet be nothing out of my father's pocket! I've only got threepence ha'-penny."

"Your father and I will talk about it," said the carpenter mysteriously, and offered no further information.

"There seems to be always some way of doing a thing," thought Willie to himself.

He little knew by what a roundabout succession of cause and effect his father's kindness to Spelman was at this moment returning to him, one of the links of connection being this project of Willie's own.

The doctor being out at the time, the carpenter called again later in the evening; and they had a long talk together—to the following effect.

Spelman having set forth his scheme, and the doctor having listened in silence until he had finished—

"But," said Mr Macmichael, "that will cost a good deal, I fear, and I have no money to spare."

"Mr Macmichael," said Spelman solemnly, his long face looking as if some awful doom were about to issue from the middle of it, "you forget how much I am in your debt."

"No, I don't," returned the doctor. "But neither do I forget that it takes all your time and labour to provide for your family; and what will become of them if you set about this job, with no return in prospect but the satisfaction of clearing off of an old debt?"

"It is very good of you, sir, to think of that," said the carpenter; "but, begging your pardon, I've thought of it too. Many's the time you've come after what I'd ha' called work hours to see my wife—yes, in the middle of the night, more than once or twice; and why shouldn't I do the same? Look ye here, sir. If you're not in a main hurry, an' 'll give me time, I'll do the heavy work o' this job after six o'clock o' the summer nights, with Sandy to help me, and I'll charge you no more than a journeyman's wages by the hour. And what Willie and Sandy can do by themselves—he's a clever boy Sandy; but he's a genius Willie—what they can do by themselves, and that's not a little, is nothing to me. And if you'll have the goodness, when I give you the honest time, at fourpence ha'penny an hour, just to strike that much off my bill, I'll be more obliged to you than I am now. Only I fear I must make you pay for the material—not a farthing more than it costs me at the saw-mills, up at the Grange, for the carriage 'll come in with other lots I must have."

"It's a generous offer, Spelman," said the doctor, "and I accept it heartily, though you are turning the tables of obligation upon me. You'll have done far more for me than I ever did for you."

"I wish that were like to be true, sir, but it isn't. My wife's not a giantess yet, for all you've done for her."

Spelman set to work at once. New joists were inserted in the old walls, boarded over, and covered, after the advice of Mortimer, with some cunning mixture to keep out the water. Then a pipe was put through the wall to carry it off—which pipe, if it was not masked with an awful head, as the remains of more than one on the Priory showed it would have been in the days of the monks, yet did it work as faithfully without it.

When it came to the plastering of the walls, Mr Spelman, after giving them full directions, left the two boys to do that between them. Although there was no occasion to roughen these walls by clearing away the old mortar from between the stones, the weather having done that quite sufficiently, and all the preparation they wanted for the first thin coat was to be well washed down, it took them a good many days, working all their time, to lay on the orthodox three coats of plaster. Mr Spelman had wisely boarded the ceiling, so that they had not to plaster that.

Meantime he was preparing a door and window-frames in the shop. The room had probably been one of the prior's, for it was much too large and lofty for a mere cell, and had two windows. But these were fortunately small, not like the splendid ones in the chapel and refectory, else they would have been hard to fill with glass.

"I'm afraid you'll be starved with cold, Willie," said his father one day, after watching the boys at work for a few minutes. "There's no fireplace."

"Oh! that doesn't signify," answered Willie. "Look how thick the walls are! and I shall have plenty of blankets on my bed. Besides, we can easily put a little stove in, if it's wanted."

But when the windows were fitted and fixed, Mr Macmichael saw to his dismay that they were not made to open. They had not even a pane on hinges.

"This'll never do, Willie," he said. "This is far worse than no chimney."

Willie took his father by the coat, and led him to a corner, where a hole went right through the wall into another room—if that can be called a room which had neither floor nor ceiling.

"There, father!" he said; "I am going to fit a slide over this hole, and then I can let in just as much or as little air as I please."

"It would have been better to have one at least of the windows made to open. You will only get the air from the ruins that way, whereas you might have had all the scents of Mr Shepherd's wallflowers and roses."

"As soon as Mr Spelman has done with the job," said Willie, "I will make them both to come wide open on hinges; but I don't want to bother him about it, for he has been very kind, and I can do it quite well myself."

This satisfied his father.

At length the floor was boarded; a strong thick door was fitted tight; a winding stair of deal inserted where the stone one had been, and cased in with planks, well pitched on the outside; and now Willie's mother was busy making little muslin curtains for his windows, and a carpet for the middle of the room.

In the meantime, his father and mother had both written to his grandmother, telling her how Willie had been using his powers both of invention and of labour to make room for her, and urging her to come and live with them, for they were all anxious to have her to take care of. But, in fact, small persuasion was necessary, for the old lady was only too glad to accept the invitation; and before the warm weather of autumn was over, she was ready to go to them. By this time Willie's room was furnished. All the things from his former nest had been moved into it; the bed with the chintz curtains, covered with strange flowers and birds; the old bureau, with the many drawers inside the folding cover, in which he kept all his little treasures; the table at which he read books that were too big to hold, such as Raleigh's History of the World and Josephus; the old oblong mirror that hung on the wall, with an outspread gilt eagle at the top of it; the big old arm-chair that had belonged to his great-grandfather, who wrote his sermons in it—for all the things the boy had about him were old, and in all his after-life he never could bear new furniture. And now his grandmother's furniture began to appear; and a great cart-load of it from her best bedroom was speedily arranged in Willie's late quarters, and as soon as they were ready for her, Mrs Macmichael set out in a post-chaise to fetch her mother.

CHAPTER XIV. WILLIE'S GRANDMOTHER.

Willie was in a state of excitement until she arrived, looking for her as eagerly as if she had been a young princess. So few were the opportunities of travelling between Priory Leas and the town where his grandmother lived, that he had never seen her, and curiosity had its influence as well as affection. Great, therefore, was his delight when at last the chaise came round the corner of the street, and began to draw up in order to halt at their door. The first thing he caught sight of was a curious bonnet, like a black coal-scuttle upside down, inside which, when it turned its front towards him, he saw a close-fitting widow's cap, and inside that a kind old face, and if he could have looked still further, he would have seen a kind young soul inside the kind old face. She smiled sweetly when she saw him, but was too tired to take any further notice of him until she had had tea.

During that meal Willie devoted himself to a silent waiting upon her, watching and trying to anticipate her every want. When she had eaten a little bread and butter and an egg, and drunk two cups of tea, she lay back in her own easy chair, which had been placed for her by the side of the parlour fire, and fell fast asleep for ten minutes, breathing so gently that Willie got frightened, and thought she was dead. But all at once she opened her eyes wide, and made a sign to him to come to her.

"Sit down there," she said, pushing a little footstool towards him.

Willie obeyed, and sat looking up in her face.

"So," she said, "you're the little man that can do everything?"

"No, grannie," answered Willie, laughing. "I wish I could; but I am only learning to do a few things; and there's not one of them I can do right yet."

"Do you know what they call you?"

"The boys at school call me Six-fingered Jack," said Willie.

"There!" said his grandmother. "I told you so."

"I'm glad it's only a nickname, grannie; but if it weren't, it would soon be one, for I'm certain the finger that came after the little one would be so much in the way it would soon get cut off."

"Anyhow, supposing you only half as clever a fellow as you pass for, I want to try you. Have you any objection to service? I should like to hire you for my servant—my own special servant, you understand."

"All right, grannie; here I am!" cried Willie, jumping up. "What shall I do first?"

"Sit down again instantly, and wait till we've finished the bargain. I must first have you understand that though I don't want to be hard upon you, you must come when I call you, and do what I tell you."

"Of course, grannie. Only I can't when I'm at school, you know."

"I don't want to be told that. And I'm not going to be a tyrant. But I had no idea you were such a silly! For all your cleverness, you've positively never asked me what wages I would give you."

"Oh! I don't want any wages, grannie. I like to do things for people; and you're my very own grandmother, besides, you know."

"Well, I suppose I must settle your wages for you. I mean to pay you by the job. It's an odd arrangement for a servant, but it will suit me best. And as you don't ask any, I needn't pay you more than I like myself."

"Certainly not, grannie. I'm quite satisfied."

"Meantime, no engagement of a servant ought to be counted complete without earnest."

"I'm quite in earnest, grannie," said Willie, who did not know the meaning of the word as his new mistress used it. They all laughed.

"I don't see what's funny," said Willie, laughing too, however.

But when they explained to him what earnest meant, then he laughed with understanding, as well as with good will.

"So," his grandmother went on, "I will give you earnest, which, you know, binds you my servant. But for how long, Willie?"

"Till you're tired of me, grannie. Only, you know, I'm papa and mamma's servant first, and you may have to arrange with them sometimes; for what should I do if you were all to want me at once?"

"We'll easily manage that. I'll arrange with them, as you say. And now, here's your earnest."

As she spoke, she put into his hand what Willie took to be a shilling.

But when he glanced at it, he found himself mistaken.

"Thank you, grannie," he said, trying not to show himself a little disappointed, for he had had another scheme in his head some days, and the shilling would have been everything towards that.

"Do you know what grannie has given you, Willie?" said his mother.

"Yes, mother—such a pretty brass medal!"

"Show it me, dear. Why, Willie! it's no brass medal, child;—it's a sovereign!"

"No-o-o-o! Is it? O grannie!" he cried, and went dancing about the room, as if he would actually fly with delight.

Willie had never seen a sovereign, for that part of the country was then like Holland—you never saw gold money there. To get it for him, his grandmother had had to send to the bank in the county town.

After this she would often give him sixpence or a shilling, and sometimes even a half-crown when she asked him to do anything she thought a little harder than usual; so that Willie had now plenty of money with which to carry out his little plans. When remonstrated with by her daughter for giving him so much, his grandmother would say—

"Look how the boy spends it!—always doing something with it! He never wastes it on sweets—not he!—My Willie's above that!"

The old lady generally spoke of him as if she were the chief if not the sole proprietor of the boy.

"I'm sure I couldn't do better with it," she would add; "and that you'll see when he comes to be a man. He'll be the making of you all."

"But, mother, you can't afford it."

"How do you know that? I can afford it very well. I've no house-rent to pay; and I am certain it is the very best return I can make you for your kindness. What I do for Willie will prove to have been done for us all."

Certainly Willie's grandmother showed herself a very wise old lady. The wisest old ladies are always those with young souls looking out of their eyes. And few things pleased Willie more than waiting upon her. He had a passion for being useful, and as his grandmother needed his help more than any one else, her presence in the house was an endless source of pleasure to him.

But his father grew anxious. He did not like her giving Willie so much money—not that he minded Willie having or spending the money, for he believed that the spending would keep the having from hurting him; but he feared lest through her gifts the purity of the boy's love for his grandmother might be injured, and the service which at first had looked only to her as its end might degenerate into a mere serving of her for the sake of her shillings.

He had, therefore, a long talk with her about it. She was indignant at the notion of the least danger of spoiling Willie, but so anxious to prove there was none that she agreed to the test proposed by his father—which was, to drop all money transactions between them for a few months, giving Willie no reason for the change. Grannie, however, being in word and manner, if possible, still kinder to him than ever—and no wonder, seeing she could no more, for the present, let her love out at her pocket-hole—and Willie having, therefore, no anxiety lest he should have displeased her, he soon ceased to think even of the change; except, indeed, sometimes when he wanted a little money very much, and then he would say to himself that he was afraid poor grannie had been too liberal at first, and had spent all her money upon him; therefore he must try to be the more attentive to her now. So the result was satisfactory; and the more so that, for all her boasting, his grandmother had not been able to help trembling a little, half with annoyance, half with anxiety, as she let the first few of his services pass without the customary acknowledgment.

"There!" she said one day, at length, triumphantly, to Mr Macmichael; "what do you think of my Willie now? Three months over and gone, and where are your fears? I hope you will trust my judgment a little better after this."

"I'm very glad, anyhow, you put him to the trial," said his father. "It will do him good."

"He wants less of that than most people, Mr Macmichael—present company not excepted," said the old lady, rather nettled, but pretending to be more so than she really was.

CHAPTER XV. HYDRAULICS.

The first thing Willie did, after getting his room all to himself, was to put hinges on the windows and make them open, so satisfying his father as to the airiness of the room. Finding himself then, as it were, in a house of his own, he began to ask his friends in the village to come and see him in his new quarters. The first who did so was Mrs Wilson, and Mr Spelman followed. Hector Macallaster was unwell, and it was a month before he was able to go; but the first day he could he crawled up the hill to the Ruins, and then up the little winding stair to Willie's nest. The boy was delighted to see him, made him sit in his great arm-chair, and, as the poor man was very tired with the exertion, would have run to the house to get him something; but Hector begged for a little water, and declared he could take nothing else. Therefore Willie got a tumbler from his dressing-table, and went to the other side of the room. Hector, hearing a splashing and rushing, turned round to look, and saw him with one hand in a small wooden trough that ran along the wall, and with the other holding the tumbler in a stream of water that fell from the side of the trough into his bath. When the tumbler was full, he removed his hand from the trough, and the water ceased to overflow. He carried the tumbler to Hector, who drank, and said the water was delicious.

Hector could not imagine how the running water had got there, and Willie had to tell him what I am now going to tell my reader. His grandmother's sovereign and his own hydraulics had brought it there.

He had been thinking for some time what a pleasure it would be to have a stream running through his room, and how much labour it would save poor old Tibbie; for it was no light matter for her old limbs to carry all the water for his bath up that steep narrow winding stair to his room. He reasoned that as the well rose and overflowed when its outlet was stopped, it might rise yet farther if it were still confined; for its source was probably in the heart of one of the surrounding hills, and water when confined will always rise as high as its source. Therefore, after much meditation as to how it could be accomplished in the simplest and least expensive manner, he set about it as follows.

First of all he cleared away the floor about the well, and built up the circular wall of it a foot or two higher, with stones picked from those lying about, and with mortar which he made himself. By means of a spirit-level, he laid the top layer of stones quite horizontal; and he introduced into it several blocks of wood instead of stones.

Next he made a small wooden frame, which, by driving spikes between the stones, he fastened to the opening of the underground passage, so that a well-fitting piece of board could move up and down in it, by means of a projecting handle, and be a more manageable sluice than he had hitherto had.

Then he made a strong wooden lid to the mouth of the well, and screwed it down to the wooden blocks he had built in. Through a hole in it, just large enough, came the handle of the sluice.

Next, in the middle of the cover, he made a hole with a brace and centre-bit, and into it drove the end of a strong iron pipe, fitting tight, and long enough to reach almost to the top of the vault. As soon as this was fixed he shut down the sluice, and in a few seconds the water was falling in sheets upon him, and flooding the floor, dashed back from the vault, against which it rushed from the top of the pipe. This was enough for the present; he raised the sluice and let the water escape again below. It was plain, from the force with which the water struck the vault, that it would yet rise much higher.

He scrambled now on the top of the vault, and, examining the ruins, soon saw how a pipe brought up through the breach in the vault could be led to the hole in the wall of his room which he had shown his father as a ventilator. But he would not have a close pipe running through his room. There would be little good in that. He could have made a hole in it, with a stopper, to let the water out when he wanted to use it, but that would be awkward, while all the pleasure lay in seeing the water as it ran. Therefore he got Mr Spelman to find him a long small pine tree, which he first sawed in two, lengthways, and hollowed into two troughs; then, by laying the small end of one into the wide end of the other, he had a spout long enough to reach across the room, and go through the wall on both sides.

The chief difficulty was to pierce the other wall, for the mortar was very hard. The stones, however, just there were not very large, and, with Sandy's help, he managed it.

The large end of one trough was put through the ventilator-hole, and the small end of the other through the hole opposite; their second ends met in the middle, the one lying into the other, and were supported at the juncture by a prop.

They filled up the two openings round the ends with lime and small stones, making them as tidy as they could, and fitting small slides by which Willie could close up the passages for the water when he pleased. Nothing remained but to solder a lead pipe into the top of the iron one, guide this flexible tube across the ups and downs of the ruins, and lay the end of it into the trough.

At length Willie took his stand at the sluice, and told Sandy to scramble up to the end of the lead pipe, and shout when the water began to pour into the trough. His object was to find how far the sluice required to be shut down in order to send up just as much water as the pipe could deliver. More than that would cause a pressure which might strain, and perhaps burst, their apparatus.

He pushed the sluice down a little, and waited a moment.

"Is it coming yet, Sandy?" he cried.

"Not a drop," shouted Sandy.

Willie pushed it a little further, and then knew by the change in the gurgle below that the water was rising in the well; and it soon began to spout from the hole in the cover through which the sluice-handle came up.

"It's coming," cried Sandy, after a pause; "not much, though."

Down went the sluice a little further still.

"It's pouring," echoed the voice of Sandy amongst the ruins; "as much as ever the pipe can give. Its mouth is quite full."

Willie raised the sluice a little.

"How is it now?" he bawled.

"Less," cried Sandy.

So Willie pushed it back to where it had been last, and made a notch in the handle to know the right place again.

So the water from the Prior's Well went careering through Willie's bed-chamber, a story high. When he wanted to fill his bath, he had only to stop the run with his hand, and it poured over the sides into it; so that Tibbie was to be henceforth relieved of a great labour, while Willie's eyes were to be delighted with the vision, and his ears with the sounds of the water scampering through his room.

An hour or so after, as he was finishing off something about the mouth of the well, he heard his father calling him.

"Willie, Willie," he shouted, "is this any more of your kelpie work?"

"What is it, father?" cried Willie, as he came bounding to him.

He needed no reply when he saw a great pool of water about the back door, fed by a small stream from the direction of the woodhouse. Tibbie had come out, and was looking on in dismay.

"That's Willie again, sir," she was saying. "You never can tell where he'll be spouting that weary water at you."

The whole place'll be bog before long, and we'll be all turned into frogs, and have nothing to do but croak. That well 'll be the ruin of us all with cold and coughs."

"You'll be glad enough of it to-night, Tibbie," said Willie, laughing prophetically.

"A likely story!" she returned, quite cross. "It'll be into the house if you don't stop it."

"I'll soon do that," said Willie.

Neither he nor Sandy had thought what would become of the water after it had traversed the chamber. There it was pouring down from the end of the wooden spout, just clearing the tarred roof of the spiral stair, and plashing on the ground close to the foot of it; in their eagerness they had never thought of where it would run to next. And now Willie was puzzled. Nothing was easier than to stop it for the present, which of course he ran at once to do; but where was he to send it?

Thinking over it, however, he remembered that just on the other side of the wall was the stable where his father's horses lived, close to the parson's garden; and in the corner, at the foot of the wall, was a drain; so that all he had to do was to fit another spout to this, at right angles to it, and carry it over the wall.

"You needn't take any water up for me tonight, Tibby," he said, as he went in to supper, for he had already filled his bath.

"Nonsense, Willie," returned Tibbie, still out of temper because of the mess at the door. "Your papa says you must have your bath, and my poor old bones must ache for 't."

"The bath's filled already. If you put in one other pailful, it'll run over when I get into it."

"Now, don't you play tricks with me, Willie. I won't have any more of your joking," returned Tibbie.

Nettled at the way she took the information with which he had hoped to please her, he left her to carry up her pail of water; but it was the last, and she thanked him very kindly the next day.

The only remaining question was how to get rid of the bath-water. But he soon contrived a sink on the top step of the stair outside the door, which was a little higher than the wall of the stable-yard. From there a short pipe was sufficient to carry that water also over into the drain.

I may mention, that although a severe winter followed, the Prior's Well never froze; and that, as they were always either empty, or full of running water, the pipes never froze, and consequently never burst.

CHAPTER XVI. HECTOR HINTS AT A DISCOVERY.

The next day after Hector's visit, Willie went to see how he was, and found him better.

"I certainly am better," he said, "and what's more, I've got a strange feeling it was that drink of water you gave me yesterday that has done it. I'm coming up to have some more of it in the evening, if you'll give it me."

"As much of it as you can drink, Hector, anyhow," said Willie. "You won't drink my cow dry."

"I wonder if it could be the water," said Hector, musingly.

"My father says people used to think it cured them. That was some hundreds of years ago; but if it did so then, I don't see why it shouldn't now. My mother is certainly better, but whether that began since we found the well, I can't be very sure. For Tibbie—she is always drinking at it, she says it does her a world of good."

"I've read somewhere," said the shoemaker, "that wherever there's a hurt there's a help; and when I was a boy, and stung myself with a nettle, I never had far to look for a dock-stalk with its juice. Who knows but the Prior's Well may be the cure for me? It can't straighten my back, I know, but it may make me stronger for all that, and fitter for the general business."

"I will lay down a pipe for you, if you like, Hector, and then you can drink as much of the water as you please, without asking anybody," said Willie.

Hector laughed.

"It's not such a sure thing," he replied, "as to be worth that trouble; and besides, the walk does me good, and a drink once or twice a day is enough—that is, if your people won't think me a trouble, coming so often."

"There's no fear of that," said Willie; "it's our business, you know, to try to cure people. I'll tell you what—couldn't you bring up a bit of your work, and sit in my room sometimes? It's better air there than down here."

"You're very kind, indeed, Willie. We'll see. Meantime, I'll come up morning and evening, and have a drink of the water, as long at least as the warm weather lasts, and by that time I shall be pretty certain whether it is doing me good or not."

So Hector went on drinking the water and getting a little better.

Next, grannie took to it, and, either from imagination, or that it really did her good, declared it was renewing her youth. All the doctor said on the matter was, that the salts it contained could do no one any harm, and might do some people much good; that there was iron in it, which was strengthening, and certain ingredients besides, which might possibly prevent the iron from interfering with other functions of the system. He said he should not be at all surprised if, some day or other, it regained its old fame as a well of healing.

Mr Spelman, in consequence of a talk he had with Hector, having induced

his wife to try it, she also soon began to think it was doing her good.

Beyond these I have now mentioned, no one paid any attention to the

Prior's Well or its renascent reputation.

CHAPTER XVII. HOW WILLIE WENT ON.

As soon as Willie began a new study, he began trying to get at the sense of it. This caused his progress to be slow at first, and him to appear dull amongst those who merely learned by rote; but as he got a hold of the meaning of it all, his progress grew faster and faster, until at length in most studies he outstripped all the rest.

I need hardly repeat that the constant exercise of his mind through his fingers, in giving a second existence outside of him to what had its first existence inside him—that is, in his mind, made it far easier for him to understand the relations of things that go to make up a science. A boy who could put a box together must find Euclid easier—the Second Book particularly—than one who had no idea of the practical relations of the boundaries of spaces; one who could contrive a machine like his water-wheel, must be able to understand the interdependence of the parts of a sentence better than one equally gifted otherwise, but who did not know how one wheel could move another. Everything he did would help his arithmetic, and geography, and history; and these and those and all things besides, would help him to understand poetry.

In his Latin sentences he found the parts fit into each other like dove-tailing; finding the terms of equations, he said, was like inventing machines, and he soon grew clever at solving them. It was not from his manual abilities alone that his father had given him the name of Gutta-Percha Willie, but from the fact that his mind, once warmed to interest, could accommodate itself to the peculiarities of any science, just as the gutta-percha which is used for taking a mould fits itself to the outs and ins of any figure.

He still employed his water-wheel to pull him out of bed in the middle of the night. He had, of course, to make considerable alterations in, or rather additions to, its machinery, after changing his bed-room, for it had then to work in a direction at right angles to the former; but this he managed perfectly.

It is well for Willie's reputation with a certain, and that not a small class of readers, that there was something even they would call useful in several of his inventions and many of his efforts; in his hydraulics, for instance, by means of which he saved old Tibby's limbs; in his house-building, too, by means of which they were able to take in grannie; and, for a long time now, he had been doing every little repair wanted in the house. If a lock went wrong, he would have it off at once and taken to pieces. If less would not do, he carried it to the smithy, but very seldom troubled Mr Willett about it, for he had learned to do small jobs, and to heat and work and temper a piece of iron within his strength as well as any man. His mother did not much like this part of his general apprenticeship, for he would get his hands so black sometimes on a Saturday afternoon that he could not get them clean enough for church the next day; and sometimes he would come home with little holes burnt here and there in his clothes by the sparks from the red-hot iron when beaten on the anvil. Concerning this last evil, she spoke at length to Hector, who made him a leather apron, like Mr Willett's, which thereafter he always wore when he had a job to do in the smithy.

It is well, I say, that the utility of such of his doings as these will be admitted by all; for some other objects upon which he spent much labour would, by most people, be regarded as utterly useless. Few, for instance, would allow there was any value in a water-wheel which could grind no corn, and was of service only to wake him in the middle of the night—not for work, not for the learning of a single lesson, but only that he might stare out of the window for a while, and then get into bed again. For my part, nevertheless, I think it a most useful contrivance. For all lovely sights tend to keep the soul pure, to lift the heart up to God, and above, not merely what people call low cares, but what people would call reasonable cares, although our great Teacher teaches us that such cares are unjust towards our Father in Heaven. More than that, by helping to keep the mind calm and pure, they help to keep the imagination, which is the source of all invention, active, and the judgment, which weighs all its suggestions, just. Whatever is beautiful is of God, and it is only ignorance or a low condition of heart and soul that does not prize what is beautiful. If I had a choice between two mills, one that would set fine dinners on my table, and one that would show me lovely sights in earth and sky and sea, I know which I should count the more useful.

Perhaps there is not so much to be said for the next whim of Willie's; but a part at least of what I have just written will apply to it also.

What put it in his head I am not sure, but I think it was two things together—seeing a soaring lark radiant with the light of the unrisen sun, and finding in a corner of Spelman's shop a large gilt ball which had belonged to an old eight-day clock he had bought. The passage in which he set it up was so low that he had to remove the ornaments from the top of it, but this one was humbled that it might be exalted.

The very sight of it set Willie thinking what he could do with it; for he not only meditated how to do a thing, but sometimes what to make a thing do. Nor was it long ere he made up his mind, and set about a huge kite, more than six feet high—a great strong monster, with a tail of portentous length—to the top of the arch of which he attached the golden ball. Then he bought a quantity of string, and set his wheel to call him up an hour before sunrise.

One morning was too still, another too cloudy, and a third wet; but at last came one clear and cool, with a steady breeze which sent the leaves of the black poplars all one way. He dressed with speed, and, taking his kite and string, set out for a grass field belonging to Farmer Thomson, where he found most of the daisies still buttoned up in sleep, their red tips all together, as tight and close as the lips of a baby that won't take what is offered it—as if they never meant to have anything more to do with the sun, and would never again show him the little golden sun they had themselves inside of them. In a few minutes the kite had begun to soar, slowly and steadily, then faster and faster, until at length it was towering aloft, tugging and pulling at the string, which he could not let out fast enough. He kept looking up after it intently as it rose, when suddenly a new morning star burst out in golden glitter. It was the gilt ball; it saw the sun. The glory which, striking on the heart of the lark, was there transmuted into song, came back from the ball, after its kind, in glow and gleam. He danced with delight, and shouted and sang his welcome to the resurrection of the sun, as he watched his golden ball alone in the depth of the air.

He never thought of any one hearing him, nor was it likely that any one in the village would be up yet. He was therefore a good deal surprised when he heard the sweet voice of Mona Shepherd behind him; and turning, saw her running to him bare-headed, with her hair flying in the wind.

"Willie! Willie!" she was crying, half-breathless with haste and the buffeting of the breeze.

"Well, Mona, who would have thought of seeing you out so early?"

"Mayn't a girl get up early, as well as a boy? It's not like climbing walls and trees, you know, though I can't see the harm of that either."

"No more can I," said Willie, "if they're not too difficult, you know.

But what brought you out now? Do you want me?"

"Mayn't I stop with you? I saw you looking up, and I looked up too, and then I saw something flash; and I dressed as hard as I could, and ran out. Are you catching the lightning?"

"No," said Willie; "something better than the lightning—the sunlight."

"Is that all?" said Mona, disappointed.

"Why, Mona, isn't the sunlight a better thing than the lightning?" said philosophical Willie.

"Yes, I dare say; but you can have it any time."

"That only makes it the more valuable. But it's not quite true when you think of it. You can't have it now, except from my ball."

"Oh, yes, I can," cried Mona; "for there he comes himself."

And there, to be sure, was the first blinding arc of the sun rising over the eastern hill. Both of them forgot the kite, and turned to watch the great marvel of the heavens, throbbing and pulsing like a sea of flame. When they turned again to the kite they could see the golden ball no longer. Its work was over; it had told them the sun was coming, and now, when the sun was come, it was not wanted any more. Willie began to draw in his string and roll it up on its stick, slowly pulling down to the earth the soaring sun-scout he had sent aloft for the news. He had never flown anything like such a large kite before, and he found it difficult to reclaim.

"Will you take me out with you next time, Willie?" asked Mona, pleadingly. "I do so like to be out in the morning, when the wind is blowing, and the clouds are flying about. I wonder why everybody doesn't get up to see the sun rise. Don't you think it is well worth seeing?"

"That I do."

"Then you will let me come with you? I like it so much better when you are with me. Janet spoils it all."

Janet was her old nurse, who seemed to think the main part of her duty was to check Mona's enthusiasm.

"I will," said Willie, "if your papa has no objection."

Mona did not even remember her mamma. She had died when she was such a little thing.

"Come and ask him, then," said Mona.

So soon as he had secured Sun-scout, as he called his kite with the golden head, she took his hand to lead him to her father.

"He won't be up yet," said Willie.

"Oh, yes, long ago," cried Mona. "He's always up first in the house, and as soon as he's dressed he calls me. He'll be at breakfast by this time, and wondering what can have become of me."

So Willie went with her, and there was Mr Shepherd, as she had said, already seated at breakfast.

"What have you been about, Mona, my child?" he asked, as soon as he had shaken hands with Willie.

"We've been helping the sun to rise," said Mona, merrily.

"No, no," said Willie; "we've only been having a peep at him in bed,

271

before he got up."

"Oh, yes," chimed in Mona. "And he was so fast asleep!—and snoring," she added, with a comical expression and tone, as if it were a thing not to be mentioned save as a secret.

But Willie did not like the word, and her father was of the same mind.

"No, no," said Mr Shepherd; "that's not respectful, Mona. I don't like you to talk that way, even in fun, of the great light of the earth. There are more good reasons for objecting to it than you would quite understand yet. Willie would not talk like that, I am sure. Tell me what you have been about, my boy."

Willie explained the whole matter, and asked if he might call Mona the next time he went out with his kite in the morning.

Mr Shepherd consented at once; and Mona said he had only to call from his window into their garden, and she would be sure to hear him even if she was asleep.

The next thing Willie did was to construct a small windlass in the garden, with which to wind up or let out the string of the kite; and when the next fit morning arrived, Mona and he went out together. The wind blowing right through the garden, they did not go to the open field, but sent up the kite from the windlass, and Mona was able by means of the winch to let out the string, while Willie kept watching for the moment when the golden ball should catch the light. They did the same for several mornings after, and Willie managed, with the master's help, to calculate exactly the height to which the ball had flown when first it gained a peep of the sun in bed.

One windy evening they sent the kite up in the hope that it would fly till the morning; but the wind fell in the night, and when the sun came near there was no golden ball in the air to greet him. So, instead of rejoicing in its glitter far aloft, they had to set out, guided by the string, to find the fallen Lucifer. The kite was of small consequence, but the golden ball Willie could not replace. Alas! that very evening he had added a great length of string—so much, that when the wind ceased the kite could just reach the river, into which it fell; and when the searchers at length drew Sun-scout from the water they found his glory had departed; the golden ball had been beaten and ground upon the stones of the stream, and never more did they send him climbing up the heavens to welcome the lord of day.

Indeed, it was many years before Willie flew a kite again, for, after a certain conversation with his grandmother, he began to give a good deal more time to his lessons than hitherto; and while his recreations continued to be all of a practical sort, his reading was mostly such as prepared him for college.

CHAPTER XVIII. WILLIE'S TALK WITH HIS GRANDMOTHER.

One evening in winter, when he had been putting coals on his grannie's fire, she told him to take a chair beside her, as she wanted a little talk with him. He obeyed her gladly.

"Well, Willie," she said, "what would you like to be?"

Willie had just been helping to shoe a horse at the smithy, and, in fact, had driven one of the nails—an operation perilous to the horse. Full of the thing which had last occupied him, he answered without a moment's hesitation—

"I should like to be a blacksmith, grannie."

The old lady smiled. She had seen more black on Willie's hands than could have come from the coals, and judged from that and his answer that he had just come from the smithy.

An unwise grandmother, had she wished to turn him from the notion, would have started an objection at once—probably calling it a dirty trade, or a dangerous trade, or a trade that the son of a professional man could not be allowed to follow; but Willie's grandmother knew better, and went on talking about the thing in the quietest manner.

"It's a fine trade," she said; "thorough manly work, and healthy,

I believe, notwithstanding the heat. But why would you take to it,

Willie?"

Willie fell back on his principles, and thought for a minute.

"Of course, if I'm to be any good at all I must have a hand in what

Hector calls the general business of the universe, grannie."

"To be sure; and that, as a smith, you would have; but why should you choose to be a smith rather than anything else in the world?"

"Because—because—people can't get on without horse-shoes, and ploughs and harrows, and tires for cart-wheels, and locks, and all that. It would help people very much if I were a smith."

"I don't doubt it. But if you were a mason you could do quite as much to make them comfortable; you could build them houses."

"Yes, I could. It would be delightful to build houses for people. I should like that."

"It's very hard work," said his grandmother. "Only you wouldn't mind that, I know, Willie."

"No man minds hard work," said Willie. "I think I should like to be a mason; for then, you see, I should be able to look at what I had done. The ploughs and carts would go away out of sight, but the good houses would stand where I had built them, and I should be able to see how comfortable the people were in them. I should come nearer to the people themselves that way with my work. Yes, grannie, I would rather be a mason than a smith."

"A carpenter fits up the houses inside," said his grandmother. "Don't you think, with his work, he comes nearer the people that live in it than the mason does?"

"To be sure," cried Willie, laughing. "People hardly see the mason's work, except as they're coming up to the door. I know more about carpenter's work too. Yes, grannie, I have settled now; I'll be a carpenter—there!" cried Willie, jumping up from his seat. "If it hadn't been for Mr Spelman, I don't see how we could have had you with us, grannie. Think of that!"

"Only, if you had been a tailor or a shoemaker, you would have come still nearer to the people themselves."

"I don't know much about tailoring," returned Willie. "I could stitch well enough, but I couldn't cut out. I could soon be a shoemaker, though. I've done everything wanted in a shoe or a boot with my own hands already; Hector will tell you so. I could begin to be a shoemaker to-morrow. That is nearer than a carpenter. Yes."

"I was going to suggest," said his grannie, "that there's a kind of work that goes yet nearer to the people it helps than any of those. But, of course, if you've made up your mind"—

"Oh no, grannie! I don't mean it so much as that—if there's a better way, you know. Tell me what it is."

"I want you to think and find out."

Willie thought, looked puzzled, and said he couldn't tell what it was.

"Then you must think a little longer," said his grandmother. "And now go and wash your hands."

CHAPTER XIX. A TALK WITH Mr SHEPHERD.

In a few minutes Willie came rushing back from his room, with his hands and face half wet and half dry.

"Grannie! grannie!" he panted—"what a stupid I am! How can a body be so stupid! Of course you mean a doctor's work! My father comes nearer to people to help them than anybody else can—and yet I never thought what you meant. How is it you can know a thing and not know it at the same moment?"

"Well, now you've found what I meant, what do you think of it?" said his grandmother.

"Why, of course, it's the best of all. When I was a little fellow, I used to think I should be a doctor some day, but I don't feel quite so sure of it now. Do you really think, grannie, I could be a doctor like papa? You see that wants such a good head—and—and—everything."

"Yes; it does want a good head and everything. But you've got a good enough head to begin with, and it depends on yourself to make it a better one. So long as people's hearts keep growing better, their heads do the same. I think you have every faculty for the making of a good doctor in you."

"Do you really think so, grannie?" cried Willie, delighted.

"I do indeed."

"Then I shall ask papa to teach me."

But Willie did not find his papa quite ready to take him in hand.

"No, Willie," he said. "You must learn a great many other things before it would be of much use for me to commence my part. I will teach you if you like, after school-hours, to compound certain medicines; but the important thing is to get on at school. You are quite old enough now to work at home too; and though I don't want to confine you to your lessons, I should like you to spend a couple of hours at them every evening. You can have the remainders of the evenings, all the mornings before breakfast, and the greater parts of your half-holidays, for whatever you like to do of another sort."

Willie never required any urging to what his father wished. He became at once more of a student, without becoming much less of a workman—for he found plenty of time to do all he wanted, by being more careful of his odd moments.

One lovely evening in spring, when the sun had gone down and left the air soft, and balmy, and full of the scents which rise from the earth after a shower, and the odours of the buds which were swelling and bursting in all directions, Willie was standing looking out of his open window into the parson's garden, when Mr Shepherd saw him and called to him—

"Come down here, Willie," he said. "I want to have a little talk with you."

Willie got on the wall from the top of his stair, dropped into the stable-yard, which served for the parson's pony as well as the Doctor's two horses, and thence passed into Mr Shepherd's garden, where the two began to walk up and down together.

The year was like a child waking up from a sleep into which he had fallen crying. Its life was returning to it, fresh and new. It was as if God were again drawing nigh to His world. All the winter through He had never left it, only had, as it were, been rolling it along the path before Him; but now had taken it up in His hand, and was carrying it for a while; and that was how its birds were singing so sweetly, and its buds were coming so blithely out of doors, and the wind blew so soft, and the rain fell so repentantly, and the earth sent up such a gracious odour.

"The year is coming to itself again, Willie—growing busy once more," Mr

Shepherd said.

"Yes," answered Willie. "It's been all but dead, and has come to life again. It must have had the doctor to it."

"Eh? What doctor, Willie?"

"Well, you know, there is but One that could be doctor to this big world."

"Yes, surely," returned Mr Shepherd. "And that brings me to what I wanted to talk to you about. I hear your father means to make a doctor of you."

"Yes. Isn't it good of him?" said Willie.

"Then you would like it?"

"Yes; that I should!"

"Why would you like it?"

"Because I must have a hand in the general business."

"What do you mean by that?"

Willie set forth Hector Macallaster's way of thinking about such matters.

"Very good—very good indeed!" remarked Mr Shepherd. "But why, then, should you prefer being a doctor to being a shoemaker? Is it because you will get better paid for it?"

"I never thought of that," returned Willie. "Of course I should be better paid—for Hector couldn't keep a horse, and a horse I must have, else some of my patients would be dead before I could get to them. But that's not why I want to be a doctor. It's because I want to help people."

"What makes you want to help people?"

"Because it's the best thing you can do with yourself."

"Who told you that?"

"I don't know. It seems as if everybody and everything had been teaching me that, ever since I can remember."

"Well, it's no wonder it should seem as if everything taught you that, seeing that is what God is always doing—and what Jesus taught us as the law of His kingdom—which is the only real kingdom—namely, that the greatest man in it is he who gives himself the most to help other people. It was because Jesus Himself did so—giving Himself up utterly—that God has so highly exalted Him and given Him a name above every name. And, indeed, if you are a good doctor, you will be doing something of what Jesus did when He was in the world."

"Yes; but He didn't give people medicine to cure them."

"No; that wasn't necessary, because He was Himself the cure. But now that He is not present with His bodily presence—now, medicine and advice and other good things are just the packets in which He wraps up the healing He sends; and the wisest doctor is but the messenger who carries to the sick as much of healing and help as the Great Doctor sees fit to send. For He is so anxious to cure thoroughly that in many cases He will not cure all at once."

"How I should like to take His healing about!" cried Willie—"just as the doctors' boys take the medicines about in baskets: grannie tells me they do in the big towns. I should like to be the Great Doctor's boy!"

"You really think then," Mr Shepherd resumed, after a pause, "that a doctor's is the best way of helping people?"

"Yes, I do," answered Willie, decidedly. "A doctor, you see, comes nearest to them with his help. It's not the outside of a man's body he helps, but his inside health—how he feels, you know."

Mr Shepherd again thought for a few moments. At length he said—

"What's the difference between your father's work and mine?"

"A great difference, of course," replied Willie.

"Tell me then what it is?"

"I must think before I can do that," said Willie. "It's not so easy to put things in words!—You very often go to help the same people: that's something to start with."

"But not to give them the same help."

"No, not quite. And yet"—

"At least, I cannot write prescriptions or compound medicines for them, seeing I know nothing about such things," said Mr Shepherd. "But, on the other hand, though I can't give them medicine out of your papa's basket, your papa very often gives them medicine out of mine."

"That's a riddle, I suppose," said Willie.

"No, it's not. How is it your papa can come so near people to help them?"

"He gives them things that make them well again."

"What do they do with the things he gives them?"

"They take them."

"How?"

"Put them in their mouths and swallow them."

"Couldn't they take them at their ears?"

"No," answered Willie, laughing.

"Why not?"

"Because their ears aren't meant for taking them."

"Aren't their ears meant for taking anything, then?"

"Only words."

"Well, if one were to try, mightn't words be mixed so as to be medicine?"

"I don't see how."

"If you were to take a few strong words, a few persuasive words, and a few tender words, mightn't you mix them so—that is, so set them in order—

as to make them a good medicine for a sore heart, for instance?"

"Ah! I see, I see! Yes, the medicine for the heart must go in at the ears."

"Not necessarily. It might go in at the eyes. Jesus gave it at the eyes, for doubting hearts, when He said—Consider the lilies,—consider the ravens."

"At the ears, too, though," said Willie; "just as papa sometimes gives a medicine to be taken and to be rubbed in both."

"Only the ears could have done nothing with the words if the eyes hadn't taken in the things themselves first. But where does this medicine go to, Willie?"

"I suppose it must go to the heart, if that's the place wants healing."

"Does it go to what a doctor would call the heart, then?"

"No, no; it must go to what—to what a clergyman—to what you call the heart."

"And which heart is nearer to the person himself?"

Willie thought for a moment, then answered, merrily—the doctor's heart, to be sure!"

"No, Willie; you're wrong there," said Mr Shepherd, looking, as he felt, a little disappointed.

"Oh yes, please!" said Willie; "I'm almost sure I'm right this time."

"No, Willie; what the clergyman calls the heart is the nearest to the man himself."

"No, no," persisted Willie. "The heart you've got to do with is the man himself. So of course the doctor's heart is the nearer to the man."

Mr Shepherd laughed a low, pleasant laugh.

"You're quite right, Willie. You've got the best of it. I'm very pleased. But then, Willie, doesn't it strike you that after all there might be a closer way of helping men than the doctor's way?"

Again Willie thought a while.

"There would be," he said, at length, "if you could give them medicine to make them happy when they are miserable."

"Even the doctor can do a little at that," returned Mr Shepherd; "for when in good health people are much happier than when they are ill."

"If you could give them what would make them good when they are bad then," said Willie.

"Ah, there you have it!" rejoined Mr Shepherd. "That is the very closest way of helping men."

"But nobody can do that—nobody can make a bad man good—but God," said

Willie.

"Certainly. But He uses medicines; and He sends people about with them, just like the doctors' boys you were speaking of. What else am I here for? I've been carrying His medicines about for a good many years now."

"Then your work and not my father's comes nearest to people to help them after all! My father's work, I see, doesn't help the very man himself; it only helps his body—or at best his happiness: it doesn't go deep enough to touch himself. But yours helps the very man. Yours is the best after all."

"I don't know," returned Mr Shepherd, thoughtfully. "It depends, I think, on the kind of preparation gone through."

"Oh yes!" said Willie. "You had to go through the theological classes. I must of course take the medical."

"That's true, but it's not true enough," said Mr Shepherd. "That wouldn't make a fraction of the difference I mean. There's just one preparation essential for a man who would carry about the best sort of medicines. Can you think what it is? It's not necessary for the other sort."

"The man must be good," said Willie. "I suppose that's it."

"That doesn't make the difference exactly," returned Mr Shepherd. "It is as necessary for a doctor to be good as for a parson."

"Yes," said Willie; "but though the doctor were a bad man, his medicines might be good."

"Not by any means so likely to be!" said the parson. "You can never be sure that anything a bad man has to do with will be good. It may be, because no man is all bad; but you can't be sure of it. We are coming nearer it now. Mightn't the parson's medicines be good if he were bad just as well as the doctor's?"

"Less likely still, I think," said Willie. "The words might be all of the right sort, but they would be like medicines that had lain in his drawers or stood in his bottles till the good was all out of them."

"You're coming very near to the difference of preparation I wanted to point out to you," said Mr Shepherd. "It is this: that the physician of men's selves, commonly called souls, must have taken and must keep taking the medicine he carries about with him; while the less the doctor wants of his the better."

"I see, I see," cried Willie, whom a fitting phrase, or figure, or form of expressing a thing, pleased as much as a clever machine—"I see! It's all right! I understand now."

"But," Mr Shepherd went on, "your father carries about both sorts of medicines in his basket. He is such a healthy man that I believe he very seldom uses any of his own medicines; but he is always taking some of the other sort, and that's what makes him fit to carry them about. He does far more good among the sick than I can. Many who don't like my medicine, will yet take a little of it when your father mixes it with his, as he has a wonderful art in doing. I hope, when your turn comes, you will be able to help the very man himself, as your father does."

"Do you want me to be a doctor of your kind, Mr Shepherd?"

"No. It is a very wrong thing to take up that basket without being told by Him who makes the medicine. If He wants a man to do so, He will let him know—He will call him and tell him to do it. But everybody ought to take the medicine, for everybody needs it; and the happy thing is, that, as soon as anyone has found how good it is—food and wine and all upholding things in one—he becomes both able and anxious to give it to others. If you would help people as much as your father does, you must begin by taking some of the real medicine yourself."

This conversation gave Willie a good deal to think about. And he had much need to think about it, for soon after this he left his father's house for the first time in his life, and went to a great town, to receive there a little further preparation for college. The next year he gained a scholarship, or, as they call it there, a bursary, and was at once fully occupied with classics and mathematics, hoping, however, the next year, to combine with them certain scientific studies bearing less indirectly upon the duties of the medical man.

CHAPTER XX. HOW WILLIE DID HIS BEST TO MAKE A BIRD OF AGNES.

During the time he was at college, he did often think of what Mr Shepherd had said to him. When he was tempted to any self-indulgence, the thought would always rise that this was not the way to become able to help people, especially the real selves of them; and, when amongst the medical students, he could not help thinking how much better doctors some of them would make if they would but try the medicine of the other basket for themselves. He thought this especially when he saw that they cared nothing for their patients, neither had any desire to take a part in the general business for the work's sake, but only wanted a practice that they might make a living. For such are nearly as unfit to be healers of the body, as mere professional clergymen to be healers of broken hearts and wounded minds. To do a man good in any way, you must sympathise with him—that is, know what he feels, and reflect the feeling in your own mirror; and to be a good doctor, one must love to heal; must honour the art of the physician and rejoice in it; must give himself to it, that he may learn all of it that he can—from its root of love to its branches of theory, and its leaves and fruits of healing.

He always came home to Priory Leas for the summer intervals, when you may be sure there was great rejoicing—loudest on the part of Agnes, who was then his constant companion, as much so, at least, as she was allowed. Willie saw a good deal of Mona Shepherd also, who had long been set free from the oppressive charge of Janet, and was now under the care of a governess, a wise, elderly lady; and as she was a great friend of Mrs Macmichael, the two families were even more together now than they had been in former years.

Of course, while at college he had no time to work with his hands: all his labour there must be with his head; but when he came home he had plenty of time for both sorts. He spent a couple of hours before breakfast in the study of physiology; after breakfast, another hour or two either in the surgery, or in a part of the ruins which he had roughly fitted up for a laboratory with a bench, a few shelves, and a furnace. His father, however, did not favour his being in the latter for a long time together; for young experimenters are commonly careless, and will often neglect proper precautions—breathing, for instance, many gases they ought not to breathe. He was so careful over Agnes, however, that often he would not let her in at all; and when he did, he generally confined himself to her amusement. He would show her such lovely things!—for instance, liquids that changed from one gorgeous hue to another; bubbles that burst into flame, and ascended in rings of white revolving smoke; light so intense, that it seemed to darken the daylight. Sometimes Mona would be of the party, and nothing pleased Agnes or her better than such wonderful things as these; while Willie found it very amusing to hear Agnes, who was sharp enough to pick up not a few of the chemical names, dropping the big words from her lips as if she were on the most familiar terms with the things they signified—phosphuretted hydrogen, metaphosphoric acid, sesquiferrocyanide of iron, and such like.

Then he would give an hour to preparation for the studies of next term; after which, until their early dinner, he would work at his bench or turning-lathe, generally at something for his mother or grandmother; or he would do a little mason-work amongst the ruins, patching and strengthening, or even buttressing, where he thought there was most danger of further fall—for he had resolved that, if he could help it, not another stone should come to the ground.

In this, his first summer at home from college, he also fitted up a small forge—in a part of the ruins where there was a wide chimney, whose vent ran up a long way unbroken. Here he constructed a pair of great bellows, and set up an old anvil, which he bought for a trifle from Mr Willett; and here his father actually trusted him to shoe his horses; nor did he ever find a nail of Willie's driving require to be drawn before the shoe had to give place to a new one.

In the afternoon, he always read history, or tales, or poetry; and in the evening did whatever he felt inclined to do—which brings me to what occupied him the last hours of the daylight, for a good part of this first summer.

One lovely evening in June, he came upon Agnes, who was now eight years old, lying under the largest elm of a clump of great elms and Scotch firs at the bottom of the garden. They were the highest trees in all the neighbourhood, and his father was very fond of them. To look up into those elms in the summer time your eyes seemed to lose their way in a mist of leaves; whereas the firs had only great, bony, bare, gaunt arms, with a tuft of bristles here and there. But when a ray of the setting sun alighted upon one of these firs it shone like a flamingo. It seemed as if the surly old tree and the gracious sunset had some secret between them, which, as often as they met, broke out in ruddy flame.

Now Agnes was lying on the thin grass under this clump of trees, looking up into their mystery—and—what else do you think she was doing?—She was sucking her thumb—her custom always when she was thoughtful; and thoughtful she seemed now, for the tears were in her eyes.

"What is the matter with my pet?" said Willie.

But instead of jumping up and flinging her arms about him, she only looked at him, gave a little sigh, drew her thumb from her mouth, pointed with it up into the tree, and said, "I can't get up there! I wish I was a bird," and put her thumb in her mouth again.

"But if you were a bird, you wouldn't be a girl, you know, and you wouldn't like that," said Willie—"at least I shouldn't like it."

"I shouldn't mind. I would rather have wings and fly about in the trees."

"If you had wings you couldn't have arms."

"I'd rather have wings."

"If you were a bird up there, you would be sure to wish you were a girl down here. For if you were a bird you couldn't lie in the grass and look up into the tree."

"Oh yes, I could."

"What a comical little bird you would look then—lying on your little round feathery back, with wings spread out to keep you from rolling over,

288

and little sparkling eyes, one on each side of such a long beak, staring up into the tree!—Miaw! Miaw! Here comes the cat to eat you up!"

Agnes sprang to her feet in terror, and rushed to Willie. She had so fully fancied herself a bird that the very mention of the cat had filled her with horror. Once more she took her thumb from her mouth to give a little scream, and did not put it in again.

"O Willie! you frightened me so!" she said—joining, however, in his laugh.

"Poor birdie!" said Willie. "Did the naughty puss frighten it? Stwoke its fedders den.—Stwoke it—stwoke it," he continued, smoothing down her hair.

"But wouldn't it be nice," persisted Agnes, "to be so tall as the birds can make themselves with their wings? Fancy having your head up there in the green leaves—so cool! and hearing them all whisper, whisper, about your ears, and being able to look down on people's heads, you know, Willie! I do wish I was a bird! I do!"

But with Willie to comfort and play with her, she soon forgot her soaring ambition. Willie, however, did not forget it. If Agnes wished to enjoy the privacy of the leaves up in the height of the trees, why shouldn't she? At least, why shouldn't she if he could help her to it. Certainly he couldn't change her arms into wings, or cover her with feathers, or make her bones hollow so that the air might get all through her, even into her quills; but he could get her up into the tree, and even something more, perhaps. He would see about it—that is, he would think about it, for how it was to be done he did not yet see.

Long ago, almost the moment he arrived, he had set his wheel in order, and got his waking-machine into working trim. And now more than ever he enjoyed being pulled out of bed in the middle of the night—especially in the fine weather; for then, in that hushed hour when the night is just melting into the morn, and the earth looks as if she were losing her dreams, yet had not begun to recognise her own thoughts, he would not unfrequently go out into the garden, and wander about for a few thoughtful minutes.

The same night, when his wheel pulled him, he rose and went out into the garden. The night was at odds with morning which was which. An occasional bat would flit like a doubtful shadow across his eyes, but a cool breath of air was roaming about as well, which was not of the night at all, but plainly belonged to the morning. He wandered to the bottom of the garden—to the clump of trees, lay down where Agnes had been lying the night before, and thought and thought until he felt in himself how the child had felt when she longed to be a bird. What could he do to content her? He knew every bough of the old trees himself, having scrambled over them like a squirrel scores of times; but even if he could get Agnes up the bare bole of an elm or fir, he could not trust her to go scrambling about the branches. On the other hand, wherever he could go, he could surely somehow help Agnes to go. Having gathered a thought or two, he went back to bed.

The very next evening he set to work and spent the whole of that and the following at his bench, planing, and shaping, and generally preparing for a construction, the plan of which was now clear in his head. At length, on the third evening, he carried half a dozen long poles, and wheeled several barrowfuls of short planks, measuring but a few inches over two feet, down to the clump of trees.

At the foot of the largest elm he began to dig, with the intention of inserting the thick end of one of the poles; but he soon found it impossible to get half deep enough, because of the tremendous roots of the tree, and giving it up, thought of a better plan.

He set off to the smithy, and bought of Mr Willett some fifteen feet of iron rod, with a dozen staples. Carrying them home to his small forge, he cut the rod into equal lengths of a little over two feet, and made a hook at both ends of each length. Then he carried them down to the elm, and drove six of the staples into the bole of the tree at equal distances all round it, a foot from the ground; the others he drove one into each of the six poles, a foot from the thick end; after which he connected the poles with the tree, each by a hooked rod and its corresponding staples, when the tops of the poles just reached to the first fork of the elm. Then he nailed a bracket to the tree, at the height of an easy step from the ground, and at the same height nailed a piece of wood across between two of the poles. Resting on the bracket and this piece of wood, he laid the first step of a stair, and fastened it firmly to both. Another bracket a little higher, and another piece of wood nailed to two poles, raised the next step; and so he went round and round the tree in an ascending spiral, climbing on the steps already placed to fix others above them. Encircling the tree some four or five times, for he wanted the ascent easy for little feet, he was at length at its fork. There he laid a platform or landing-place, and paused to consider what to do next. This was on the third evening from the laying of the first step.

From the fork many boughs rose and spread—amongst them two very near each other, between which he saw how, by help of various inequalities, he might build a little straight staircase leading up into a perfect wilderness of leaves and branches. He set about it at once, and, although he found it more difficult than he had expected, succeeded at last in building a safe stair between the boughs, with a hand-rail of rope on each side.

But Willie had chosen to ascend in this direction for another reason as well: one of these boughs was in close contact with a bough belonging to one of the largest of the red firs. On this fir-bough he constructed a landing-place, upon which it was as easy as possible to step from the stair in the elm. Next, the bough being very large, he laid along it a plank steadied by blocks underneath—a level for the little feet. Then he began to weave a network of rope and string along each side of the bough, so that the child could not fall off; but finding this rather a long job, and thinking it a pity to balk her of so much pleasure merely for the sake of surprising her the more thoroughly, he resolved to reveal what he had already done, and permit her to enjoy it.

For, as I ought to have mentioned sooner, he had taken Mona into his confidence, and she had kept Agnes out of the way for now nearly a whole week of evenings. But she was finding it more and more difficult to restrain her from rushing off in search of Willie, and was very glad indeed when he told her that he was not going to keep the thing a secret any longer.

CHAPTER XXI. HOW AGNES LIKED BEING A BIRD.

But Willie began to think whether he might not give Agnes two surprises out of it, with a dream into the bargain, and thought over it until he saw how he could manage it.

She always went to bed at seven o'clock, so that by the time the other people in the house began to think of retiring, she was generally fast asleep. About ten o'clock, therefore, the next night, just as a great round moon was peering above the horizon, with a quantity of mackerel clouds ready to receive her when she rose a yard or two higher, Willie, taking a soft shawl of his mother's, went into Agnes's room, and having wrapped her in the shawl, with a corner of it over her head and face, carried her out into the garden, down to the trees, and up the stair into the midst of the great boughs and branches of the elm tree. It was a very warm night, with a soft breath of south wind blowing, and there was no risk of her taking cold. He uncovered her face, but did not wake her, leaving that to the change of her position and the freshness of the air.

Nor was he disappointed. In a few moments she began to stir, then half-opened her eyes, then shut them, then opened them again, then rubbed them, then drew a deep breath, and then began to lift her head from Willie's shoulder, and look about her. Through the thick leaves the moon was shining like a great white fire, and must have looked to her sleepy eyes almost within a yard of her. Even if she had not been half asleep, so beheld through the leaves, it would have taken her a while to make up her mind what the huge bright thing was. Then she heard a great fluttering as if the leaves were talking to her, and out of them came a soft wind that blew in her face, and felt very sweet and pleasant. She rubbed her eyes again, but could not get the sleep out of them. As last she said to Willie, who stood as still as a stone—but her tongue and her voice and her lips could hardly make the words she wanted them to utter:

"Am I awake? Am I dreaming? It's so nice!"

Willie did not answer her, and the little head sunk on his shoulder again. He drew the corner of the shawl over it, and carried her back to her bed. When he had laid her down, she opened her eyes wide, stared him in the face for a moment, as if she knew all about everything except just what she was looking at, put her thumb in her mouth, and was fast asleep.

The next morning at breakfast, her papa out, and her mamma not yet come down, she told Willie that she had had such a beautiful dream!—that an angel, with great red wings, came and took her in his arms, and flew up and up with her to a cloud that lay close by the moon, and there stopped. The cloud was made all of little birds that kept fluttering their wings and talking to each other, and the fluttering of their wings made a wind in her face, and the wind made her very happy, and the moon kept looking through the birds quite close to them, and smiling at her, and she saw the face of the man in the moon quite plain. But then it grew dark and began to thunder, and the angel went down very fast, and the thunder was the clapping of his big red wings, and he flew with her into her mamma's room, and laid her down in her crib, and when she looked at him he was so like Willie.

"Do you think the dream could have come of your wishing to be a bird, Agnes?" asked Willie.

"I don't know. Perhaps," replied Agnes. "Are you angry with me for wishing I was a bird, Willie?"

"No, darling. What makes you ask such a question?"

"Because ever since then you won't let me go with you—when you are doing things, you know."

"Why, you were in the laboratory with me yesterday!" said Willie.

"Yes, but you wouldn't have me in the evening when you used to let me be with you always. What are you doing down amongst the trees always now?"

"If you will have patience and not go near them all day, I will show you in the evening."

Agnes promised; and Willie gave the whole day to getting things on a bit. Amongst other things he wove such a network along the bough of the Scotch fir, that it was quite safe for Agnes to walk on it down to the great red hole of the tree. There he was content to make a pause for the present, constructing first, however, a little chair of bough and branch and rope and twig in which she could safely sit.

Just as he had finished the chair, he heard her voice calling, in a tone that grew more and more pitiful.

"Willie!—Willie!—Willie!—Willie!"

He got down and ran to find her. She was at the window of his room, where she had gone to wait till he called her, but her patience had at last given way.

"I'm so tired, Willie! Mayn't I come yet?"

"Wait just one moment more," said Willie, and ran to the house for his mother's shawl.

As soon as he began to wrap it about her, Agnes said, thoughtfully—

"Somebody did that to me before—not long ago—I remember: it was the angel in my dream."

When Willie put the corner over her face, she said, "He did that too!" and when he took her in his arms, she said, "He did that too! How funny you should do just what the angel did in my dream!"

Willie ran about with her here and there through the ruins, into the house, up and down the stairs, and through the garden in many directions, until he was satisfied he must have thoroughly bewildered her as to whereabouts they were, and then at last sped with her up the stair to the fork of the elm-tree. There he threw back the shawl, and told her to look.

To see her first utterly bewildered expression—then the slow glimmering dawn of intelligence, as she began to understand where she was—next the gradual rise of light in her face as if it came there from some spring down below, until it broke out in a smile all over it, when at length she perceived that this was what he had been working at, and why he wouldn't have her with him—gave Willie all the pleasure he had hoped for—quite satisfied him, and made him count his labour well rewarded.

"O Willie! Willie! it was all for me!—Wasn't it now?"

"Yes, it was, pet," said Willie.

"It was all to make a bird of me—wasn't it?" she went on.

"Yes—as much of a bird as I could. I couldn't give you wings, you know, and I hadn't any of my own to fly up with you to the moon, as the angel in your dream did. The dream was much nicer—wasn't it?"

"I'm not sure about that—really I'm not. I think it is nicer to have a wind coming you don't know from where, and making all the leaves flutter about, than to have the wings of birdies making the wind. And I don't care about the man in the moon much. He's not so nice as you, Willie. And yon red ray of the sun through there on the fir-tree is as good nearly as the moon."

"Oh! but you may have the moon, if you wait a bit. She'll be too late to-night, though."

"But now I think of it, Willie," said Agnes, "I do believe it wasn't a dream at all."

"Do you think a real angel carried you really up to the moon, then?" asked Willie.

"No; but a real Willie carried me really up into this tree, and the moon shone through the leaves, and I thought they were birds. You're my angel, Willie, only better to me than twenty hundred angels."

And Agnes threw her arms round his neck and hugged and kissed him.

As soon as he could speak, that is, as soon as she ceased choking him, he said—

"You were up in this tree last night: and the wind was fluttering the

295

leaves; and the moon was shining through them"—

"And you carried me in this shawl, and that was the red wings of the angel," cried Agnes, dancing with delight.

"Yes, pet, I daresay it was. But aren't you sorry to lose your big angel?"

"The angel was only in a dream, and you're here, Willie. Besides, you'll be a big angel some day, Willie, and then you'll have wings, and be able to fly me about."

"But you'll have wings of your own then, and be able to fly without me."

"But I may fold them up sometimes—mayn't I? for it would be much nicer to be carried by your wings—sometimes, you know. Look, look, Willie! Look at the sunbeam on the trunk of the fir—how red it's got. I do wish I could have a peep at the sun. Where can he be? I should see him if I were to go into his beam there—shouldn't I?"

"He's shining past the end of the cottage," said Willie. "Go, and you'll see him."

"Go where?" asked Agnes.

"Into the red sunbeam on the fir-tree."

"I haven't got my wings yet, Willie."

"That's what people very often say when they're not inclined to try what they can do with their legs."

"But I can't go there, Willie."

"You haven't tried."

"How am I to try?"

"You're not even trying to try. You're standing talking, and saying you can't."

It was nearly all Agnes could do to keep from crying. But she felt she must do something more lest Willie should be vexed. There seemed but one way to get nearer to the sunbeam, and that was to go down this tree and run to the foot of the other. What if Willie had made a stair up it also? But as she turned to see how she was to go down, for she had been carried up blind, she caught sight of the straight staircase between the two boughs, and, with a shriek of delight, up she ran.

"Gently, gently! Don't bring the tree down with your tremendous weight," cried Willie, following her close behind.

At the end of the stairs she sprang upon the bough of the fir, and in a moment more was sitting in the full light of the sunset.

"O Willie! Willie! this is grand! How good, how kind of you! You have made a bird of me! What will papa and mamma say? Won't they be delighted? I must run and fetch Mona."

So saying she hurried across again, and down the stair, and away to look for Mona Shepherd, shouting with delight as she ran. In a few minutes her cries had gathered the whole house to the bottom of the garden, as well as Mr Shepherd and Mona and Mrs Hunter. Mr Macmichael and all of them went up into the tree, Mr Shepherd last and with some misgivings; for, having no mechanical faculty himself, he could not rightly value Willie's, and feared that he might not have made the stair safe. But Mr Macmichael soon satisfied him, showing him how strong and firm Willie had made every part of it.

The next evening, Willie went on with his plan, which was to make a way for Bird Agnes from one tree to another over the whole of the clump. It took him many evenings, however, to complete it, and a good many more to construct in the elm tree a thin wooden house cunningly perched upon several of the strongest boughs and branches. He called it Bird Agnes's Nest. It had doors and windows, and several stories in it, only the upper stories did not rest on the lower, but upon higher branches of the tree. To two of these he made stairs, and a rope-ladder to a third. When the house was finished, he put a little table in the largest room, and having got some light chairs from the house, asked his father and mother and grandmother to tea in Bird Agnes's Nest. But grannie declined to go up the tree. She said her climbing days were over long ago.

CHAPTER XXII. WILLIE'S PLANS BUD.

Either they were over, or were only beginning; for, the next winter, while Willie was at college, grannie was taken ill; and although they sent for him to come home at once, she had climbed higher ere he arrived. When they opened her will, they found that she had left everything to Willie. There was more than a hundred pounds in ready money, and property that brought in about fifty pounds a-year—not much to one who would have spent everything on himself, but a good deal to one who loved other people, and for their sakes would contrive that a little should go a long way.

So Willie was henceforth able to relieve his father by paying all his own college expenses. He laid by a little too, as his father wished him, until he should see how best to use it. His father always talked about using never about spending money.

When he came home the next summer, he moved again into his own old room, for Agnes slept in a little closet off her mother's, and much preferred that to a larger and more solitary room for herself. His mother especially was glad to have him under the same roof once more at night. But Willie felt that something ought to be done with the room he had left in the ruins, for nothing ought to be allowed to spoil by uselessness. He did not, however, see for some time to what he could turn it.

I need hardly say that he kept up all his old friendships. No day passed while he was at home without his going to see some one of his former companions—Mr Willett, or Mr Spelman, or Mr Wilson. For Hector, he went to see him oftenest of all, he being his favourite, and sickly, and therefore in most need of attention. But he greatly improved his acquaintance with William Webster; and although he had now so much to occupy him, would not be satisfied until he was able to drive the shuttle, and work the treadles and the batten, and, in short, turn out almost as good a bit of linen as William himself—only he wanted about twice as much time to it.

One day, going in to see Hector, he found him in bed and very poorly.

"My shoemaking is nearly over, Mr Willie," he said. "But I don't mind much; I'm sure to find a corner in the general business ready for me somewhere when I'm not wanted here any more."

"Have you been drinking the water lately?" asked Willie.

"No. I was very busy last week, and hadn't time, and it was rather cold for me to go out. But for that matter the wind blew in through door and window so dreadfully—and it's but a clay floor, and firing is dear—that I caught a cold, and a cold is the worst thing for me—that is for this poor rickety body of mine. And this cold is a bad one."

Here a great fit of coughing came on, accompanied by symptoms that Willie saw were dangerous, and he went home at once to get him some medicine.

On the way back a thought struck him, about which, however, he would say nothing to Hector until he should have talked to his father and mother about it, which he did that same evening at supper.

"I'll tell you what, Hector," he said, when he went to see him the next day—"you must come and occupy my room in the ruins. Since grannie went home I don't want it, and it's a pity to have it lying idle. It's a deal warmer than this, and I'll get a stove in before the winter. You won't have to work so hard when you've got no rent to pay, and you will have as much of the water as you like without the trouble of walking up the hill for it. Then there's the garden for you to walk in when you please—all on a level, and only the little stair to climb to get back to your own room."

"But I should be such a trouble to you all, Mr Willie!"

"You'd be no trouble—we've two servants now. If you like you can give the little one a shilling now and then, and she'll be glad enough to make your bed, and sweep out your room; and you know Tibby has a great regard for you, and will be very glad to do all the cooking you will want—it's not much, I know: your porridge and a cup of tea is about all. And then there's my father to look after your health, and Agnes to amuse you sometimes, and my mother to look after everything, and"—

299

Here poor Hector fairly broke down. When he recovered himself he said—

"But how could gentle folks like you bear to see a hump-backed creature like me crawling about the place?"

"They would only enjoy it the more that you enjoyed it," said Willie.

It was all arranged. As soon as Hector was able to be moved, he was carried up to the Ruins, and there nursed by everybody. Nothing could exceed his comfort now but his gratitude. He was soon able to work again, and as he was evidently happier when doing a little towards the general business, Mr Macmichael thought it best for him.

One day, Willie being at work in his laboratory, and getting himself half-stifled with a sudden fume of chlorine, opened the door for some air just as Hector had passed it. He stood at the door and followed him down the walk with his eyes, watching him as he went—now disappearing behind the blossoms of an apple-tree, now climbing one of the little mounds, and now getting up into the elm-tree, and looking about him on all sides, his sickly face absolutely shining with pleasure.

"But," said Willie all at once to himself, "why should Hector be the only invalid to have this pleasure?"

He found no answer to the question. I don't think he looked for one very hard though. And again, all at once, he said to himself—

"What if this is what my grannie's money was given me for?"

That night he had a dream. The two questions had no doubt a share in giving it him, and perhaps also a certain essay of Lord Bacon—"Of Building," namely—which he had been reading before he went to bed.

He dreamed that, being pulled up in the middle of the night by his wheel, he went down to go into the garden. But the moment he was out of the back door, he fancied there was something strange going on in his room in the ruins—he could not tell what, but he must go and see. When he climbed the stairs and opened the door, there was Hector Macallaster where he ought to be, asleep in his bed. But there was something strange going on; for a stream, which came dashing over the side of the wooden spout, was flowing all round Hector's bed, and then away he knew not whither. Another strange thing was, that in the further wall was a door which was new to him. He opened it, and found himself in another chamber, like his own; and there also lay some one, he knew not who, in a bed, with a stream of water flowing all around it. There was also a second door, beyond which was a third room, and a third patient asleep, and a third stream flowing around the bed, and a third door beyond. He went from room to room, on and on, through about a hundred such, he thought, and at length came to a vaulted chamber, which seemed to be over the well. From the centre of the vault rose a great chimney, and under the chimney was a huge fire, and on the fire stood a mighty golden cauldron, up to which, through a large pipe, came the water of the well, and went pouring in with a great rushing, and hissing, and bubbling. From the other side of the cauldron, the water rushed away through another pipe into the trough that ran through all the chambers, and made the rivers that flowed the beds of the sleeping patients. And what was most wonderful of all—by the fire stood two angels, with grand lovely wings, and they made a great fanning with their wings, and so blew the fire up loud and strong about the golden cauldron. And when Willie looked into their faces, he saw that one of them was his father, and the other Mr Shepherd. And he gave a great cry of delight, and woke weeping.

CHAPTER XXIII. WILLIE'S PLANS BLOSSOM.

In the morning, Willie's head was full of his dream. How gladly would he have turned it into a reality! That was impossible—but might he not do something towards it? He had long ago seen that those who are doomed not to realise their ideal, are just those who will not take the first step towards it. "Oh! this is such a little thing to do, it can't be any use!" they say. "And it's such a distance off what I mean, and what I should give my life to have!" They think and they say that they would give their life for it, and yet they will not give a single hearty effort. Hence they just stop where they are, or rather go back and back until they do not care a bit for the thoughts they used to think so great that they cherished them for the glory of having thought them. But even the wretched people who set their hearts on making money, begin by saving the first penny they can, and then the next and the next. And they have their reward: they get the riches they want—with the loss of their souls to be sure, but that they did not think of. The people on the other hand who want to be noble and good, begin by taking the first thing that comes to their hand and doing that right, and so they go on from one thing to another, growing better and better.

In the same way, although it would have been absurd in Willie to rack his brain for some scheme by which to restore such a grand building as the Priory, he could yet bethink himself that the hundredth room did not come next the first, neither did the third; the one after the first was the second, and he might do something towards the existence of that.

He went out immediately after breakfast, and began peering about the ruins to see where the second room might be. To his delight he saw that, with a little contrivance, it could be built on the other side of the wall of Hector's room.

He had plenty of money for it, his grannie's legacy not being yet touched. He thought it all over himself, talked it all over with his father, and then consulted it all over with Spelman. The end was, that without nearly spending his little store, he had, before the time came for his return to the college, built another room.

As the garret was full of his grandmother's furniture, nothing was easier than to fit it up—and that very nicely too. It remained only to find an occupant for it. This would have been easy enough also without going far from the door, but both Willie and his father were practical men, and therefore could not be content with merely doing good: they wanted to do as much good as they could. It would not therefore satisfy them to put into their new room such a person—say, as Mrs Wilson, who could get on pretty well where she was, though she might have been made more comfortable. But suppose they could find the sickly mother of a large family, whom a few weeks of change, with the fine air from the hills and the wonderful water from the Prior's well, would restore to strength and cheerfulness, how much more good would they not be doing in that way—seeing that to help a mother with children is to help all the children as well, not to mention the husband and the friends of the family! There were plenty such to be found amongst the patients he had to attend while at college. The expense of living was not great at Priory Leas, and Mr MacMichael was willing to bear that, if only to test the influences of the water and climate upon strangers.

Although it was not by any means the best season for the experiment, it was yet thoroughly successful with the pale rheumatic mother of six, whom Willie first sent home to his father's care. She returned to her children at Christmas, comparatively a hale woman, capable of making them and everybody about her twice as happy as before. Another as nearly like her in bodily condition and circumstances as he could find, took her place,—with a like result; and before long the healing that hovered about Priory Leas began to be known and talked of amongst the professors of the college, and the medical men of the city.

CHAPTER XXIV. WILLIE'S PLANS BEAR FRUIT.

When his studies were finished, Willie returned to assist his father, for he had no desire to settle in a great city with the ambition of becoming a fashionable doctor getting large fees and growing rich. He regarded the end of life as being, in a large measure, just to take his share in the general business.

By this time the reputation of the Prior's Well had spread on all sides, and the country people had begun to visit the Leas, and stay for a week or ten days to drink of the water. Indeed so many kept coming and going at all hours through the garden, that the MacMichaels at length found it very troublesome, and had a small pipe laid to a little stone trough built into the garden wall on the outside, so that whoever would might come and drink with less trouble to all concerned.

But Willie had come home with a new idea in his head.

An old valetudinarian in the city, who knew every spa in Europe, wanted to try that of Priory Leas and had consulted him about it. Finding that there was no such accommodation to be had as he judged suitable, he seriously advised Willie to build a house fit for persons of position, as he called them, assuring him that they would soon make their fortunes if they did. Now although, as I have said, this was not the ambition of either father or son, for a fortune had never seemed to either worth taking trouble about, yet it suggested something that was better.

"Why," said Willie to his father, "shouldn't we restore a bit of the Priory in such a way that a man like Mr Yellowley could endure it for a little while? He would pay us well, and then we should be able to do more for those that can't pay us."

"We couldn't cook for a man like that," said his mother.

"He wouldn't want that," said his father. "He would be sure to bring his own servants."

The result was that Mr MacMichael thought the thing worth trying, and resolved to lay out all his little savings, as well as what Willie could add, on getting a kitchen and a few convenient rooms constructed in the ruins—of course keeping as much as possible to their plan and architectural character. He found, however, that it would want a good deal more than they could manage to scrape together between them, and was on the point of giving up the scheme, or at least altering it for one that would have been much longer in making them any return, when Mr Shepherd, who had become acquainted with their plans, and consequently with their difficulties, offered to join them with the little he had laid aside for a rainy day—which proved just sufficient to complete the sum necessary. Between the three the thing was effected, and Mr Yellowley was their first visitor.

I am sorry to say he grumbled a good deal at first at the proximity of the cobbler, and at having to meet him in his walks about the garden; but this was a point on which Mr MacMichael, who of course took the old man's complaints good-humouredly, would not budge, and he had to reconcile himself to it as he best might. Nor was it very difficult after he found he must. Before long they became excellent friends, for if you will only give time and opportunity, in an ordinarily good man nature will overcome in the end. Mr Yellowley was at heart good-natured, and the cobbler was well worth knowing. Before the former left, the two were often to be seen pacing the garden together, and talking happily.

It is quite unnecessary to recount all the gradations of growth by which room after room arose from the ruins of the Priory. When Mr Yellowley went away, after nearly six months' sojourn, during the latter part of which, so wonderfully was he restored by the air and the water and the medical care of Mr MacMichael, he enjoyed a little shooting on the hills, he paid him a hundred and fifty pounds for accommodation and medical attendance—no great sum, as money goes now-a-days, but a good return in six months for the outlay of a thousand pounds. This they laid by to accumulate for the next addition. And the Priory, having once taken to growing, went on with it. They cleared away mound after mound from the garden, turning them once more into solid walls, for they were formed mainly of excellent stones, which had just been waiting to be put up again. The only evil consequence was that the garden became a little less picturesque by their removal, although, on the other hand, a good deal more productive.

Yes, there was a second apparently bad consequence—the Priory spread as well as grew, until it encroached not a little upon the garden. But for this a remedy soon appeared.

The next house and garden, although called the Manse, because the clergyman of the parish lived there, were Mr Shepherd's own property. The ruins formed a great part of the boundary between the two, and it was plain to see that the Priory had extended a good way into what was now the other garden. Indeed Mr Shepherd's house, as well as Mr MacMichael's, had been built out of the ruins. Mr Shepherd offered to have the wall thrown down and the building extended on his side as well—so that it should stand in the middle of one large garden.

My readers need not put a question as to what would have become of it if the two proprietors had quarrelled; for it had become less likely than ever that such a thing should happen. Willie had told Mona that he loved her more that he could tell, and wanted to ask her a question, only he didn't know how; and Mona had told Willie that she would suppose his question if he would suppose her answer; and Willie had said, "May I suppose it to be the very answer I should like?" and Mona had answered "Yes" quite decidedly; and Willie had given her a kiss; and Mona had taken the kiss and given him another for it; and so it was all understood, and there was no fear of the wall having to be built up again between the gardens.

So the Priory grew and flourished and gained great reputation; and the fame of the two doctors, father and son, spread far and wide for the cures they wrought. And many people came and paid them large sums. But the more rich people that came, the more poor people they invited. For they never would allow the making of money to intrude upon the dignity of their high calling. How should avarice and cure go together? A greedy healer of men! What a marriage of words!

The Priory became quite a grand building. The chapel grew up again, and had windows of stained glass that shone like jewels; and Mr Shepherd, having preached in the parish church in the morning, always preached in the Priory chapel on the Sunday evening, and all the patients, and any one besides that pleased, went to hear him.

They built great baths, hot and cold, and of all kinds—from baths where people could swim, to baths where they were only showered on by a very sharp rain. It was a great and admirable place.

After the two fathers died, Mona had a picture of Willie's dream painted, with portraits of them as the two angels.

This is the story of Gutta Percha Willie.

About Author

Elizabeth Yates wrote of Sir Gibbie, "It moved me the way books did when, as a child, the great gates of literature began to open and first encounters with noble thoughts and utterances were unspeakably thrilling."

Even Mark Twain, who initially disliked MacDonald, became friends with him, and there is some evidence that Twain was influenced by him. The Christian author Oswald Chambers wrote in his "Christian Disciplines" that "it is a striking indication of the trend and shallowness of the modern reading public that George MacDonald's books have been so neglected".

Early life

George MacDonald was born on 10 December 1824 at Huntly, Aberdeenshire, Scotland. His father, a farmer, was one of the MacDonalds of Glen Coe and a direct descendant of one of the families that suffered in the massacre of 1692.

MacDonald grew up in an unusually literate environment: one of his maternal uncles was a notable Celtic scholar, editor of the Gaelic Highland Dictionary and collector of fairy tales and Celtic poetry. His paternal grandfather had supported the publication of an Ossian edition, the controversial Celtic text believed by some to have contributed to the starting of European Romanticism. MacDonald's step-uncle was a Shakespeare scholar, and his paternal cousin another Celtic academic. Both his parents were readers, his father harbouring predilections for Newton, Burns, Cowper, Chalmers, Coleridge, and Darwin, to quote a few, while his mother had received a classical education which included multiple languages.

An account cited how the young George suffered lapses in health in his early years and was subject to problems with his lungs such as asthma, bronchitis and even a bout of tuberculosis. This last illness was considered a family disease and two of MacDonald's brothers, his mother, and later three of his own children actually died from the ailment. Even in his adult life, he was constantly travelling in search of purer air for his lungs.

MacDonald grew up in the Congregational Church, with an atmosphere of Calvinism. However, his family was atypical, with his paternal grandfather a Catholic-born, fiddle-playing, Presbyterian elder; his paternal grandmother an Independent church rebel; his mother was a sister to the Gallic-speaking radical who became moderator of the disrupting Free Church, while his step-mother, to whom he was also very close, was the daughter of a Scottish Episcopalian priest.

MacDonald graduated from the University of Aberdeen in 1845 with a master's degree in chemistry and physics. He spent the next several years struggling with matters of faith and deciding what to do with his life. His son, biographer Greville MacDonald stated that his father could have pursued a career in the medical field but he speculated that lack of money put an end to this prospect. It was only in 1848 when MacDonald began theological training at Highbury College for the Congregational ministry.

Early career

MacDonald was appointed minister of Trinity Congregational Church, Arundel, in 1850, after briefly serving as a locum minister in Ireland. However, his sermons—which preached God's universal love and that everyone was capable of redemption —met with little favour and his salary was cut in half. In May 1853, MacDonald tendered his resignation from his pastoral duties at Arundel. Later he was engaged in ministerial work in Manchester, leaving that because of poor health. An account cited the role of Lady Byron in convincing MacDonald to travel to Algiers in 1856 with the hope that the sojourn would help turn his health around. When he got back, he settled in London and taught for some time at the University of London. MacDonald was also for a time editor of Good Words for the Young.

Writing Career

MacDonald's first novel David Elginbrod was published in 1863.

George MacDonald is often regarded as the founding father of modern fantasy writing. George MacDonald's best-known works are Phantastes, The Princess and the Goblin, At the Back of the North Wind, and Lilith (1895), all fantasy novels, and fairy tales such as "The Light Princess", "The Golden Key", and "The Wise Woman". "I write, not for children," he wrote, "but for the child-like, whether they be of five, or fifty, or seventy-five." MacDonald also published some volumes of sermons, the pulpit not having proved an unreservedly successful venue.

After his literary success, MacDonald went on to do a lecture tour in the United States in 1872–1873, after being invited to do so by a lecture company, the Boston Lyceum Bureau. On the tour, MacDonald lectured about other poets such as Robert Burns, Shakespeare, and Tom Hood. He performed this lecture to great acclaim, speaking in Boston to crowds in the neighborhood of three thousand people.

MacDonald served as a mentor to Lewis Carroll (the pen-name of Charles Lutwidge Dodgson); it was MacDonald's advice, and the enthusiastic reception of Alice by MacDonald's many sons and daughters, that convinced Carroll to submit Alice for publication. Carroll, one of the finest Victorian photographers, also created photographic portraits of several of the MacDonald children. MacDonald was also friends with John Ruskin, and served as a go-between in Ruskin's long courtship with Rose La Touche. While in America he was befriended by Longfellow and Walt Whitman.

MacDonald's use of fantasy as a literary medium for exploring the human condition greatly influenced a generation of notable authors, including C. S. Lewis, who featured him as a character in his The Great Divorce. In his introduction to his MacDonald anthology, Lewis speaks highly of MacDonald's views:

This collection, as I have said, was designed not to revive MacDonald's literary reputation but to spread his religious teaching. Hence most of my extracts are taken from the three volumes of Unspoken Sermons. My own debt to this book is almost as great as one man can owe to another: and nearly all serious inquirers to whom I have introduced it acknowledge that it has given them great help—sometimes indispensable help toward the very acceptance of the Christian faith. ...

I know hardly any other writer who seems to be closer, or more continually close, to the Spirit of Christ Himself. Hence his Christ-like union of tenderness and severity. Nowhere else outside the New Testament have I found terror and comfort so intertwined. ...

In making this collection I was discharging a debt of justice. I have never concealed the fact that I regarded him as my master; indeed I fancy I have never written a book in which I did not quote from him. But it has not seemed to me that those who have received my books kindly take even now sufficient notice of the affiliation. Honesty drives me to emphasize it.

Others he influenced include J. R. R. Tolkien and Madeleine L'Engle. MacDonald's non-fantasy novels, such as Alec Forbes, had their influence as well; they were among the first realistic Scottish novels, and as such MacDonald has been credited with founding the "kailyard school" of Scottish writing.

Chesterton cited The Princess and the Goblin as a book that had "made a difference to my whole existence", in showing "how near both the best and the worst things are to us from the first... and making all the ordinary staircases and doors and windows into magical things."

Later life

In 1877 he was given a civil list pension. From 1879 he and his family moved to Bordighera, in a place much loved by British expatriates, the Riviera dei Fiori in Liguria, Italy, almost on the French border. In that locality there also was an Anglican church, All Saints, which he attended. Deeply enamoured of the Riviera, he spent 20 years there, writing almost half of his whole literary production, especially the fantasy work. MacDonald founded a literary studio in that Ligurian town, naming it Casa Coraggio (Bravery House). It soon became one of the most renowned cultural centres of that period, well attended by British and Italian travellers, and by locals, with presentations of classic plays and readings of Dante and Shakespeare often being held.

In 1900 he moved into St George's Wood, Haslemere, a house designed for him by his son, Robert, its building overseen by his eldest son, Greville.

George MacDonald died on 18 September 1905 in Ashtead, Surrey, England. He was cremated in Woking, Surrey, England and his ashes were buried in Bordighera, in the English cemetery, along with his wife Louisa and daughters Lilia and Grace.

Personal life

MacDonald married Louisa Powell in Hackney in 1851, with whom he raised a family of eleven children: Lilia Scott (1852), Mary Josephine (1853-1878), Caroline Grace (1854), Greville Matheson (1856-1944), Irene (1857), Winifred Louise (1858), Ronald (1860–1933), Robert Falconer (1862–1913), Maurice (1864), Bernard Powell (1865–1928), and George Mackay (1867–1909?).

His son Greville became a noted medical specialist, a pioneer of the Peasant Arts movement, wrote numerous fairy tales for children, and ensured that new editions of his father's works were published. Another son, Ronald, became a novelist. His daughter Mary was engaged to the artist Edward Robert Hughes until her death in 1878. Ronald's son, Philip MacDonald (George MacDonald's grandson), became a Hollywood screenwriter.

Tuberculosis caused the death of several family members, including Lilia, Mary Josephine, Grace, Maurice as well as one granddaughter and a daughter-in-law. MacDonald was said to have been particularly affected by the death of Lilia, her eldest.

Theology

According to biographer William Raeper, MacDonald's theology "celebrated the rediscovery of God as Father, and sought to encourage an intuitive response to God and Christ through quickening his readers' spirits in their reading of the Bible and their perception of nature."

MacDonald's oft-mentioned universalism is not the idea that everyone will automatically be saved, but is closer to Gregory of Nyssa in the view that all will ultimately repent and be restored to God.

MacDonald appears to have never felt comfortable with some aspects of Calvinist doctrine, feeling that its principles were inherently "unfair"; when the doctrine of predestination was first explained to him, he burst into tears (although assured that he was one of the elect). Later novels, such as Robert Falconer and Lilith, show a distaste for the idea that God's electing love is limited to some and denied to others.

Chesterton noted that only a man who had "escaped" Calvinism could say that God is easy to please and hard to satisfy.

MacDonald rejected the doctrine of penal substitutionary atonement as developed by John Calvin, which argues that Christ has taken the place of sinners and is punished by the wrath of God in their place, believing that in turn it raised serious questions about the character and nature of God. Instead, he taught that Christ had come to save people from their sins, and not from a Divine penalty for their sins: the problem was not the need to appease a wrathful God, but the disease of cosmic evil itself. MacDonald frequently described the atonement in terms similar to the Christus Victor theory. MacDonald posed the rhetorical question, "Did he not foil and slay evil by letting all the waves and billows of its horrid sea break upon him, go over him, and die without rebound—spend their rage, fall defeated, and cease? Verily, he made atonement!"

MacDonald was convinced that God does not punish except to amend, and that the sole end of His greatest anger is the amelioration of the guilty. As the doctor uses fire and steel in certain deep-seated diseases, so God may use hell-fire if necessary to heal the hardened sinner. MacDonald declared, "I believe that no hell will be lacking which would help the just mercy of God to redeem his children." MacDonald posed the rhetorical question, "When we say that God is Love, do we teach men that their fear of Him is groundless?" He replied, "No. As much as they were will come upon them, possibly far more. ... The wrath will consume what they call themselves; so that the selves God made shall appear."

However, true repentance, in the sense of freely chosen moral growth, is essential to this process, and, in MacDonald's optimistic view, inevitable for all beings (see universal reconciliation).

MacDonald states his theological views most distinctly in the sermon "Justice", found in the third volume of Unspoken Sermons. (Source: Wikipedia)

Lightning Source UK Ltd.
Milton Keynes UK
UKHW041604181219
355558UK00001B/59/P